A Monk Jumped Over a Wall

Other books by Jay Nussbaum

Blue Road to Atlantis

Jay Nussbaum

A Monk
JUMPED OVER A WALL

The Toby Press

A Monk Jumped Over a Wall
First edition 2007

The Toby Press LLC
POB 8531, New Milford, CT 06776-8531, USA
& POB 2455, London WIA 5WY, England
www.tobypress.com

ISBN 978 1 59264 201 4, *paperback*

A CIP catalogue record for this title is
available from the British Library.

Printed and bound in the United States
by Thomson-Shore Inc., Michigan.

To Betty: Fifteen years ago in Central Park my vision was permanently compromised by the sight of you, and the rest of the world has been black and white to me ever since. And to Taylor and Brian: We gave you the gift of life. Who knew you'd use it to do the same for us.

Chapter one

"D on't blame yourselves," Carter Boston says to the couple staring at him from across the mahogany conference table. I listen quietly from two seats to his left. "No one's saying it was your fault. For what it's worth, I think you're two very courageous people." He smiles sadly and they nod. "But life isn't fair; it's a cliché but it's true. You know, Typhoid Mary infected an entire city but never caught typhoid herself—go figure. You got sick, lost your job, missed a bunch of mortgage payments—go figure." He turns his palms up. "It's not my job to assign blame or figure out why fate deals us the hand it does. I'm just a lawyer." He sighs and adds quietly, almost to himself: "A lawyer, unfortunately, with pretty straightforward marching orders. I have to collect on this loan for my client. I don't have to like it, but I have to do it. If we can't work out something today you leave me no choice but to foreclose."

Ira Finowitz kicks me softly under the table. Seven of us are sitting in Conference Room IV at Greer, Babcock and Drew. Five are attorneys; the other two are an overwhelmed married couple trying to appear calm. But we're quite a show of force, the five of us. Carter Boston is a partner in the Litigation Department, and Heather

Sherwin, seated on Boston's opposite side, heads up our Real Estate Group. The rest of us are a troop build-up on the border, there to remind the Eagans how outgunned they'll be if we decide to sue. Our client, Stan Eiderhorn, bought a package of 1,200 mortgages not too long ago from Parker National Bank. Because all the loans were in default, he paid just forty-three cents on the dollar for them. Then he handed them over to us to plow through. To him, it's just a numbers game. The more deals he can settle without wasting time and money on trials, the better his return.

But he doesn't have to sit here. He doesn't have to turn away from the silent plea for mercy that fills the eyes of the women, or the futile, jut-jawed pride of the men. Who am I kidding? He'd love it. He's not absent because it's too hard to watch. He's absent because he's busy scouring the country for more loan packages to buy at forty-three cents on the dollar. Worse, who am I to criticize him? I'm helping.

An hour ago, Finowitz bet me that the Eagans would cave in today and agree to a deed-in-lieu deal. Deed in lieu of foreclosure— give us the deed to the house without a fuss and we won't have to sue. Lunch is riding on the outcome, but I'd be rooting for the Eagans anyway. One day, I hope to have the authority to turn down clients like Stan Eiderhorn, but I'm just a first-year associate at Greer Babcock. Friday, in fact, will mark the end of my first year here. It's been all the talk among the first years: how big a raise we'll get, how we'll all finally be second-year associates and have first years of our own to boss around.

"But Mr. Boston," comes the unsteady voice of Jared Eagan, a wisp of a man who looks a bit like an old law school professor of mine, "I'm no deadbeat. I'm working again. It's not what I had before, but it's a job. I can make the payments. Wouldn't that be best for everyone?" He doesn't know about the Eiderhorn discount, of course. The last thing Eiderhorn wants is to be a bank, collecting a measly eight percent for the next thirty years. If we get the deed today and flip the house within three months, Eiderhorn's internal rate of return will exceed 300%.

Boston rubs his hand over his face and exhales. "I wish I could help you," he says. "But it's the numbers. You're too far behind, and my client has children who need to eat too." He draws absently on the yellow legal pad in front of him. Big numbers, broad strokes that define the Eagans' impossible situation. "96" he scratches and underlines, then says, "Your original mortgage was ninety-six thousand, principal balance today around ninety-two. But you also owe back payments of thirty-three thousand, which makes one hundred twenty-five thousand dollars."

"But that's not true, Mr. Boston," Emily Eagan points out. She leans forward in her chair and explains as though Carter Boston cares. She might as well be trying to talk a Rottweiler out of a steak. "We owe four thousand, three hundred seventy-five dollars. Look, I wrote it out." She produces from her purse a red diary, opens it and slides it across the table. The unlatched lock buzzes against the mahogany as it glides toward Boston. Calculations written in green ink cover the page.

He barely looks down. "We've been through this," he says, beginning to lose patience. "Your interest rate was eight point eight percent until you went into default. The default pushed the rate to eighteen percent, plus penalties and fees. You agreed to all that when you took out the loan."

"We had no choice," Emily says. "We needed that loan. You should've seen where we were living. Our son was going to be starting school…"

But Jared has picked up on the real issue. He places a hand over his wife's. She stops speaking and looks at her husband.

"What fees?" he asks Boston.

I'm hoping he has the gumption to pursue that variable, because that's where they have a valid dispute. The fees are ludicrous, most of them pulled out of thin air by Parker National and Eiderhorn. But Boston is too good. He has his own book to offer, and his is typewritten, bound in a green marble laminate folder. It contains technical terms and boldfaced disclaimers. As the Eagans are trying to make sense of it, the intercom buzzes. "Mr. Boston, your conference call is ready."

"I have to take this," Boston says as he rises from his chair. I'm not surprised. In all my time at Greer I have yet to see Boston get through a meeting uninterrupted by other business. His work ethic is legendary here. Other partners tell stories about him. "Why don't we take a break," he suggests. "You can get some lunch—there's a good deli across the street—and we'll meet back here in an hour."

"Mr. Boston," Mr. Eagan rises and extends his hand, which Boston accepts, "I know you're just doing your job."

❧

Ira and I take the elevator down, cross over Madison Avenue and go into Marino's Delicatessen. I love Marino's. It's got a deli counter that makes everything from meatball parmesan to veggie wraps, and a salad bar with chicken au gratin, sushi, fajitas and kung pao pork. Oh, and salad.

"Why do they even bother with a menu?" Ira muses as we scan our selections from the deli counter.

"I know you're just doing your job," I mutter for the seventh time since we stepped out of the meeting.

"Let it go, J.J."

"Boston loves this, you know. He's going back to his Long Island estate tonight and won't spend a minute worrying about where the Eagans will sleep."

"Who's next?" demands an obese man behind the counter. He's staring at me, but I've been too distracted to live up to New York City deli counter protocol. "Who's next?" he repeats, more a threat than a question.

"Southwestern chicken on a kaiser roll to go," Ira blurts, which sets the man to work and earns me a reprieve.

Ira Finowitz started at Greer the week before I did. I carried an empty briefcase into the office we'd be sharing to find him behind his desk talking on the telephone and tumbling a pen across his knuckles. Cradling the phone with his head and neck, he stood and offered a smile and a long, bony hand cast down at a 45-degree angle. Other than his height and utter lack of bulk, the main thing I remember noticing about him was his sleepy eyes. They got sleepier as the months progressed. Greer Babcock pays high salaries and expects long hours in return.

"You're making too much of this," he tells me now. "They borrowed money to buy a house, they couldn't pay, so they have to give back the house. It's sad but it's not unfair."

"The guy lost his job because he got asthma."

"They'll make do."

"They've got kids."

"We'll let them keep those."

"It's not funny, Finny."

"Funny Finny."

"I'm serious. I've been evicted. I know how it feels. We must've moved a dozen times when I was a kid, and it's not like my father was lazy—guy worked like an animal. It is unfair. It's really unfair."

I notice him looking down at me, his mouth pulled to one side. "I didn't know."

I wave off his pity. "It's okay. I didn't mean to be dramatic. I know you can't save people from themselves, I know that. But twelve hundred loans," I pause and draw a deep breath, "it just feels so, I don't know, rote. And draining."

"And we've still got a long way to go."

I scan the sandwich choices. "You always want to be a lawyer, Finny?" I ask.

"Yeah," he says, "far back as I can remember. You?"

"Nope."

"What was your first choice?"

"You won't laugh?"

"I'll surely laugh, J.J."

"I wanted to be a cop."

"And after you turned nine?"

"No kidding. My dad used to get in trouble for his drinking, so his law firm hired an ex-cop to keep an eye on him. A lot of times, he was the only thing keeping the rest of us safe. We got pretty close. Used to tell me about being a cop. Dairian Davis."

"So what happened?"

"Didn't have the guts."

"Getting shot probably hurts," he allows.

"No, I didn't mind that. Getting shot would've been easy compared to—"

"Who's next?"

"Southwestern chicken on a kaiser roll to go!" I blurt.

Ira nods appreciatively. "Nice."

"I hate chicken."

"Still nice."

"Thanks," I smile, but when I notice the Eagans enter the deli, I can't turn away. Jared isn't just thin; he's gaunt. He and Emily hold hands as they walk directly past Ira and me, not noticing us. I watch as they each take less salad than it would take to satisfy a rabbit, then sit at a table in the back room.

I know you can't save everyone. I know that implicit in the assertion of personal freedom is the freedom to fail, and that the taste of fighting your way back is something to savor. But isn't there any middle ground in the leap from that premise to the casual ease with which we ignore the suffering of others? Some non-patronizing form of compassion we could offer that wouldn't suffocate freedom? Carter Boston once told me that he'd shed genuine tears the day he heard the news about the World Trade Towers. But the people who died in those buildings were the same ones we cut off in traffic every day. They were the people we dismiss when our legs outrun theirs and win us the only taxi on a rainy night. And they were the same people whose homes we foreclose on without trying just a little harder for a noble solution. Why do we mourn their deaths but care so little about their lives?

Mr. Eagan had been an E.M.S. technician until asthma cost him his job. He could've been there that day for all I know, digging through the rubble and searching for victims as the rest of the city ran for cover. Ira notices me watching the Eagans.

"I know what you're thinking, and don't do it," he says.

"What am I thinking?"

"You're going to buy them lunch," he says. "J.J., don't do it. They'll resent you. They need their self-respect more than they need a plate of baba ganoush."

"You have no idea what I'm thinking, Finny."

I take my sandwich, wrapped in white deli paper, and walk toward their table. Ira follows me. When I notice him, I stop.

"Ira, go back to work. You don't want to be here for this."

"What are you planning to do?"

I don't answer him. "Ira, trust me, go back to work. If you're here, it'll just put you in an awkward position."

He's too damn smart. His eyes widen immediately, and he points a long, skinny finger in my face. "J.J., you're a golden boy at this firm—don't screw it up. In three days, we're getting our one-year evals, big raises...you're on a partnership track, for crying out loud."

"No one's going to know."

"Don't do it."

"Stay or go, Ira," I shrug. "It's up to you."

He holds up his hands, palms toward me, and takes a step back. "Fine, I'm going. I don't want to hear anything anyone can ask me about later."

I watch him leave, then continue to the Eagans' table.

"Declare bankruptcy," are the first words out of my mouth.

They look up at me. "You're one of the ones from upstairs," Emily says.

I sit without being invited. I have no time to waste. I can't afford to be seen sitting here. "Declare bankruptcy," I repeat. "It'll change everything. Go upstairs and tell Mr. Boston that you don't accept his offer, then get a Yellow Pages and call a bankruptcy lawyer. File today," I emphasize.

Mr. Eagan stiffens. "I'm no deadbeat. I'm not declaring bankruptcy."

"If you want to keep your home, you'd better declare. If we know that you're in Chapter 7, that we'll have to go through the bankruptcy court to collect our money, we'll cut you a much better deal."

"Forget it. I owe what I owe. The bank gave me ninety-six thousand dollars to buy my house and I promised them I'd pay them back ninety-six thousand dollars. That's what I'm going to do."

He starts to stand to leave, but I grab his arm, keeping him seated. My fingers nearly touch. I check over my shoulder, then lean toward him. "Listen to me, Mr. Eagan. Our client bought your loan from that bank for about fifty thousand dollars. He paid pennies on the dollar because it was a bad loan. Your bank's not even involved anymore. They've already written off the loan and it's got nothing to do with them. If Mr. Boston wanted to break even, he could settle this for about fifty thousand bucks."

"Fifty thousand?" Jared is aghast. "I could figure out some way to come up with fifty thousand."

"Yes, but he's not going to accept that. Don't you get it? He's not looking to break even."

They're quiet for a moment, glancing up at me with nervous eyes, trying to decide if they can trust me. They look at each other as I check the front door of Marino's to see if anyone from the firm is coming in.

"Look, I've got to go," I finally tell them. "Do what I say."

❧

Five of us reconvene in the conference room an hour later and sit looking at each other for twenty minutes, wondering where the Eagans are. Ira is looking at me suspiciously, but I don't acknowledge him. Finally, Carter Boston's secretary peeks her head in the door.

"Mr. Boston, I just heard from Mr. Eagan."

"And?"

"He said an emergency came up and asked if it would be okay to meet again on Friday."

"Is he still on the phone?" Boston asks as he reaches for the receiver.

"No sir."

"Why the hell didn't you keep him on the phone, Louise?"

To everyone around him, Carter Boston has it made. He's the thirty-seven-year-old son of two wealthy Rhode Island lawyers. He's a Harvard graduate and full partner at Greer. Last month, he was on the front page of the *New York Law Journal* for a class action he settled for eight figures. But Boston has never been as convinced by his successes as he's been by his failures, and everyone around him has to live with that.

"I tried to put him through, Mr. Boston," Louise explains. "He hung up."

Boston leans back in his chair and crosses his legs. Above one droopy sock, his pallid, hairless ankle comes into view. "This makes no sense. An hour ago, they were ready to go deed in lieu, I'm sure of it. Now they're buying time?"

"They said they had an emergency," someone points out, but Boston just rolls his eyes.

"Did anyone talk to them after I left the room?"

"We all headed straight to lunch," Ira says.

"Goddamn it," Boston concludes. "If they file a seven, I'm going to go ballistic. Screw it, I've got a deposition to get ready for anyway. Finowitz, get them on the phone before you leave tonight. Tell them if they're not here ten A.M. Friday, I'm suing."

Chapter two

It's Friday, the big day. One by one, the second-year associates are being summoned to the office of Ted Dietz, managing partner, to get reviews and raises. Ira's in with him right now. Ira's a future star and everyone here knows it, so I'm sure he'll be treated well. He says the same about me, but I'm not so sure.

I had my recurrent nightmare last night. It's been a week now, and it's always the same. In it, I'm at my desk drafting interrogatories when suddenly I look up to see all my clients from the past year gathered at my office door. When I ask them what they want, they just stare at me. I grow self-conscious, but I've been carrying on this charade for so long that I don't break easily. "What?" I finally prompt, and Stan Eiderhorn—who in the dream has a vulture's curved beak where his nose should be—speaks for the group. "You don't," he pauses to peck a mite from his ruff, "know *anything*, do you?" Instinctively, I place myself between the mob and my law books.

"No," I admit, "I don't. But they're my books, and if anyone wants to know what's in them, they have to ask me."

I'd like to spend some time considering this thinnest of reeds on which my professional life rests, but it's just a dream, and I've got other concerns here in the real world. Like, for instance, the upcoming Dietz meeting, and also the fact that I can't seem to find the bag of weed I stashed in my bottom desk drawer yesterday. I notice my suit jacket hanging by a hook on the back of my office door—it's been too hot lately to wear it—and decide to check in there. I haven't smoked since college, but last week Ira said we should get high at lunch today to celebrate our raises. I know he was kidding; I just want to see what he'll do if I call his bluff. Good thing my younger brother is home for the summer, otherwise I wouldn't even know where to get the stuff anymore. I've never liked drugs; they have a bad effect on me. Last time I smoked pot I wound up at a bakery demanding sweetbreads. Leo gave me the bag a few days ago and rolled one to remind me how. I brought the bag here and put it in my desk.

"J.J.," comes the voice through my speakerphone, "Mr. Dietz will see you now."

I hear that voice all the time, and though I'm pretty sure it's my secretary, I've got no definitive proof where it comes from.

"J.J., did you hear me?" the voice repeats.

"Yes," I say as I pull on my suit jacket and check the pockets. Empty.

Greer occupies nine floors in a high-rise office building on Madison and 50th. We're two hundred fifty attorneys, and in addition to New York City, we have offices in Los Angeles, Chicago and Florida. The firm is broken up into five departments: Probate, Corporate, Real Estate, Tax and Litigation. I'm in litigation. We're on the thirty-ninth floor, along with the real estate group. The partners are all on forty-four, so I have to go upstairs to see Dietz.

I step out of my office and make my way toward the elevator bank at the far end of the hall. Unlike the threadbare industrial carpeting in the individual offices, the halls of Greer, Babcock and Drew are covered in a deep burgundy Axminster blend. I love the feel of my shoe sole when it sinks into it. It feels like I'm getting somewhere. I despise my days here, but according to everyone I know, I'll be able to choose from a variety of better options after I get a few years of experience. Deferred gratification is a common theme among associates.

When the elevator arrives, I step on and hum along with a gentrified Barry Manilow instrumental as I ascend. On forty-two, the doors open and Carter Boston steps on.

"Afternoon, Mr. Boston," I say as I step to the side.

"Son," he acknowledges pompously.

The doors open again on forty-four and I silently chastise myself when I realize I'm still humming along with Barry Manilow. Boston steps out ahead of me and greets four partners who pass us with racquetball rackets in hand.

"Good luck," he tells them.

"Good luck to you," one of them responds, then notices me and mumbles a generic greeting my way.

Something about the speed at which his glance passes by disquiets me, but he's on the elevator so fast, and Boston has turned the corner ahead of me so fast, that I'm not able to make any sense of it. Alone now, I turn the corner in Boston's wake. The atmosphere up here is much different than on thirty-nine. The walls are oak, and lined with case books so old and so beautiful that they seem like art. Even the secretaries seem like art, like representations of secretaries—efficient, serious, attractive but not inappropriately so. I don't know where they get them. I never see women like these on the outside.

I notice that my shoe is untied and, as I sink to one knee to tie it, someone nudges me. It doesn't take much to knock someone over from that position, and I fall onto my back, both feet sailing up into the air. Ira Finowitz stands over me, smiling.

"Probably not the place for it, Finny," I say as I get up and straighten myself out.

"I just came from Dietz," he whispers, clearly excited.

"And?"

He looks back over his shoulder to where the secretaries sit, then turns his back to them. "Twenty percent," he says.

"Wow."

"I'm going to go call my wife. Are we set for lunch?"

"Really? You want to?"

"Definitely."

"I've got it in our office, but—"

"Great. Come get me when you're done in there. Oh, and J.J., remember to act surprised. Dietz says it's firm policy not to discuss salary with peers."

When I get to Dietz's office, I pause by the closed door to steady myself. The room is bigger than my apartment and reeks with its authority over me. The chair I'll be forced to sit in sits obliquely in front of Dietz's desk, while Dietz himself always sits obliquely the other way. He has a lazy left eye too, so I'm constantly craning my neck to get into what I can only hope is a polite line of sight. As a final obstacle, the chair faces a credenza on which is displayed a framed photograph of Dietz's unnecessarily sexy teenage daughter, wearing cutoff denim shorts. Her hands are in her pockets, her arms tucked shyly to her sides, amplifying her breasts in a white T-shirt. I've spent a lot of time in that chair over the past year, trying simultaneously to square my shoulders, torque my head, corner my eyes and ignore his daughter long enough to hear what the guy is saying.

Tentatively, I peek my head in. Dietz is behind his desk dictating a letter into a Dictaphone, the microphone pressed up against his mouth as he speaks. His bottom lip is always glistening with saliva, and I live in constant fear of ever having to use his Dictaphone.

Feeling pretty good about myself and the money coming my way, I joke, "Sorry, I didn't know you were having lunch."

He looks at me quizzically. "Have a seat, J.J."

I sit down, sneak a quick look at his daughter's thighs, and turn toward Dietz. He avoids my eye. Something must be bothering him.

"Is everything okay?" I ask.

"Just waiting for someone," he answers, then looks toward his door when Carter Boston enters. "Ah Carter, good," he says.

I glance from Dietz to Boston and back again.

"J.J.," Dietz begins, removing his glasses and rubbing the bridge of his nose between thumb and forefinger, "you've been with us for a year now." My ears perk up in anticipation of the words, twenty percent, even though I already know something else is happening. "We need to discuss your work."

"Yes, sir."

"It's not good," he concludes.

I glance over at his daughter. She is thumbing her nose at me. I focus back on him. "It's not?"

"No," Boston adds eagerly. "It stinks."

"Stinks?"

"Carter, please," Dietz says. "You asked to sit in, not run things."

"Sorry."

"Stinks?"

"It doesn't stink, J.J.," Dietz continues. "It's just not as good as it once was. After your first six months here, Mr. Boston here told me you were the best new associate we'd hired. But since then, you've changed. You've become obstinate, uninspired."

"Slovenly," Boston adds.

"Slovenly?"

"Carter," Dietz warns.

"Sorry."

"Slovenly?"

"Mr. Boston is referring to the length of your hair," Dietz shrugs. "But that doesn't concern me. As a matter of fact..." He pauses.

"Mr. Dietz, what is it?" I ask.

"There are reasons one becomes managing partner," he chuckles to himself, then replaces his glasses and looks at me. "They tell you it's your management ability when they give you the job, but that's butter and biscuits. They make you managing partner when they decide you're a better diplomat than you are a lawyer. I've never relished conflict the way Mr. Boston does, which is why I'm beating around the bush now. But," he sighs and picks up a sheet of paper, "we have a serious problem with you."

"What kind of problem?"

"Ethics," he says.

"Ethics?"

Over my shoulder, Carter Boston hands me a bouquet of flowers in a glass vase. I stare at him, confused. "Read the card," he says.

My hands tremble as I fumble to remove the card from the

envelope. What kind of tribal ritual is this? I read the embroidered card, a floral vine running vertically down its left side. The message is written in green ink.

> *Mr. Spencer,*
> *Thanks so much for your help the other day. We're deeply "indebted" to you.*
> *Love,*
> *Emily and Jared Eagan*

"They filed for bankruptcy Wednesday," Boston says. I stare down at the card because I'm afraid to look up. "You know how much harder you've just made it to collect on this note? You cost our client—and us—a lot of money."

"J.J.," Dietz adds, "more important than the money, this is a serious breach of attorney-client confidentiality."

"I can explain," I say.

"There's nothing to explain," Dietz shrugs. "Look, I like you. You're a bright young man. I sincerely believe you're still going to enjoy a bright future somewhere." He pauses and looks at Boston, who nods in return. "Unfortunately, it isn't going to be here."

"You're firing me?" My stomach is in knots, my throat tight. It all happened so fast, and it sounds so irreversible. No one has even asked me to tell my side. I'm sure this is a personality clash with Boston, but Dietz isn't interested. I stare from one to the other. They're still not inviting a conversation. "Can't we talk about it?"

"I'm afraid not. The decision's been made."

"Why can't we talk about it?"

"There's nothing to talk about," Boston says. "*Res ipsa loquitur.*"

Legal jargon: the thing speaks for itself. My legs have only been crossed for a few minutes, but already the left one has gone to sleep. I uncross them and try to speak, but am too preoccupied by the podiatric orgasm now spinning my head.

"It's clear you haven't got the stomach to be a quality litigator," Boston says evenly. The feigned compassion in his eyes is proof positive of how much he's enjoying this. "There's a lot of good probate work out there now."

I try to maintain my composure. A part of me wants to turn over Dietz's desk and mule kick Boston out the window. But the bigger part—the part that always finds itself pruning the beanstalk with the giant still in hot pursuit—isn't ready to accept the change that has already happened.

"Please don't do this to me," I say.

"You did it to yourself."

"I'm not talking to you," I explode, and suddenly find myself standing, facing Boston with my hands clenched into fists. I can feel my breath as it passes heavy over my dry lips. My jaw is so numb I can barely form words. I turn to Dietz. "It's one mistake. This isn't about that, Mr. Dietz, you have to believe me. It's him. He just, he—"

"J.J., calm down." Dietz holds up his hands. "Losing your temper will only make things worse."

Boston has backed up to the window. He looks like a frightened child, and it feels so damn good to have even a false sense of control for a moment. I'm furious with myself for having been blindsided. I should've known the minute Boston walked into that office what was going on. If you look around the cauldron and all you see are cannibals, you're dinner.

"Please give me a chance with another partner, Mr. Dietz."

"It wouldn't matter," Dietz insists. "It's not Mr. Boston, it's you. You're not suited to this firm."

"What does that mean?"

"We're a very serious, clean-cut place. We're squares, as young people say."

"Young people forty years ago."

"J.J.—"

"I am all that," I insist. "I'm square, I swear. Just give me a chance with another partner and I'll prove it to you."

"Show him," Boston calls from across the office.

"It's not necessary," Dietz answers.

"Show me what?"

"Show him."

Dietz rolls his eyes, then slowly reaches into the bottom drawer of his desk. He produces a clear plastic bag which he holds by two fingers. The bottom inch of the bag is filled with weed. I can't think of a thing to say in my defense.

"J.J., how could you?"

The truth is, I don't know. I've got nothing to say. I have the right to remain silent and I do. I have the right to remain stiff and blank, my mouth dumbly ajar and my career in tatters.

"Monday morning," Boston says, "I'm filing a formal complaint with the State Bar Association, stating that you lack the character and fitness to practice law, and I'm going to ask to have you disbarred. When I'm done with that, I'm going to devote my life to foreclosing your friends, the Eagans."

Silently, I turn to the door and leave. I try to stand straight, to pretend that I'm on my way to better things, but in the elevator I slump against the wall and cover my face with my hands. I walk through the halls of the thirty-ninth floor feeling as though everyone I pass already knows. My goal is to gather my belongings and leave quickly, before anyone can ask me to explain. I hurry past the break room, where Finny is refilling his coffee. He asks me if I remembered to act surprised.

Chapter three

Not knowing exactly why, I find myself at the garage that stores my car. Within minutes, I'm driving the streets of midtown Manhattan, headed nowhere, staring at nothing. A taxicab cuts me off and I scream obscenities even though both of us have our windows shut and besides, he's already way ahead of me. It feels good though, so I continue to scream for a while. I head east toward F.D.R. Drive and curse at that for a while, then exit at Twenty-Third and give Madison Square Park a piece of my mind.

Relax, I think, and a thought occurs to me. I open the glove compartment and, sure enough, there's the joint Leo had rolled. I smoke it as I drive.

My cell phone rings but I turn it off. I'm not ready yet to tell people that I've lost my job. I'm relieved that my father is long since out of my life and doesn't need to find out. I turn left onto Third Avenue and drive north. What's the rest of my family going to say? Leo will just make a joke to bypass the awkward moment. Then I think of my mother. My success is more important to her than it is to anyone, including me. I graduated second in my high school class and all she could think to say at graduation was that I needed a haircut. I can't imagine how she'll react to this.

At Third Avenue and Fortieth, I notice an available, legal parking space right in front of an Irish pub. It seems like divine intervention. I crush out the quarter-inch of joint remaining and climb unsteadily out of the car. I hack out two violent coughs and swallow as I rub my eyes, then push open the door to the pub.

A bouncer sitting on a bar stool inside the door takes no notice of me as I pass him by and sit at a table away from the bar. I swallow beer after beer and still can't get my mother off my mind. My failure ought to be just mine, but it isn't.

"You looking for trouble?" I hear someone say, and I look up to see an old man with a veiny red nose. He's wearing a flannel shirt half untucked, pushing aside his greasy gray hair and wobbling as he motions for me to stand.

"Huh?" is my answer.

"'Cause if you're looking for trouble, mister, you just found it."

"I already got plenty, thanks."

"Wanna fight?" he persists.

"Wanna beer?" I ask.

His face registers comprehension ever so slowly, and suddenly lights up. He likes me a lot now and cackles as he sits across the table from me.

"The hell's a young big shot doing here in the middle of the afternoon?"

"Is it the middle of the afternoon?" I check my watch and see that he's a few hours off. It's past four. "I don't know, Gus. May I call you Gus?" He doesn't answer, but I always wanted a drinking buddy named Gus. "What am I doing here," I repeat. "I guess I'm thinking about my mother, and about when my father left. Trying to figure out why he couldn't just go quietly."

"I got shipped out to Korea...March '51 I'm pretty sure," he points out.

"He and my mom both grew up poor. You think it's worse when you accept your lot in life or when you don't?"

"Sergeant always woke up first," he adds as the waitress puts a beer in front of him.

"My father never accepted it."

He just stares at me.

"See, Gus, my dad earned his college degree at night, then got his law degree the same way. My mom, she used to say we all had a dream by the tail, and even if that kind of thing can make your life crazy for a while, you don't want to let go because that would be worse. So she raised me and my brother alone pretty much—my dad worked all day and studied all night. She told us that, one day, it would all be worth it." I have to shake my head at the notion. "I never knew what she meant by that. I mean, I just wanted my dad home. I couldn't figure out what it was he was planning to buy us that would be better than that. You know?"

He purses his lips and waves off the thought. "Ah, medics don't know crap."

"So you've been there," I nod. "You're right—he wasn't doing it for us. But what did he think was going to happen? What did he think, that we were all home studying for our law degrees too, all those years? We were who we were!"

"Settle down over there," the bouncer calls.

I lean closer to Gus. "I remember the first time he and my mom came home from his firm's Christmas party. They come in the door, and I hear her pleading, 'Jerry, talk to me. What did I do wrong? Talk to me.' My father goes into the kitchen and pours a jelly glass full of whiskey." I display the size of the glass with my hands. "Me and my little brother, Leo, we're watching from our doorway down the hall. We'd just moved to this new apartment on the Upper West Side. Big celebration, that was—finally leaving the Brooklyn walk-ups. Signing a real lease, no more midnight moves with the marshal breathing down our necks. But here's the problem, Gus—my mom's Brooklyn born and raised, and my father, even though he is too, he doesn't want it anymore. You know? He wants to be Manhattan now, and the rest of us, I guess, are like a daily reminder of who he really is."

Gus is fast asleep now, his head slack left like a deflated balloon on his shoulders.

"So my father finally says to her, 'You want to know what's wrong? I'll tell you,' he says. 'Did you see any other wife dancing the way you did tonight?' You never saw a face drop like my mom's did when he said that." I look away for a moment and stare at the bottles of alcohol lined up behind the bar. I take a deep breath to relax my mouth, then take a few more. "You know," I emphasize to the sleeping body in front of me, "this was the first firm dinner. Their big arrival. And I guess, up until he said that, she thought she'd done pretty well. She says, 'I danced the way I always dance,' and that's when he lost it. 'But we weren't at one of your low-rent nightclubs! That's not how you dance at a cocktail party!'"

"If I have to come over here again," the bouncer says as he hovers menacingly above me, "you're out."

"Sorry," I say, holding up my hand to reassure him, then turn back to Gus. "Like she's supposed to know what the hell to do at a cocktail party. Son of a…he was the one in school all those years, not her. She was home with us. That was their deal—she holds down the fort so he can go improve himself." I take another long drink of beer. "Improve himself," I shake my head. "I liked him better the old way.

"You ready for the worst part?" I ask. "She asks if there was a school *she* could go to, you know, to learn how to behave properly, how to fit in. I think that was the saddest thing I ever heard in my life. Know what he said?"

My head is now supported only by the heel of my left hand cupped under my cheekbone, my hand in turn supported only by the elbow perpendicular beneath it. We sit in silence for a while. The light from outside dims as the sun moves behind a cloud. But though I'm silent, I'm still immersed in the memory of that night. I remember my father looking away from my mother. He was facing directly toward Leo and me. He didn't see us but I saw him perfectly. His eyes were half-closed like he was tired, but the muscle in his jaw kept popping and falling, popping and falling. And I found myself yearning for something human in him, something compassionate and youthful. Even now, knowing how it all turned out, I still yearn for it, sure that if he could have just tapped in for a moment to the man he must have been when they first fell in love, everything would be different today. Come on, Dad. Say something nice. Hug her.

"'There's no such thing as white trash school,' he finally said, and started to walk down the hall toward us, toward his bedroom.

"That's when Leo went after him. It was just a whiffle-ball, but man," I'm laughing now, "did it pop when it bounced off my dad's forehead. And holy cow, he just went nuts—I mean nuts. Kicked a hole in the sheetrock and took off after Leo. From there, it's kind of a blur. I defended Leo but he took a nasty beating. My mom's screaming, 'Respect your father, respect your father!'

"Finally, she runs from the room, and twenty minutes later, the cops come and take my dad out." I drain the rest of the beer. "Bet that was more embarrassing at the water cooler the next morning than his wife's bump-and-grind. Not that it mattered; they loved him there. Because he was a workaholic, and guys like my dad, they think that means people really like you. But why couldn't he just leave that first night? Just go, you know? Why put us through another hundred nights like that?

"After he finally moved out—my mom, it was like she couldn't turn it off. She was going to improve her lot if it killed her. She got her real estate license, but she's not all that great at it. So it came down to me and Leo. Suddenly, nothing was good enough for her anymore. It was always, 'What are you waiting for, a round of applause?' She loved that expression." But really, I lean back into my chair and think, it wasn't so much what she said as what she didn't say. I wasn't asking for a round of applause, just a pat on the back, just once.

Feeling hungry, I stand unsteadily, pay for my beers and Gus's, and stick a twenty-dollar bill into his shirt pocket as he sleeps. I push open the door to the pub and squint against the glare.

Chapter four

I see Docks restaurant right across the street from the pub, so I tuck in my shirt and gather myself to rejoin proper society. It's pretty empty, but the hostess says, yes, they're serving dinner. I get a window table that looks out onto the corner of Third Avenue and Fortieth Street, and order another beer. I'm trying hard to feel liberated, but I'm still just a year removed from last summer's degrading job search. I'd thought that graduating high in my law school class would have made me an appealing prospect, but the interviewers all saw right through me. Everyone but Dietz. He bought it all. He even said, when he saw on my resume that I was into karate, that it "spoke volumes about my character." People really have a misconception about karate.

Now I'm going to have to start interviewing all over again, and with a spotty record. That's if I don't get disbarred, I realize, remembering Boston's threat like a punch in the gut.

The waitress brings my beer and stares as I immediately drain it. "The crabcakes, please," I exhale, "and can I have another beer with a shot of your worst whiskey?"

Her green eyes narrow. "What do you mean, 'worst'?" she asks. "Our cheapest?"

I wave my hand in the air. "Money is no object," I assure her. "Just bring me the worst whiskey you have."

She rolls her eyes and walks away. I remember one morning when I was still in law school, talking to a lawyer I happened to be seated next to on a train. He'd been staring out the window, but by the folded legal journal on his lap I knew he was a lawyer, so I struck up a conversation. When he asked me why I wanted to practice law, I said I thought it would be a fulfilling career, and he laughed. He actually laughed—a bitter, hostile laugh. I asked what was so funny, and he turned back toward the window. "Might be different for you," he said, "but I hate my life. Spend my days talking to people who are either angry at me or scared of me—everyone always posturing, bluffing, threatening. Sure kid, real fulfilling. Welcome to the life. I hope you like your car."

"My car?"

"That's what you get in return. A real nice car."

"If you're so miserable, why don't you do something else?"

"My wife likes her car too."

"More than a happy husband?"

"No contest." He never once took his eyes off the window.

Another hour or so passes and, full of crab, beer and legitimately offensive whiskey, I am staring in amazement at my beer mug, which appears to be melting. I should really smoke pot more often. The waitress might be asking me something, but she's so far away that it doesn't matter. I think of Dairian Davis. Dairian was the retired cop who worked security for my father's law firm. His job was to keep my dad from killing the rest of us and getting disbarred or thrown in jail—a tragic loss of billable hours, either one. Whenever my father would get drunk and violent, we'd call Dairian and he'd come over and calm things down so that my mom didn't have to call the cops. Sometimes he'd wrestle him to the ground, but usually, all he had to do was put his heavy arm around my father's shoulder and talk quietly. He stayed on call even after my father left us and took up with a refined Connecticut divorcee, which was lucky because one very bad night, Dad must've remembered how angry he still was with all of us, and he came back.

Things got wild that night, my father reeling around the kitchen swinging a half-full bottle of whiskey and rambling the most spiteful things I'd ever heard. My mother screaming at him to leave. She called Dairian and tried to hold out until he arrived, but when Dad shattered his bottle against the wall, spraying glass everywhere, she attacked him with a metal teapot. He hit her and I dove in. But he was so big, and the room was so filled with his madness. It felt like charging into a burning house. He pinned me to the wall, his forearm under my chin, lifting me almost off my feet. Dairian arrived and threw himself into the fight just as my mother was closing in again with the teapot. Dairian got hit, his head sliced open by the spout of the teapot. He dragged my father out of the kitchen and into the living room, and when they fell together to the ground, I couldn't tell exactly what Dairian was doing, but he had his forearms up by my father's head on the ground, and in a few seconds, my father was unconscious. I watched in amazement from the kitchen doorway, knowing that one day I'd learn how to do that.

Dairian stayed for a while that night after he'd carried my father out. He closed the door to my and Leo's bedroom and sat at the foot of my bed, a bloody washcloth pressed to his head just above his right temple. He told us cop stories and I felt so safe with him there, his back against the wall, one arm over his knees, talking to us in his calm baritone. It was comforting, like sitting by a fireplace and listening to the pouring rain hit a sturdy roof.

"Why'd you become a policeman, Dairian?" Leo asked as the three of us sat in the darkness, the only light a streetlamp nine stories down. Leo was on my bed, his legs crossed, and I was under my blanket. Dairian faced ninety degrees from me, a single fleck of hallway light reflecting off his crop-circle haircut.

"All evil needs to win is a bunch of good men doing nothing," Dairian answered.

"Is our dad evil?" I asked.

"Don't know," Dairian said. He refolded the washcloth and pressed it back to his head. "Probably not. But promise me something boys, don't you waste too much time in trying to figure him out, you hear? One day, some shrink's going to tell you you got to do that to be happy, but it ain't true. It don't matter anymore why he does what he does. What matters is you don't let him get to you."

"He's kind of hard to ignore," Leo noted.

Dairian drew a deep breath and I saw his silhouette nod. "I know," he said. "Thing is, I never met a man who could honestly say he'd never been bullied in his life, somehow or some time. My dad used to make me stand up to 'em all, every last one of 'em, but that don't always work either. And even if it does work," he paused and felt the cut on his head, "it changes you. So just shrug 'em off. Every damn bully you meet, survive 'em then let 'em go. If they got to punch you or yell at you, so be it. But don't let 'em hit any deeper than that. Don't carry 'em around forever."

"What choice do we have?" I asked. "Even now that he's gone he comes back."

"You always got a choice, J.J., you understand that? You always got a choice. Your dad'll be gone for good one day, and when he is, you can spend the rest of your life trying to get even with a memory, or you can just tell him to fuck off."

I'd never heard Dairian curse before. Leo and I giggled, like I'm giggling now, as the waitress gives up on me and walks away. But I stopped giggling when our bedroom door opened. I flinched, thinking it was my father, but it wasn't; it was my mother. Her breathing had subsided, but her hair was still wild from the fight. She looked at me and Leo. "You two," she brushed her hair aside and lifted her chin, "are going to take every damn thing that son of a bitch ever did, and double it."

I notice a commotion outside the window of the restaurant. A crowd has gathered, and through the gaps, I see a bicycle messenger stopped on the side street between Docks and the pub, one leg down. He wears a filthy gray tank top and baggy shorts down to mid-calf. His helmet is tied to the rear of the bike. From where I sit, I can see that he's pointing his finger at someone in front of him and shouting, spit flying from beneath his fu manchu mustache. His right hand is already clenched into a fist, the muscles of his forearm taut. Someone in the crowd shifts just enough for me to see Gus, standing directly in front of the bicycle, his feet planted.

"'Cause if you're looking for trouble, mister," I hear Gus's muffled voice through the window, "you just found it."

"For the last goddamn time, old man," the messenger yells, "give me back my damn bag."

"Wanna fight?"

The messenger climbs off his bike and it clatters to the pavement. I see him slap Gus hard with his open right hand, his bottom lip curled beneath his teeth.

"Damn it, Gus," I stagger to my feet and run toward the door. I glance back to the table for just a moment when I think I see my fork curl three of its four tines and direct an obscene gesture toward me. I break into a stumbling sprint out of the restaurant and turn the corner, shouting, "Leave him alone, man. Leave him alone."

When I reach them, the messenger aims his index finger at me. "Mind your damn business."

"Just leave him alone," I repeat, and I can hear that I'm already out of breath. "He's crazy."

"If you know him, tell him to give me back my damn bag. I got no time for this."

People are too close to each other, I sense that right away. So I wedge myself between the two men and try to take the bag, but Gus is stronger than I thought. He wheels away from me and throws a wild punch, which I evade easily. If only the messenger had done the same.

Gus's fist bounces off the messenger's temple, sending him into a frenzy. He hits Gus hard in the eye and breaks past me as Gus falls to the street. I dive on top of him and wrap my arms around his shoulders, trying to pry him off. But his shoulders are sweaty and I slide off to the left. He lands two more punches to Gus's face, which is bleeding now. This time, I dive at him from the side and tackle him off Gus. He wraps his arm around my neck and rolls on top of me. I look to the crowd for help, but their removed stares make it clear that they are here as spectators only. As the messenger throws punches, a paint-covered hiking boot kicks at my head. It's Gus.

We roll toward the cars that have stopped to watch, as some farther back in the line of traffic begin honking their horns. But my head is starting to clear and I'm throwing as many punches as I'm taking. With the hubcap of a car pressed against my face, I realize with dismay that although I've studied quite a lot of karate in my life, it's of little use now. We're on the ground, and I can't kick or punch well from here.

My tie is trapped beneath my shoulder and it's choking me, so I roll onto my stomach. I want to get my knees under me, but can't because the messenger has pulled himself to his knees over my back and is punching repeatedly. I try to duck my head but the thuds on my skull hurt, and with each one, my face grinds into the pavement. Gus isn't helping matters either, still kicking at me from the side. But it's also not so bad. Somehow, it's just what I've been needing tonight. Maybe this is how it starts, and by tomorrow night, I'll be approaching perfect strangers with the greeting, "You looking for trouble?"

I push with my hands and finally get my knees under me. As I lift my torso, the messenger loses his balance and slips off me to the right. I spin and throw a punch that hits nothing but air. But the spin has left my back to him, and when I see him get to his feet and come at me, my right leg surprises me as it extends in a perfect mule kick that catches him square in the chest. He spills over onto his back and somersaults heels over head, all the way to his chest. A police siren wails in the distance. He notices it at the same time as I, scrambles onto his bike and pedals away. I stagger to the curb, dizzy and nauseated. Uphill across Third Avenue, I see a police car heading east on Fortieth Street with its sirens on. But it's closer to Lex than Third and the traffic isn't budging. I seize the opportunity, find my car on Third Avenue and flee.

Chapter five

Driving north on Third Avenue, I can barely keep my head up. Cars on both sides of me honk. My stomach spasms and I vomit on the floor, spattering my feet. Still, I know I have to keep going. I'm in enough trouble as it is. But within moments, I glance at the rearview mirror and see a police car winding its way through traffic behind me. If I can just stay steady, I think, maybe it's not even the same car. I wonder if he could've possibly seen me back there. Maybe Gus told him. "It's the silver Pontiac, officer. License plate HDG-496. Wanna fight?"

I stare straight ahead, trying not to look at the rearview mirror, as though that might make the police car go away. My senses are clearing, and although my shoulder, throat and eye are killing me, I start feeling that I'm going to get out of this. That's when the police car appears directly behind me, all siren and lights.

What I notice first in the mirror is not the cop but my own right eye, swollen shut. Blood is smeared across my upper lip and cheek. I wipe the blood on my shirt tail as I pull over to the right and stop the car, then tuck in my shirt again to hide the red stain. My head is much clearer now, and I check the mirror to see the cop step out of his car. Other than the eye, I feel okay. I can do this. After a deep breath, I roll down my window and he leans in.

"What happened to your face?"

This is great. It must not be the same cop whose car turned onto Fortieth Street. I respond quickly. "I'm a boxer," I say. "Just came from the gym."

"Nice suit."

"Thanks."

He stands for a moment and arches his back, emitting a soft grunt as he braces his right hand against his lower back. He looks up Third Avenue into the distance, then leans back in. "You know how fast you were going?"

I can't believe my luck. Speeding. Speeding is all he's thinking. I've talked my way out of speeding tickets before, and even if I can't do it now, a ticket's no big deal.

"I think I was going forty, officer," I say. They love it when you call them "officer."

"Afraid not," he answers.

My head is spinning again but I resolve to keep my eyes steady and not pass out. All I have to do is get through the next few moments. I can't be as drunk or high as I feel, even if the cop's badge now has a little skull growing out of it.

"I suppose I could have been going forty-five or fifty, officer," I concede. My tongue feels like a giant slug in my mouth.

The cop does not answer, but the way he rolls his eyes indicates that my estimate is still so far off as to not even be worthy of a reply. I'm getting a bad feeling.

"Well, the speedometer isn't perfect, officer. I guess fifty-five isn't out of the question, officer."

"Stop calling me that."

"Sixty? Are you saying I was going sixty? Okay, well, maybe, but only because my friend here is sick."

He looks at me through heavy eyelids. "Son—"

"We were at the gym boxing in our suits and—"

"Son, shut up. You're drunk, you're stupid, and," he says after a pause, "you were going four miles an hour."

Chapter six

Y
ou ready?" Ira asks.

I look up from the wooden bench on which I am seated, just outside Hearing Room 4 at the Office of the State Bar Disciplinary Committee in downtown Manhattan. It's the Wednesday before Labor Day weekend, and instead of spending it looking forward to a few days at the beach, I'm here fighting for my career. Not long ago, I would've handled the moment with a joke, but I don't think I've ever been this scared and I can't muster the energy to fake it. Beside me, my mother sits with her hands folded, her silver hair in a bun. That was her own touch. I didn't want her here at all, but Ira said it would help, and the more austere she presents herself, the better. I'm in no position to argue. Ira's really gone out on a limb for me. When word reached the office that I'd been arrested, he went to Dietz and demanded that he be allowed to represent me, both criminally and before the Disciplinary Committee. That they'd agreed to the latter was a shock; it's not often a law firm files a complaint then defends the person they're complaining about. When Ira told me, I'd felt conflicted—half grateful, half jealous that in the same time it took me to place my career on life support, he'd built up enough goodwill to make demands and succeed. Dietz had resisted, but Ira is blue chip and the firm didn't want to alienate him.

"I don't know," I finally answer, but when he reaches out with one of his giant, skeletal hands, I allow him to pull me to my feet. "I honestly don't know if I can do this. I can't feel my mouth. How am I going to talk if I can't feel my mouth?"

"He's ready," my mother puts in as she stands. She'd been angry with me when I first told her what had happened, punishing me with silence one night over dinner, breaking it only to respond to my observation that I'd helped the Eagans with her standard offer of a round of applause. But since then she'd been great.

"You'll surely do this," Ira says, adjusting my burgundy tie. "You look great, very lawyerly. And I'm going to do the talking."

"Charcoal is really better on him," my mother notes.

"No," Ira tells her. "Navy blue for court, always. Conveys sincerity. It's going to be okay, J.J.," he assures me. "I promise. Just remember, same thing we said in criminal court—it was an isolated incident."

"But it's not an isolated incident, Finny," I say, thinking of the criminal case that's still pending. "It's D.U.I., it's fighting in the streets, it's…," I whisper the last word. "…drugs."

"Don't forget breaching attorney-client confidentiality."

"Oh yeah, thanks." I rub my forehead. "How did I make such a mess of things?"

He lays a hand on each of my shoulders to steady me. "I'm just playing with you," he smiles. "Which I wouldn't do if I were worried. Now repeat after me—one incident. Four prongs, one incident. A good man sees an injustice being done, and steps in…" I start to protest his depiction but he raises a flagpole forefinger. "…despite the personal career risk of which he is only too well aware." I can't suppress a smile, so I sigh and look away. He gives my shoulders a shake and I look back at him. "Facing the prospect of losing the one and only career he's ever wanted—all he ever wanted to do with his life—he cracks. He cracks—it's poetic. He suffers a nervous breakdown. And, looked at individually, nothing he did was so terrible." He counts off on his fingers, "Fighting in defense of a helpless old man, D.U.I. in panic and a *recreational amount* of marijuana that was really only a misguided joke. One incident. One incident. If you don't believe it, they're not going to believe it."

"He believes it," my mother says.

"Mom, please."

"And we've got a good, strong group of character witnesses."

"Is Josie here yet?"

"Who's that?" my mother asks.

"My old law school professor."

"Our ace in the hole," Ira adds, "the legendary Professor Steele."

"Is he here?"

"Not yet."

"Not yet?"

"He'll be here."

"Maybe I should call him."

"He'll be here," Ira repeats. "I spoke to him last night."

The thought of Josie hearing about this from Ira saddens me, but I just couldn't call him myself. In fact, I'd argued to leave him out of it, but Ira insisted. Josie's won cases before the U.S. Supreme Court, appeared on *Larry King Live*. Ira knows the value of celebrity.

"But we've got another surprise for you," my mother coyly arches her eyebrows.

"What's that?" I ask.

"Who," she corrects.

My patience is thin. "Whatever. Who's that?"

"You'll see," she sings.

"Mom, this isn't a birthday party."

"Okay, enough," Ira says. "Showtime." I can see why the firm is so high on him. My faith in Ira is the only thing getting me through the idea of the four people in the next room having my life in their hands. If his plan is for me to lay out bare the mess I've made of things, promise never to do it again, and beg for forgiveness, I will. I nod at him and force a smile.

We enter the hearing room and I pause to take in my surroundings. The room has none of the courtly oak charm of a real courtroom.

At the front, two long tables are pushed together, with three empty chairs behind them, facing us. The panel wouldn't dream of entering before I do. Directly in front of those tables, ten feet away, is another, with two chairs facing the panel. That's where Ira and I will sit. To the right, two more chairs. One's for the stenographer. The other—a makeshift witness chair—sits isolated a few feet away, between the stenographer and the judges. Finally, against the far wall, is a bench like the one outside the room. I nod to the people sitting there, my character witnesses.

"Someone should call Josie," I say again to Ira.

"He'll be here."

My mother gives me a kiss, then joins the other witnesses: Ed Coleman, my best friend from law school, and my brother Leo.

We've just settled into our seats when a voice commands, "All rise," and I begin to get up, only to have Ira pull me back down, looking irritated.

He is glaring at the side of the room and, following his gaze, I see he is looking at Ed, who is laughing at his joke. Although he is being reprimanded simultaneously by my mother and Ira, Ed's eyes are on me. His smile fades and he nods just a bit. He's reminding me: they're not judges. They're just lawyers like you. I return his nod. It brings me back to more certain days.

Boston
Four Years Earlier

Chapter seven

The Charles River flows in a blue serpentine directly through the center of the city, with Boston University Law School rising eighteen stories above its southern bank. About five miles northeast but clearly visible on a nice day is the golden dome of the Statehouse, and following the direction of the Charles and out of sight, Storrow Drive. Across the river, the Marriott and M.I.T. form part of the unassuming, pleasant skyline of Cambridge. I can still see it all in perfect detail, and if I close my eyes, I can even feel it.

It was late August and the banks of the Charles were desolate. In a few weeks, once the undergrads started their fall semester but before the weather turned rust, those banks—they called it B.U. Beach—would be lined with co-eds in bikinis. Tan frat boys would be tossing footballs or Frisbees, depending on their political leanings. Sailboats and windsurfers would skim across the river surface and the air would smell like coconut oil. But that day, with only the graduate schools in session, the morning sun shone on empty grass as the incoming freshman class of B.U. Law gathered as a unit for the first time. We stood in a courtyard outside the law school, waiting for them to open the doors and begin orientation. Everyone milled about casually. I'd already said hello to the few people I recognized from my alma mater, Brandeis University, in nearby Waltham. We'd endured a few moments of stilted conversation, silently realizing that we weren't going to be any more friendly now than we had been then, and we moved on. But I remember noticing, while talking to them, that no one seemed to have a compelling reason for being here, starting law school. Neither did I, really. I had a vague notion of wanting to be a prosecutor, but nothing concrete. Mainly, it seemed we were treating law school as an extension of college, the last safe port for the generalist. The music had stopped and we saw no open chairs in the working world, so we just kept circling.

There's a nagging premonition that terrifies the generalist toward the end of college, that post-graduate life is about to narrow into a laser beam. You realize that you've spent the last four years parsing Kierkegaard, Fitzgerald and Einstein, but suddenly they'd hightailed it, leaving in their place a corporate world offering choices like ad space sales, plumbing fixtures and retail annuities. For the next forty-three years. Worse, you realized that most of your choices were derivative. Only one guy sews the sheet. Another guy stress-tests it, one more packages it, and others on down the line approve it, broker it, advertise it, distribute it, sell it, account for it, critique it, wash it and mend it. So much reflected glory, so little opportunity to sew.

At least law school delayed decisions. Everyone had assured us and we reassured one another that, at the very least, it would be a good degree to have. "A good degree to have," that was our mantra.

I was staring out at the river, as I'd do a thousand more times over the next three years, watching it move through the city, main channel and tributaries, when someone tapped me on the shoulder from behind.

"Excuse me, but is your name J.J. Spencer?"

A hand was thrust toward me.

"Yes," I accepted the hand. "Hi."

"I'm Aaron. Aaron Bocian." The first thing I noticed about him was his dynamic smile. I know it doesn't make sense to infuse physical features with meaning, but his smile was thrilling, all white confidence and joy. His eyes smiled too, along with his cheeks (caved into perfect dimples), chin, ears and forehead. Certainly, I'd just met the happiest, most enlightened person in Massachusetts. I caught myself when I feared I might be falling in love.

"Have we met?" I asked him.

"I was a high school friend of Eileen Tirico. She told me to look you up here."

"That was nice of her. So she's forgiven me for the senior formal, I guess."

"I wouldn't go that far."

"How did you know who I was?"

"Eileen said to look for a guy in a T-shirt and patched jeans, and if he stares you in the eye when you speak to him, that's J.J." I looked away. "She said that whenever you're uncomfortable in a situation, you wear a T-shirt and patched jeans—which she says accounts for the senior formal—because you have a narcissistic need to envision yourself as the opposite of whatever stereotypical group you happen to be involved with at the time." His attention was distracted as the doors to the auditorium opened to the courtyard and a few students began filing in. He watched them but kept talking. "That you don't understand that no one is so unique that they can't be labeled with some stereotype, and if you are that unique, you're doing it on purpose, which is worse." Silently, I watched his distracted profile, amazed at the amount of information he'd managed to absorb about someone he'd never met. "What are you staring at?" he asked when he noticed the silence and turned back to me.

"And my feet?" I shrugged. "Did Eileen fill you in on the degenerative bone condition in my feet?"

But Aaron knew I was being sarcastic and nodded his head as though I'd just confirmed some other personality flaw about which Eileen had warned him. He did, however, go on to tell me about the time he'd been threatened with a degenerative bone condition of his own, called a slipped epiphysis.

"You see, the top part of the femur is called its epiphysis. And when the epiphysis slips posteromedially off the metaphysis..."

I wasn't listening anymore. Aaron was from that particularly challenging school of storytelling where no detail is considered surplus, so he included everything. He also had an amazing memory, so his stories tended to get very long. The truth is, he could have been telling me about anything and I wouldn't have been listening. My girlfriend, Jennifer, had broken up with me the night before.

I'd met Jennifer Reed during my senior year of college, while I was on winter vacation in Jamaica with friends. She was a freshman at Boston College, also in Jamaica on vacation. I was in the hotel pool when she first appeared in a white bikini and I swear, the water came to a boil. She was stunning, with a melodic voice free of any accent despite her having grown up in suburban Boston. I was immediately attracted to her—we all were—but it wasn't until I'd spent time with her that I really fell. She had such a clear vision of the future—something I lacked at the time. She was the one who first suggested to me that I take the law school admissions test, and it felt good to have a direction. I told her about my childhood dream of being a cop, and she kind of rolled her eyes and said, "You think too small—with your looks and brains, if you want to fight crime, think district attorney. Maybe even judge," she added with a quick arch of her brown eyebrows. By the end of my first week back at school, I'd gotten the application forms to take the LSATs and I was on my way. Life's no different than the Charles—it's got a main channel, but there are so many tributaries, so many destinations. Veer right and you're in the Statehouse, veer left and you're in the Combat Zone.

"...but interestingly enough, the epiphysis never actually slips," Aaron continued into the layer of dead air between us. "It stays in the acetabulum and is held there by the ligamentum teres. The femur distal to the epiphysis slips anterolaterally, you see, but when you look at it on an x-ray, it looks as though it's the epiphysis that's slipped."

"Uh-huh."

"And they don't even really put a pin in it, as many people believe. It's actually percutaneous cannulated screw fixation...."

In a single, sun-soaked week, Jennifer had given my life direction, then packed up my heart in her luggage alongside her white bikini and bottle of coconut rum, and left me unable to carry on the simplest of conversations without invoking her name. We'd continued to see each other once we'd returned to school, because Boston College was just a few miles from Brandeis. After I graduated, we'd spent the summer together in Boston, her living at home in Sudbury while taking summer classes at B.C., me waiting tables, trying to save up money for the three years of law school when I'd have less time to work. In June and July we talked about our future goals, but it was always our respective future goals. Then one night in early August, as we strolled through Faneuil Hall, she very casually used the word "we" in describing the kind of neighborhood she wanted to live in. She was too beautiful to question. But a week ago, her high school sweetheart called from Chicago with a surprise. He said that being apart from her during the past year had been too hard, and so he'd decided to transfer. He'd be starting at B.C. in a week. She came to my apartment last night and told me.

"I don't know what to do," she'd said, sitting on my bed with her legs crossed. I sat a few feet away, feeling helpless. She did, in fact, know what she was going to do. She was just having trouble working up to it. I felt sorry for her. Despite her outward confidence, there was always something fragile about Jen, something I'd never understood, but which made her all the more beautiful to me. So I waited. "I'm crazy about you," she finally said, "but we've only been together a few months. Jeff and I have four years."

"What are you saying, he's tenured?"

"No, but I don't know how else to decide." Then her eyes widened and she sat up on her knees, closer to me. "Break up with me," she said.

"What?"

"Break up with me. That'll be best for everyone."

"Stop it."

"I'm serious."

"Jen," I began, but stopped. We stared at each other in silence. "Just do it," I finally said.

She frowned, and I wondered whether she was disappointed in me for not fighting harder for her. She sort of shook her head, then stood and walked to my bedroom door.

"Please don't hate me," she said, and left.

"...but I was never real big on skiing anyway," Aaron continued, "so I guess I can live without it."

"Uh-huh."

"Anyway, we should go get seats before the auditorium fills up."

We?

Chapter eight

The law school auditorium was a large room with seats ascending at a steep angle from the front row to the last. The Dean approached the podium and adjusted the microphone to his height, while Aaron shifted nervously by my side.

"Why do they all have books?" he asked. "J.J., they have books."

"They're just notebooks," I whispered out of the side of my mouth. "Relax, you've got three."

"But look down there. They have textbooks."

"Big deal," I reassured him. "You've got more pens than anyone in the room."

"You think we're falling behind already?"

"Are you serious?" I asked when I saw the terror in his eyes. "How can we be falling behind if we haven't even had a class yet?"

"So why do they have textbooks?" he demanded.

"I don't know. Maybe they were left back."

"They don't leave you back here, J.J.," he said. "They just throw you out."

I pulled back to consider him at a distance. His eyes were

wide and the perfect smile had vanished somewhere beneath a sweaty, inflated upper lip. A squeaking sound escaped his mouth as the lip lost air, and I realized then who Aaron really was, smile notwithstanding, like the moment the salesman emerges in an otherwise dignified, silver-haired gentleman.

"Oh," I exclaimed, "I see. You're nuts."

He just stared.

"But I'm not telling you anything you didn't already know, am I?"

He shook his head silently. Somewhere, Eileen Tirico was looking at today's date circled on her calendar, throwing her head back and cackling triumphantly.

The dean opened his talk by telling us how special we were for having chosen to go to law school. When he said he was confident that he was looking out at the next great generation of lawyers, Aaron took exception.

"He shouldn't do that," he muttered.

"Do what?"

"Call us lawyers. We're attorneys."

"Aaron, we're not shit. Besides, what's the difference?"

"Would you call a physician a doctor?"

"Yes."

"Would you call a professor a teacher?"

"That woman's taken more notes than you."

After the dean had finished, a heavyset Asian professor took the stage and congratulated us, saying that one can attain no more powerful a form of knowledge than the rules by which one's society operates. All over the room, heads nodded, and I wondered what was going on at that moment at the nation's other graduate schools. Surely in a business school somewhere there was a dean explaining to the incoming freshmen that the most powerful knowledge is the knowledge of how to acquire wealth. Art schools saying it's the knowledge of how to culturally define its civilization to future generations. Medical schools, how to save lives. Dental schools, how to save teeth. Accounting schools, how to save money. And on and on and on. And the truth is, no one has got any more real power than anyone else, because anyone can do whatever he damn well pleases, except maybe Jai Alai referees who, as near as I can tell, can't seem to do a blessed thing.

"At this point," he concluded, "I'd like to turn matters over to my esteemed colleague, Professor Josiah Steele. Professor Steele is widely considered to be the nation's foremost expert on constitutional law. He is a former clerk to the United States Supreme Court, and following a distinguished career in the private sector that included a victory before the U.S. Supreme Court, he decided to devote himself to academia—our gain. He's authored several textbooks and legislations, and most recently wrote the *amicus curiae* brief that resulted in a landmark decision before the Supreme Court of Massachusetts. In short, he's going to be fitted for his black robe long before me, the son of a gun."

"This is the guy," Aaron whispered to me.

"What do you mean?"

"Meanest son of a bitch in the school. They call him the Advocates' Devil. I heard that if you can make it in his class, you can make it anywhere."

"Isn't that New York?"

"I'm telling you, it's true. My senior advisor told me."

"You have a senior advisor?"

"Christ, J.J., didn't you even read your orientation packet? We all have one." He quickly thumbed through my packet—which I actually had started reading, but it was three inches thick—and showed me the name of my advisor. "With all due respect, J.J.," he said, "your problem is, you think you're still in college just because this all looks like college. But you're on a different level now, and if you don't start moving your legs, the treadmill's going to throw you off."

"Maybe you're right," I nodded.

"Do you have Steele for Con Law?"

"Yeah. You?"

"Yeah, God help us."

With a newfound sense of humility, I turned back to watch Professor Steele as he pushed a mop of sand-blond hair behind his ears. He was a man of slight build, whose shoulders arched back at an unusual angle. His nose dominated his face: a long, angular nose with lima bean nostrils. He offered a wan smile and silently scanned the room. When he started speaking, I was taken aback by the frailty of his voice. It was not the sort of voice I imagined would lead to, or result from, such a list of accomplishments.

"Professor Katahira is a dear friend who exaggerates my contribution," he began apologetically, and I found myself leaning forward to hear. "You may indeed be the next great generation of lawyers, as Dean Perelman suggests, but more likely, you are not a monolith. You are future litigators, deal-makers, CEOs and tortured artists. You are everything." He smiled.

"He doesn't seem mean," I whispered to Aaron.

"It's all available to you here," he continued, "if you remain open to finding it. Law can lead in many directions, both substantively and professionally. However, if you're laden with preconceptions about what a lawyer is, or you're in it for recognition or status, you will likely develop into a well-paid, mindless drone. Many of you will do that...the bulk of you, I daresay."

"Yeah, he's a peach," Aaron answered.

I noticed that neither his voice nor his manner had altered a bit during the seamless transition from welcome wagon driver to mass character assailant.

"I tell you this in the hope that it will inspire you toward a nobler search, which will lead you to greater heights and allow you to add your own unique verse to the powerful play. However, I'm only too well aware of the allure of cold cash, and you will surely face that. But for now, you needn't concern yourselves with it. You have three years ahead of you during which you will have the luxury of focusing on only the law—a stirring, fluid, poetic pursuit if ever there were one. Enjoy it. During your first year in particular, I offer you three pieces of advice, and I humbly urge you to heed them. One: Work hard every day and don't fall behind. It's too hard to play catch-up. Two: As you've probably noticed, our law school is built vertically. With only two classrooms per floor over eighteen stories, you'll spend a lot of time on elevators and those elevators can move quite slowly. Use them anyway. Forsake the stairs, however fit you are. Ours is an age of automation—glory in it. But if you happen to be sharing an elevator alone with a professor, please don't feel the need to make conversation. We'll appreciate you all the more for it. Finally: In class, ask questions. I appreciate the sense of exposure the classroom setting engenders, but don't let that deter you. Even if it's just a term of law with which you're unfamiliar—ask. After all, your professors know that you're not yet lawyers. We'll happily provide you with a definition, and you'll be surprised at how many of your silent classmates will thank you later."

His eyes suddenly shifted and I followed the direction of his gaze to a large, bearded man in the front row, whose hand was raised. Steele seemed surprised to see someone taking him up on his offer already, but he acknowledged him. "Yes, you have a question?"

"Well, since you offered," the man said lightly, and a soft laughter puckered from different sections of the auditorium. He pushed his wire rim glasses up a bit farther on his nose. "You used the term *monolith* earlier. That's one I'm not familiar with."

"Well," Steele said gently, staring directly at the man, "that's not so much a legal term as it is a regrettable defect in your general education. Dictionaries cost $34.99 in the college bookstore, and there's a wonderful café there as well. Try the biscotti."

The room fell utterly silent. The bearded man sat motionless in the heat of seven hundred eyes trained on him. He stared straight ahead.

"Damn," I whispered. It sure wasn't college. I turned to Aaron, who was staring directly at me, his eyes wide in encephalitic shock.

"Any other questions?" Steele asked brightly, scanning the room of tightly tucked hands. "Okay, well then, I'll see you in class. Have a grand time of it."

Chapter nine

The first few weeks of law school were tough but bearable. I lived on Beacon Street near Cleveland Circle in a three-bedroom apartment that I shared with two female friends from college who had decided to brave the working world instead of going to graduate school. I knew I was a last resort when they asked me to live with them. It certainly would've been easier for them if they'd been able to find a woman, but they couldn't, so they chose me over a stranger. The complications had been minimal so far, mainly because all I ever did was study.

Yesterday, I spent my Sunday at the law school library while they held a housewarming party. By the time I got home the party was winding down, so I joined them and two remaining guests for pizza and a game of *Battleship*. I mismanaged two aircraft carriers and ran a heavy cruiser aground before my teammates remembered what busy days Mondays were for me, and suggested I go the hell to bed.

When I heard my alarm clock ring this morning, I rolled heavily to my left, swatted it silent, then rolled back to my right and opened the window over my bed. Bits of summer still hung in the air, but autumn comes early in New England and it was easy to smell the change already. I thought about Jennifer, about my packed Monday schedule, about how much life had changed over the past few months. Lying there, as tired as I was, as unsure as I was of myself, my motivations and my future—for now it all seemed okay. Autumn mornings in Boston are like that.

Across the room, I saw that a piece of paper had been slid beneath my closed bedroom door. On moving day, one of my roommates, Amy, had pulled me aside and asked whether there was anything she could do to help me with what she said she knew must be a difficult transition. I asked if I could give my brother Leo her email address, because I didn't have a home computer and the ones at school were inconvenient. She agreed and I asked what I could do for her, since she was in as much of a transition as I. She said I could respect my fellow creatures and the divinity that resides as much in them as it does in any of us by eating less meat, and we sealed the deal that night over a gluten-free veggie chalupa.

Like a club fighter trying to beat a ten count, I dragged myself from bed, picked up the printed-out email and got back under the covers. Leo was just starting his freshman year at Emory, and I was eager to see how he was doing.

Hi J.J.,

> If there's one thing I hate it's a guy you hardly know who says hello to you every damn time you pass. I mean, I don't mind saying hello to anyone from time to time, but some people just seem to get you locked into having to say it all the time. I don't even know this guy! The only thing we've EVER said to each other is hello. Plus, the guy I'm talking about is stationary, and therein lies the genius of his evil plan. He works in food services serving hot food during lunch. I never even buy hot food during lunch, I go for the cold sandwiches. But I still have to walk past him every day to get my lunch, and that's where he gets me. Then, if I have to

go back for a napkin or something, I find myself looking down or checking my watch because I don't want to have to say hello three times in 45 seconds. I know he does it on purpose. Isn't that harassment or assault or something? It must be something. Tell me J.J., does the world get more stressful than this after college? I hope not—I don't think I could handle it.

School's okay so far, but the freshman social life isn't easy. I almost met a girl today, but when I ran up from behind to introduce myself, she was mean to me. Maybe I was running faster than I realized. But you see, Emory only has about 3,000 women, and me being a freshman, only the freshmen women will even talk to me. So that's 750 girls, with 39 who I set my sights on at the beginning of the year. The upperclassmen cherrypicked the best 32 of those, and five of the remaining seven are going around with freshmen athletes. This leaves two, Aurora Namphihu and Wilhemina Maplebeck. Wilhemina is tall and tan and young and lovely and critically psychotic and constantly under heavy sedation, and when she passes, each guy she passes goes "What the hell was that?"

Aurora is an exchange student from Antananarivo, here to do her thesis on the Madagascan mudfly and its reaction to being injected with radioactive isotopes while being chanted to in psychoanalytic jargon. And I'm so desperate I spent nine hours today building a pond margin for the egg clusters to breed, whaddaya think of that?

Other than all that, being a freshman is easy...he said two months before mid-terms. Gotta go now—I think I just heard Marvin Gaye coming from the pond margin!

Love,
Leo

I put Leo's note aside, lingered in bed for another minute, then got up. Professor Steele's Constitutional Law class started at ten, and he was known to embarrass stragglers. I dressed, grabbed my books and gym bag, and opened my bedroom door, to find two notes taped to the other side. The first was from Lauren:

> J.J., The bags of garbage by your door were left by me. I don't think it's too much to ask that you carry them out to the dumpster every now and then. Thank you, Lauren.

I looked down. No garbage. I opened the other note, which was in Amy's handwriting:

> J.J., In case you're wondering, I took the garbage out. Don't tell Lauren.

A good heart, that Amy, I thought as I left the apartment and crossed to the center of Beacon Street to the T stop. One good thing about Mondays, they might've been loaded with classes, but the ten o'clock start meant I got to avoid rush hour. Tuesdays through Fridays, I was lucky to squeeze onto the bottom step into the train. It was always an awkward moment when a woman occupied the second step up, but still a damn sight better than when it was a guy. Today I got to relax in a seat and review my case notes about the day's topic, freedom of choice, as the T clattered its way to school.

Once there, I went into the law school to the elevator banks. Everyone had Monday morning fog in their eyes as three elevators simultaneously unloaded on the fifteenth floor. We filed into the 120-seat classroom and migrated toward our assigned seats. The Advocates' Devil hadn't arrived yet.

"Am I the only one who notes the irony of studying freedom of choice from an assigned seat?" Ed Coleman asked no one in particular. Ed had a voice like a Harley-Davidson with a southern twang.

"That's an inciteful comment, Mr. Coleman," Bernie Nockowitz called from the front row.

"Why, thank you, Mr. Nockowitz," Ed said.

"No, I mean inappropriately provocative," Nockowitz clarified. "Intended to incite, not full of insight. No freedom's absolute—the freedom of speech doesn't allow you to advocate the violent overthrow of the government."

"You calling me a commie, boy?"

"Was communism in the reading?" Aaron Bocian asked, his head swiveling back and forth.

"I didn't mean to—"

"I will kick your Greenwich Prep butt before I let you denigrate this great nation of ours, Mr. Nockowitz."

By then I'd made my way to my assigned seat, just one to Ed's right. "Why do you torment him?" I asked.

"Ah, Monday morning, J.J. Gotta wake myself up somehow."

"I've heard jogging is nice."

"Son," he said, "if you ever happen to wake up at five A.M., look out your window and see me running, you grab a shotgun and come to my aid because it means something's chasing me."

"Anyway, it's our fault, you know, the assigned seats."

"Yeah, I know."

There has been waged—I suppose since the days Abraham Lincoln was taking class notes on a slate—an ongoing battle of wills between professors and students. It's counterintuitive at its root, because it essentially boils down to the professor trying to cram knowledge into a student and a student doing his best to avoid learning. Maybe it's because most people's first experience of learning involves being force-fed subjects we're not especially passionate about: arithmetic, penmanship, table manners. By the time we get to choose for ourselves what we'd like to learn, turning our heads so the strained peas slop to the floor is a habit.

In an open-seating class, the unprepared law student unfortunate enough to be called upon has the upper hand. The professor—who's rarely familiar with the students' faces—is helpless as long as the student just stays quiet. The professor scans the room, your classmates scan the room, and you scan the room. If there are no assigned seats, you're untouchable. You get marked absent, but that's better than the embarrassment of having to admit that you hadn't read your cases. In response to this, professors long ago developed the seating chart, where they could fill in each grid with the corresponding student's name and look students in the eye when they call on them.

ᴈ❧

"But is it possible to take the notion of civil liberties too far?" Steele asked.

He always wore a suit and tie to school, in lieu of his leisure attire of leathery wings backlit by the flames of hell. The suit jacket came off as soon as class began. He paced in shirtsleeves, back and forth on the raised podium, his hands in his pockets. "Who can tell me what the Thirteenth Amendment says?"

He looked up at us, his lips relaxed in a slight smile. When no one volunteered, a barely perceptible sigh expanded his chest. He rolled his eyes, then casually wandered back toward his lectern and the dreaded seating chart. He negotiated a sip of coffee around his nose and said, "Mister"—letting the "r" hang in the air as the males of the species tucked our heads and narrowed our eyes,—"Shaughnessy?" His eyes rose from the chart and landed on Big Dan Shaughnessy, seated directly in front of me, just one row below. I think a whimper might have come out of me because Ed on my left, and Lisa Fascitelli, directly behind me, both laughed.

"Yes?"

Steele took a few steps toward us and shrugged his shoulders. "Can you tell me what the Thirteenth Amendment to the Constitution of the United States says?"

After a long pause, Dan said, "I'm sorry, sir, no."

Steele looked at him for a moment, pursed his lower lip, then returned to his chart. "Ms. Fascitelli?" he asked. He looked at Lisa.

Lisa was a natural beauty who'd been called on in three classes already, hadn't answered a single question correctly, yet continued to show up unprepared. She didn't read the cases. She didn't brief the cases. As far as I could tell, she didn't know there *were* cases. She sat behind me now, intermittently peeling off her nail polish and writ-

56

ing a letter onto yellow perfumed paper. When she heard her name, she calmly met Steele's eyes. He prompted her with his own, but she just smiled graciously and shook her head.

"Okay, let's try again," Steele persisted. He looked down, then up a third time in my direction. "Mr. Coleman, can you help us?" I noticed a peculiar pattern. Dan Shaughnessy in front of me—miss. Lisa Fascitelli behind me—miss. Now Ed on my left. Was Steele playing *Battleship* too?

"Sir, the Thirteenth Amendment states that neither slavery nor involuntary servitude, except as a punishment for a crime whereof the party shall have been duly convicted, shall exist within the United States, or anyplace subject to their jurisdiction," Ed answered.

"Thank goodness, a lawyer," Steele said. "That in mind, Mr. Coleman, why do you think the Court, in—"

"Sir," Ed interrupted, "I see I've unfairly raised your expectations. Fact is, I've been blessed with an autographic memory, which I've used to my advantage throughout my schooling as a way to avoid having to put in a sincere effort. And I was sure hoping I'd be able to do the same here. I've known the amendments by heart since the seventh grade, sir, but if it's a reasoned Socratic exchange you're after, might I recommend my good friend here, Mr. Spencer."

He put his right arm around my shoulder and nodded at me. I stared at him in disbelief. I tried to turn toward Steele but couldn't get my neck to comply. The odd thing was, I *had* read the cases for the day. I'd briefed them. And I knew that getting called on was inevitable. Everyone would get called on at least once in every class—it was preordained. The fact that it hadn't happened to me yet in Steele's class was just luck. And since I was prepared, now would've been as good a time as any to face it. But it's like hearing your transmission fail—there's never a good time for it.

My neck still locked, my teeth gnashing, I slowly turned my shoulders clockwise until they were perpendicular to the podium, enabling me to see Steele. He was staring directly at me, an expectant look on his face. I flashed back to a high school dance, when I'd tried to break up a fight and gotten punched by a football player. I'd taken my time on the floor since it seemed the safest place to be, but when

I finally looked up, he was still standing over me, beef and jerky, his fists balled up and eager for more. "I don't know what you're waiting for," I'd said then. "Our fight is over. You've won."

"Professor Steele," called a voice from across the room, "I'm not sure where we're going with this. I thought the case for today was the baseball free agency case: Curt Flood v. Major League Baseball." It was Irwin Smuck, who made you pronounce his last name with a hard *u* and had not yet completed a single class session without volunteering his opinion. Ordinarily, I cringed at the sound of his voice, but today it seemed to be accompanied by heavenly chimes.

Steele took a seat on the ledge of the podium, legs dangling. "You say you don't know where we're going with this, Mr. Smuck," Steele said slowly. "But actually, what your question makes abundantly clear is that you have no idea where we're coming from. Can anyone help Mr. Smuck?"

"I suspect plenty have tried," Ed offered.

"Anyone?" Steele asked, ignoring Ed. "Anyone at all," he repeated. "How about someone from the low end of the curve. I'll give away a free point right now to anyone who can help Mr. Smuck—trust me, for some of you, that point's going to look awfully good in May."

No one said a word. Steele glared at us, moving deliberately from one mute face to another. "Hopeless," he said, then stood and turned toward the blackboard, pinching his nose between his thumb and forefinger. Suddenly, from his seat on my right, Aaron Bocian sprung out of his chair like a felon under white light interrogation.

"Alright—stop it! I know you're talking about me! You think I don't know? I know!" He became belligerent. "I didn't read it, okay? Okay, that's what you wanted, you son of a bitch, you got it! I went to a movie last night! I shouldn't have, but I did, and you know what? I'm proud of myself! That's right, proud! Damn proud! What are you gonna do, send me up the river? I'll be back!" He paused when he realized that everyone, including Steele, was staring dumbfounded at him. Aaron pivoted toward the back of the room, then looked down at me, his eyes calming when he saw me. I inverted my palms and shrugged my shoulders. He knew me as an ally, and

I suppose seeing that even I was confused, he slumped back down into his seat.

"Any-who," Steele continued. "Let's try this again. Ms. Letour," he said, "let's just start with the facts of the case in Flood v. Major League Baseball. Can you give me a brief summary of what happened?"

As Emily Letour spoke, I read quickly through my notes, still expecting to be called on.

"So," Lisa Fascitelli whispered softly into my ear from behind, "I hear you've got it bad for some Boston College chick."

I looked up at her in amazement. How could she be so calm? He'd eviscerated her—didn't she even care? And now she wanted to make small talk?

"I need to look over my briefs, Lisa," I whispered back.

"I'd let you look over my briefs," she said, "but I'm not wearing any."

Behind us, Emily Letour was giving a creditable recitation of the facts of the case, in a soft but confident voice.

"And yet," Steele was saying when I managed to drag my attention from Lisa's state of undress, "the Court used the Thirteenth Amendment as a philological basis to free Curt Flood from his contract. What was the Court's reasoning?"

With the attention on Emily, I relaxed enough to understand. Congress passed the Thirteenth Amendment in 1865, just after the Civil War, to put the final legislative touches on the Emancipation Proclamation and formally outlaw slavery. The fact that the Supreme Court was willing to apply it to the case of a professional baseball player demonstrated just how far an aggressive court could stretch constitutional language.

Emily explained this rather eloquently, after which I heard, from what seemed like miles away, my name called again. Through the hot flush and cold sweat, the best I could discern was: "Mr. Spencer, please describe the meaning of meaninglessness using the theory of infinity, and give three examples." I flipped frantically through my case briefs, though I knew the futility of expecting to find an answer in there.

"Hold onto your briefs," Lisa smirked, blowing softly on her nails.

I said something through my suddenly necrotic jaw, and it earned me a nod of, if not approval, at least tolerance from Steele. He turned to field a comment from Mr. Smuck, buying me time.

"How did I do?" I asked Ed. "What did I say?"

"Don't you think it would make golf a better game if you were allowed to play defense?" he replied.

"Mr. Spencer, do you agree with Mr. Smuck?" Steele asked.

"I'm sorry, sir, I didn't hear what he said."

"Stay awake, Mr. Spencer," he scolded, then continued. "He said that the Court got it right in Flood, that just because professional athletes are paid millions doesn't change the fact that being forced to play for a team other than one of their choosing is tantamount to involuntary servitude and therefore outlawed by the Thirteenth Amendment."

"I guess he's entitled to his opinion."

"Entitled to his opinion?" he said disdainfully. "Do me a favor, Mr. Spencer, leave it to family therapists and other touchy-feelies to see other," he curled his fore- and middle fingers in the air, "realities. We're attorneys. Our clients rely on us to obliterate opposing points of view. Now, come on, Mr. Spencer—let him have it. Get on a high horse and tell us about the differences between slavery and baseball. Or if you can't accomplish that, just lay into his unfortunate family name."

"Okay," I said with some hesitation, "I don't agree with him."

"Good. Why not?"

"Well, because the Court's not doing its job." Maybe I remember it as more than it really was, but I could swear I heard a collective gasp rise in the room.

"They're going to lynch you," Steele said.

"All I mean is that the Court's job is to interpret laws, but here it seems like they're trying to write a new one, which is Congress's job."

Steele stared somewhat toward me, somewhat past me. His head teetered ever so slightly on his shoulders. He turned broadside, silently pacing the room. It seemed to last forever.

I turned to Ed. "Is there any sound coming out of my mouth?"

He wasn't listening, absorbed as he was in sketching in his notebook a golfing green, with one golfer trying to putt and the other planted in front of the cup like a goalie. "Think about it," he was muttering, "you open up the youth market; you need all sorts of new equipment...."

"In other words, Mr. Spencer," Steele said, "your contention is that the nine most perfectly wired legal minds in the world should stay out of the business of creating societal rules, and instead, defer to politicians." My mind didn't think that at all, but to my dismay, the skull that housed it seemed to be nodding. "Spiro Agnew, Joseph McCarthy, Gary Condit, Gary Hart," he continued, calmly taking another sip of coffee, "these are the people you would choose to make our laws?"

"Well, no."

"So courts should be allowed to make laws?"

"'kay."

"On the other hand, we can't fire a Supreme Court Justice, Mr. Spencer, you know that, don't you? We don't vote them in and we can't vote them out. Should anyone who answers to no one be permitted to govern everyone? Does the name Pol Pot ring a bell, Mr. Spencer? Stalin, Hussein, Noriega?"

"But that's what I—"

"You're waffling, Mr. Spencer. Which is it? What do you believe?" I said nothing. "Do you believe in anything?"

I was hopelessly confused. And I was tired, embarrassed and completely out of my league. "Until now, I believed in God."

"One blown debate and you're an atheist? Listen," he said, addressing the class at-large, "that's what this is all about—debate, strong opinions, educated opinions. Even Mr. Spencer's opinion. Sure, it can be tough sometimes—Mr. Spencer's sitting there right now battling to regain bladder control—but he's allowed us to consider a wonderful, perplexing question. How far should a court go? Is our Constitution a set of strict rules, or a legal-philosophical framework, to which we are expected to apply our better judgment? Most scholars say the latter. In fact, many consider the framers veritable prophets for realizing that they couldn't predict the future and drafting a document that's intentionally vague, to allow future generations to mold it to their circumstances. But then, if that's the case, why have a Constitution at all? England doesn't have one. England's law is comprised of hundreds of years of case law, and yet here *we* are, continually trying to cram into a round hole, a peg that no one ever even knew would exist when they drilled the hole. Good work, Mr. Spencer—someone grab him a mop and a fresh diaper so we can continue."

Chapter ten

All day, I thought of Professor Steele and fumed over how he had embarrassed me. During Civil Procedure class, I was so worried that I might be called on again that I genuinely felt short of breath. I ate lunch alone because I didn't want to have to talk about it. I tried to imagine what educational benefit could possibly result from disrespect and I came up empty. Ed sought me out in the student lounge and told me not to take it so seriously, that the only person Steele had embarrassed had been himself, but it didn't feel that way. Even at the end of the day, during my legal research seminar, I felt like people were staring at me.

Still, when six o'clock came and the legal research seminar ended, I resolved to put Steele out of my mind, and I grabbed my gym bag. I took the stairs instead of waiting for the elevator, and broke into a full sprint when I reached the lobby. I ran out the door, across the courtyard and weaved through Comm Ave's westbound traffic to catch the T, then hurled myself through the doors just as they were closing. My right ankle didn't make it, and people on the train rolled their eyes when the doors had to open and shut again to let me in. I should've waited for the next train, but karate class would be starting soon and I didn't want to be late.

Twenty minutes later, the T dropped me on the outskirts of South Boston and I walked along Postal Road in the twilight toward the *dojo*. I crossed over Postal at my usual spot, following the obsolete railroad tracks, tramping the weeds under my shoes. As I walked beneath the fading sky, I watched the former sheet metal factory grow with my approach—an industrial blight that was my Shaolin Temple.

When I reached the building, I went in and climbed the stairs to the third floor. On the door was a sign reading: VERNON PAUL ZACHARY ACADEMY. From the landing I could hear on the opposite side of the heavy steel door the sounds of punches and kicks against the *makiwara* and heavy bags. I removed my shoes and left them with the others. My stomach started to churn as I pushed open the door and put my foot in the jam to hold it. The squeak of the rusty hinges stopped abruptly. I bowed, then clapped twice in honor of the pictures of the late masters, the sound reverberating off the cinder block walls. "*Konban wa*," I announced, then bowed once more and stepped inside.

"*Konban wa*," a few answered by rote.

"*Konban wa*, J.J.," called Manny. Manny was an amazing martial artist, who'd taken me under his wing when I'd first shown up here a few weeks before. I'd first taken karate as a gym class at Brandeis, then gotten a letter of referral from the sensei there to the Zachary school.

I hadn't wanted to change *dojos*, but when I'd told Sensei Mysko that I'd rather commute from Boston to Waltham to keep training with him, he just smiled. He said I'd learn more from Sensei Zachary in a year than he could teach me in a lifetime.

"Just be prepared though," he'd warned me one night, "he's pretty unorthodox."

"Unorthodox?"

"After I tested for my black belt, he pulled me aside and said there was one more thing I had to do to get it. He pointed across the room to a woman he knew I liked but was too shy to approach, and said I'd have to ask her out. I figured he'd spoken to her about me, but he said, 'Never once. In fact, I'm pretty sure she'll turn you down. That's why you have to ask.' It took me three weeks to give in, wearing that damn brown belt every day. When I finally asked her, she turned me down flat."

"That was cruel," I said, but he shook his head.

"He doesn't have a mean bone in his body. He was doing it for me. He thought it was important for my development."

Around the room now, students were stretching, practicing *kata* or hitting one of the two heavy bags that hung by thick chains from the twenty-foot ceiling. Manny was slamming his shin repeatedly into the *makiwara*, a vertical plank of wood wrapped in tape and bolted into a stand that itself was bolted into the floor. I winced at his routine as I continued silently into the locker room and removed my clothes. I stepped into my heavy white cotton *gi* pants and pulled the drawstring tight. If it comes loose during a workout, protocol requires you to step off the floor to re-tie it. By the time you unwrap your *obi* and jacket to fix the drawstring, you can miss an entire *kata*. Next I put on my *gi* jacket, still cold from a day hung in my law school locker. Finally, the *obi*. Mine was brown, and I wore it with less pride than I'd worn my green before. The green belt had been an accomplishment—the first step up from white. The brown was an albatross—still a long way from black, and who knew what I'd have to do to get that.

Holding the *obi* in front of me, I lined up its center with my own. I wrapped it from front to back, doubled it over and tied it in front. After checking to see that the knot was right and the belt wasn't twisted, I snapped the knot secure, drew a deep breath and left the locker room. I paused to bow by the edge of the warped planks of gray-painted applewood that comprised the floor, then stepped on. In a corner of the cavernous room, I found an open spot and stretched.

There was a lot of chatter around me. A new Zachary story seemed to be circulating and people were debating whether it was true. Everyone knew that sensei had been growing frustrated with Manny. He wanted him to teach more classes but Manny had been reluctant. Zachary concluded that Manny had a problem accepting responsibility. So yesterday morning, according to the story, he took Manny for a drive, pulled into a parking lot, steered the car toward a wall and dove into the back seat. I glanced at Manny, practicing elbow strikes against the heavy bag, his eyes straight ahead. I wouldn't dare ask.

"Line up," Zachary announced as he sauntered toward the front of the room, his shoulders rolling with each step.

He faced the class as we lined up in front of him, eight across and four deep. We lined up in order of rank, with the exception of the brown belts. Though we outranked the white and green belts, we lined up behind them, in the back row, so that when the class turned 180 degrees during exercises, they'd still have someone to watch.

Zachary dropped onto one knee, then both. We did the same. Bracing himself on one fist, he spun his back to us and looked up at the row of etchings and photographs—the masters—some still living, some long gone. After a moment, he brought his hands out from his sides and we did the same. Everyone clapped twice, bowed, then clapped once more. The simultaneous clap of sixty-six hands raised the dust off the floor and I had to close my eyes. When I opened them again, I couldn't believe what I saw. In the row ahead of me— Professor Josiah Steele.

I blinked in disbelief. Though his back was to me, he was three rows off to my right, his three-quarter profile clear to see. It was him all right, the angel of the bottomless pit, right here in my sanctuary. His tail cleverly tucked into his *gi* pants, he sat silent, modestly awaiting Zachary's instructions.

The blood rushed to my face as I stared at him, every insult ringing in my ears. I wanted to leave right then and there, find somewhere else to work out. But something caught my attention. Around his waist, Steele wore a white belt. Not only white, but perfectly clean, still with its original creases, tied incorrectly. This was probably the first karate class of his life, I realized, which meant that I was now his superior.

I glared at his profile, thinking of all the things I could do to him. But there were limits. Zachary insisted that senior students show compassion toward juniors, damn it all. If I went too far with Steele, Zachary might expel me. But just look at him, pretending to be human in that twenty-dollar *gi*. Maybe it would be worth expulsion.

I watched Steele all through the stretching and calisthenics, until Zachary told everyone to choose partners for arm pounding. I immediately tried to find anyone other than Steele to work out with, or maybe I walked directly toward him.

My loins girt about with truth, my feet shod with faith, and the breastplate of justice over my heart, I stepped forward and confronted the Explorer of the Left Hand Path. I could hear the wailing of damned souls leaking from his ears, could feel the fiery breath of the Accuser.

"Aren't you a student of mine?" he asked. No seating chart here.

I lifted my chin. "A student I be," I said.

"How's that?"

"Huh?"

"J.J.," Zachary called, "would you take Josie off to the side and help him with his *obi*?"

That sounded odd—*Josie*. Steele turned from Zachary back to me with a furrowed brow.

"He means your belt," I said. "It's twisted." He looked down and started to untie it, but I stopped him and led him off the floor. "You're not allowed to fix anything on the floor."

"Why are they hitting each other's arms?" he asked after we finished re-tying his belt.

"It's called *kotekitae*," I said. "Arm pounding. It toughens the forearms, helps you block better."

"Looks painful."

"It is. Come on, I'll show you."

Steele and I faced each other, and I stared directly into his undead eyes. *Throw a left punch, oh Moloch, Messenger of Odin, Tempter of the Canaanites, Aztec God of Pain*, I thought. "Throw a left punch," I said.

"Like this?"

"Well, yes, but preferably with your thumb on the outside of your fist. Good, now just hold it there."

Then, savoring it like my first incredulous touch of a woman's smooth flesh, I slowly but firmly smashed the inside of his extended forearm with the inner edge of my right forearm, my elbow at a right angle, my palm facing my own face. It was so satisfying that I didn't even mind the puff of hot air that licked across my cheek as the flames of hell everlasting escaped his mouth along with a Tic-Tac. I followed this with a circular block with my left arm, moving his punch to the outside of my left. Then I lifted my right fist over my head and accelerated downward, hitting the forearm that he held dutifully extended. His eyes watered but he otherwise showed no pain. Now it was his turn. I threw a left punch and held it there as I guided him through the blocks.

He hit me very softly with both strikes. He's trying to lower the stakes, I thought, but I'd have none of it. As I saw it, I was already being nicer than he deserved, because there's a nerve that runs across the thumb side of the wrist that I could've been targeting, but had intentionally avoided. I recalled no such tether on his mouth earlier in the day. The more I thought of it, the harder I hit him.

He knew exactly what was happening. And though I knew that taking it easy on him here might lead him to return the favor in class, I didn't care. Appeasement is fundamentally dishonest. I continued to lay it on and he continued to take it, both of us knowing that the leverage would shift again in fourteen hours. He'd destroy me in class by day, and I'd destroy him here by night, and we made a silent pact to live honestly with each other.

"Line up!" Zachary finally called.

Steele started to walk away but I grabbed him roughly by the shoulder. He stared at me, flustered. I directed his attention to the other pairs around us, all of whom were exchanging bows. He bowed to me and I bowed back, and as I was leaning forward, I whispered, "Want a mop and a fresh diaper, Professor?"

⁂

"Manny," I said during a water break, "are you leading the sparring tonight?"

He was bent over the water fountain, slurping with abandon. "Yeah," he exhaled, then cupped two handfuls of water and splashed them across his face. He stood erect, pushing the water through his black mullet. "But only the *dans* are doing freestyle. Sensei said I should have the rest of you do some choreographed stuff. Why? You want another crack at the little guy you were beating up?" He smiled.

"You saw that?"

"Hell, yeah—what's the problem, man?"

"He's a professor of mine."

He held up one hand. "Enough said—he's yours all night."

"Actually, no," I said. "That's what I wanted to ask you. Could you not pair us up?"

"Why not?"

"I don't know, he...he gets me too mad. I look at him, and I just boil. I can't keep my head."

He leaned forward and spoke out of a corner of his mouth. "That's the beauty part—you don't have to here. Everyone sensei lets in signs a waiver. You think you're the first guy to jump ugly? Man, I remember one time—"

"No, Manny, please. Seriously, I'm afraid of what I might do." I could see that he was disappointed, whether in my lack of commitment or emotional discipline, I don't know. "Maybe in a week or so, but not tonight—I had a bad time with him in class today. It's just, it's not...please, okay?"

"You serious, counselor?" That's what he called me when I let him down. I wished it didn't matter to me.

"Yeah," I said with some hesitation, "I'm sure."

He looked at me and shook his head, then just turned and walked away, leaving me feeling soft and lawyerly. We drilled for another fifteen minutes, until Zachary called us back into line.

"Black belts, over here for sparring. Manny, *kyu kumite* with the *kyu* ranks."

Manny bowed toward Zachary, then motioned for the rest of us to follow him.

"Everyone know *kyu kumite*?" he asked, and only Steele did not. "It's your first class, right?" he asked Steele, who nodded. "Okay, well, *kyu kumite* is a beginners' sparring drill. '*Kyu*' means beginner, and '*kumite*' means sparring. What those guys are doing over there," he indicated the black belts, "is *jyu kumite*, freestyle sparring. You'll get to that, but for now, this is better. And you're in luck—we've got one of our best *kyu kumite* teachers right here tonight. J.J., you'll be working with, I'm sorry, what's your name?"

"Josie," Steele said softly.

"You'll be working with Josie."

For a long moment, my eyes met Manny's, but he just stared at me, the hint of a smile curling one corner of his mouth. "Give me two straight lines, facing each other," he said. "People facing the wall, you'll be the attackers, other side defends, and we'll alternate. J.J., Josie, don't worry about keeping up. Okay, let's go—*kyu kumite* one, let's see it."

"Right punch," I said, and Steele threw a right punch, which I blocked with a right circle block. "Left punch," I said, and he threw a left that I blocked with a left circle block. With his left arm blocked to the outside of mine, his entire left flank was open. I punched to the ribs but pulled up short of contact. So far, so good.

"Other way," Manny called.

It took Steele longer to do the defenses, but he caught on fast. His technique was poor, of course, but he remembered the choreography immediately. In fact, through our first four sets of attacks and defenses, I don't think I ever had to show him anything twice. Still, we fell behind the others because I had to make corrections to his technique. I was determined to keep my head, to show Manny my discipline. And I have to say, Steele made it easy. He wasn't strong but he was more fluidly athletic than I would've thought. And he kept trying, never recoiling from contact or acknowledging the subtext. We even shared a couple of laughs, when a few times he anticipated my punches or kicks, whipping out tense, sloppy blocks before I had even attacked.

"Number five," Manny called. "How are you guys doing over there?"

"We're fine," I answered.

"Josie, you got good legs," Manny noted. "Let me see some mustard on these roundhouse kicks, okay?"

"Okay."

That was a trap.

The fifth sequence in *kyu kumite* is painful when you kick too hard, even for advanced students. Most of our blocks yield—absorbing and redirecting the attacker's force—but the block called for in the choreography of *kyu kumite* five meets force on force. The harder Steele kicked, the harder his shin would get hit.

The sequence began with a straight punch and front snap kick, both of which I deflected. Then I saw him wind up for the first roundhouse kick. He threw his entire body into it, and it came at me hip high, fast and unbalanced. I tucked my right elbow, locking my arm in place by pulling down hard with my latissimus dorsi muscle. His shin slammed into the outer edge of my right forearm and his planted leg wobbled. I felt ridiculous, but couldn't even give him time to withdraw his leg, as instinct was surely screaming at him to do. I couldn't do that because the choreography now called for me to sweep across my body with my other forearm and attack his calf muscle. This is the most brutal part of the block, because the biomechanics of kicking leave that muscle relaxed and therefore vulnerable. Feeling Manny's eyes on me, knowing that he was waiting to see what I'd do, I finished the block.

Steele was suffering and was past the point where he could hide it. He stared at me in disbelief, his face flushed, his mouth agape.

"Come on, Josie, finish your attack," Manny shouted. "Right roundhouse, right roundhouse!"

The disbelief gave way to determination, and he wound up to throw the exact same kick with the opposite leg. But I couldn't do it to him. So as the right kick came, I pivoted away and blocked it more softly. Then I came across with my opposite forearm, scooped it under Steele's leg and helped the leg to continue along the course of its arc. Letting it pass my body under its own momentum, I tossed his foot down and to the side, leaving Steele with his back to me. I grabbed his shoulder and punched past his head. He flinched as the punch passed him, spun around as I took a step back, and stared at me. He put weight on the leg to test it, and smiled when he realized that he was okay.

"Very sweet, counselor," Manny chided. I didn't look at him. "Other side."

"You okay?" I asked Steele before I attacked.

"My shin," he answered.

"Let's go!" Manny shouted.

His voice jolted me, and I attacked without thinking, forgetting that I was working with a beginner. He never had a chance. The straight, right punch connected cleanly with his chest, sounding like a work boot falling off a high shelf onto a kettle drum. Steele's circular block, designed to defend against the first punch, finally came as my right front snap kick was returning from his midriff. I paused when I realized what I had done, and took a lot off the left roundhouse kick to give him a chance to regain his composure. But he was, if not angry now, certainly overwrought, and moving too fast. He did well with the crossblock. Since I hadn't kicked hard, it didn't hurt either his arm or my shin. Then I threw the right roundhouse. He managed to trap it and began to throw it. But you're not really supposed to throw the leg, you're supposed to allow it to continue along its arc and lead it downward, so that the attacker can't continue his spin and hit you with a backfist or spinning kick. There's another reason too, especially when working near one of the *dojo* walls.

"Throw it down," Manny shouted, but he was too late. Still pumped with adrenalin, Steele threw my foot as though it were a tetherball. I spun from right to left with my right leg extended, my spin stopping abruptly when my foot slammed into the cement wall of the *dojo*. I felt a crack. As my foot fell to the floor, I found that Steele's foot was somehow occupying the exact spot on which my own already broken limb sought to land. My ankle twisted violently beneath my body weight, and I sprawled to the floor.

"Oh God!" I screamed, writhing in pain. I covered my face with my hands, feeling a fire in my leg. Someone rolled me onto my back and pulled my hands aside. Gasping for breath, I looked up. Overhead, the ceiling fan whirled clockwise and the ring of faces staring down at me whirled counterclockwise. I closed my eyes and went dark.

Chapter eleven

The foot was broken in three places. Impact with the wall caused the first two breaks, and the third happened when I rolled the ankle as I fell. In the hospital emergency room, a young doctor wrapped a fiberglass cast around my leg as Amy leaned against the far wall, still half asleep. I watched her as the doctor worked, her long dark hair pulled back in a ponytail, her eyes heavy. I had crawled into her room at five o'clock in the morning after refusing to let her take me to the hospital the previous night. She didn't complain. We drove in the darkness toward the hospital, and I kept waiting for a reprimand, a tease—even a yawn—but she just drove, comforting me occasionally with, "almost there, almost there."

"Okay, that should do it," the doctor said, turning away to go wash his hands in the sink near Amy.

"It's too tight."

"It's swollen," he called back over his shoulder. "It has to fit for ten weeks."

"Ten weeks?"

"Afraid so. Here, take these," he said, handing me two small pills and a paper cup full of water. "They're painkillers, and I'm going to send you home with a prescription for more. But don't take too many. Wait until you need them. And you should stay in bed for a week."

"A week?" I almost choked up the pills. "I have class in an hour."

"Not today, I'm afraid."

"I can't miss a whole week; I'm first year law. I'll never catch up."

"A week," he repeated. "I need your word."

"I can't give it to you."

"You don't need his word," Amy yawned, pushing off the wall. She came over and sat on the edge of the gurney. "You have mine."

"You're going to keep me in bed?"

"I'll do whatever it takes," she shrugged, playfully beginning to untie the drawstring of her navy blue sweatpants.

I looked at the doctor, who was staring at Amy. "Um, doctor?" I asked.

He blushed when he realized he'd been staring, but who could blame him? He wasn't much older than I. And Amy looked beautiful this morning. The ponytail held her hair off her face, accentuating her blue eyes. But it wasn't just that. In her naturalist, hippie way, Amy had a naked quality about her, even when dressed. I'd seen her effect on men ever since college, and I'd be lying if I said she didn't sometimes have that effect on me. But she'd always had a boyfriend when I was single, and I'd always had a girlfriend when she was single, and before either one of us knew it, we had a friendship that had outlasted the boyfriends and girlfriends. But sometimes, the way we flirted with each other, I couldn't help but wonder what it would be like to make love to her.

She stared back at the doctor now, her eyes amused. "Irresistible, aren't I, dad?" she asked, then motioned toward me. "Even he's thinking I might be serious, and he's still in love with his ex-girlfriend."

"True on every level," I admitted.

"Yes, well," the doctor stammered, "so that's a week in bed, come back and see us in ten weeks and we'll probably be able to take it off then."

"How about karate?" I asked.

He looked back at Amy.

"He's being literal," she laughed.

"Oh, God, I'm so sorry. Karate—what, with the kicking and punching people?"

I nodded.

"Oh no, not for some time, I wouldn't think."

"Some time?"

"It's a bad break," he explained. "You're not going to be able to kick things for a long while."

"How long?"

"I don't know," he said. "Six months, a year…I really can't say."

"A year?" I laid back on the gurney, held my hands to my head and stared at the ceiling. My foot throbbed in the cast. My silent deal with Professor Steele suddenly seemed pretty lopsided: he'd destroy me in class by day and I'd destroy him in the *dojo* beginning next year, assuming he wasn't better than me by then. I'd tugged on Lucifer's cape.

"Is your boyfriend okay?" I heard the doctor ask.

"Oh, we're just friends," Amy was quick to say.

The lights dimmed, steam wafted up from a street vent and, off in the distance, a saxophone began to play.

"I'm Howard," his voice dipped an octave.

"Amy."

"Where are you from, Amy?"

"Upstate New York—Ithaca."

"Me? I'm fine," I offered. "Never better, tip-top."

"I know Ithaca," Doctor Howard said. "I have family there. Do you know Beth Dodd?"

"I was homeschooled," she answered. "I didn't know a lot of people my age."

"Homeschooled, really? Your parents sound like interesting people."

"Cornell professors, environmental activists, brown socks and Birkenstocks—you know the type."

"You are the type," I said.

"I did get to run track with the high school team," she added, ignoring me.

I sat up and felt my head spin. "Whoa."

Howard never took his eyes off Amy. "I'm a runner too," he said. "You ever do the reservoir out by Cleveland Circle?"

"I love the reservoir."

"Maybe we could run it together one day. I'm supposed to be at a barbecue Saturday. Want to run, then go with me?"

"That sounds nice."

"Arrowroot and seitan burgers," I put in before lying back down.

"You're a vegetarian?"

"*Non-genetically modified* vegetables," I emphasized.

"I'm sure there'll be pasta," he said.

"Udon noodles, you hyena."

"You know what?" Howard persisted. "We don't even have to eat there. We could just hang out a while, then go out for lunch. Or we could skip the run, and—"

"Cannibal."

"Would you excuse me for a minute?" I heard Amy say, then felt a pillow over my face. "I'd love to go to the barbecue," I heard her muffled voice through the pillow.

As we drove home through morning rush-hour traffic, I stared out the window in silence. Amy tried to cheer me up, but all I could think was that college had just ended, and I'd already lost my girlfriend, my free time, and the use of a leg. Watching Comm Ave pass by out the window, my head felt heavy. Though my foot throbbed, it didn't bother me. It was more of a curiosity, and I looked at my watch, wondering if the second hand was synchronized to the throbs.

"Can we stop at school, Ame?"

"What for?"

"I need to get some things from my locker."

She looked at me askance. "You're not going to classes today, J.J."

"I know."

"I'm serious."

"I know," I repeated.

"And I'm not really going to sleep with you to keep you in bed."

"Ame, I know all that," I said. "But it's bad enough that I can't be in class—I can at least keep up with the reading."

We were on Comm Ave anyway, so she pulled the car up alongside the curb in front of the law school and threw it into park. "What books do you need?"

"Conlaw, Torts, Civ Pro, Conlaw and Torts."

Her eyes narrowed. "How many of those pills did he give you?"

"And Civ Pro."

She rolled her eyes. "Where are the lockers?"

"Basement, I'm number 34J. 18-12-7...12-7-18-12. Hike!" I started laughing.

"I'll figure it out. Don't you move, dad," she warned.

But as soon as she got out of the car and disappeared into the school, I pulled the crutches from the back seat and wobbled in after her. She was in the basement, so I headed immediately for an upper floor. I got lucky—an elevator was waiting. It was full of people, but when they saw my condition, someone got out and ev-eryone compressed to make extra room for me. Standing upright for the first time in a while, fluid filled my foot. It felt ready to explode. By the time the elevator reached my floor, I was perspiring and dizzy. Some-one helped me into the room for my upcoming Torts class and led me to my seat. Bernie Nockowitz, who sat directly in front of me in Torts, even took a different seat for the day so I could keep my foot elevated. These are wonderful people, I thought. Why doesn't anyone like lawyers?

As class began, I struggled to pay attention. But my foot throbbed. My mind was foggy. Under the best of circumstances, Professor Vermilyea's lectures were at least as strong a soporific as whatever it was they'd fed me at the hospital. Today, near as I could tell, he had given up the pretense of teaching, or even separating his lecture into individual words. Only a monotonous hum came from his lips, as the ventilation system pumped ether into the air and the wall clock clacked like a woodpecker.

I thought of Amy. Poor Amy. It's hard to be born without the capacity to deceive. It leaves you so helpless. I could picture her right now, standing by the car, confused, with an armload of my books. I might have turned myself in right then had the door not burst open. The entire class sat in stunned silence as an angry hippie with a naked quality stormed down to my seat and dragged me from the room.

She didn't talk to me all day, but finally forgave me when the good doctor Howard called later that night and asked her out.

New York
Present Day

Chapter twelve

I no longer inhabit a world that tolerates people born without the capacity to deceive. The world I've chosen regards such people as children, with no idea of how the world really works. These children, meanwhile, regard the inhabitants of my world as pitiable cynics who happened one day to come upon their last remaining hope clinging by its fingernails to the edge of the abyss, and decided with great weariness to just stomp the damn hand. If only I felt at home in either world, maybe I wouldn't be sitting here right now.

Ira and I watch as three austere men in dark suits take their seats directly in front of us. They're the New York State Bar Association Disciplinary Committee, and they don't even glance in my direction as they settle into their seats and whisper into each other's ears. The one in the center appears to be in charge. He makes notes with a burgundy Mont Blanc pen, still not bothering to look up. He's overweight, and his neck bubbles over his collar like a soufflé. Ira waits patiently, his notes spread out on the table in front of him.

From behind me, I hear the door to the room open. Relieved that Josie's finally arrived, I turn to the rear of the room, as does Ira. All three members of the disciplinary committee look up too. But when the door opens, it's an old black gentleman, holding his fedora hat to his chest with both hands. He wears a tattered gray suit, the jacket unbuttoned and a little too big on him.

"This is a private session, sir," the center judge says.

The man has a bit of confusion in his eyes, but doesn't turn around and leave. Instead, as the panel returns to their whispering and writing, he scans the room. Just as he acknowledges my mother on the witness bench, I realize who I am looking at. It's Dairian Davis. He's old and tired after so many years, but it's him. I recognize him by his dignity.

Seeing him, I feel safe, at least for the moment. I'm behind a closed bedroom door under a heavy blanket. He's seated at the foot of my bed, leaning against the wall with his arms resting on his bent knees. The door won't open, and even if it does, Dairian will stand and plant himself between my father and me. He won't have to utter a word to say that he's not clearing the way. But he's out of his element here, and the panel doesn't need to get around him to get at me.

The years must have been hard on him. His face has lost its fullness. The fingers holding the hat are crooked, with deep, dark creases in the knuckles. His eyes continue to scan the room until they find mine. It's not anger I see in them, not even disapproval. Maybe it's dismay, as though he doesn't understand what we're all doing here. I feel my lips curve upward into a hesitant, sheepish grin, like the night he rushed over to our apartment and I had to admit that my father's tantrum that night was my fault, because I had used one of his ties and a bottle of alcohol to try my hand at a Molotov cocktail.

"Sir, I said this is a private session," the judge repeats when he realizes Dairian is still here.

"He's with me, Your Honor," my mother calls, half standing.

"Oh, fine then. Take your seat please, sir; we're about to begin."

Only then does Dairian take his eyes off me and turn to join my mother.

"For crying out loud, Ira," I whisper, "why is he here?"

"Your mother insisted," he replies. "Said he was sort of an uncle. What's wrong?"

"You couldn't have brought anyone to make me feel worse."

"Mr. Finowitz," the center judge says now, "are you ready?"

"Yes sir," Ira answers.

"You have all your character witnesses?"

"We're missing just one, sir. But I spoke to him last night and he's on his way. He's from out of town."

"That would be Professor Steele."

"Yes."

"Mr. Spencer," the judge turns to me, "I assume you understand how serious the charges against you are." I nod as he continues. "Your former employer, Greer, Babcock and Drew, has filed a formal complaint against you for breaching attorney-client confidentiality—which if true is quite disgraceful in itself, but with your list of ethical transgressions, it's hard to say which of them is worst."

"I'd ask that the panel refrain from drawing any conclusions until we've had a chance to develop the facts and put them in proper perspective," Ira interrupts.

"Counselor, this isn't a courtroom," the judge says, "and I'll remind you that we didn't even have to grant you this hearing; it's a courtesy. So let's proceed with that in mind." He picks up just the upper half of a piece of paper in front of him and tilts his head up to look down at it. "Mr. Spencer, you're also accused of driving while intoxicated, possession of illegal narcotics, brawling in the streets, and...what's this?" he leans to his right and shows the paper to his colleague on the panel. I can't hear what the man says, but the judge looks at me over the top of his glasses and asks: "Running out of Docks restaurant without paying for your dinner?"

"I paid them," I say quickly, then turn to Ira. "I went back and paid for that dinner the next day." I start to explain that I'd run out of the restaurant to help Gus, then just forgotten to go back, but Ira puts his hand on my forearm on the desk and I hush up. I can't even bring myself to look in Dairian's direction.

The judge removes his glasses and addresses Ira. "I know the purpose of this hearing isn't to decide guilt or innocence; it's to decide whether Mr. Spencer has the character and fitness to practice law in the state of New York. But I have to say, Mr. Finowitz, I don't see that happening if all you have are excuses. Some of these charges better not be true."

"That's why I suggested delaying this hearing until my client's criminal proceedings are over," Ira says.

"As I told you, our rules say that hearings must be held expeditiously."

"And as I told you, Mr. Carlysle," Ira raises his voice a bit, "'expeditiously' is a subjective word, and in this case—"

"Are we going to hear from a witness or not?"

"Our first witness is Mr. Spencer's mother, Ms. Beverly Spencer."

"His mother?" Carlysle repeats.

"Yes sir."

He rolls his eyes as another judge leans forward. "What time is Professor Steele expected?"

"He'll be here," Ira says. "Our first witness is Beverly Spencer."

The judges look at each other and smile.

"Can't we just stipulate that she thinks he's wonderful?" the third one smirks.

"Our first witness is Beverly Spencer."

They all lean back in their chairs as my mother walks stiffly toward the witness chair. The stenographer's hands pause above her keyboard as my mother takes her seat. With Ira leading, she recounts some basics for the committee—who she is, where she lives—then nods along as Ira says: "As Mr. Peabody here was kind enough to point out, mothers generally think well of their sons. So instead of summarizing his character, would you instead give this committee specific illustrations of it? And please, confine your remarks to facts and not opinions." As he says this last part, he smiles toward Peabody, who nods and returns the smile. Out of a tense situation, he creates a moment of community—he's so good, it's scary.

"My son has never been in trouble in his life," my mother begins, and I already know she's decided to blur some facts because she knew about the Molotov cocktail. It didn't ignite, but Leo and I did drop it from a ninth-story window onto my father's parked car. "He was always an excellent student, and never wanted to do anything else with his life but be a lawyer."

I look immediately to Dairian when she says that, and I see his head cock to the side and his brow furrow. When I see him begin to turn toward me, I look away.

She talks for a while more about my lifelong quest to be an attorney and my excitement when I got the letter saying I'd passed the bar exam. She tells them about the celebratory dinner my family had when I got the job at Greer, Babcock and Drew, not mentioning—perhaps not even having noticed—the fact that I barely ate.

"Mrs. Spencer," Carlysle says when she's finished, "as a mother, what do you think of your son's driving under the influence of alcohol? His possession of illegal narcotics? Were you aware of your son's substance-abuse issues?"

"He doesn't have substance-abuse issues," Ira shouts. "That's a logical leap that's beyond ludicrous."

"Fine, strike my last sentence," Carlysle says. The stenographer adds the words, 'Strike my last sentence,' because she's not allowed to actually strike anything. "Mrs. Spencer?"

"Your Honor, you have to understand where J.J. comes from," my mother says, and I'm immediately concerned about where she's heading with this. "He had a mean drunk of a father who left us when J.J. was just ten. The fact that he's even got this far…"

"Do you think your son's alcohol problems could be inherited from his father?" Peabody asks.

"I never thought of that," my mother tilts her head. "Maybe."

"Mom!"

"I mean, no," she says as she looks at me. "That's definitely not where his alcohol problems come from."

"Oh God." I drop my head into my hand.

"Mrs. Spencer," Ira leaps in, "you don't really think your son has alcohol problems, do you?"

"You're leading the witness, counselor," Carlysle warns.

My mother is scrambling now. "No, he doesn't have alcohol problems…"

"Mrs. Spencer…"

"No, now you're trying to get me to say stuff," she persists. She closes her eyes, takes a deep breath and holds up her hands. "Everyone shut up so I can talk."

Ira starts to speak but I grab his arm. My mother's a gentle soul, but they've just awakened the bear. Leo and I used to hear the same words when we got out of hand.

"She's okay now," I say, and Ira trusts me.

"My son doesn't have a drinking problem—believe me, I know what one looks like. He lost his job that day. He went to have a few—big deal. You grow up in the home he did and let's see if you're sitting there like big shots. J.J. went to four grade schools, three middle schools and two high schools, and he was straight As in all of them. He would've been valuditorian when he graduated except he was only at the school for a year and a half, and he paid his own way through college." Peripherally, I see Ira look at me but I don't acknowledge it. "Any of you pay your way through college?" she challenges Peabody, who looks down at his notes. "I didn't think so. He had a bad day," she adds. "He's had a lot of good ones too." She doesn't wait for anyone to tell her to step down, just gets up when she's done and comes over to me. The stiffness is gone from her walk, replaced by a Brooklyn strut. "I love you," she says as she takes my head in her two hands and kisses me on the cheek. "These clowns ain't half what you are."

Chapter thirteen

We break for lunch after Leo's test mony. As we're leaving the hearing room, my main goal is to avoid having to face Dairian. I stay on Ira's right side as everyone else exits from the left. The last people I expect to approach from the right as we step outside the room are Emily and Jared Eagan. I haven't seen them since the day in the delicatessen, and haven't heard from them since their ill-advised thank you note.

"Oh thank God, there you are," Emily exclaims breathlessly when she sees me. She shakes her head once to clear the hair from her eyes. "You have to help us, Mr. Spencer."

I look at her, then past her to Jared. He looks even thinner, and his eyes are red-rimmed, but I'm too preoccupied with my own troubles at the moment to give it much thought.

"Help you?" I turn back to Emily. "You're the reason I'm in this mess. How could you send flowers to my office? You got me fired, you know."

If she hears me, she doesn't show it.

"We filed bankruptcy just like you told us to do, and Mr.

Boston said it was the worst advice we could've gotten. He's suing us for everything."

"He was already suing you for everything," I say, but she shakes her head.

"No—he says he would've cut us a very nice deal if we hadn't filed, but now he's going to ruin us."

"How did you know where I was?"

"Mr. Boston told us," she says, moving closer. "He said, 'You want to see who you're taking advice from? Go down to 61 Broadway. He's being disbarred for incompetence.' Is that true?"

I can feel the blood fill my face. "He said what?" I imagine him sitting with his legs crossed, his hairless white ankle in full view, an arrogant sneer on his face, and at the moment, I want nothing more than revenge.

"Are you really being disbarred?" Jared asks, standing a step behind his wife, perspiring. His breaths are heavy.

"Are you okay, Mr. Eagan?"

"Just a little episode," he explains. "I'm okay."

Emily looks at him, then back to me. "I rushed him too much getting over here and he lost his breath. Use your inhaler again, baby," she says, fishing it out of her purse and holding it for him. She turns to me as Jared takes long, slow breaths with the inhaler. "I'm so sorry we got you fired," she tells me. "It was a stupid thing to do, sending the flowers. It never occurred to me..."

She doesn't finish the sentence and I wouldn't have answered anyway, because I can't take my eyes off of Jared. She notices this and turns to him. I look up at Ira and he takes his eyes off them long enough to meet mine. He shakes his head so slightly that I don't know if he means to convey his disapproval of what he knows I'm about to say, or sympathy for the Eagans' plight.

"Look," I say, "we're just taking a short break here; I can't concentrate on this right now. But if you give me your address, I'll come by tonight. Say around eight?"

"Would it help if we came in there and explained what happened?" she asks.

"No thanks, it's okay."

"But what if they disbar you?"

"They won't," I say, feigning confidence.

"I'll be there tonight too," Ira adds.

Chapter fourteen

The Eagans live in a two-story town house in a community on the border of Queens and Nassau Counties. Ira and I arrive at a little past eight and park in the driveway they share with their neighbor. Ira has said little during the drive out, and I notice him looking up at the house as I step out of the car and lock the door.

"It's not too late to change your mind," I say. He continues to stare at the Eagans' home. "Finny, I've already made my bed, and you've been more than a good friend by defending me. There's no reason for you to risk your career." I point to Little Neck Parkway a hundred yards away. "Drive this road another mile north and I'm sure you can find a diner to grab a cup of coffee for an hour."

The expression on his face when he removes his gaze from the house and fixes it on me tells me he's considering the offer. I'd be very happy if he took it.

"Hey, I'd do the same thing in your shoes," I say. "You're a great lawyer and you're going to have a great career at Greer. Five years from now, you'll take on just the clients you want to represent, and Carter Boston will be working for you. But not if you hold secret meetings with people the firm is suing."

He walks around to the front of the car and sits back against the hood. He looks up at the house again, then down at his shoes.

"You think anyone ever really gets there, J.J.?"

"Where?"

"To turning down the Stan Eiderhorns of the world. I don't know, I think maybe the lawyers willing to turn down the Stan Eiderhorns never get started with them in the first place. The rest of us—hell, J.J., there are reasons we're with Greer now instead of with a non-profit, Greenpeace, I don't know. Maybe the D.A.'s office or public defender."

"Well—" I come around the front of the car and sit next to him "—I'm not with the D.A. because they wouldn't hire me."

He waves me off. "That's not true," he says. "You got seduced. We all get seduced. You got turned down by the Manhattan D.A. You could've applied to Queens, Nassau, Brooklyn, Westchester. We get seduced, and comfort ourselves with the notion that an ignoble road can lead to a noble destination."

"Can't it?"

He thinks for a while, then shrugs. "I don't know, but I suspect that, eventually, you become whoever you spend your days being."

The Long Island Expressway is just a few hundred yards to the south, and we pause when the sound of screeching brakes fills the air. We wait a moment for crunching metal, but it doesn't come. Another close call. Somewhere, a lawyer is putting his business cards back in his pocket and pressing his shoe back on the accelerator.

"Hey, Finny," I say, "don't you think golf would be a better game if you could play defense?"

"What?" he laughs.

"Defense," I repeat. "You know." I pantomime a golf club in my hands and plant myself right in front of him, challenging him to putt past me.

"Always a joke," he smiles, and steps past me toward the Eagans' walk. "Come on, let's go ruin my career."

I join him and put a hand on his shoulder. "It's cool—I'll defend you."

Emily appears at the door just as I'm about to press the door-bell. "I thought I heard someone out there," she smiles. "Come in, come in. Thank you both so much for coming."

She leads us through the entryway to the living room. The house is immaculate, although a strong, musty odor hangs in the air. She notices Ira lean his head back a bit and inhale, a quizzical expression on his face. "I know," she says apologetically, "it always smells this way. You're probably trying to figure out why we want to keep the place."

Jared enters from the kitchen, which is separated from the living room by an open doorway. He carries a tray of cheese—a cheddar cut into cubes—and crackers.

"Oh, you didn't have to go to any trouble," I say.

"No trouble at all," he answers, placing it on the coffee table before us. "We're just so grateful for your coming out all this way, especially with everything you're going through."

"Well, I got you into this."

"We could say the same."

"You look much better," Ira notes.

"Yeah," Jared answers. "I'm fine as long as I don't exert myself too much."

"I shouldn't have rushed him," Emily adds.

Jared turns back toward the kitchen. "Beer?" he asks.

Ira and I both decline, then ask the Eagans to bring us any loan documents they have, as well as letters and notices from Parker National, Eiderhorn or Greer. As they fill the coffee table with papers, I scan the photographs hanging on the wall.

"Kids asleep?"

"Thank goodness," Emily smiles.

"Where are your bankruptcy docs?" Ira asks.

"At the lawyer's," Jared says.

"We should see those," he says, and Jared makes a note to call the bankruptcy lawyer in the morning.

For the next two hours, Ira and I read through stacks of documents, making notes and pointing out things to each other. For the most part, they're documents we've already seen, since we've been handling their case from the other side. But there are a few new items. We make two piles—one containing papers that are relevant and might help, and the other, useless forms.

"Is there a restroom I could use?" I ask after a while.

"Of course," Emily answers, "but the one down here isn't working. Let me show you upstairs."

As she leads the way, the musty smell gets stronger. I revert to mouth breathing, subtly, so she doesn't notice. After I leave the bathroom, I make my way alone back toward the stairs leading down to the living room. I pause on the landing when I notice something on the wall, down by the floor where the molding meets the carpet. It's a common wall with the bathroom I just left. I check to make sure no one is watching me. Ira is seated on the couch with his back to me, hunched over the papers. The Eagans are catty-cornered on either side of him, staring at him while he reads. I kneel down to get a closer look at the wall, and pull back the corner of the carpet just a bit. Beneath it is a green-black slime. It trails along the floor and disappears behind the sheetrock. The musty smell is because of the mold, but it's not something to mention now. They seem desensitized to the smell, and wouldn't have the money to fix the problem anyway. I continue down the stairs and sit beside Ira. As we work, I notice more dark spots along the living room walls. We ought to let Eiderhorn have this place for free, I think, if he could stand it for an hour with the windows closed.

Another thirty minutes or so pass and I'm starting to run out of energy. I didn't realize until now how long a day this has been. But Ira just keeps going. When Emily brings some French bread pizza into the room and sets it down on the table, a dog follows her in.

Ira looks up from the papers with a smile on his face. "Hey, is that a border collie?" he asks. "Come here, boy," he calls to it, taking a small piece of cheese to entice it. "I had one of these when I was a kid," he says as he pets its head and feeds it cheese.

Jared watches proudly until the dog tries to get on the couch. "Dali, no," he reprimands.

"Dalai?" I ask, "as in Dalai Lama?"

"Salvador Dali," he says. "We're fans."

"Eggs on a plate without a plate," I smile.

His eyebrows arch up. "You know your Dali."

"Friend of mine, more than me," I explain, which reminds me that I should really try to call Josie tonight to see what's going on. "Listen," I say as I stand, "we should really be on our way. We have another day of hearings tomorrow."

"Did you see anything in these papers you think could help us?" Emily asks.

"Give us some time to think about it," I say as we're saying goodnight by the front door. "And call your bankruptcy lawyer to get the rest of the papers. I'll speak to you tomorrow."

"At least now we won't accidentally call you at work," Jared jokes.

"Hey, that's right," I remember. "Listen, guys, please, please, please—don't tell anyone that Mr. Finowitz was here tonight."

"We won't," they assure me, but that's not good enough.

"No, listen to me," I say. "This is really serious. Ira's taking a huge risk in trying to help you. He'd lose his job too if anyone found out. So no one—you hear? No one. Not your kids, not your best friends—please."

⁂

In the driveway outside the house, I pause. It's a beautiful evening, but with the lights off the Long Island Expressway just a short distance away, the night sky is drowned out.

"How far out of the city do you have to drive to see stars?" I ask as Ira walks around to the passenger side of my car.

He stares straight up, his long neck and protruding Adam's apple forming a triangle. "A lot farther than this," he says, then adds, "I don't think there's anything we can do to help these people, J.J."

I look down from the blank sky, walk around to my side of the car, and rest my forearms on the roof. "There has to be," I say. "It's my fault."

"Your advice was perfect. They messed themselves up by sending those flowers. If they had filed the seven and Boston never found

97

out that you were involved, he would've cut them a good deal. He's using them to get back at you."

"There's got to be something we can do."

"I don't know," he says. "Eiderhorn knows what he's doing—he doesn't leave a lot of loose ends."

I nod along but my mind is racing, trying to organize all the moving parts. There's always one that can help. I notice a light turn on in a bedroom of the house. "We shouldn't talk here," I say, and we get into the car.

Traffic back to the city is bumper to bumper. I'm a little surprised—traffic the week before Labor Day weekend is usually lighter because everyone's on vacation. Three lanes compress down to two just over the Queens border, and the two are repainted and rerouted. Near Junction Boulevard, cement dividers funnel the two lanes into one narrow canal. Just what the Long Island Expressway needs: a log flume. But even after the road opens up again to three lanes, the going is slow.

"I don't get volume traffic," Ira observes. "Granted, there are a lot of cars, but we're all going in the same direction."

"So how do we get Boston to treat the Eagans objectively?" I wonder aloud.

"Hey," Ira brightens, "I didn't know you were almost valuditorian."

I laugh at the memory of my mother's testimony. "Shut up, she did great."

"You think if the valedictorian and salutatorian got married and had kids, they'd all be valuditorians?"

"I was proud of her."

"Me too," he nods, looking ahead. "Know what else I didn't know? I didn't know you put yourself through school. I learned a lot about you today. You really do love the law."

"How do you figure?"

"Your mother. She said you never wanted to do anything but be a lawyer."

"I told you—I wanted to be a cop. Wasn't until I met Jennifer that I decided on law."

"How is Jen?"

"Beats me."

"Boy," he inhales, "I think she's probably the most beautiful woman I've ever met close up. I'll bet if you charted the firm's billable hours, you'd see a big drop-off coinciding with her visits."

"So you're saying the firm was behind the break-up?"

"Maybe she'll come back."

I sigh and throw the car into neutral as we come to a complete stop three miles from the Midtown Tunnel. "It's so tiring, though." I lean back and face Ira. "Is your marriage this tiring?"

It's not the fact that he shakes his head that strikes me, as much as the small, reflective smile that lifts the corners of his mouth. It tells me that maybe relationships don't have to be tiring.

"Work doesn't make you tired either, does it?" I ask.

"Nope," he answers. "You?"

"Oh yes," I exhale.

"Come on, J.J., you've got as much energy as anyone I know."

"Maybe tired is the wrong word. It makes me weary."

"Weary's the same as tired."

"No it's not. When I'm tired, I need sleep. When I'm weary, I need change."

"Well, you sure got yourself a heap of that."

I throw the car back into gear as traffic starts to move. "I did, didn't I?"

"You're going to call Steele when you get home, right?" I nod. "Because if he's not going to show, we're going to have to scramble to get another professional reference."

"He'll show, Finny," I say. "He's not some contact I made in school; he's a friend."

"So you say."

"He'll show."

"How close a friend?"

"Very close." He stares at me from the passenger seat, but I don't look at him. The traffic is finally picking up speed and I want to make some progress while I can. "Ira, trust me," I say.

"It's just that you never struck me as the type to stop by the professor's office with mini-muffins. I'm surprised you're friends."

Boston

Chapter fifteen

I stayed home from classes for a full week, just as I'd been ordered to do by the doctor whose presence I awakened to in my apartment this morning, and who by the by made a variety of ungodly rheumatic sounds in the shower while I tried to eat a soft-boiled egg for breakfast.

I gave up on the egg, wrapped some sponge around my crutch handles and strapped on Amy's backpack. I'd once sworn never to wear a backpack, but needed my books for class. After a week at home, it was time to get back into the fray. On the T to school, I thought about the dream I'd had the night before, in which I'd been engaged in a chess match against Jennifer. The pieces were made of black and white ivory, and every time I tried to move one of my white pieces, it turned black. Still, I persisted, even after my mother appeared, trying to tip my king. I held off my mother with one arm and waited for Jen's move. She wouldn't look at me. Her upper lip, beaded with sweat, rested on her fore-knuckle. Her eyes oscillated over the board. But these are the only pieces in the game, Jennifer. Either you have an option or you don't. Give in, be mine. I love you, and there must be some level of romantic logic that suggests you therefore love me too. That may make as much sense as pouring red wine over spilled seltzer, but it's all we have. Life is all we have. I'll admit it—I have no choice because I'm in love with you. How it goes, only time will tell. Let's let time tell.

"It don't mean nothing," Ed repeated for the fourth time as we stepped off the elevator on the sixteenth floor and made our way toward Con Law. It would be the first time I'd see Professor Steele since the night in the *dojo* a week before.

"I'm dreaming about chess, Ed," I persisted. "Don't you see what that implies?"

"It don't imply nothing."

"She came to my castle. My castle," I repeated for emphasis. "I think something's about to happen."

"Come on, J.J., make a lay-up." He held the door for me and I went into the room. I pivoted on the top landing to face him. It was a clean pivot. I was getting quite good with the crutches. "It's your dream, not hers. Until you can show me that she's visiting your castle"—he said the word with contempt—"in *her* dreams, it don't mean a thing. We already know *you're* obsessed. Now," he arched an eyebrow, "I think we ought to talk about the wrestling match with your mother."

"Not wrestling," I clarified. "Besides, you can't go by her. No one's ever good enough for her. Hell, I'm not even good enough for her."

"See, now that, I think, means something."

Professor Steele was already down at his lectern surrounded by students when we entered the room. He looked up at me as I hopped the steps down to my row, both crutches in my left hand, Ed steadying me by the elbow. I ignored him and continued to my seat. After removing my casebook, notebook and a pen from my backpack, I looked up again. He was still watching me.

"Some party, huh?" he said.

I had entertained the hope that guilt might convince him to show a bit of compassion toward me in class, but the fact that he thought it an appropriate subject to joke about showed how wrong I'd been. I'd made my bed when I decided to enter into this honest, brutal, ever-reversing relationship with him. Now I was on his turf, and wasn't even going to have the satisfaction of seeing him that night in the *dojo*. I returned his grin.

"Seriously," he continued, "how are you feeling?"

"Not so bad," I answered. I'm not sure what I meant by that, seeing as how my foot was broken in three places.

He stood there nodding for what seemed an awfully long time, his lips pursed. Then he turned back to the disciples. What was it they talked about up there? Is it really possible to have genuine questions that need answering before and after every class session of every subject? Don't they ever just read it, hear it, get it and move on?

"Ms. Jhangiani," Steele said once class began, "strictly from a legal perspective, what would you say is the most unsettling thing about the case of Skokie v. Frank Collin?"

Asha rummaged through her notes, trying to reconcile them with the casebook.

"The answer isn't in there, Ms. Jhangiani. I'm asking you for a personal opinion. What was most unsettling to you as a future attorney?"

"If I may, I shall say that it is the way that the National Socialist Party chose Skokie for their demonstration of Nazism. Skokie was a Jewish suburb of Chicago, with many residents who had survived the death camps. With so many other places available to them, I fail to see why, short of simple cruelty, they felt the need to march in Skokie."

"Okay, Ms. Jhangiani, now that you've stated the monumentally obvious, tell me," he leaned forward and raised his voice, "*as an attorney*, what do you find most unsettling?"

"That the court allowed them to do it?"

"Don't use the inflection of a question, Ms. Jhangiani because, again, I'm asking for your personal opinion. There's no right or wrong answer. Now—with conviction this time—what was most unsettling to you as an attorney?"

"That the court allowed them to do it."

"Wrong. Ms. Constantine, can you help Ms. Jhangiani?"

I tried to concentrate, but couldn't get my mind off my dream.

I'm not like Ed; I think dreams have meaning. I was trying to figure out what, when I heard: "Mr. Spencer, can you tell me why?"

I slowly looked up at the sound of my name. It was the only sound I'd heard for the past thirty-five minutes.

"Why?"

"Yes, why?"

Why. An interesting question to be asked of someone working without a frame of reference. Why indeed. My mind was a complete blank. Tabula rasa. Newborn baby, post-diluvian, one hand clapping—deeply spiritual. People pay handsomely to spend weekends in New Age spas, drink carrot juice, commune with dolphins and walk hot coals to get this feeling. But this wasn't the time for it. My face must have reflected what was going on behind my eyes—nothing—because Steele just shook his head and moved on to someone else.

"You know," Aaron Bocian whispered as Steele continued with the lecture, "I heard that Steele offered to represent the Nazis in the case, but they thought it would hurt their public image."

"You're putting me on."

"It's true; I heard it from a third-year."

"Mr. Spencer," Steele said as the hour wound to a close, "may I see you up here for a moment?"

"What's he want to see me for?" I asked Aaron.

"I have no idea."

"Arrogant son of a bitch," Asha growled as she gathered her books to leave. "I'd like to smash his skinny face."

Apprehensively, I made my way down toward the front of the class, where Steele was waiting for me. The zombies lumbered toward him, casebooks in outstretched hands and lips puckered.

"Not today," he announced before they could surround him. "Find me later in my office if you have something you need to discuss." I watched them shuffle out the door, then turned to Steele.

"You wanted to see me?"

"Yes," he said as he packed his books into a black leather brief-case. "Tell me about the leg."

"Broken," I shrugged.

"How long do you have to wear the cast?"

"Ten weeks."

He winced, then pushed his hair behind his ears. "I don't know what to say—" he looked down, then up at me again "—I'm sure you know it was a mistake."

"I know," I answered, shifting on the crutches. "It's okay, no big deal."

"Don't worry, your grades won't suffer if you hate me. If I failed everyone who hated me around here…"

Though he left the thought unfinished, something in the way he said it struck me. It had never occurred to me that Josiah Steele, condescending and spiteful, didn't want to be hated. But what did he expect? Did he think his constant stream of ridicule would lead to an invite and a foam finger at the hockey games? Seeing this side of him emboldened me.

"Can I ask you something?"

"Of course," he answered.

"How did you manage to get your foot all the way over there under mine?"

It lightened the mood. "I was trying to catch you," he laughed.

"Really? You're quick," I said. "Honestly, to do that, you must be awfully quick."

"I played tennis in college. Okay, let's go."

"Go?"

"We're going to lunch."

"I've already eaten."

"We're going to lunch," he repeated.

Chapter sixteen

Chef Chang's was past its noon rush hour, but still very active when we arrived. I felt uncomfortable being there with Steele.

"Professor," the host bowed, rushing over as we entered. "You come on good day. I tell chef you here."

"*Ni hao,*" Steele answered in singsong as he returned the bow.

He took a seat at a small round table near the kitchen. I paused, scanning the room for other law students.

"The adamantine Gates of Hell are hereby thrown open, Mr. Spencer—boldly stride in and have a spring roll."

"You know?" I asked as I sat across from him.

"Of course I know."

"Is it true you offered to represent the Nazis at Skokie but they were worried it might ruin their public image?"

"Skokie was in 1978, Mr. Spencer. Just how old do I look to you?" When I didn't answer, he said: "I'm thirty-nine."

I tried not to show my surprise, but it was at least ten years younger than I'd thought. And I really don't know why. When I looked at him more closely, his face wasn't old at all. Tired, but not old. We ordered a couple of beers and the waiter brought them quickly, along with a bowl of fried Chinese noodles. The noodles went quickly, a sacrifice to Steele's hunger and my anxiety. He ate fewer than I, because his routine slowed him down. Before eating, he'd heat each individual noodle. He took the red glass candleholder with the plastic white mesh stocking and moved it in front of him, then held a noodle over the flame. When it started to smoke, apparently, it was ready.

"Do you think thirty-nine is too old to take up karate?" he asked as he put a smoldering noodle into his mouth.

"Sensei Zachary didn't start until he was twenty-nine," I said.

"He's an interesting man," Steele said. "But a little unusual, huh?"

"A little?"

"When I first met him, I asked what style of karate he taught and he said it didn't matter."

"*Don't* matter," I corrected him. "He tells everyone that. Don't matter."

"Why?"

"He says it either makes sense or it doesn't, and either way, the name's irrelevant."

Steele nodded.

"You sure you want to be a part of that crazy place?"

"Yes," he said. He stared at a noodle, the flickering light of the candle reflecting in his eyes. "Very much so."

"They say he once made his class train blindfolded in the Boston Commons at midnight, to teach helplessness."

"You're trying to get rid of me," he said. "It won't work. What else do you know about him?"

"Not much," I said. "He served in Okinawa; that's where he learned. They say when he was younger, he was a hell of a fighter...oh, I'm sorry—no offense."

Steele sighed. "Mr. Spencer...J.J., I'm not as bad as people say." He paused and looked out the window onto Beacon Street, as though he'd just recognized a familiar face. He looked for another moment, then turned back to me. "At least, I didn't used to be. Tell me more. Does Zachary ever talk to you about the history of martial arts? Takuan Soho, Musashi…any of the ancient masters?"

"Not really."

"How about the spiritual component?"

"Spiritual component?"

"Yes, the defense as an attack, *wei wu wei*?"

"Way-woo-way? There's one guy who yells that all the time when women spar with each other, but sensei tells him to shut up."

He laughed. I just made Josiah Steele laugh. "Well, don't you know where the guy got that?"

"I assumed it was a derivation of 'woohoo.'"

He chuckled again and pushed his hair behind his ears. "*Wei wu wei* is from an ancient text called the *Tao te Ching*. It means 'action through inaction.'"

"Oh," I nodded, more interested in catching the eye of the waiter to get another bowl of noodles. "What's the other thing you said?"

"The defense as an attack." He thought for a minute, looking back out onto Beacon Street, then leaned back in his chair as the waiter came over with another bowl of noodles and set down two menus in front of us. He looked up at the ceiling and recited: "When you take up the sword, the idea is to kill an opponent. Even though you may catch, hit or block a slashing sword, all of these are just opportunities to kill. This must be understood: If you *think* of catching, hitting or blocking, you will thereby become unable to make the kill. It's crucial to think of everything as an opportunity to kill."

"John and Yoko?"

"Miyamoto Musashi, the greatest swordfighter in history. Why don't you know about him?"

"Why do you?"

"I didn't just fall into your *dojo*, J.J. I've been studying the life of the samurai for years. I finally realized that I couldn't learn any more by reading. I had to train, as they did."

"But Professor Steele, we're not training as they did—we're just working out. They devoted their lives to it."

At first, he seemed disappointed, but was distracted when the waiter set a large bowl in the middle of our table.

"Chef say, special for you, Professor," the waiter said.

"*Duo jie*," Steele responded with a slight bow of the head. "*Guo guo hai mot ye?*"

When the waiter replied, Steele drew back his head, clearly surprised. I noticed that his head bows got deeper, more grateful.

"Do you know what this is?" he whispered excitedly to me once the waiter had left. I shook my head. "It's a very famous soup, called A Monk Jumped Over a Wall." He took the ladle and maneuvered some of the floating debris. "The story is that a rich man had a very important guest coming to a banquet he was hosting, so he told his chef to create a soup that was made from the best of everything. Look," he said, leaning forward, "that's shark fin. This is abalone, here's goose feet. Some ginseng. Ah, you know what this is? Gallbladder." He scooped some into the ladle and put it in my bowl.

I looked down at it, then back at him. He watched me expectantly. "All due respect, Professor," I said, pushing the bowl back toward him, "but Con Law's just one grade."

"Come on, just try it. It's not even on the menu—they made it special for us."

"That's what Socrates said. Seriously, I'm not eating it."

"Mr. Spencer, where's your spirit? You're a martial artist, for goodness sake. These are very expensive ingredients. You know what this could cost us?"

"Our lives?"

He put some in his own bowl and tasted a spoonful. "It's magnificent," he exclaimed.

I watched him, interested, but not enough to taste it. "Why's it called A Monk Jumped Over a Wall?"

"Ah," he said, clearly happy to have been asked, "legend has it that, while the chef cooked the soup, an ancient monk in a nearby monastery was so overcome by the smell of it simmering that he renounced his vows, scaled the stone wall of the monastery and turned his back on the monastic life forever."

I stared at him for a moment, then leaned forward and inhaled. "Smells okay," I shrugged. "I wouldn't upend my life over it."

"It's a metaphor. Think of it—how often have you smelled something cooking beyond the walls of your life and fought the temptation to leap? The monastery's safe and warm, the world outside chaotic, ruled by thieves and brigands. But once you've smelled the soup, can you ever be happy in the monastery again?"

I thought about it, but couldn't see the romance. Climbing a stone wall, diving off into uncertainty, and for what?

"I'd stay," I said. "No soup could be worth the risk."

"Unless the real risk were in staying," he countered. "Unless you never belonged inside those walls in the first place, and the scent of that soup made your safe, warm life in the monastery unbearable. Surely, there were other monks there that never even noticed the smell. So is it the story of a soup's aroma or a monk's tortured soul?"

He'd said too much; we both felt it. An awkward silence followed and, somehow, I knew that this was why I was here.

"But maybe," he continued cautiously, "it didn't have to be all or nothing. Maybe a bowl of soup a day would've made the monastery more bearable." He watched me. "Do you understand?" I shook my head. "I know I've only been coming to the *dojo* for a few weeks, but I've found something there, I'm sure of it. I think about it all the time. I practice at home. Unfortunately, with my class schedule, I can only get there a couple of times a week. That's not enough soup. You know?"

"You want me to train you," I realized.

"I thought we could make a deal. You mentor me in karate and I'll mentor you in law. We'll set aside two hours a week, one hour for each of us." One of my crutches slid off the other and fell to the floor. Steele picked it up and put it back in its place. "I admit, I feel a little foolish asking you this after what I did to you. But you don't have to do anything physical, just coach me. And you'll be healed soon enough. What do you say?"

"I don't think I'm qualified," I defer.

"Yes you are," he answered. "I've asked around the *dojo* about you. You won the New England championship last year."

"Brown belt championship," I pointed out. "It's no big deal."

"Uh huh," he said, unconvinced. "And you're the only one Manny'll spar with when he's got a tournament coming up. So will you do it?"

Before I could answer, a very pretty woman approached us with a long, confident gait. Steele's face lit up as she wound her way through the tables.

"*Chulo*, baby," she smiled, "what are you doing here?"

"Having lunch with a student. What are you doing here?" He stood up to kiss her, and I stood as well.

"I was supposed to meet Melissa but she didn't show. I've been at the bar for the last ten minutes."

"I thought I saw you outside," he said.

I watched in amazement. The kiss, the obvious delight they took in the other's presence—the total evaporation of the Josiah Steele I had come to know.

"Hi, I'm Terry Steele," she said with a very slight Texan drawl. She extended her hand and I took it. "You must be the poor fellow *Chulo* crippled."

"Honey, please."

"Oh relax, he knows his foot's broke." She turned back to me. "You're lucky you didn't know him when he took up wood-burning."

We sat back down, Steele giving his seat to his wife and waiting while the waiter brought another chair. As they shared the soup and talked, I stared at her, unable to believe that this was the wife of a law professor. I knew they were allowed to marry, but surely not women with long, fine auburn hair and big round eyes. Not women who dressed in jeans and white oxford shirts.

Terry asked me where I was from, and I told her a little about Brooklyn and the move to Manhattan. She said she was from Fort Worth, but hadn't been back in years. I asked Professor Steele what his home town in Colorado was like, having read that in his bio. Being with them was relaxing, until I saw Aaron Bocian and Bernie Nockowitz enter the restaurant. I was responsible to them for being with Steele; I was responsible to the Steeles for my classmates' reaction. Nockowitz came in first, and the unlit pipe nearly fell out of his mouth when he saw us. He jabbed Aaron, whose eyes would've shot across the room and onto our table if they could. Nockowitz puffed on his pipe and used his forefingers as horns, while Aaron laughed, something Steele saw but assiduously ignored. I'm quite sure that if people knew how utterly transparent we all are, we'd behave very differently. I tried to ignore them too, but Terry noticed, and wanted an explanation.

"Tell me the truth, J.J.," she said, "what's Professor Steele like in class?"

I looked at Steele, hoping he'd help me out of this. But he just looked away, so I did my best. "He's great," I said. "I mean, his lectures are very thought-provoking—"

She looked back toward Aaron and Bernie, who were now seated at a nearby table. "Then why are those two idiots holding candles under their chins?"

"He's just, you know, he doesn't give you a free pass."

She wasn't convinced. "*Chulo*, what's going on?"

"It's nothing," he demurred. "Every teacher at school has some nasty nickname."

"What's yours?"

He sighed and looked at me. "Well, it seems to change pretty often," he said. "What's it this year, J.J.? The Prince of Darkness, The Dragon of the Abyss?" He said this with false bravado; I could tell he was embarrassed.

"We're students," I made light of it. "We're just playing."

"I don't like this," she said.

"I'm not crazy about it either," Steele said.

"No, not that. I want to know how you behave that leads to this."

"Terry, I told you, it's just a nickname."

"Then tell me some of the other nicknames, J.J. Don't look at him—look at me. Who do you have for Torts?"

"Vermilyea."

"What's his nickname? Don't look at him; look at me."

"He doesn't have one," I admitted.

"Civil Procedure?"

"Blake."

"Nickname?"

"Um...Aiden."

"That's his name, J.J."

I didn't say anything. Why did I feel like I was betraying Steele, when he'd so surely earned his moniker?

"What's going on with you?" she said to Steele. "Who are you when you leave our home?"

He pushed his hair behind his ears and looked away, but then quickly back to her. "I don't know," he admitted. "Maybe it's because these poor kids think they're getting into something glamorous, and I just want them to find out now if they're cut out for a lifetime of civilized hostility." She rolled her eyes, which bothered him enough to persist. "A lawyer trades in animosity. In most kinds of law, a lawyer takes his client's affronts as his own, and that's hard. A lot of the time, it's miserable. The world becomes a game of wits, filled with potential liability. You get so buried under trivial details and doomsday hypotheticals, you can't even see the sun. And if you do, you try to figure out what it wants from you. Maybe I want them to know up front."

"Big Bird Scheffer," I remembered, but they ignored me.

Her brown eyes wide and attentive, she leaned closer to him, seeming to try to see into him. Her long hair fell to one side and covered his hand on the table. She flipped it away with a shake of her head and covered his hand with her own. "Then why not just tell them that?" He said nothing, so she turned to me. "Josie Steele is the most gentle, considerate man I've ever met," she said, but the sentiment didn't match the way she said it. It was an assertion, a pronouncement that I was damn well going to hear. Her eyes blazed into me.

"Terry, please," he said, "this is embarrassing."

"He said he became a man the first time he saw Carole King barefoot on the cover of *Tapestry*."

"Terry!"

I realized that her determination wasn't aimed at me, but Steele. Now she turned to him, and her voice softened as she continued. "We have a little boy, Ben, named after Josie's father. He's eight. They're best friends. They both love bubble wrap."

Steele looked down at his soup and rafted the ingredients around.

"We met in Morocco," she continued. "We were both living in Spain at the time, and you could take a ferry across the Straits of Gibraltar, dock at Ceuta and spend the day in the Kasbah in Tangier. We fell in love, then lived together in Barcelona. He would sing me to sleep at night. He gave museum tours and I was a student. It was so romantic—we'd go weeks without putting on a pair of shoes. He used to tell me that looking at me was the first time he'd ever been comfortable in a woman's eyes, and that's how he knew it was safe to fall in love. He still sings me to sleep sometimes."

She fell into thought, then nodded, satisfied that she'd covered enough. She looked at me and smiled, then turned back to him. "You're too good for that big bad persona, *Chulo*," she said, and stood to leave.

Steele followed her, but paused for a moment and looked down at me. "I trust I can count on your discretion. Think about the mentoring."

"Oh, I'll do it," I said quickly. "I'll definitely do it."

"Good."

Chapter seventeen

I was just about to leave my apartment for school when the phone rang. It was my mother, worried about Leo. She said he'd decided to major in philosophy but didn't seem to be enjoying it.

"He'll be fine, Mom," I reassured her as I leaned on my crutches, my backpack already on. "Leo's always fine."

"He's not always fine," she answered. "That's just how he hides."

"Okay, so he hides a little. Mom, he's only eighteen; he'll figure things out."

"But he's all over the place," she said. "He doesn't even know what he wants."

"He's supposed to be all over the place. I was when I was eighteen."

"And look where it got you."

"What does that mean? I'm in law school."

"Sure, but come on, it's not like it's Harvard or anything."

"I'm blushing."

I heard a puff of air that was either a sigh or complete disregard for what I'd just said. "I'm sorry, you know what I mean. I just worry about him. He's not like you. I always knew you'd get by."

"I'll tell you what—I'll try to give him a call later today. Right now, though, I've really got to get going. I've got class at ten."

"What class?"

"Constitutional Law."

It got suddenly silent on the other end of the line as she tried to compose herself.

"Mom, don't cry—it's just a class."

"I'm just so proud of you," she struggled to say. "My baby studying the Constitution. I'm just—"

"It's okay, I understand."

"You know I didn't mean anything by the Harvard thing, right?"

"Of course."

She sniffed and I could hear the scented tissue scraping out of the Kleenex box. "It has, like what, twenty amendments, right?"

"Twenty-seven."

"Look how he knows right off the top of his head. You're going to be a great lawyer, better than your father. Name me a few Amendments."

"Aw, Mom…"

"Just three, please?"

Ordinarily, I didn't mind these requests for maternal dirty talk, but I really was late. "Okay, okay," I said, "Free speech, Suffrage and, and…oh for crying out loud…"

"Apportionment of Representatives?"

I pulled the phone away from my ear and looked at it.

"Yeah—how did you—?"

"Go, you're going to be late," she said. "Go make *Law Review* for me."

Law Review, I scoffed as I left the apartment. Out of 120 people, ten would get invites—not the best odds.

At school, I settled into my seat and Aaron sat beside me. At the lectern, Steele was preparing to begin class.

"What was that yesterday?" Aaron smiled.

"It was nothing. He took me to lunch to apologize for breaking my leg." Aaron looked at the floor, shook his head and laughed. "You know," I continued, "you and Nock weren't especially discreet."

He slowly raised his eyes from the floor. "He didn't…"

"Oh, absolutely, he saw you."

He glanced at Steele, then back to me. "But he doesn't know…"

"He sure does," I said. "He knows all the nicknames. He knows everything people say about him."

"I told that idiot not to make the horns."

"Yeah, you were a lot better with the candle."

"He's going to fail me. Oh God, he's going to fail me."

"He's not going to fail you," I said. "But you might want to be on your toes today."

"Why, did he say something?"

"No, I'm just saying—"

"Now you tell me? Why didn't you call me last night?"

"Why'd you have to act like an ass?"

"Mr. Nockowitz," Steele opened the class by asking, "where in the Constitution is power divided between the federal government and the states?"

From several rows to our right, Bernie said, "Article Four, I think."

"Article Four, Section…"

Steele was leading him on. It wasn't in Article Four at all.

Bernie flipped madly through his textbook. In the comfort of his living room, he'd be able to find the section easily. But with everyone watching and the professor waiting, it's like trying to find a relief parachute. Steele pulled a chair up beside the lectern, sat down and took out an apple. He crunched quietly, evoking laughter. Beside me Aaron tried to find the Constitution but could barely find his textbook. I moved his hands off the book and turned it to the right page.

"Quite alright, Mr. Nockowitz," Steele said between bites. "I can see that your colleague, Mr. Bocian, is champing at the bit to help you. Mr. Bocian?"

There goes the upper lip again. The guy must be part blow-fish.

"Section Two?" Aaron blurted.

"Just so we're clear—it's your contention that Article Four, Section Two is what divides power between the federal government and the states?"

Aaron's eyes had gone their wild way again, disconnect sequence locked.

"No," I tried to say under my breath, but Aaron had lost his hearing.

"Read me Article Four, Section Two, Mr. Bocian."

Aaron ignored the page I'd found for him, and turned to Article Four, Section Two. He read on and on, hoping something relevant would come up. Hands rose around the room as it became apparent that nothing would.

"Pass me a beer, would you, Mr. Bocian?" Steele interrupted.

"Excuse me?" Aaron looked up from his book.

"Well, if we're going to spend all day on a fishing trip together, I'd like to have a beer."

"Tenth Amendment," I urged Aaron. As he just stared ahead at Steele, who had gone back to his apple, I pushed his hand off his book and put my finger on the Tenth Amendment. He looked at me and I nodded. "Trust me."

"Tenth Amendment," Aaron called out.

Steele nodded and, immediately, I knew two things. First, the answer was right. And second, I had just pushed Aaron into white water after he'd capsized in a stream.

"Very good, Mr. Bocian," Steele said. "The powers not delegated to the United States by the Constitution are reserved to the states," he quoted. "So tell me—if everything not explicitly given to the federal government remains a state power—just where do the feds get off involving themselves in the civil rights of state citizens? Anything in the Constitution give them that right?"

"Article Four, Section Two?"

"Is that what you think, or are you just going to keep saying that until it's right?"

"Yes."

"Yes, what?"

"Yes sir."

"No, I mean which is it?"

"Which is what?"

Steele rolled his eyes. "Okay, Abbot, take a breather and see if Costello can help. Mr. Nockowitz, for the sake of the dubious future of the law firm of Bocian & Nockowitz, under what authority does the federal government legislate civil rights?"

"I don't know," Bernie admitted.

"Not enough malpractice insurance in the world to cover the havoc you two are going to wreak one day," Steele mused, and I started to get angry. However insensitive Aaron and Bernie had been in the restaurant, it didn't justify this. Or maybe it did, but still, a professor should be above some things. I wanted to do something about it but feared the consequences.

"Mr. Bocian, looks like you're on your own. So I ask you again, what gives the federal government that right?" Steele persisted. Unfortunately, Aaron had plummeted into hysterical blindness just moments before, and now stared alternately down at his book and then at the space he knew I was occupying, then back to the book and back at me. "He can't help you with me watching, Mr. Bocian."

An idea came to mind, but it was reckless. Steele would resent me, and I couldn't afford to make such a powerful enemy, make myself vulnerable, particularly now that I was actually in favor with him. I couldn't squander the goodwill. We were going to study together, and not just Con Law—any subject I wanted. That actually *could* put me on *Law Review*. My allegiance was to my family, not to a couple of guys I'd just met. Around me, some people were smiling, but most of the class seemed uncomfortable. It was clear that Aaron didn't know the answer. If Steele were more interested in teaching the class than punishing Aaron, he'd have just moved on to someone else. But the price was too high. Damn the price. Everything has a price.

"We're waiting, Mr. Bocian."

As Steele stood and sauntered along the podium toward the other side of the room, I got up on my good leg. I tried to speak, but it was harder than I'd expected. I wanted to ask him exactly what he meant when he said he became a man the first time he saw Carole King barefoot on the cover of *Tapestry*. Humiliate him the way he was humiliating Aaron. But the words wouldn't come. Steele was still facing the other way. He didn't know that I was standing. It wasn't too late. Sit the hell down, J.J., explain later to anyone who asks that you were just stretching your leg.

"Excuse me," I said weakly, fairly certain that I'd just added the word, *Chulo*.

He faced me, fear in his eyes. Forget the Carole King thing, just ask why we can't make a better use of our time.

"Yes?" he asked, but I was unable to speak.

The silence couldn't possibly have lasted as long as it seemed. He stared at me and I stared back. Maybe this would be enough; maybe the implied threat would get us through this. I met his eye, daring him to make me say more.

"I think the Civil Rights Act was based on the interstate commerce clause, sir," I said.

His mouth open just a bit, he blinked several times. He began to speak but thought better of it, and instead, made his way slowly, silently toward his lectern.

"Don't you think a leaf sucker would make more sense than a blower?" Ed tugged at my sleeve, but I ignored him.

I remained standing, not sure what would happen next. Years ago, my family used to take annual summer trips to a waterfall somewhere in northwestern New York. At the pool at the bottom of the falls was a diving board ten foot above the frigid water. The board had great spring, and I used to love leaping as high as I could off of it. For that fleeting moment, when I was helpless, suspended in the air, knowing how cold the water was and that in just another second I'd be in it—it was one of the most exhilarating feelings I'd ever known. I felt like I was above the cold water again.

Steele consulted his seating chart then looked up. "Mr. Anatole," he finally said, and class continued. I sank back into my seat. An hour later, he dismissed us. We made our ways into the aisles and up the stairs toward the back landing and the exit door. I was the last one to reach the landing. I turned back toward Steele and for a moment, thought about going to talk to him, but the distance between us was still too great. He was seated beside his lectern, apple in hand, staring at nothing. I turned back toward the landing.

"Mr. Spencer," he called. "I'm sure you've already figured out what this means for our deal."

"Yes sir," I replied.

"Well, you're wrong. I'll see you Thursday in my office, four o'clock."

Chapter eighteen

In the elevator after class, I was a hero. People congratulated me for my courage in standing up to the Advocate's Devil. Aaron and Bernie wanted to buy me lunch, dinner, a regional airline. But I was drained. I needed to get away from school, away from the praise, so I hobbled along Comm Ave toward Kenmore Square, thinking I might get a slice of pizza or kill time at the bookstore. But as I made my way, my mood grew darker. An old man approached, carrying a cane. He closed his shoulder to me as we passed, a habit of advanced age, I supposed. How awful it is to live in fear. How awful to be helpless. I sit in classes praying for my name not to be called. Unable to negotiate my crutches and a lunch tray simultaneously, I wait for others to get hungry so I can eat. I pine for a girl I haven't seen in weeks. I'm alone. I'm alone, I'm hurt, and I'm not sure I just sided with the good guys. A lump lodged in my throat. I stepped on an uneven crack in the sidewalk and the pain in my foot buckled me.

"Damn it!" I shouted, my eyes glazing over. As people stopped and stared, I hurled my crutches into the middle of Comm Ave and sat down on the curb, rubbing my eyes with my thumb and forefinger.

Someone pulled his car over and returned my crutches, laying them down beside me.

"Here you go, pal," he said. "Take it easy, everything's going to be all right."

I nodded, embarrassed by his kindness. Forget the bookstore— I just wanted to sleep, so I caught a T home.

In the darkness of my room, I felt fingertips brush through my hair.

"Isn't it a little early for bed?" Amy whispered.

"Huh?"

"Come on, wake up J.J. We're going to a movie."

I rolled toward her and though I was still mostly asleep, I could feel stiffness in my neck and back. Stress, I supposed. "A movie?"

She took some strands of my hair between her thumb and forefinger, and moved them off my brow. "Lauren and I are going to see a movie and we decided that you're coming too."

"Lauren decided?"

"Believe it or not."

I looked at her in the darkness, and her sad smile comforted me. The hallway backlight outlined her face and hair.

"You're good friends," I said, "but I've got studying, and my neck hurts."

"You're coming," she repeated, standing to go. "No one can survive on just books."

"Okay," I said. "Give me a minute to get dressed. Hey Ame, have you got anything for a sore neck?"

"I've got Alleve."

"Okay, but before you go, could you give me something for my neck?"

She smiled and sat back down. "Are you okay?" she asked. "Do you need to talk?"

I loved the way she said "talk"—T-O-K. I liked it so much, along with the lilt in her voice, that I couldn't even answer her at first. But then I swallowed hard and told her what had happened in class.

"Dad, you shouldn't worry when you make noble choices."

"They don't always work out, Ame."

"Sure they do. They always do—just not necessarily in a straight line." She stood and started to leave, pausing by the door. "This year might get tougher before it gets easier, dad. Any time you want to talk, you know I'm here, and—"

"I know Ame, thanks," I cut her off. When someone tries to talk me out of sadness, I wind up arguing to legitimize the sadness, which makes me even more sad. But I could never leave Amy unfed. "I will, I promise."

Amy and Lauren both had to be up early the next day for work so we came straight home after the movie. Lauren held the door for me and I was walking inside as the phone started to ring. When the caller needed two syllables and three notes to complete the word, "Hi," I knew it was Jennifer.

We hadn't spoken in a long while, and as much as I'd fantasized about hearing her voice again, I never envisioned it happening at ten thirty on a Tuesday night. After a few rounds of "fine, how are you" she said that she was in the neighborhood.

"I'm with a friend at a party in Brookline. Is it okay if we just pop by for a friendly little visit?" I didn't much like the use of the word "friendly," and I wasn't sure why Brookline was in the neighborhood while her dorm room three miles away wasn't, but damn, I wanted to see her.

I tried my best to match her casual tone. "Sure, why not?"

Amy and Lauren wished me luck and went to sleep, and a few minutes later, there she was at my front door, the apparition incarnate. She looked fantastic, even though it was clear that both she and her friend had been drinking. Her hair was cool from the night air and it felt wonderful against my cheek when we hugged. Her hair never tickled; there was never a strand off on its own agenda, getting into my eye or mouth. It was soft and full, and I would've never let go if decisions like that were mine to make. She wore Tiffany for Women, of course. I kissed her on the corner of her downturned mouth, then turned to welcome her friend, who was behind Jen, leaned against the door jamb perusing the mailboxes.

We separated and I hopped backward a pace to let them in.

"What happened to your leg?" Jen asked when she noticed.

"Karate accident."

"Aw, is it broken?"

"Three places."

She took it in stride. She takes everything in stride. I suggested that we talk in my room instead of the living room, so that I could sit on my bed with the leg elevated. Her friend took a step and stumbled to her right. She was more drunk than I'd realized. Jen steadied her by the arm and led her down the hallway.

"So how's Sir Galahad?" I asked once we were in my room, immediately reproaching myself for having caved into that disabling impulse so soon.

"Fine. How's the Polynesian chick?"

I tried to remember what lies I'd told when we last spoke. I did have dinner with a Hawaiian girl one night, but just because she happened to be sitting next to me at a sushi bar.

KING INVENTS PAWN, SHOWS OFF WITH WASABI, SPIT-TAKES SEA URCHIN AND FLEES IN DISGRACE.

"She's fine," I nodded, wincing at the memory of how completely sea urchin at terminal velocity can splatter across the plexiglass of a sushi bar.

Jen sat at my desk while her friend lay down on the floor by the bedroom door.

"So how's school?" she asked.

"Has its ups and downs."

"Trini's dating a guy on the *Law Review* at B.C.," she motioned toward her now snoring friend.

"Is she okay?"

Jen got up and knelt over Trini, lifting her chin. "You want me to take you home, sweetie?" she asked.

"No, I'm fine," Trini mumbled.

"If you need to leave, just let me know," she said, then added to me: "I love her. She's my best friend at school."

"She looks like she should be home."

Her eyebrows arched as she stood upright. "You trying to get rid of me?"

"No," I said quickly, then shrugged. "I guess maybe I was trying to get rid of her."

"J.J...."

"I know, I know. Just a friendly visit."

She came over and sat beside me on the bed, looking at me with rich, brown eyes. "Actually, Jeff and I have been fighting a lot," she confessed. I must have reacted to that, because she felt compelled to add: "We're not going to break up or anything, but he just frustrates me sometimes."

"How so?"

"He's a great guy and I love him and all, but he just doesn't have any direction." They were the darkest brown eyes I'd ever seen, so dark that it was hard to differentiate between the iris and the pupil. "One day he's pre-med, now he's Ag and Life Sciences." And the whites were dramatically white—bright, healthy white—setting off the brown like the moon in a clear country sky. "Which is fine, freshman year. But he's a senior, you know? Time to get realistic." They weren't quite almondine. Closer to the shape of a perfect skipping stone—almost round, but with a tapered end for leverage. She combed her hair back with her thumb and forefinger, displaying her near olive skin and the catenary curve of her jawline. "I don't know— what do you think? Am I being too impatient with him?"

"You're the most beautiful woman I've ever seen."

"J.J.," she scolded softly, "we're friends."

"When did that happen?"

"Maybe I should go."

"No, don't. Sure, we're friends." In her quiet stare, I realized that she was actually awaiting an answer. "I don't think you're too impatient, Jen. He's twenty-two, it's time to grow up."

"Maybe you're right. You knew by twenty-two that you wanted to be a lawyer, I remember when we met."

"You think I'll be a good one?"

She thought for a few seconds, then nodded her head just slightly. "I do," she said. "Sometimes you get distracted, but once you leave school and settle down I think you'll be great. Thing is, you can't be afraid to stand up to people to get what you want. There's nothing wrong with that."

"I'm not afraid to stand up to people."

"No, of course not. It's just not maybe as natural for you as it might be for others. Anyone who grew up like you did," she shook her head. "How could you not hate conflict?"

"You should've seen me today," I blurted, regretting it immediately. I didn't want to tell the story again; I didn't want to think about school. But at least we were talking about me and not Galahad.

"What happened today?"

"Don't you think we should wake her?" I asked again, as Trini rolled to her back on the floor.

"I'll get her some water," Jen said. "Want some?"

I declined and she left, returning a moment later with a glass of water. "What happened today?" she asked me as she propped Trini up and helped her drink.

"Nothing big—a professor was picking on a couple of friends of mine in class, and I sort of told him to lay off."

Her eyes widened. The water ran down the side of Trini's face. "You talked back to a professor?"

"No, I didn't talk back—you're getting it on her shirt—I just told him that I thought he was being unfair."

She shifted position to support Trini's upper body on her chest for better leverage to pour the water into her mouth. "He's allowed to be unfair," she said to me. "He gives the grades."

Chasing after someone's approval is like jogging down a hill. It's chaotic, it's clumsy, and it only gets worse the longer you let it continue.

"So, Ag and Life Sciences," I nodded. "What is that?"

"J.J."

"Jen, it's no big deal. Actually, I think he appreciated it," I said. "He did, he appreciated it. He likes me."

"How close are these friends?"

"They're, I don't know…it doesn't matter."

"Well, if you're going to jeopardize your future for them…"

"I'm telling this all wrong," I held my hands up. "Honestly, it was nothing. I spoke up, he said it was cool, we're fine." Then I remembered my trump card. "I actually had lunch with him yesterday."

"With the professor?" she brightened. Trini grimaced and jerked her head away from the water, so Jen put the water aside and let Trini put her head down on her lap. Jen gently stroked Trini's hair and looked at me. She's always been like that with her friends: tender, nurturing. I've never heard her say a bad word about any of them.

"Just the two of us, well, and his wife," I continued.

"Oh, so you have a relationship. J.J., that's great, that can be really valuable." I nodded along. "I'm sorry, I didn't understand the context. Wow, see, you know how to manage your life. It's too bad the situation…I think Jeff could learn a lot from you."

It took all my strength not to offer to have a talk with him. As much as I needed Jen's approval, I didn't need it that bad.

"I could talk with him if you'd like," I said.

"No, that's okay," she answered. "I think that would just be too weird. But thanks."

We passed a bit more time talking about school, then yawned simultaneously and laughed.

"I guess I should be getting her home," she indicated Trini.

We woke Trini and made our way toward the front door.

"It was great to see you again."

"It really was," she answered, facing me.

I couldn't decide whether to peck Jen's cheek or try to really kiss her. I settled on another noncommittal kiss on the corner of her lips, but as I leaned forward, she wrapped her arms around my neck and held me there. We kissed gently, romantically. The thought crossed my mind that the kiss could escalate if only Trini weren't standing behind Jen, arms folded and foot tapping. I waved goodbye to her behind Jennifer's back but she didn't budge.

"Oh boy, I drank too much," she said breathlessly as we separated. She patted me on the left side of my chest. "Forgot what a good kisser you are. We'll speak again soon."

She turned and linked arms with Trini and they left. I stood in the doorway for a long while, feeling lonelier than ever. The kitchen was right beside the front door. I went into it, opened the refrigerator door and stared. We had beer, but I wasn't in the mood. The cold pasta leftovers were Lauren's. Amy's Mulliga-tofu soup was a non-starter. I closed the refrigerator and hobbled back toward my room, but stopped in the hallway in front of Amy's door.

It was late. She'd surely be sleeping. On the other hand, just last weekend she'd come into my room while I'd been studying to ask me to interpret something Doctor Howard had said. I turned the door handle quietly and stepped into her room, leaving the door ajar behind me for light. She was a restless sleeper and was only partly covered. She wore a half-shirt and panties, and one long, bare leg lay atop her blanket. I'd never seen her like this. I couldn't believe what a beautiful leg it was. A pillow was between her legs. I sat down on the edge of the bed and covered her with the blanket before waking her. Then I put my hand on her shoulder and shook it softly.

She squinted and cupped one hand over her eyes to shield them from the hallway light. "J.J.? What's wrong?"

It took me a moment to answer.

"Jen just left," I finally said.

"How did it go?" I sighed and sank to my knees alongside the bed, and rested my arms next to her. She put the flats of her fingers on my arm. "What happened?"

"She kissed me."

She watched me, frowning when she realized that I wasn't buoyant.

"And then she left," she said.

I nodded and rested my forehead on the bed. "Why'd she come here, Ame?" I looked up again. "Is she doing this just to torture me?"

"No, dad, she's not mean."

"Then why?"

"Sometimes a girl puts a few acorns away for winter."

"Are we onto a different topic?"

She smiled and rolled onto her side toward me, propping

her head up on her bent arm. "She might want you, she probably does—just not yet. This was probably her way of checking to see if she still had the option."

"You really think she's that manipulative?"

She didn't answer at first. She sat up under the covers and pulled her knees up, resting her arms over them. "Could you close the door a little? The light's bothering my eyes."

I got up and closed the door most of the way, then came back to the bed and knelt beside it.

"Well?" I prompted.

"No," she said halfheartedly, "I don't think she's necessarily being manipulative. Look—she probably didn't even think it through; it's instinct. Was she drinking?"

"Yeah."

"See? That's all it was. Women, we do that kind of thing."

"You ever do it?"

"No," she admitted, but added: "I probably should. Howard said he'd call tonight."

"We do that," I nodded.

"You ever do it?"

"Yeah," I admitted, then laughed along with her. "Argh!" I rubbed my hands sharply over my face and through my hair. "I feel so helpless."

"I know," she said. "But you don't have to be. You can make choices, you know. You don't have to invite her over just because she asks."

"You've seen her, right?"

"She is a knockout. I'm just saying, you don't have to like a girl just because she likes you. You can decide who you like. You're a pretty amazing guy."

"Might even be a lawyer one day."

"See, that's just it—you're not amazing because of who you're going to be. You're amazing because of who you are."

"You don't believe people can make something of themselves?"

"I think people can be true to who they are, and when they get really true, they've made something of themselves."

"I don't understand a word of what you say, Ame," I said as I climbed up onto the bed and put my arms around her, "but I really love you." She hugged me back and we stayed like that for a while. She smelled wonderful. I don't know why women waste money on Tiffany for Women; it's nothing compared to a warm, honest sleep.

New York

Chapter nineteen

It's Thursday, the second day of hearings. Ed and Dairian take their turns on the stand during the morning session, then we break for lunch. When we return to the hearing room a little after two o'clock, Carlysle is seated at the witness bench reading the *Law Journal*. He looks up as we enter.

"Any word from Steele?" he asks. Ira shakes his head. Carlysle is visibly upset, and makes a bit of a show of closing his newspaper.

"He'll be here," Ira assures him. "You have to understand, this is a very important man, and he's coming all the way from Boston to vouch for Mr. Spencer."

"Apparently not."

"Give me a minute," Ira says as he takes his cell phone from his pocket. "I'll try him again." He walks over to the window to get a better signal, and dials off a card that he's taken from his pocket. We watch him but Ira doesn't return the eye contact. Finally, I see him purse his lips and disconnect the line. He looks at us and shakes his head.

"Why don't we talk in chambers, Mr. Finowitz," Carlysle says, standing. He walks out the back of the room.

"Chambers? What chambers?" Ira asks me. "This isn't a court-house."

"Must be a room back there, I guess."

"Well, let's go," he says.

"I wasn't invited."

"You're surely invited—let's go."

In the hallway behind the hearing room, Carlysle is waiting. The other two judges are back there too, leaning against the wall, one with his arms folded, the other staring at his shoes.

"I'm going to be straight with you...Ira," Carlysle says. "I've got plenty of work to keep me busy at my real job and I don't want to waste another day on this. Under normal circumstances, this case wouldn't even require a hearing. Speaking only for myself, it's pretty straightforward. Maybe we suspend his license, maybe we disbar, I don't know. We can always go back and revisit things after the criminal case anyway. The reason we made an exception for you is because of Professor Steele. The testimony of a man of that standing would impact this committee a lot more than your client's family and beer buddies. And second—and I'm being perfectly candid with you here—I wanted to meet him. I've followed his career for years and I was intrigued when you said you could produce him. But I'm not going to let this thing drag on past the holiday weekend. So here's the deal: you produce Steele by tomorrow morning and I think this committee might look more favorably upon your client. If not..." he shrugs his shoulders. "I'll see you both at ten."

They walk down the hall and disappear around the corner.

"That's why they gave me the hearing?" I ask Ira. "Because they're star-struck?"

Ira stuffs his hands into his pockets and leans against the wall. "I knew if I could get them to listen to the whole story, they'd see that you're a good man who made a mistake. I never told them Steele would be interested in networking or invite them to contribute a chapter to his next book, but I knew they'd be thinking it. I just never thought he wouldn't show. Why isn't he here, J.J.?"

"I don't know," I say, but my thoughts are elsewhere. "Finny, we've got to take another look at the Eagan file."

"Would you forget about that already, J.J.? There's nothing we can do for them. Let's concentrate on you."

"Eiderhorn bought the loan as a package. With twelve hundred deals, there's always a couple that have deficiencies."

He sighs and sinks to the floor, sitting with his back against the wall, his knees bent. "What kind of deficiencies?"

"I don't know, chain of title, recording error." I begin to pace the hallway. "Did Parker originate that deal?"

"Doesn't matter—a ministerial error isn't going to stop a foreclosure, you know that. Not even in bankruptcy court."

"The fees are ridiculous."

"Surely are, but that'll just affect the payoff," he says, "not the foreclosure. J.J., you're stuck on the fact that Eiderhorn bought the loan at pennies on the dollar, but that's not legally relevant. He owns the loan and he's legally entitled to collect on it."

"Okay, so maybe I can't stop the foreclosure. Maybe I can cut a better deal to pay it off—maybe I can help them get a hard money loan."

"You're going to put them in one of those sixteen-percent, ten-point deals?"

"Just for a year. Or maybe they could get a bank loan if I could convince Eiderhorn to let them settle with him cheap enough."

"You think? With their credit?"

"I don't know, I don't know. Damn it," I slap the wall. "There's got to be a solution." I stop pacing and lean against the opposite wall from where Ira sits.

"What's that house worth, anyway?" he asks.

"I don't know, why?"

"Well, maybe the loan's under water. If the house is worth less than what they owe on the loan, the bankruptcy court might cram it down some."

"That's a good thought," I say. "And I bet they owe back taxes—that'll take priority over the mortgage. That's another negotiating chit."

"None of them great, though."

"Well, they're all small. But it could be our only hope is to gather a bunch of small chits. I'm going to call my mother."

"There's a Freudian segue."

"She's a broker," I explain. "I'm sure she has some broker friends who do deals out there. They can help me get a read on the value of the house."

"I've got to get back to the office. I'll go through the file again, see if there's anything in there we can use."

"See if the old title report's in there. Maybe there's some cloud, some exception to title that would give us leverage."

"Okay, but don't get your hopes up. Parker National wouldn't have made the loan in the first place if there were."

"And write down how much they owe in back property tax."

"Okay. But still, our best chance is if the loan is under water—that would be real leverage."

"Hey," I realize, "that's right. Sometimes banks reappraise loans before they sell them. See if you can find a new appraisal in the file."

He shakes his head. "I'll look, but I wouldn't go by it even if it's in there," he says. "The appraiser wouldn't have been able to get into the house. He'd have to evaluate it by what it looks like from the outside. You've got to make sure your mom knows just how run-down this place is inside."

I hold out my hand to him and, when he takes it, pull him to his feet.

Chapter twenty

After stopping at my apartment to change out of my suit, I take the 4 train to Grand Central and walk east along 44th Street. My mother lives in the nearby Turtle Bay area, at 47th and Second. I'd moved her there when I got the Greer job. She'd been living in a place at 39th and Park, no more than a mile away, but the density of Manhattan makes it a completely different neighborhood. She had wanted to live in Turtle Bay for years, and with the Greer job, I could finally afford to contribute enough to her rent to let her make the move.

"Afternoon, counselor," says the doorman, Nick, as he holds the door open for me. He had taken an immediate liking to my mother when he heard her Brooklyn accent, since he lives just a few blocks from one of our old places. He's a neighborhood kid whose barrel chest and calloused knuckles never seem comfortable in the polyester yellow blazer the management company makes him wear. He loves calling me "counselor." It's an inside joke between us, that guys like us never really leave the neighborhood.

"Hi, Nick."

"So let me ask you something," he begins, although his version removes the last letter from "let" and inverts the "S" and "K" in "ask." He lifts his chin toward me. "Some guy wraps a tie around your throat" (no "H"), "you snap his elbow or what?"

"Depends," I answer. "Are we in a department store?"

"Whatever," he dismisses. "Cause some big *mamma lucca* stole a cab from me last night—right when I'm leaving here," he points, "right out here—and I'm just wondering, if I wrapped his tie around his throat, am I okay?"

I extract myself from the conversation as quickly and subtly as I can. Nick is obsessed with fighting, and ever since my mother told him that I did martial arts, it's all he ever wants to talk about with me. I know that if I don't manage this exchange carefully, I'll be down here for half an hour explaining why Bruce Lee and Mighty Mouse would never actually have occasion to fight. After a couple of minutes, he slaps me on the back and says, "Always good to see you, counselor."

I get onto the elevator and press the fourteenth floor. A man in a warm-up suit stares me down as he presses the twenty-fifth, then leans back against the wall and basks in his victory. When the doors open at fourteen, I step off the elevator and walk down the hall to my mother's door.

"How did it go today?" she asks as she seats me at the kitchen table and puts a bowl of soup in front of me.

"Not so good," I say. "Dairian did as well as he could, but Josie's the key and he still hasn't shown up." I look around the apartment and realize how quiet it is. "Where's Leo?"

"Well, you know, he's off for school tomorrow morning, so he's been out with friends every minute."

"Are you okay, Mom? You seem…I don't know…."

"Yeah, I'm fine. So what's this you said on the phone? Why do you need to know about housing costs on Long Island? Why move out there when New York City has everything?"

"Mom, I told you, I'm not looking to move. It's for a client." I take from my pocket a piece of paper on which I'd written the Eagans' address. "Here," I give her the paper. "I need to know the value of this place."

She considers the address, her eyes unfocused. "Little Neck," she says to herself. "That's Queens or Nassau?"

"Right near the border. It's Queens."

"Let me call Evelyn." She stands.

There's a thump in the hallway outside and she starts.

"You sure you're okay?" I ask.

She looks at me but doesn't respond. I don't pursue it because I have no reason to believe otherwise and I'm more interested in her call to Evelyn. She sits on the sofa and dials the phone.

"Evy?" she says. "It's Bev. Listen honey, I need you to pull some comps for me."

I wander into the hallway, the walls of which are covered by framed pictures of me and Leo. No one else is up there, not even her. She's run out of room at eye level, so the photos go all the way down to my waist. There's one taken at my college graduation, me and Leo arm in arm, sporting broad smiles and Leo wearing my mortarboard. Below it is a black and white of me seated on the steps in front of our last place in Brooklyn. In the living room, my mother is scribbling on a yellow pad, happy she can help me with something. So what if she's demanding—look at this wall.

She tosses the pad onto the sofa beside her, leans back and crosses her legs. The conversation with Evelyn turns social, and when she notices me watching her, she picks up the pad and silently offers it to me.

I sit next to her while she talks on the phone. On the pad are several numbers. I'm not sure what to make of them. They range from $119,100 to $198,400.

"Don't use that one," she says to me, cupping her hand over the receiver and indicating the $198,400. "Evelyn said it was a gut rehab." She assumes by my furrowed brow that I don't know what she's talking about. "Evy, hold on a minute. My big shot lawyer son doesn't know what a comp is."

"Mom, I know what a comp is. But this range is so wide."

"These are the other places that sold in that same community over the past six months," she says to me. She's enjoying her expert status. "Comps—comparable sales."

"I know that, I just—"

"You look at these and get a pretty good idea of what yours is worth. But like I said, don't go by the 198; it was a gut rehab."

"Could you ask her what she'd estimate for a very rundown two bedroom?"

My cell phone rings before she can answer. I see on the screen that it's Ira. The comps can wait. I excuse myself and go into her bedroom.

"Finny, what did you find out?"

"Nothing," he answers. "The file's in Boston's office. I need you to help me come up with an excuse to tell him I need to see it."

There's a hollow sound to the call.

"Is there something wrong with your phone?"

"I'm on my cell," he says. "No offense, but I don't think the firm would appreciate me making calls to you."

"They know you're representing me."

"Yeah, it's belt and suspenders, I know."

His misgivings make me realize how thoughtless I've been, casually involving him in my crusade. He's risked political advantage at the firm by demanding permission to represent me, then risked his entire career by joining me when I went to the Eagans' home last night. That he'd done it of his own volition only gives me more responsibility to protect him like he's protecting me.

"You know, Finny, let me take it from here on my own."

"Don't get offended. I'm just being careful."

"I'm not offended. I just don't want your career in my hands. I think I've proven my gift for managing one."

"I'm a big boy."

"But too good a friend. You've been sticking out your already preposterously long neck too far."

"Well, we can talk about that later. Did you get the house values?"

"Yes, but I don't think they're going to help much. The Eagans owe 125, and it looks like the place could be worth anywhere from 120 to," I look at the sheet, "I don't know, maybe 135."

"That's something."

"But not much. I could've knocked out a lot of the fees anyway. Their principal balance is ninety-two. That means the bankruptcy court won't cram it down, and if Eiderhorn's in for, say, fifty-three thousand, he can still foreclose, sell the place, and turn a profit."

"So where does that leave us?"

I wander to the front door of my mother's bedroom as I think. Down the hallway, in the living room, she hangs up the telephone and folds her hands on her lap. She stands and gets her purse, then returns to the sofa with it. She fishes around in it and comes out with a pack of cigarettes. Her fingers drum on the package, then she puts them back, sets the purse aside and refolds her hands on her lap.

"We've got to figure out a way to see that file," I say to Ira.

"Can you think of some excuse I could give Boston?"

I think for a minute, chewing on my lower lip. "No," I conclude. "Whatever you say, he'll suspect something."

"And I really doubt we're going to find anything in there."

"Probably not, but—"

I'm interrupted by the buzz of the intercom. I see my mother lurch from her seat and walk stiffly toward it. I hear Nick's voice on the other end but can't make out what he's saying. My mother speaks with him, then waits by the front door of the apartment.

"Something's going on here, Finny," I say, watching as my mother rubs a thumbnail perpendicular between her two front teeth. "I've got to go. Can you meet me for dinner tonight, around seven?"

"Let me see…what time is it now—five-thirty. Sure, seven's fine. Let's meet uptown. What's that pizza place, you know, the one on 85th and Broadway where we went with that guy?"

"You mean Ed, my friend from law school?"

"Yeah, Ed."

"I know the place. I don't know the name, but I know the one you're talking about. I'll see you there."

I disconnect the line and walk toward my mother, stopping several feet away. She's still working on the thumbnail and leaning sideways against the foyer wall, watching the door. She senses my presence but doesn't turn toward me immediately. Her head is cast at a slight downward angle. When I hold my stare on her, only her eyes move. She looks at me out of the corners of them.

"What's going on?" I ask. "Who's here?"

She doesn't say anything. She's not ignoring me; just doesn't seem to be sure what to say.

"Who is it, Leo?"

"Sometimes you got to do what you got to do," she says.

"What does that mean?" I ask, although I already know.

We both hear the elevator doors open, and a gray fear envelopes her. It's familiar and I know it well, though I haven't seen it in a long time.

"You didn't," I say.

"Sometimes you got to do what you got to do. He's well-connected. He can help you."

"I don't want his help, and besides, why would he even care? I haven't seen him in years."

"Me neither."

The doorbell rings and before I can protest, she takes a deep breath and opens it. The air leaves the apartment as my father steps inside.

Boston

Chapter twenty-one

H_{i J.J.,}

Trouble in the pond margin. Two weeks ago, it somehow attracted a ferocious colony of red paper wasps that devoured the mud flies and commandeered the margin. I tried using pesticide but they put it in their daiquiris. A guy in the Entomology Department suggested diatomaceous earth. He said it was like microscopic shards of glass that I could blow into the margin and it would slice the wasps' exoskeletons and kill them like dogs—which I guess, evolutionarily speaking, is more than fair. Well, I did it this morning and the wasps got very busy with it right away. After watching them all day today, the best I can figure is that they're building some sort of diatomaceous mirror ball. I need a new plan and fast, because Professor Larvae says the several hundred wasps I now board could easily be several thousand within a couple of weeks. Needless to say, my roommate has put in for a transfer.

In other news, it was great to see you during intersession. I loved Boston and by the way, your roommate's in love with you. I didn't even mind the cold weather. Actually, I love Boston in the spring, summer and fall—it's the other nine months you can keep. And not another word about dinner—it was my pleasure to treat. I'm just sorry I had to pick your pocket to be able to. But now vacation is just about over, and I'm starting to get my first semester grades in the mail. I aced the Philosophy of Religion course we talked about, but I'm thinking of switching my major to Psychology anyway. I just think we might make too much of both philosophy and religion, and understanding either is really a matter of understanding the minds that create it. Take David and Goliath, for example. What's the big deal? Basically, some big jerk was messing with David's neighborhood so David threw a rock at the guy's head. Me and you used to do the same thing with the Naccarato brothers and wasn't nobody around looking to make us kings.

Big party tonight. It's the last major bash before classes start (as though they slow anything down). One of the Jewish frats is throwing the party, and the theme is "Come As Your Favorite Hasidic Animal." I'm going as a svordfish. Get it? A sVordfish! It ought to be great. I won't tell you what I'm using as a spear, but dear God, I hope svordfish is kosher. Oops, gotta go! Carolyn Dubasch, on the second floor, just found out that we snuck into her room during her post-dinner nap and clipped her hair to use as *payes*. I'll write more tomorrow.

Love,
Leo

Hi again,
Well, it's tomorrow, and I wish it weren't. No

one panic, but the pond margin is empty, and there's a muffled but undeniable buzzing coming from beneath my bed. I'd like to do something about it but I'm too hung over to move anything but my eyes. I just lifted my right hand to scratch my head and cracked myself in the eye with an empty whiskey bottle. I wonder what happened last night. I wonder why my beard is in my mouth, especially since I don't have a beard. Someone is sleeping next to me and I'm afraid to look. Someone please shut those wasps up! I'd better wrap this up later J.J.; I think I'm falling back to sleep...or maybe slipping into a coma. Please send natural predator!

    Love,
    Leo

    P.S. Just a thought. If the fish at the bottom of the sea consider the water their sky, and know of nothing existing beyond that, why is it not possible for our sky to be no more than a similar illusion? Just the water of some greater, more vast universe, with creatures far more advanced than us, existing above our sky? Discuss.

Because, I thought as I put Leo's emails away, skewered pizzas don't hang from the clouds. All those philosophy courses are starting to get to the kid. Leo's right though—we make too much of philosophy. Life's tough, enough said.

I used this thought to keep me warm as the T stopped on Beacon Street, some 400 yards from the law school. It was pitch black outside and sub-zero to boot, and I paused on the bottom step of the T with the doors wide open in front of me, staring out into the tundra before stepping off. It was on nights like this that I wished I had chosen a southern law school. The January air in Boston didn't care a whit about the lining of your overcoat. On windy days, the cold would cut right through fleece, down, wool or whatever else you had on, and gnaw voraciously on your chest. And even when the wind didn't blow, the air bit. Nights were that much worse. And February was just around the corner, straining at its leash.

It felt strange to be wearing a suit and tie at school, but this was the night of my big moot court oral argument. I'd been looking forward to it ever since getting into school, my first chance to argue a case in front of judges. A pretend case, admittedly. Megalomaniacal third-year law students posing as judges, sure. But still, it felt real to me.

Several weeks earlier we were told to choose partners, and Ed Coleman and I decided to work together. Ed's a legitimate genius, number one in his college class, though I'm the only one he's told that to. It had been a week since we submitted our fifty-page brief, and tonight I'd finally get a taste of what it would one day feel like to be a D.A. The theater, the drama, fighting the good fight. As I walked in the darkness toward the school, I imagined that I was walking Centre Street, downtown New York. The scents from hot dog vendors' carts filling the air, bleating mid-week traffic—I stride purposefully past all of it toward the courthouse, focused on the felon I'm about to take off the streets. D.A.s should get to wear uniforms, like cops and firefighters, so they don't have to remain anonymous as they walk the streets they protect. People should buy them drinks at bars, wink and refuse taxi fares, slap them heartily on the back as they pass.

Tonight, however, I wouldn't be fighting for any particularly laudable cause. The case Ed and I had been assigned involved a stick-fight that broke out during a professional hockey game. Our client was the instigator and winner of the fight. And as unappealing as I find my client, my job is to convince the court that the other player had assumed the risk of having a third eye socket carved when he made the voluntary decision to play professional hockey.

At least that's what Josie Steele told me I had to do when we discussed it yesterday, during my weekly mentoring hour. Steele had really kept to his word on that. We'd been meeting once a week since September, and had both benefited. I felt like I had my own private interpreter to translate law into English, and his karate was actually starting to look like karate. He'd gotten nicer in class too, since we had clashed that day. He was still demanding—even caustic, occasionally—but hardly ever malicious.

I tried to run the last fifty yards to school to get out of the cold, but though I had gotten the cast off weeks before, my leg was still weak. The run became a ridiculous gallop, and I gave up and walked the rest of the way. Inside, I took the elevator to the ninth floor and entered the room. By day it was an ordinary classroom, rows of ascending seats, an aisle of stairs down the center, a podium up front. But tonight, a lectern had been set in the aisle between the two halves of the first row, facing the front, creating something of an appellate court design. Fittingly, our seats were to the right of the aisle, and those of the bleeding heart liberals trying to destroy the very fabric of professional hockey—unmitigated violence—to the left.

I was reviewing my notes when Ed silently took his seat beside me.

"Ready?" I asked.

"Ready."

I noticed that he wasn't carrying anything. "No notes?"

"Don't need them."

"Forgot them?"

"On the T."

The judges entered the room and took their seats. I was surprised to see they were actually wearing black robes.

"Counsel for the appellant," one of them announced, and I rose and stood behind the lectern. I was nervous, but ready. The fluttering in my stomach felt good—it meant I was pushing the borders of my comfort zone. The path of least resistance is no way to live.

I looked up at the judges, seated behind a long table on the podium, four across. "May it please the court," I began, "I am J.J. Spencer, attorney for the appellant." And that's as far as I got. Apparently, I'd come at feeding time, and the judges set upon me like a mountain lion on a three-legged gazelle.

"Counselor, your brief says…" "Counselor, does this mean that…" "Surely you aren't saying…" They all seemed to be talking at once. I fought them off bravely, not to mention politely. "May it please the court, what I am saying…" "Counselor that's preposterous."

"But Your Honor…" "Yes, that's true Your Honor, but…" It was infield practice against five hitters. "Counselor, your adversaries say that…" "May it please the court, my learned adversaries overlook the fact that…" "Yeah, but…I know that, but…yeah, but I, but…"

And then it was over. The dust settled and I stood for a moment, bewildered. I staggered back to our table and slumped into the chair next to Ed. After one of our adversaries went, it was Ed's turn.

"May it please the court, I am Edward Horacio Coleman, attorney for the appellant and lineman for the county."

The gang of four, unimpressed by his attempt at humor, attacked with abandon.

"Counselor, I believe your brief misstates the law," called a red-headed judge seated to the far right.

"May it please the court," Ed answered immediately, "*I* did the research—don't tell *me*."

I buried my face in my hands.

"Counselor, I'm incredulous at your defense. Your entire argument is based on the notion that hockey would lose its fan base without fighting. And my rejoinder would be, who cares? By your logic, we should allow gladiators, as long as people are willing to pay to see them."

"Don't get me started on outlawing gladiators, y'Honor." I could swear his southern accent was getting more pronounced. "It's a sadness for all of us but *habet, hoc habet*. Point is, that ain't your call. Violence is part of hockey; hockey's legal. Case closed. Who's up for foosball?"

"I don't contend that hockey should be golf, but—"

"Hey, may it please the court, can I ask you something? Don't you think golf would be a better game if you could play defense?"

"I don't contend that hockey should be golf," the judge repeated, his eyes closed, "but your adversaries argue that, while their client might have consented to certain kinds of physical contact during a game, he didn't consent to being attacked with a stick. What do you say to that?"

Ed was indignant. "I say they ought talk to their client, for he was heard clearly and without question to say—as he was entering the game for the first time—'Dang, I love this game, especially the stickfighting.'"

One of our adversaries looked open-mouthed at me—as though I had any more control over Ed than anyone else—while the other leapt to his feet.

"Objection Your Honor!" he shouted.

"No hockey player in history ever said 'dang,'" added a judge.

Suddenly, it seemed as though everyone was objecting. I was half tempted to do so myself. Typically, there are no objections in moot court because it's an appellate court, not a trial. But this was now a case of first impression.

"Objection to what, son?" Ed demanded, facing our adversary.

"It's hearsay!"

Ed turned back toward the judges and fixed his eyes on them. "Y'Honor, this is not hearsay since it is not offered to prove the truth of the statement, but only to show his client's state of mind at the time of the incident." His eyes still forward, his right hand rose in the direction of our learned adversaries, and to my dismay, the center finger of that hand emerged from the pack.

Chapter twenty-two

I know this is all a big joke to you, Ed," I said as we sat in a local bar an hour after losing moot court, "but you were playing with my grade in there too."

He wasn't paying attention. He looked toward the window and stood up halfway. "Is it snowing?" he asked himself. "Is it damn snowing? We might get a day off tomorrow," he rejoiced, rushing outside.

I looked around the bar at the dim lighting, wobbly tables, wobbly customers. Linda Ronstadt was singing *Blue Bayou* while a group of unshaven men with cigarettes hanging out of their mouths played billiards. Despite losing our oral argument on all four judges' cards, Ed and I weren't in that bar to drown our sorrows. Moot court was over, and that was cause for celebration. One more obstacle out of the way in first-year law. I was disappointed though. It hadn't been anything like I'd expected, even before Ed started his sideshow.

"Gang, gang, the hail's all here!" Ed announced with arms wide when he reentered the bar. He brushed the snowflakes off his hair as he returned to the booth. "Let's have another round, J.J. Ain't going to be no school tomorrow."

"I still want an explanation," I leaned forward. "I hitched my wagon to your star and you messed up."

"Hey, how about a watch that could also predict the weather?" he said. "I could call it the Tropical Storm Watch."

"Ed."

"Or a motorized toilet."

"Ed."

"The commodorcycle."

"Ed!"

"I told you, I lost my notes on the T."

"That doesn't excuse what you did. You could've cost me."

He looked at me and exhaled. "Okay, what's it going to take to get you past this? If I admit I got a little out of hand and apologize, will you drop it? Come on J.J.," he continued, "it's pass/fail, and we know they don't fail anyone who turns in a brief, much less one as good as ours. So what can they do, send us to moot-jail?"

I suppressed a smile. He was right, but I didn't want to let him off the hook that fast. He'd still taken more liberties than he should've.

"I'm sorry, J.J. I am."

"Alright," I conceded.

"What I want to know," he slapped both hands on the table, "is what kind of shots we're doing."

"We are doing Sambuca," I slapped my own hands on the table. A guy lining up what I suppose was a very important shot at the pool table glared at me. Our waitress looked over from her seat at the bar and Ed held up two fingers. When she brought two beers, we ordered the Sambuca.

"So," he asked as he tried to balance the salt shaker on a few grains of salt, "any new word from Jennifer?"

"You wouldn't believe me if I told you."

"Come on now, out with it."

"Talked to her two nights ago," I said. "Remember when she came by my apartment drunk a while back, and we kissed?"

"Remember? I'm still waiting for you to talk about anything else."

"Well, this time she had just finished her last final exam, and they were all in someone's room, drinking again—"

"She drinks too much," he said as the waitress put our Sambuca shots on the table.

"Cheers."

"Cheers."

"And she left the room to come call me. Guess what she said just before hanging up."

"That's rhetorical, right?"

"I love you," I said.

"So when do I meet your folks?"

"I'm serious. She told me she loves me."

"Dang, that girl's crazy."

"Wait, it gets better. Yesterday afternoon, she calls again. Apologizes for calling me in that condition, and tells me to ignore the whole thing."

"Ignore the whole thing."

"Yeah, just ignore it. The jury will strike the defendant's last remark from the record."

"You know what they say," he began to point out, but I was already one step ahead of him.

"Not only do I know what they say, I told her what they say. That since alcohol's a depressant, it depresses inhibitions, so you do and say things when you're drunk that you'd like to do and say but are afraid to do and say when you're sober."

"They tend to use fewer words to say it, but that's what they say," Ed nodded. "So what did she say when you said what they say?"

"Ah, she denied everything, said that's not the case with her, and we'll talk again real soon."

He stared at me, shaking his head slowly side to side. "J.J., why you putting yourself through this?"

"Because I love her," I said, feeling suddenly sad.

"That ain't no reason."

"You ever been in love?"

"You mean before you confessed your feelings for me just now?" I didn't say anything. "No," he admitted.

"Well," I took another drink, "one day you'll know what I'm talking about. You don't choose it, and if it chooses you, you don't fight it." My head felt heavy. Ed seemed farther away than he was. I looked down into my glass. "You just trust it, and no matter where it takes you, you go. Because even if it takes you through hell, you survive. And even the burns, they're okay, you know? They brand you. They leave you with something, I don't know...something."

"But why would it take you through hell in the first place, is my point."

"I don't know," I said. "Love's a miracle; maybe you're supposed to have to earn it."

"What a romantic."

"Okay then, you tell me—why would I choose this? Over the past few months, this woman has annihilated me. Why do you think I still want her back?"

He seemed to sober up for a moment. He stared at me without blinking, and clipped off each word: "Because men hate losing."

I shook my head. "This is who I am."

"Fine, but wearing your heart on your sleeve like that is why it gets crushed, you know. I respect the fact that you're willing to do it, but me, I'm more calculating. I'll know when to be sincere."

"You better," I warned him. "Because if you don't know when to turn it off, the woman of your dreams will pass you by because she won't know it was you."

The day after wasn't pretty. Fortunately, Ed had been right about the snow and classes were cancelled all over the city. I lay in bed for much of the morning, feeling nauseated, heavy-headed, and guilty for reasons I couldn't define. I lifted the window shade and let the stark white snowy landscape stab my eyes. Snow silences the world, gives you space to think. Why do I feel guilty? I deserved to blow off a little steam last night; it was my first courtroom appearance ever. I'd been nervous about it for weeks.

I rolled to my left and noticed that a note had been slid beneath my bedroom door. I didn't bother to get it. What happened after I got home last night? I remembered calling Jennifer; maybe I woke her up and was feeling bad about that.

But as it came back to mind, she hadn't been upset with me for calling. In fact, we'd had a nice conversation. I remember her telling me she was sure moot court hadn't gone as badly as I thought, that I was going to be a great prosecutor one day, on the level of—and then she couldn't come up with the name of a famous prosecutor to use as an example. I suggested Menchel, the guy from the Manhattan D.A.'s office and she said, no, she knew him and I wasn't going to be quite that good. And she said to stop apologizing for calling so late and just to make sure to drink a big glass of water before going to sleep. Did I tell her that I loved her? I hoped not. King passes out on board, scattering pieces and dismantling all previous strategy.

No, I hadn't, I was sure of it. So things were fine with Jen, no need to tip the king. And the headache now compressing my eyeballs wasn't even costing me class time. I couldn't have offended Ed because Ed's not offendable.

Then I remembered: it was as I was returning to my bedroom after having gone to the kitchen for the large glass of water. I passed by Amy's room, stopped and stood in the hallway. I went back to her door and grasped the handle but didn't turn it. We'd been spending a lot of time together lately, commiserating about our respective love lives. She'd been out with Doctor Howard several times, but the relationship had stalled. She wanted a monogamous relationship but he'd balked, and it wasn't her way to force things.

It had been just a few hours before sunrise and my instincts told me to rush back to my room and lock myself in until this feeling passed. But I missed her, and I longed to stare into her eyes across the darkness. But it was so selfish. I only wanted to look into her eyes because of how they looked at me. Then I thought of her legs, and her face backlit by the hallway light, and the way she said "talk" and called me dad. I put it all on my shoulders when I pushed open the door to her room, unable to see even my own hand in front of my face.

I stood still as my eyes adjusted to the darkness, and I made out the outline of her bed, and her on it. She was wearing a half-shirt and panties, and like the last time, one leg was beneath the blanket, the other atop it, a pillow in between. I removed the pillow and lay down beside her. I touched her bare thigh lightly, just my fingers, and she opened her eyes and smiled as though she'd been expecting me. Neither of us spoke. She rolled to her back and I rolled toward her and kissed her. In another few moments, our clothing was gone. We made love and when she fell asleep, I went back to my room. When I woke up again, the apartment was empty.

I looked back to my bedroom door and the note slid beneath it.

Chapter twenty-three

I approached the note with great trepidation. I picked it up off the floor but paused before reading it. With it crumpled in my hand, I went to Amy's room just to make sure her things weren't gone. It was absurd, of course. Even if the note did contain words of heartbreak and violation, she couldn't be gone yet. So with very little solace at the sight of her full room, I sat down on her bed and unfolded the note. Just a few hours before, we'd rolled around that bed together, and now it seemed so cold.

"Call me, 847-9000," was all it said.

I went back to my room, picked up the phone and dialed. A woman at the switchboard answered, and forwarded me to Amy's extension.

"Amy Adler," she said.

"Hi," I said, trying immediately to sound contrite. To my surprise, her voice brightened at the sound of mine.

"Well, good morning, incubus," she said. "How're you feeling?"

"Embarrassed."

"Well don't be," she said. "That's why I told you to call. I didn't want to come home tonight to a lot of tension. Now, I've thought about this all morning, so just hush up and listen."

"Okay."

"First of all, I knew what was going on. You didn't force me to do anything, you didn't take advantage of me, none of those self-serving male clichés. Next, I know you're not the one-night stand type—we care about each other." I started to speak, but she continued: "We also both know that we're not in love with each other; we're in love with people who make us miserable. But that doesn't mean it has to affect our friendship if we sleep together from time to time." It took me a moment to process what she'd just said, like hearing a phone number recited with the wrong cadence. "Thing is, we could really help each other through hard times right now. How many people can turn to someone they love when they need some warmth?"

"We love Lauren too, don't we?"

"Excuse me?"

"I'm just kidding."

"I know," she said softly. "But actually, I've thought about that too, and I think that, as much as possible, we should be discreet. I don't want to make her uncomfortable."

"Ame, I have to admit, you leave me speechless."

"I know it's unconventional, but we know who we are. And the nice thing is, I know that you'll always be rooting for me to work things out with Howard, and I'll root for you and Jennifer, or whoever else."

"You really think it's going to be that simple?"

"I don't value simplicity in my relationships. Look J.J., we've been friends for a long time. As long as we honor that friendship and respect each other, I think everything will be fine. Besides, I've got a feeling Jennifer is coming home soon."

"Whose home?"

We were already comfortable again. But the change in the relationship became apparent when, before we hung up, she said, "Oh by the way, tonight I'm the one going out with friends for drinks. And that late-night attack you pulled makes you fair game too, any time of night."

"Okay," I exhaled, "see you later, succubus."

"Far out, incubus."

Chapter twenty-four

Oh no, not again," I thought when I awoke, facedown on a Civil Procedure textbook, a rancid combination of perspiration and drool coating the right side of my face from temple to jaw. I rubbed my eyes and, ever so slowly, rotated my head side to side, then up and down. Outside the second-story window was an exquisite spring day, but I hadn't left the library since morning. I'd even packed a lunch so that I wouldn't have to waste time in the cafeteria.

"Psst," I said to Asha, seated opposite me at the library table, "what time is it?"

"Five-thirty," she answered, then noted the film on my face. "Someone needs to make an absorbent textbook, don't you think?"

Oh, wonderful, J.J., I thought as I dried my face on the inside of my collar. I'd been sleeping for nearly an hour. Final exams were less than two weeks away—fine time to be turning narcoleptic. But I was so weary. Classes had ended the week before, and like my classmates, I'd been studying incessantly. My typical day started early in the morning and went past midnight, with breaks only for meals. I was sleeping just a few hours a night. It was a brutal schedule that would only intensify over the coming weeks, but I had no choice.

None of my professors had given mid-terms, meaning that each final exam would cover the entire first year, August to May. One year, one test. Winner-take-all.

Undaunted, I shook the cobwebs from my head and continued reading where I had left off. My textbook was open to page 423. I wonder how Leo is doing with his exams? No, no—not now. Come on, concentrate. I began to read.

Stare decisis is a principle of policy and not a mechanical formula of adherence to the latest decision, however recent and questionable, when such adherence involves collision with a prior doctrine more embracing in its scope.

I'm sorry, I was with a customer. What was that?

I say—"*Stare decisis* is a principle of policy…" What's a principle of policy? How would that differ from a policy of principle? I was growing daunted. I sat up straighter in my seat. This never helps but I always do it when the battle is becoming hopeless, like the foundering situation comedy that starts casting guest stars.

"*Stare decisis…*"

Wait—I know what that is. Or am I thinking of *res judicata*? Or *ab initio*? *Res ipsa loquitur*? "Why am I studying American law in an American school and talking LATIN?!"

"Shhh—I'll feed your eyeballs to my cat!"

"Sorry, Asha, I didn't realize…sorry." I grit my teeth and looked down again.

"*Stare decisis is a principle of policy and not a mechanical formula of…*"

When did I scrape that knuckle? Why can't the T serve sandwiches? How is Leo doing? Why's there no umlaut in the word "umlaut?" Why *isn't* defense allowed in golf?

The bathroom, I thought. That's what I need. Splash some cold water on my face; I'll be a new man. I got up from my seat and left the library, very little limp left in my walk. In April, when I'd gone for my last follow-up appointment, the doctor had said that my foot had healed perfectly. He said I was free to return to karate whenever I chose. I was even considering testing it a little tonight, when Josie and I would meet for our weekly session. Just the week before, Zachary had promoted Josie from white belt to green belt. I was happy for him, though a little envious that he was continuing to improve and I wasn't.

I pushed open the bathroom door and went in. I leaned over the sink and turned on the cold water, catching it in my cupped hands and splashing it onto my face. Then I looked up at the mirror. The head facing me had unkempt hair and the imprint of a textbook running down its right side. I pointed a finger at it. "You don't deserve to do karate tonight," the head told me.

"But I've got to start training again if I want my black belt," I replied as I wiped away the water.

"You're not in Boston to get a black belt; you're here to get a law degree."

"Karate's more fun."

"Fun don't feed the bulldog."

"Aw, give me a break; law school's tough."

"Your father did it…and held down a full-time job."

"He was fueled by the dream of getting rid of all of us."

"So? You want to be outdone by him? You want Mom to have to tell him you flunked out of law school and listen to him laugh and call you all Brooklyn trash?"

"I'll flatten him if he does."

"Then he'll call you unrefined."

"God, he loved that word."

"It's a good word."

"It's an okay word."

"Well, you're going to hear it if you flunk out, and so will Mom."

"Don't worry, Mom," I said as I wet my hair back. "I'll do it. We'll show him. We're going to take everything he ever accomplished and double it. You can bring my diploma to his office, shove it in his face and do your cocktail party bump-and-grind."

"No karate tonight, then?"

"No karate."

"Good boy."

"Drop dead."

Chapter twenty-five

At night, I dressed to go to Josie's. It would be the first time I'd ever been to his home—he had such a big office that we usually just met up there and moved the furniture aside to do karate. But with my increased study schedule, I hadn't been able to meet him during the day.

"Can I talk to you?" Amy asked as she stood in the kitchen boiling a pot of pasta for dinner.

I already had the front door to the apartment open. "Can it wait until I get home tonight?"

"When will you be back?"

"Not late. Maybe ten."

"Okay, we'll talk then."

As I left the building and crossed Beacon Street to catch the T to Brookline, I thought about Amy, and the relationship we'd started the night of moot court. On so many levels, it made no sense. We weren't dating but we were passionate. We weren't in love but we were intimate. At times, I didn't understand Amy any better than I had understood Jen, but with Amy, it never hurt. We'd fallen into each other's beds because the people we were in love with were each, in different ways, unavailable. Howard was there in body but not soul. Jen called occasionally but that's all it was. Maybe I needed the passion and Amy needed the intimacy. For whatever reason, it worked, whatever it was. It didn't exist during the day, only at night.

One of us would wake the other and we wouldn't say a word, just make love—tender or wild, intimate or impersonal, free and loud on nights Lauren was out. But then there were nights like the one last week, when she woke me and knelt silently by my bed. When I turned to her, through the darkness I saw the tear tracks down her cheeks, and another droplet pooled on the ledge beneath each eye, about to spill over. She climbed into my bed and we held each other for a long while before she told me what had hurt her. We talked until morning, and it never even crossed our minds to make love.

The T arrived and I climbed on. I sat near the front and stared out the window.

I'd never slept with anyone like Amy before. Sometimes I'd awaken just slightly in the middle of the night and cradle around her, and her sleeping body would always move toward me. She'd wrap her arm around mine and hold it to her heart. No one I'd shared a bed with had ever done that. Even Jennifer would just lie motionless when I'd curl up to her. I'd dated other women who would snort an angry, unconscious snort, an instinct I'd always considered revealing. In the glare of day, we all learn to behave so as to get what we need. But in sleep our personas are bypassed, and the true self emerges. In times of need, the true self is all that a man can depend upon. Even in sleep, all of Amy's instincts were embracing. And yet I wasn't in love with her, and she wasn't in love with me.

The T finally stopped and I pulled out the piece of paper on which I'd written the directions to Josie's apartment building. I was surprised when I got there. It was nicer than my building certainly, but not as much as I would've thought. With his credentials, I wondered for the first time why he hadn't stayed in private practice. Surely it would be more lucrative than teaching. After they buzzed me in, I rode the elevator to the third floor, where his wife was waiting in their doorway.

"J.J., it's nice to see you again," she said, and surprised me when she followed that with a hug, and a kiss on the cheek. Some people just know how to hug. "I've been telling Josie to invite you over ever since he told me how you put him in his place in class that day."

"Oh, I didn't—"

"It's okay," she said. "It was great for him."

She took my coat and we talked for another few minutes before Josie appeared in the archway between the foyer and family room. I thought he'd be wearing his *gi* pants, or at least sweats—we usually did the karate before the law. But he was still in his work clothes. "Sorry, I got caught on a phone call," he said, offering his hand. "Do you drink coffee?"

"I started about a week ago."

"Terry, would you show him to my office while I get some coffee?"

"No, you two get started," she said. "I'll get the coffee. Tea for you, *Chulo?*"

"Please."

"What about karate?" I asked. "Don't you have anything you want to work on?"

"Finals are close," he answered. "I thought we should give you the whole two hours."

"Wow, thanks."

He led me through the family room and we stepped over and around toys and small socks as we crossed it. The walls were decorated with paintings, reproductions of classic pieces I recognized from Art History class at Brandeis: Dali's *Eggs on a Plate without a Plate*, de Goya's *Clothed Maja*, Velazquez's *Don Luiz de Gongora*, which I'll never forget because they made us travel all the way into Boston to see the original.

"These are beautiful," I said, standing in front of the Dali.

"They're just repro's," Josie answered. "There are some originals in my office, but no one so famous."

We turned down a hallway that opened up to the right, passing a closed door with a woodcarving of a baseball mitt and bat hanging on it. On the bat, painted in royal blue, were the words, "BEN'S ROOM." Past that, at the end of the hall, was Josie's office.

As we entered, I was taken aback not only by the amount of art-work, but how it was displayed. In other homes I'd been in, the art was there to decorate the house. Here, the room revolved around the art. It was as though the walls' only function was to frame the paintings and tapestries, the floor there only to support the bases that held the sculptures. I strolled slowly around the room, look-ing at it all.

"All Spanish artists?"

"Except this one," he said, laying his hand gently on a statu-ette.

I went over to it and knelt down. "It's beautiful."

"It's Mayan," he said.

"I wasn't going to touch it."

"But the rest are Spanish—Terry and I used to live there," he explained.

"That's right, I remember you telling me. When was that?"

"We left Madrid thirteen and a half years ago."

"Wow, Madrid. That must have been great."

"Oh, we lived everywhere—Madrid, Barcelona, Toledo, Valen-cia—anywhere they had a good museum. We were married in Bar-celona," he said wistfully as he ran his hand over a painted wood sculpture. "Spent our honeymoon wine tasting in Jerez de la Frontera. That's where we got this. Young guy, Gracielo. Don't know if he ever made a name for himself, but it's lovely, don't you think?"

"Yes."

He sat down behind an antique, cherry wood desk strewn with papers, and I pulled a folding chair alongside it.

"So when are you coming back to the *dojo*?" he asked, chang-ing the subject.

"As soon as exams are over," I answered, laying open my note-book on his desk. "Did you work out your problem on that *kata*?"

"Manny worked with me on it Tuesday night," he nodded, "but it led to another problem."

"That always happens, doesn't it?"

"Always. Okay then," he clapped his hands together, "what've you got for me?"

We worked for almost two hours, going through two cups of coffee and tea, respectively. When Terry brought in our third cups, she said to Josie, "I'm switching you to herbal," and then turned to me. "And you're on decaf."

"Good idea," Josie said. "In fact, J.J., we should finish up so you can get some sleep."

"I'm down to my last question."

"Hit me."

"Okay. What happens when someone's civil rights are violated, not by the government, but by a private entity that has some attributes of a government?"

"Such as?"

"Such as a private township," I read from my notes, "a large-scale community association..."

"A company town," he added.

"How would the law apply in that case?"

"Well," he began, "first I need to disabuse you of the notion that there's any such thing as 'that case.' Situations differ—cases often turn on their specific facts. How many people live in the town? How much choice do they have to live elsewhere? What other attributes of municipal government has the association or township appropriated for itself?" He sipped his tea. "Not to mention, what court are you in? Who's the judge? Where does he or she live? When is he or she up for reelection, or has she a lifetime appointment?"

I was dumbstruck.

"What's the matter?" he smiled. "You look upset."

"What are you, kidding me?"

"No, I'm not kidding you," he said simply. "Don't expect to find consensus on every rule."

"So you wouldn't ask about that on the exam."

"You're leading the witness, counselor. Is this direct or cross?"

"What?"

"Nothing," he smiled. "In trials, you're allowed to lead a witness on cross-examination, but not on direct." I said nothing. "Direct is when you question your own witness," he explained, still getting nothing but a furrowed brow from me. "Forget it—don't worry about trial law. You'll learn about that next year in Evidence. Take Katahira for that if you can."

Something about the breadth of his mastery of law, or maybe the realization of how much more I still had to learn, overwhelmed me. I'd been walking around thinking the learning was almost over because my first year was almost over. Before I could name it, I was fighting off a full-scale panic attack. Josie tried to settle me down.

"J.J., relax," he said. "I'm sorry, forget all the trial stuff. It's not important now. But you asked me what I'd put on the exam and we had agreed not to talk about that. Perhaps I was awkward in how I tried to avoid the question."

"But you wouldn't ask us about something if there's no consensus on the law, would you?"

"Yes," he said emphatically, "yes I most certainly would."

"So what are we supposed to do? If there's no agreement on the law, how can we…what are we supposed to do?"

"The same thing you would do if it came up in court—argue your position. I'm not interested in finding out who has the best rote memory—you might want to warn your friend Ed—I want to see who understands the reasoning behind the laws, and who can apply them to a fact pattern. If you know the elements a court will consider in deciding whether a private entity such as a company town is sufficiently similar to a state to apply the Fourteenth Amendment to it, then you simply discuss those elements and do your best to reason through the situation. Your ultimate conclusion is unimportant; it's the rationale you follow I'll be looking for."

I stared noncommittally toward a wall tapestry, then looked back at him. Eventually, he continued. "The problem with the academic setting is that it fosters the illusion that questions necessarily have answers. Tell me something: does Sensei Zachary teach moves at the *dojo*?"

"Moves?"

"Yes, you know—someone grabs you here, you do this. Someone pushes you there, you do that."

"Oh," I shook my head, "no."

"Why not?"

"Because you never come up against the exact situation that the move works against, so chances are, it wouldn't work."

"Precisely," he said, turning his palms upward. "And rarely does the situation occur in law where a rule can be applied in practice as it is in the classroom. We don't learn karate; karate learns us. We train our bodies to move a certain way so that our reactions are instinctive. We learn the logic behind rules of law so that we can extrapolate it to any situation."

He sat back, and I turned back to the wall. "That's discouraging," I muttered.

His laugh was one of exasperation. "Why?"

"Because the exam's in three days. It's too late to learn all that now."

"Too late? Do you want to be a great attorney or a great test taker?" I said nothing. "It's not late at all. You're just starting. You know what it takes to excel at something, to go from competence to greatness?" I shook my head. "Freedom of spirit. Because without exploration, even a great mind is condemned to mediocrity. Learn the rules of law like you learn the fundamentals of karate, but don't think of them as the ceiling; think of them as the floor. And for God's sake, don't smother your freedom with mundane concerns like exams, because if the freedom dies, it will be too late."

"But exams aren't mundane," I answered. "I need good grades to get a good job."

"Jobs are mundane too. Look at these paintings," he said, holding his left arm aloft. "Do you think the men who created these were concerned about the job of being a painter, or do you think they painted with all their heart, day in and day out, the natural result being that they were painters?"

I said nothing. I didn't understand his point and didn't want to pretend.

"A man who's true to his inner flame doesn't seek to define himself through his work; he seeks to express who he already is," he continued. "And that can't be suppressed by the circumstances of his life—his job or grade point average. Lech Walesa's first job was as an electrician. Copernicus was a doctor."

He stood up and paced the room for a moment, then sat down on the edge of his desk and faced me. "I don't mean to overstep boundaries. But why do you want to be a lawyer? Is your father a lawyer?"

"Yes, but that's not it." He watched me, unconvinced. It made me laugh. "Believe me, I'm not looking to follow in the old man's footsteps."

"It's not always admiration that leads a young man to follow his father, you know."

I do know, I thought—*you* don't. You couldn't possibly know, and neither could your son, not in this quiet, viable household. I have an ability to look away from someone without actually turning away, simply by unfocusing my eyes. He understood and didn't press any farther. "Then what?" he asked. "Do you feel you have a gift for law?"

"A gift? I never really thought about it that way. I did well in school. I think being a D.A. would be pretty cool…." I left the thought where it was and shrugged.

"Okay," he nodded. "That's a good start. And, for what it's worth, I think you could be a wonderful lawyer. Just promise me you'll think about it, not only in the context of who you want to be, but also who you already are." He stood and wandered to the other side of the room, where the tapestry hung. He straightened it, then gently brushed his fingers beneath its fringe. "Talent can be a trap, J.J.," he said. "Even love can be a trap. You have no responsibility to your talent, and the only responsibility to love, is to love. Passion alone is never a trap. And your responsibility to your passion is to follow where it leads."

"Daddy, you woke me up," a little boy said from the open office door. Like his father, Ben had fine, blond hair and a willowy physique. His eyes squinted against the light as he reprimanded his father.

"Come here," Josie told him, and when Ben did, Josie lifted him, then returned to his chair and sat with the boy on his lap. He brushed Ben's hair behind his ear. Lost for a moment in Ben's sleepy profile, he sighed softly. "Of course," he said to me while still looking at his son, "sometimes your passions do collide."

180

I thought all night about how calm Ben was on his father's lap, as trusting of it as if it had been a bed. And I thought about traps and responsibilities. I thought about it on the T heading home; I even thought about it when I went to bed, just after Amy told me that she and Howard had decided to move in together, and that whatever it was we'd shared, was over.

New York

Chapter twenty-six

I t's not just that he looks so much smaller than when I'd last seen him, more than fifteen years ago. Nor is it his barely detectible recoil upon seeing that I'm now bigger than he is that most strikes me as the three of us stand frozen in each other's presence. It's how civilized he looks. It's just a man in the doorway now, not the roiling force of nature I remember from my youth, whose whereabouts I had to take account of as first order of business any time I walked into our apartment. His hair is the fine coated silver of the dignified gentleman, and wrinkles ray out from the corners of his blue eyes as he smiles at my mother. Beneath his navy blue suit he wears a powder blue shirt with a white collar, and a crimson necktie. A white handkerchief is folded perfectly into his breast pocket. He stands calmly in the doorway waiting to be invited inside. Just an ordinary man, like thousands of others I've passed on the street. His eyes hold steady on my mother.

"You look good, Bev," he says.

"You too," she answers. She smiles but I know it's forced. Only for one of her children would she have ever allowed him back into her life.

He turns to me. "Don't worry, kiddo, I'm not expecting a hug. How about a handshake for the old man?"

He extends his hand. But it's the same hand that beat my mother, connected by the wrist to the same forearm he once shoved under my chin and up into my throat. My feet are melted clay, seeping into the cracks between the slats of hardwood. I want both to attack and to run. He retracts his arm.

"You call me for a favor and won't even shake my hand?"

"I didn't call you."

"He didn't know anything about it, Jerry," my mother explains. "Give him a minute. He'll come around."

"No I won't," I say. "I'm leaving."

"Jerry, come in and sit down," my mother says, ushering my father into the living room as she clutches my shirtsleeve. I try to remove her hand, so she readjusts her grip. Her fingernails dig into my triceps. "Me and J.J. are going to talk in the kitchen for a second. You want a drink?"

"No thanks," he replies eagerly as he sits on the sofa. "I don't drink anymore. Just wine."

She nods at him as she pushes me into the kitchen. Inside, I yank my arm away.

"Damn it, Mom, that's my skin."

I lean against the counter and rub my arm.

"Shake it off, you panty waist." She moves closer. "Look, no one hates this more than me," she whispers. "But if I can take him for a few minutes, so can you."

"Panty waist?"

"If you were drowning, would you care who pulled you out of the water?"

"How are you spelling that?"

"Now listen, I don't like asking him for help either. But the fact is, he might be able to do something. He's done us enough harm over the years, God knows; it's only right he does something good."

"But I don't want to owe him anything."

"I'm the one who called him," she taps her index finger on

her chest. "So if anyone'll owe him, it's me, and I'll make sure he knows that."

"I don't want you owing him either."

"Well, that's none of your business, is it?"

I sigh and look away. Knowing she's won, she heads back toward the living room. I follow behind. "Panty waist?"

"Shh."

"What does that even mean?"

"Shh!"

She sits in a chair beside the sofa; I remain standing. I'm still not planning to stay long. My father takes a fat Macanudo cigar out of his breast pocket.

"Been a long time," she begins.

"Long time."

"So tell me, what's new?"

"Nothing much, still working hard. Can't complain."

"Who'd listen anyway, right?"

"Heather and I got separated," he adds a bit clumsily.

"Yeah, I ran into your sister a while ago. She told me. What's that, four?"

"Three."

They laugh cheerlessly, then it fades to silence and becomes awkward.

My mother breaks the silence, motioning toward his cigar and beginning to stand. "Let me get you a match for that."

"No," he defers. "I'm good."

I wish I had a match. A match, maybe a few gallons of gasoline. He keeps the unlit cigar in his hand and gestures toward me with it when he speaks. "Your mother tells me you're into karate now." I nod. "I got my own karate. I call it a hammerless thirty-eight with a Packmeyer grip."

"Jerry…"

"I'm just joking. For crying out loud, I can't joke?" She stares at him. "Okay, fine, tell me what's going on."

As my mother explains, my father nods along, a slight frown on his lips. Occasionally, he puts the cigar in his mouth and slowly twirls it. Just one match and maybe a quart of gasoline. If he proves quicker than he appears, I'd be just as happy to douse myself. Self-immolation would be a comparatively painless way to end this family reunion.

When my mother finishes, my father exhales and leans back into the sofa. He stares toward the window and shakes his head. Then he looks at me.

"For crissake, kiddo. Breaching attorney-client confidentiality? Why you want to go and do a stupid thing like that for?"

He seems genuinely concerned. I meet his eye, defiantly at first, then not.

"They had no one else to help them," I say.

He stands and wanders toward the sliding glass door that leads out to the balcony. He's looking more at the glass door than through it, and rolling up and back onto the balls of his feet. There's something sincere in this, and it makes me resent him all the more for blurring the stark, graphite lines of the caricature I've spent years creating. "I'm sorry, Bev," he says, then walks back to the sofa and puts a hand on my mother's shoulder. "It's my fault. I should've come around more."

He passes her and sits on the arm of the sofa, facing me. "Your mother's a good woman," he says as though she's left the room. "She might seem unrefined, but you could do a hell of a lot worse than her. Still, there's some things a *father's* got to teach a son. Kiddo," he leans forward, "take it from a guy who's seen it all—you've got to grow the hell up. That's all there is to it. 'They had no one else to help them'? No one's got anyone to help them. Your job is to represent your client's interests to the best of your ability, case closed."

I press my tongue to the roof of my mouth and take a deep breath. "You're gone fifteen years and think you're going to lecture me about—"

"Let me tell you something," he interrupts loudly. "I've been a lot poorer in my life than these people have ever even had nightmares about. You know who helped me? Me. I helped me. This guy, Eagan, wants to keep his house? Fine, it's up to him to figure out a way to do it. I know, I know—he lost his job, boo-the-hell-hoo. You know what—deal with it. I've lost jobs. I dealt with it. Your mom knows," he points to her. "She saw you about to lose your license so she dealt with it. She called in the big guns—me." He counts off on his fingers. "You didn't give Eagan asthma; you didn't fire him; you didn't miss his mortgage payments; you didn't foreclose. You deal with your life and let Eagan deal with his."

"I don't want to live like that."

"No, no," he says. "You don't get the high ground here. You're helping one couple—one couple. What do you want, a reward?"

"I was hoping for a round of applause."

"I write dozens of checks a year to charity. I sponsor an under-privileged kid in Biafra, or Congo, I forget which. I send money to Make a Wish, Outward Bound, U.J.A. Which of the two of us you think does more good?"

"You don't know if your kid's in Biafra or the Congo?"

"Who cares?" he shouts. "You think he gives a damn? What do you think he'd rather have—love notes from you or cash from me?"

Every rich man I've ever known who built his fortune on bodies face down in the mud could recite this same speech, almost verbatim. They must teach it somewhere.

"Well, good for you."

"Yeah, good for me. Damn good for me. You know what they call me in my office?" I don't answer. "A.D. Know what that stands for?"

"Affective disorder?"

"American dream, that's what, wise guy. Because I started with nothing, and by the time I was forty, I was a full partner. I make more rain now than any other two partners combined. I got a Ferrari parked downstairs and a townhouse on West 65th. And I still help a thousand times more people than you."

"Fine," I shout, holding my arms wide, "that's what you do. You're a saint and Ayn Rand will massage your comb-over in heaven. I saw two people who needed help and I tried to help them. That's what I do."

"Comb-over?"

I look to my mother. She regrets bringing him here, I can see it. "I'm sorry, Mom, but I've had enough of this." I turn back to my father. "You think I've forgotten everything? I don't recognize you because you show up in a nice suit? I know who you are. I know exactly who you are. I remember everything."

"Comb-over?" he stands.

Instinctively, I take a fighting stance. If someone's going to take a beating today, it's not going to be me. "Take one step and I'll lay you out, I swear to God." My face is flushed and my arms feel cold.

"Enough, you two," my mother shouts, launching herself between us. But she doesn't have to. My father is smiling broadly.

"Well, what do you know," he laughs. "Used to be I thought Leo would be the only man in the family. Good for you, kiddo. Got a little of the old man in you after all."

"Jerry," my mother tries to say evenly, "we need an answer. Can you help us or not? Do you know this guy, Carlysle?"

"Yeah, I know him," he says. "I could probably help you."

I hate the fact that this gets my attention. I drop my hands to my side.

"Does he owe you a favor or something?" my mother asks.

"Bev," he shakes his head and chuckles, "people don't help me because they owe me a favor. They help me so I don't owe them an ass-kicking."

"That's a yes?" she persists.

"I'll do my best." He puts his cigar back into his mouth and angles it upward. "I'll give him a call. You'll keep your license, kiddo. But if I ever hear about your playing with confidentiality again, I'll personally disbar you. You got that?"

"Thank you," I mutter. "I'm sorry about all the—"

"Ah," he waves me off, smiling toothily around the cigar. "Come here," he says. "I like how you stood up to me. You surprised me." I hesitate. "Come here; one handshake won't kill you."

I exhale and shake his hand. "Look, I've really got to go. I'm meeting someone uptown."

"Where uptown?"

"Upper West."

"I'll give you a lift," he says, then turns to my mother. "Listen,

Bev," he removes the cigar from his mouth, "what would you say to dinner one night? Must be a long time since you've been out nice. You think I might deserve that?"

Behind his back, I shake my head vigorously. She sees but doesn't acknowledge me. Through languid eyes, unsmiling, resigned, she answers: "Sure, that would be great."

"You going out of town for the long weekend?" She shakes her head. "Great, me either. How's Saturday night?"

"Fine."

"So, kiddo," he cuffs me on the shoulder, "you ever been in a Ferrari?"

Chapter twenty-seven

Traffic snarls near the 59th Street Bridge and, silver Ferrari Spider or not, I'm not enjoying life in a convertible. The fumes rise and mottle the summer air as cars fight their way out of the city. Even though it's only Thursday, a lot of people seem eager to get the jump on Labor Day weekend. My father forces his way into a left turn from two lanes over, to head west. I'm happy to see the traffic start moving more smoothly once he does; I'm supposed to meet Ira in fifteen minutes.

"I'm not saying there's anything wrong with karate," he shouts as we drive north on Madison. "I'm just saying, it doesn't exactly pay the rent, does it?"

Fortunately, there's no need to answer. He's been pontificating on a variety of subjects ever since we set out from my mother's place, and the few questions he's posed have been strictly rhetorical. Which is good, because I'm too upset to hold a conversation. I don't want my mother getting involved with him again. And I'm sure she wouldn't have accepted his invitation to dinner had she considered it anything less than the *quid pro quo* for his help. I'm so angry I want to scream. The fact that I'm the cause of it all makes me angrier still.

"Not that I didn't get into the occasional scuffle as a young man," he adds, as I notice the sun begin to cool from yellow to orange, "but I won most of my fights anyway."

I know this to be true because I was on the other end of many of them.

"So what do you think of the car? Incredible, isn't she?" We turn left onto 96th Street to cut through Central Park. I remember going to Central Park with Josie the last time he came to New York, and I make a mental note to call him and see when he's planning to show up for the hearings.

To my right as we make the turn, I see Mount Sinai Hospital a few blocks north. "Maybe if you get on my good side I'll let you drive her one day." It's the perfect place to open the door and roll myself out of the car, I think. Someone's bound to drag my mangled torso to the hospital. How much blood could I possibly lose in four blocks? "Life," he chuckles softly. "It's so unpredictable. That's why I never let anything get me down, never let anyone stand in my way." A cabdriver tries to squeeze in front of us at a light and my father takes a moment from his philosophical discourse to fling an obscene gesture at him. "Deal with it, buddy," he shouts when the cabdriver curses him, then continues, to me or himself, I'm not sure and he's probably not either. "Deal with it, that's my motto. Like this guy here," he indicates the cabdriver, "he wants to get in front of me and I don't want him to. So I deal with it, no hesitation. Someone else, he'll wring his hands forever over what to do, but at the end of the day, I get everywhere I want to get."

"Dad," I say, disgusted by the taste of the word on my lips, "this thing with Mom."

"What about it?" I don't know how to say this. "What?" he repeats.

"I don't think it's the best idea."

He glances over at me as he drives, twice, to make sure he heard me right. I can't see his eyes because he's wearing sunglasses. He purses his lips and bobs his head back and forth. We stop at a red light on the western edge of the park, and he removes the glasses to look at me.

"She seeing someone?"

"No," I admit. "Look, I appreciate what you're doing for me, but Mom...she's been through enough. You know? Can't you just leave her be?"

"Don't you think that's up to her?"

"Yes, and if you want to wait until we're finished with our business, I'll back off, I promise. But right now, you're not really leaving it up to her."

"Hey," he puts his sunglasses back on, "if someone's arm's twisted, it's still their arm."

"What does that mean?"

He shifts the car back into gear and continues west. "Give your mother some credit," he says. "And while you're at it, give me some. I'm not as bad as you think. Believe it or not, we're a lot alike, you and me." He turns south down Broadway. "Maybe that's why you hate me so much." If I were behind the wheel right now, I'd pull into a parking lot, aim the car for a concrete wall, jump into the back seat and not even care if he got us out of it.

"Are you helping me just to get back in with Mom?"

"What if I am?"

"It's wrong, Dad. It's just wrong."

"What if I know I'm good for her, that I'm different now?"

"Then tell her that. After we've finished our business."

"Hey, she called me. I didn't call her."

"You're just dealing with it."

We stop at another red light, at the corner of Broadway and 94th Street. He looks straight ahead. "Maybe I am," he checks himself in the rear view mirror. "Look, she made the decision she wanted to make: I made the decision I wanted to make." He turns to me. "And you, kiddo, in all your self-righteousness—you made the decision you wanted to make."

I stare at his profile, and I've never felt such hatred before. And maybe he's got a point. But this decision he thinks I've made, it's not yet irreversible. Which is good, because it's a bad tradeoff. It's always a bad tradeoff when your soul's part of the deal.

I check the stick shift and see that the car is idling in neutral.

I'm in the mood for an irreversible decision. So in one motion, I turn the key, remove it from the ignition and hurl it into the center of Broadway, just as the light turns green and traffic starts to move.

"Deal with it," I say. He looks at me wide-eyed and speechless, then scrambles out of the car after the keys. He runs into the middle of Broadway, dodging cars and shouting at drivers to stop. I get out and shout above the cacophony of blaring horns: "I don't need your help, I don't want your help, and stay the hell away from my mother!"

Chapter twenty-eight

I walk briskly down Broadway, glancing back periodically to see if he's coming after me. At the first corner, 93rd Street, I consider turning left and taking another route to the restaurant so he can't find me. But I stay on Broadway, walking fast, occasionally jogging, continuing to check behind me and flinching every time I think I hear a 12-cylinder engine or .38-caliber gun.

I'm so unsettled that it jolts me when my cell phone rings from the pocket of my suit jacket. I take out the phone and flip it open.

"Hello?"

"Where are you?" Ira asks.

"Just a few blocks away. I'm sorry—I'll explain when I get there."

After disconnecting the line, before putting the phone away, I dial my mother's apartment. It takes five rings, but eventually she answers.

"Mom, it's me," I say. "Listen, I can't really talk. I just wanted to let you know that, if Dad calls, you don't have to go out with him."

"What did you do?" she demands.

"I told him I didn't want his help."

"What?!"

"I don't want him back in my life, Mom. I don't want him in your life."

"Well, that was a really stupid thing," she says. She's trying to sound angry but not pulling it off. It's just volume; there's no spirit beneath it. The truth is, she's relieved. Throwing the keys into the street felt good, but this, letting my mom know she's off the hook, this feels great. Of course, she doesn't give up easily. "I'm going to give him another call," she says. "Maybe I can smooth things over."

"I wouldn't bother."

Her voice softens. "What did you do, J.J.?"

"Just trust me," I smile. "We're way past the point of smoothing anything over. Listen, Mom, I'm at the restaurant and my friend's waiting inside. I'll tell you everything later. It's more of a visual anyway."

She sighs loudly, tells me I'm a fool and thanks me. I check the phone before I close it and see that it reads 7:21 P.M. Inside, Ira's sitting on a red vinyl couch that runs the entire length of the right-hand wall of the restaurant. He's in shirt sleeves, his suit jacket beside him. There's a rectangular table in front of him with two chairs on the opposite side. He's biting into a slice of pizza when I enter. On the table is a slice for me. Still on edge, and perspiring from the hurried walk, I pull out a chair and sit. I apologize and tell him about what just happened. He laughs when I get to the part where I threw the keys into the middle of Broadway.

"So," he sips his ginger ale through a straw, "have you come up with an excuse for me?"

"Excuse?"

"I needed you to come up with a reason I can give Boston for needing to see the Eagan file."

"Oh, right," I remember. I drink some of my soda and consider but decide against the pizza. I need a few minutes more to let my stomach calm. "Problem is, no matter what you say, he's going to suspect something."

"Then we don't get to see the file," he mumbles as he chews.

He swallows and adds: "Which means all we've got for leverage is the threat of a cram-down, and it's a pretty weak threat. Unless…"

"I'm listening."

"What if I go back tonight, after Boston's left for the day?"

"I don't know," I hesitate. "If you get caught sneaking around his office—"

"So what? I tell them I needed to see a file. I've been on the Parker National deal for a year." It sounds good in theory, but I'm sure it wouldn't be so simple if it actually came to that. "J.J., do you want to help the Eagans or not?"

"I do, but not at the risk of your career."

"I won't get caught if…" He stops himself mid-sentence and leans back in his chair. "You know what?" he holds out his hands, palms inverted. "I don't need your permission. I'm going tonight."

"Then I'm coming with you," I say.

"Surely you jest."

"Why not?"

"Well, for starters, because I don't like losing, and you and your professor friend are already making my job hard enough. I don't want to have to explain breaking and entering, too." I don't respond, and he adds: "It's the only way we're going to see the file, J.J., you know it as well as I do. I'll be careful. I'll go at, like, 3 A.M."

"There could still be people there. Hell, even Boston's there sometimes at 3 A.M., the psycho. You need a lookout. Let me go with you." We sit in silence for a few minutes, then an idea occurs to me. "Wait a minute," I smile. "We're missing the obvious. If we go tonight, the place could be crawling with people. But tomorrow's Friday, and it's a long weekend."

"Boston spends every Labor Day weekend out on his boat."

"And most of the associates will be gone too. Improves our chances."

"Would you stop with the collective pronouns," he laughs. "What do you think you're going to do, hypnotize me?"

"Finny, there's no way I'm letting you do this alone. If you're going, I'm going."

"And your negotiating leverage here would be what, exactly, counselor? The way I see it, it's my key card, my decision."

"I'll camp outside your apartment tomorrow night. Explain that to Joanne."

"I won't go home. I'll just stay after work."

"You're good," I nod. "Oh, you're good. But you're forgetting one very important detail." I smile and keep nodding.

"And that would be?"

I continue nodding because I've got absolutely nothing say. Here's where I used to flip over the checkers board when Leo and I were kids. "Come on, Finny, let me go."

"Begging? That was your last chit?"

"Fine," I sit back in my chair. "But you'd better stay after work because I'm going to follow you home if you leave."

"Deal. Now, more importantly, let's think about what I could look for in the files." He takes out a yellow pad and we begin making notes, marking down anything that could constitute a defect in the loan. After a while, we're about out of ideas.

"I've got to go to the bathroom," he stands. "Get me another soda, would you?"

He walks past the counter into the back of the restaurant, and I go to buy two more sodas. As I'm sitting at the table waiting for him to return, I'm still uncomfortable with the risks he's taking. Getting caught tomorrow night would be much worse for him than he's admitting, and he knows it. But he's right—as long as he's the only one with a valid key card, he gets to make the decisions. That's it, I realize, the key card.

I look toward the back of the restaurant, to make sure he's not coming back yet. I have to move fast; I might've already missed my chance. Quickly, I slide from my chair to the red vinyl couch, and fish through Ira's suit jacket, hoping his wallet will be in there. In the inner breast pocket, I find it. I don't bother to look up again; if he comes back now I don't lose anything. In a sleeve of his wallet, I find his key card and stuff it into my pocket. Then I check my own wallet. I'm relieved to see that I hadn't bothered to throw out my key card, even though the firm certainly disabled it as soon as I was fired.

Other than that, it's identical to Ira's card. I put it into his jacket and throw his jacket back onto the chair.

I'll go to the firm tonight. I'll go alone. Ira won't have to get involved at all, a worthy double-cross. By the time he realizes what's happened, it'll be Friday.

Chapter twenty-nine

I say good night to Ira outside the pizza place, then go home to relax and try to get a few hours sleep. Several hours later, my alarm clock goes off. It's a little past 2 A.M. I can't believe I have to get up. I'm so tired, and today's going to be a long day of hearings, but I need to get a look at that file. And I've got to do it now. I'm due at my mother's apartment at six to pick up Leo and drive him to the airport so he can go back to school. And I told the Eagans I'd be at their place around six-thirty to pick up their bankruptcy papers.

I choose my clothing carefully so as to blend in. If I get caught breaking into Greer on top of all the other charges against me, I'm finished as a lawyer. If someone I know sees me there it won't matter how I'm dressed, but I need to at least be able to fool security guards, new hires and other strangers. It would be less risky to go tomorrow night, but this is the only way to keep Ira out of it. I leave myself unshaven, and put on a suit and tie, then loosen the tie. I want to look like a sleep-deprived associate who hasn't left the office all day. Associates usually wear suits during all-nighters. It's not required, but no one wants to keep a change of clothes in the office and admit to themselves the reality of their working hours.

I stop at an all-night deli and buy some coffee and doughnuts, then enter the lobby a little past three. I sign in under my own name. It wouldn't help to make one up—building security insists on seeing a picture I.D. Fortunately, this doesn't derail my plan. I'm not planning to steal documents or do anything else that would compel the firm to go back and check the sign-in sheet or review security camera tapes. I'm just going to look through the file, gather information, and leave everything just as I found it.

The elevators are all open and waiting. I get onto one quickly, just in case anyone from the firm is on his way downstairs. I hold the key card to the plate on the elevator and when it automatically registers the 39th floor, I curse under my breath. Ira's card, of course, doesn't provide access to the 44th floor, where Boston's office is. I'll have to use the stairwell and hope the door isn't locked on 44.

At 39, the elevator doors open and I peek out before stepping off. To my right are the set of thick glass doors that lead into the office. No one is at the front desk. For several seconds, I stay on the elevator, staring through the glass doors to gauge the level of activity. It's busier than I would've thought. I recognize a few of the associates who pass by. They're from the real estate group. There's probably a deal that has to close before the weekend. Every few seconds, someone walks past the door. One woman even looks up toward the elevator banks and I nearly tear my ear off my head as I hurriedly withdraw into the elevator. It's not going to be easy to run from here to the stairwell without being seen, but I only have another few seconds before the elevator starts buzzing. Check over your shoulder as you run to make sure no one has seen you, I remind myself as I crouch and brace my right hand against the open door. I take a deep breath then break for the stairwell.

In the stairwell and out of sight again, I stand upright and take a moment to calm down. I don't think anyone saw me, but can't be sure; I forgot to check over my shoulder. I climb five stories, to where the door is marked "44," then turn the handle slowly, silently. I have no idea what my next step will be if it's locked. It turns completely and I hold it steady, listening through the door to make sure no one is coming. It's silent. I crack open the door and peek through. The place is empty; I should've known. Partners don't work the graveyard shift; that's what associates are for. Still, I move to the glass door carefully. I enter silently and head for Boston's office.

It takes a while to find the Eagan file, but eventually I do, on the credenza beneath a tackle box. Though I'm pretty sure there aren't any partners around, I still have to be careful. I don't want to be seen by anyone, not even the cleaning crew. Boston has an enormous, L-shaped desk, so I take the file and lie down on the floor behind it. For the next two hours I work my way through the documents, checking everything. I find an appraisal that Parker National must have commissioned. The value comes out at $160,000, which I'm sure is way too high. But as Ira had pointed out, the appraiser only took photographs of the outside of the townhouse. A good appraisal really needs to take account of the interior condition too. If the appraiser had had access to the interior of the house, he wouldn't have valued it a penny higher than $120,000, maybe even less. Eiderhorn would know this too, of course, but that $160,000 valuation will help him in bankruptcy court. He'll negotiate hard and try his best not to come off that number.

The loan documents themselves are flawless. If I were teaching a course in transactional law, I couldn't find a better loan to use as an example. The promissory note and mortgage are intact, and not only signed by Emily and Jared, but initialed by them on every page. It's recorded perfectly, the title exceptions are routine, even the damn notary did exemplary work. We're in trouble.

As I'm trying to find the real estate tax bills to see how much the Eagans owe, a rumbling sound comes from the hallway outside. In my state of fatigue, I can't tell whether it's the wheels of a cleaning cart, a partner's irritable bowel, or a fine Italian sports car. I still haven't seen everything I need to, but I might not have that option. I check my watch and see that it's past five. I still need to go back home to shave and make myself otherwise presentable for the hearings today, then get Leo to drive him to the airport.

I gather everything off the floor and return it to the file. I've made sure not to remove more than one item at a time, and to note exactly where things came from each time I removed something. It's important to leave the file just as I found it, so as not to arouse suspicion. I can't take any chances. If Boston senses anything amiss, he's bound to suspect Ira. I put the file back under the tackle box and peer out Boston's office door.

Down the hall, a cleaning cart turns the corner. I duck back into the office and behind the desk to wait. The cart passes by Boston's office and continues into Dietz's. Quickly, I return to the stairwell. Having gotten this far, I can't let myself be caught now, so I avoid the elevator entirely, and instead take the stairs all forty-four flights. I exit the stairwell into the lobby, and turn immediately toward the street exit.

"Hey!" someone shouts from behind.

My first instinct is to run. But my legs are a little rubbery from so many stairs, and besides, security has my name on the sign-in sheet. There are security cameras everywhere. The guard has no reason to mention this to anyone tomorrow unless I give him a reason now. So I turn back, my mind whirling with explanations, excuses, and counter-charges—for what, I have no idea.

"You got to sign out, sir," he says.

"Oh, I'm sorry," I smile. "Sometime around midnight, I start forgetting stuff."

"I don't know how you guys do it."

"You're doing it. Have a good night, now."

I make sure to walk out of the building at a leisurely pace, then head north on Madison, relieved until it occurs to me that the Eagans are no better off now than they'd been yesterday. I realize that I haven't accomplished anything yet, like at the end of law school, when my brief euphoria ended with the realization that I still had a lawyer's life to live.

Boston
Third-Year Law

Chapter thirty

Through the heavy rainfall, and through the leaves that the wind whipped and pasted to the sliding glass door leading out to my patio, I saw the headlights of Josie's minivan as he turned onto Kelton Street.

I had moved into this tiny studio apartment nearly two years earlier, just after my first year of law school had ended. I'd had little choice after Amy announced that she and Howard had decided to move in together and Lauren told me in the same moment that she'd gotten a place of her own, leaving me alone in the three-bedroom apartment. Passive eviction, I guess. Amy promised to stay in touch but never really did, because Howard didn't like having me around. Occasionally, she'd sneak in a call from her office, but not often. And the one time I'd called her at home, it led to a big fight between her and Howard, so I didn't call again.

Josie's car pulled up to the curb in front of my building. I slid open the patio door, slung one leg then another over the railing, and tucked my head as I trampled the landscaping in my rush to get out of the rain. He handed me a cup of coffee as I climbed in.

"Thought you might need it," he said.

"I need something," I answered, wondering where I was going to find the enthusiasm to exercise on such a soaked and miserable night. "Thanks."

When I'd been in college, I'd heard stories of friendships emerging between students and teachers. Real friendships, I was told, life-long bonds, often rooted in some shared noetic passion. But, personally, I'd never even come close. Professors, for me, had always remained two-dimensional figurines at the front of a lecture hall, and I felt sure that, in their eyes, I was but a cardboard cutout folded into a seat. I didn't resent it; these were our jobs. They were supposed to feed me information and I was supposed to yak it back onto a bluebook page every three months. Nothing personal; just business. And law school would've been no different had it not been for the *dojo*. Josie and I had become close friends, but not because of law. During first year, we'd gotten to know each other mainly through our study sessions, where he'd roll his eyes over my articulation of constitutional principles and I'd berate him for kicking too slow. But after first year ended, we stopped talking about law. My leg was fully healed and I returned to training three or four nights a week. We car pooled to the *dojo*, sought out one another for sparring or two-person drills during class, stopped for pizza on the way home. I'd been to his apartment for dinner many times, had gotten to know his wife and son. Most of the time, I didn't even think of him as a professor.

As we drove to the *dojo*, I stared through the windshield at the heavy March rain. On the floor between us, I noticed his gym bag.

"Tell me you brought it tonight," I said, tapping the bag.

"Yes," he answered, "I brought it. Still don't feel right about it, though."

Sensei Zachary had recently promoted Josie from green belt to brown belt, and Josie had made the mistake of continuing to wear his green belt. When asked, Josie had said that he didn't yet feel worthy of a brown belt. Zachary said Josie must not consider him much of a sensei if he didn't think he knew a brown belt when he saw one.

"Don't feel self-conscious," I said. "You deserve it."

"So do you."

"He'll let me know when I'm ready."

"Everyone in the *dojo* knows you're ready right now. Even Manny."

"They're just jealous. I'm going to set the record for the longest-held brown belt in history and they just wish it was them."

He looked at me and smiled, then turned back toward the road. "I was sure he'd invite you to test before you graduated. He knows you're moving back to New York soon, doesn't he?"

"He knows."

We pulled up to the *dojo* and I was glad to end the conversation. Talk of graduation was bound to lead to talk of my job search, which was as stagnant as my quest for a black belt. We were a little late on arriving, so we hurried inside and went into the locker room to change into our *gis*. I watched Josie wrap a brown belt around his waist. He put it on with a trace of awe, something I knew he'd eventually grow out of, just as I had done. I was happy for him—he was a devoted student and had grown into a good sparring partner. Though much smaller than I, he was a tactician—and a left-hander to boot—so fighting him wasn't easy.

Out on the floor, I spent extra time stretching, trying to wring the cold weather from my joints. Josie stretched beside me, his hair still damp from the sprint from the car to the *dojo*. We looked at each other and rolled our eyes.

"Oil," he gasped. "Need oil."

Warm-ups were a misnomer; no matter what I did, I couldn't seem to get loose. The *dojo* windows were air-tight, but it didn't matter—the chill was coming from inside me. I knew that if the class could ever manage to break a collective sweat, my muscles would warm and everything would be okay. But the steady percussion of raindrops battering the windows rang in my head. Even Manny, whose intensity never faltered, called the count with more sigh than bark in his voice. When Zachary told everyone to choose a partner for sparring, Josie and I found an open corner and squared off.

I felt sluggish and mechanical as we started to spar, and was taken aback when Zachary appeared at my left shoulder.

"J.J., is it raining?" he asked.

"Yes, sensei," I answered, continuing to spar.

"You didn't let me finish," he said, stepping so close to me that I had to stop and face him. "Is it raining in Bangkok?"

I looked at Josie, who shrugged. "Pardon me, sensei?"

"Is it raining in Bangkok?"

"I don't know."

He nodded.

Josie stepped forward to join us.

"Is it raining in London?"

"Probably."

"Is it raining in Boston?"

"Yes."

"Is the rain in Boston touching you any more right now than the rain in Bangkok or London?"

"No."

"So why should the rain that doesn't touch you in Boston affect you any more than the rain that doesn't touch you in London and Bangkok?"

"I'm sorry, sensei," I said, realizing that he was calling me undisciplined. "I've only been out of the rain for twenty minutes. I'll warm up and do better."

"How privileged we all are," he smiled, "that we can afford to be so easily influenced. If this were four hundred years ago, and we were training outside"—his voice began to rise as he took a step back—"with swords instead of empty hands, and the rain had turned the earthen floor to mud, and Josie were leaping toward you, sword overhead," he simulated, grasping his left thumb in his right hand and raising it high above his head, then slamming his foot down onto the hardwood with a violent shout as he exploded toward me, then immediately calmed again—"could you afford to wait until you warmed up?"

I felt the floor beneath my bare feet reverberate from the force of his attack, and for just an instant, was sincerely, biologically afraid.

It wasn't anxiety, that slowly advancing sense, cognitive and civilized, that I'm somehow not the equal of my future challenges. It was real fear, a primal flood of white water. My heartbeat sped to increase blood flow. My breathing grew shallow to preserve oxygen. Everything outside the tunnel of attention between me and Zachary vanished. It passed immediately of course, because my rational mind quickly concluded that I wasn't in danger, but he had made his point. I could be training more realistically.

Manny overheard and interjected as only he had the leeway with Zachary to do. "Come on, V.P.," he appealed, "it's not four hundred years ago. These guys are lawyers, not swordfighters."

Zachary shook his head slowly. "I wouldn't waste five minutes here, Emanuel, if all I were teaching was how to kick and punch. We're learning how to live, and the winds of circumstance are as fickle as the weather. The martial artist who lets a rainy night weaken his training will also let it weaken his work. He'll let a supervisor's bad mood lead to a fight with his wife; he'll let a flu derail his dreams.

"You have to be stronger than that," he said to me. "No true martial artist ever relinquishes his sword to circumstance. He continues to hear his own, clear voice, regardless of what else is going on. Because he knows he can't trust anything—anything—but that voice."

He focused on me now, his eyes squinting just a bit. His body was still, as though he was trying to figure something out. I feigned interest in two green belts sparring a few feet away.

"*Yame*," he called to them and they stopped sparring. Then he turned back to me. "What do you want out of your life, J.J.? What do you need? What don't you need? More important, what will make these choices—your own clear voice, or circumstance?" When I said nothing, he pointed his finger at Josie and twirled it a bit, saying, "*Tzuzukete*." Thinking the lesson had passed, I bowed to him. Josie and I exchanged bows and continued sparring.

But as we circled, Zachary snuck up behind me and slapped me lightly on the back of my head. I turned to him.

"Ignore me," he said. "Keep sparring."

But every time I tried to, he'd slap me again, or push me off balance by my shoulders, or sweep my feet.

"You're not sparring me," he insisted when I turned to him again. "Concentrate on Josie."

So I threw a front snap kick and tried to advance, but Zachary pulled me back by my belt.

"Advance," he shouted, as others began to take notice. "Advance!"

But he had me by the belt, so I broke free of him, walking right into a side kick to the ribs from Josie.

I threw up my arms. "What are we doing?"

"You're focusing on a goal and ignoring circumstance. Now go," he insisted. "Go!"

I sensed Josie's leg rising toward me and pivoted out of the way. His leg continued on its arc toward Zachary, who slid to his right in time to avoid it.

"What do you acknowledge?" Zachary persisted. "What do you disregard?" I threw a combination, leading with a right jab to get Josie's hands up, then following with a low kick to his thigh, as Zachary swept my legs out from under me and yelled, "Has the rain turned to sleet?" I landed hard on my hip, but used the new position to sweep Josie's leg. He landed on top of me and scrambled back to his feet, and it was chaotic and beautiful, and free. "Listen for your voice." Josie tried to grab me as I was on the ground but I pulled away, tearing open my *gi* jacket. I spun on my back, lashing out at him with my right leg to drive him backward and give me room to stand. His hair flew into his eyes. My belt rode up to my bare ribs. It came untied and I slung it to the side as I stood, and we exchanged another flurry of punches and kicks.

By the time I heard Zachary call *Yame* to end the sparring, he was shouting it repeatedly and pulling me backward. Manny wrapped his arms around Josie, and only then did I come back to myself. My hip ached and I realized that I'd bruised it when I fell. But it hadn't slowed me down, not a bit. I'd been so focused on the fight that I'd been able to ignore the distraction. As I caught my breath, I saw that the entire school had stopped their own sparring to watch.

"V.P.," Manny called, still with Josie in a bear hug, "I just had an idea. We got two lawyers beating each other's brains out here. We could charge a cover."

Some people laughed but Zachary ignored him. "Line up," he shouted, and everyone fell into rank. "Take stances."

This was the identifying characteristic of the V.P. Zachary *dojo*: stance. Our style of karate—whatever it was—had one fundamental stance from which all *kata* began, and in which all *kata* ended. And once you took your stance, you weren't allowed to break it for any reason, until the *kata* was complete. Zachary called *kata* a sacred dream, so sacred that even if the *dojo* itself caught fire, it would dishonor him, his teachers, our *dojo* and ourselves to awaken from it. Complete your *kata*, he would say, then bow and run. We took it as a figure of speech. We hoped to hell it was just a figure of speech.

Energized by the sparring, I stood now in stance, my hands in a modified sparring position, my elbows tucked near my ribs, my feet at shoulder-width. I chose a point far in the distance and stared straight ahead at it as Zachary walked from student to student, testing stances and making silent adjustments. He took his time, and with forty people in class that night, ten minutes passed before he reached me.

My arms felt heavy and I could feel the throbbing more prominently in my hip. He threw a kick at it and I winced when it landed, and he shook his head no. He stood directly in front of me and stared me in the eye, and when I just slightly averted my eyes, again he shook his head no. He walked behind me and spoke into my ear. "Has the rain turned to sleet?" I didn't respond and he said, "Good." But when he circled again to my front and moved to kick at my injured hip, I buckled a little, shying away from the impact I anticipated.

He sighed and walked away, and from the corner of my eye, I saw him go into his office. The mirror that covered the front wall was fogged with the steam of our sweat. The fog was thicker on the lower half of the mirror, and my legs seemed invisible, faded into mist. When Zachary reappeared, he held a glass jar in his hand.

He unscrewed the jar's lid, and I watched in disbelief as a bumblebee flew out and made its way to the rafters twenty-five feet above. As I stood locked in my stance, I could think of nothing but that bee, somewhere up there in the rafters, surveying the target-rich area. I heard it buzzing. I felt its faceted compound eyes on my neck, no doubt sensing the bowl of Honey Nut Cheerios I was now regretting having had for dinner. A man in the row of black belts bowed, saying, "I'm sorry, I'm allergic," and strode off the floor. Zachary stood in front of me again, and preoccupied as I was, I didn't recoil at all when he kicked at my hip. He nodded, smiling slightly. Hoping his next move wasn't going to be the application of a dollop of honey to my nose, I was completely unprepared for what did happen.

Beyond him, the front door to the *dojo* began to open, and Jennifer Reed—whom I hadn't seen in more than a year—stepped inside. For a moment I actually believed it was connected to me, was somehow Zachary's doing, but the way he followed my stare over his shoulder, shook his head and smiled when he saw her, told me it wasn't.

She was as beautiful as ever, and I relinquished my sword, my concentration, my bee, and everything else I thought I'd learned that night as I watched her take a seat in the row of spectator chairs. It was all I could do to keep my arms up. Zachary walked away from me to the front of the room, bowed us out of stance and told us to choose new partners for more sparring.

I hid behind people and watched as Zachary walked over and welcomed her. Life gives you so little time to prepare for its most important moments. You worry about grades and step in front of a moving car; you obsess over a bee and the love of your life shows up. I hoped she was here to find me—trading kicks and punches in a sweaty *dojo* had never been her style—but wasn't sure.

Standing between me and Jennifer, Manny was beckoning me to spar. Only because walking across the room backwards would've called attention to myself, I took a deep breath and faced up to the moment. I wiped my face on my *gi* jacket and walked in her direction toward Manny. She saw me.

"J.J.," she exclaimed, and the surprise in her voice saddened me. I had no right to be disappointed—it had been more than two years since we'd dated—but I'd never stopped thinking of her.

"Jennifer?" I started to pass by Manny but he grabbed me by the sleeve.

"Flirt later, Casanova," he said too loudly, and I shut my eyes in embarrassment.

"It's okay," she held up a hand. "Don't let me interrupt."

"We'll be done in a couple of minutes," I said.

"We'll talk then."

"You know her?" Manny asked me as we found an open space.

"My ex-girlfriend."

He looked at me suspiciously, then at Jennifer, then back to me. "Come on, no one breaks up with women like that."

"I didn't."

"Ah, Jeez," he winced, "and I embarrassed you. I'm sorry."

"It's okay."

"No," he shook his head, "that's not cool between friends. Tell you what, we'll impress her with you now."

"What do you mean?"

"Tonight, you're Chuck Norris. Come on, bust me up."

I didn't think much of the idea, but bowed anyway and began sparring. Over Manny's shoulder, I saw Zachary leave Jennifer. Her attention turned to me and Manny. I threw a few distracted kicks, each of which he let land.

"Come on," he implored, "show her what you got."

"She doesn't care what I've got," I whispered back.

We rotated 180 degrees, until I had my back to her. Still, I could feel her presence. I threw the best combination I knew, a fake sweep into a mule kick. I'd never once connected with something like this on Manny before, but he let it through. My heel sank into his midsection, and I could actually feel his abdominal muscles yield just enough to make it look real.

"Come on!" he said again, more urgently this time.

But it was no use; she was still the most disruptive woman I'd ever known. I felt exposed. Out of sheer frustration, I snapped a front kick at Manny and to my amazement, it landed legitimately. I followed it with everything I knew—roundhouse kicks, back-fists, sidekicks, elbows, complex Sino-circular blocks that only ever really work in cheap karate films and *Underdog* cartoons. Amazingly,

Manny made it all look real. I'd seen him spar a lot and always get the upper hand, but that was nothing compared to this. To make sense of the motley array of martial twaddle I was subjecting him to was impressive.

After a while, Zachary called an end to the class and we lined up in rank for the formal bow out. At his signal, we sank to our knees and waited in *seiza* position. We closed our eyes and drew deep breaths through our nostrils, releasing the air with a soft, collective whistling through our mouths.

"*Hai,*" Zachary said softly, our signal to open our eyes. "*Rei,*" he said, and we bowed. Forty right palms rested on the smooth, sweaty floor, then forty left palms did the same. Forty heads bowed, low enough to let our forearms lay horizontally on the floor. Zachary returned the bow, though his was slightly different than ours. Only his right hand touched the floor; the left remained by his side, a vestige from feudal Japan, when one hand always stayed to guard the sensei's sword.

"*Domo arigato gozaimashita,*" we said in unison.

"*Gokuro sama,*" he answered.

Using his right fist for leverage, Zachary spun 180 degrees on his knees to face the portraits of the masters.

"*Hai,*" he repeated and the entire class bowed in the direction of the photos. This time, Zachary placed both hands on the floor as he bowed. We sat up and waited. Zachary slowly brought his hands out from his body as we followed, and all forty-one of us clapped twice in unison, fast and firm. We bowed again and clapped once more. Zachary spun to face the class, we bowed once more, then leapt from our knees to our feet, bowed a final time, and broke into applause. Some headed for the locker room, others dispersed to different parts of the *dojo* to keep training. Josie approached from my left.

"Are you in a rush to get home tonight?" he asked.

"No."

"Great, I'll see you in about twenty minutes."

He jogged to a corner of the room to join a gathering of brown belts, and I made my way off the floor.

Jennifer was waiting for me near the spectator chairs. When I reached her, she surprised me by embracing me despite my sweat-soaked *gi*. My hip was throbbing, so I leaned against the wall as we talked. When I finally summoned the nerve to ask why she had come, she shifted on her feet.

"There've been three attacks on campus this semester," she said. "I know I used to tease you about all this, but I finally decided it made sense. You always spoke so highly of this place, so…" She shrugged.

"J.J.," Manny interrupted, "I need some time on the bag. Give me a hand?"

I introduced Jen to Manny, then we accompanied him to the heavy bag. He took a fighting stance on the opposite side of it, several feet away. When he nodded, I drew the 110-pound bag backward, then slung it at him as hard as I could. The purpose of the drill is to practice pivoting out of the way of an attacker without wasting any movement. He waited calmly as the bag reeled toward him, pivoting out of the way at the last possible moment. I caught it on its return and quickly threw it back at him, trying to change the angle to make him account for it. Time and again, he avoided the bag, never off balance, never wasting any motion. Every step was smooth. He never got hit, never moved too soon. I'd done the drill myself, and knew how hard it was to wait for the last instant before pivoting out of the way. I also knew that the bag could knock a man clean off his feet with even a glancing blow.

Jen and I continued to talk, standing close to hear one another over the hollow acoustics. I pointed out the different exercises that people were doing in different parts of the room and explained the uses for some of the equipment. But I regretted what I couldn't bring myself to say. I couldn't seem to tell her how much I missed her. I couldn't say that my life had never been the same since she left. I couldn't ask if she was still with Galahad, or if she ever thought of me.

It hurt to have her so close. It literally hurt. She didn't stand next to me; she invaded me. I felt it in my stomach. Her scent spun my head. Her hair was just inches away, and when the bag would come back too close to her, she'd turn her shoulder into me for protection, and it felt so goddamn good I nearly cried.

In time, Manny excused himself and, not knowing how else to keep her there, I asked Jen if she'd swing the bag at me a few times.

"I can't throw that thing."

"You don't have to," I said. "Just back up with it and let it go."

She looked at me skeptically but agreed to try. In time, she was enjoying it, even putting some muscle into her throws and trying to hit me.

"This is helping you?" she called.

"It's great."

"But we're going so slow. You and the other guy did it fast."

"He's a lot more advanced than I am."

"Oh, please, you creamed him when you fought. I was watching."

"I did okay," I said with false modesty as I narrowly dodged the bag.

"You did better than okay. You took him apart. He should give his black belt to you."

I knew immediately that I should disagree, but it felt too good. Still, that didn't make it any less awkward to hear Manny say: "Yeah, maybe I should do that."

He stood about five feet behind and to the left of Jennifer, by the front door, about to leave, glaring at me. He was waiting for me to come clean with Jen, but it had been his idea to make me look good.

Jen hadn't heard him. I looked at him, silently pleading with him to continue out the door. His glare eased. He dismissed me with a wave of his hand then started to pull the door open as I heard someone yell.

"J.J., look out!"

I turned back as the 110-pound blue pendulum flew toward me. Beyond it, Jennifer covered her face, her shoulders raised, braced for impact. At least one of us was.

When I came to, I was lying on the floor, several feet from the heavy bag, which still swayed triumphantly. Josie and Zachary pulled my underarms until my head was as high as theirs. I don't know if it meant I was in love with them too, but my stomach felt just as queasy around them as it had around Jen. They told me I wasn't badly hurt and I was in too much pain to argue. Jennifer rode with me and Josie on the drive back home, and they helped me inside. At some point, Josie became not in my apartment anymore, and Jennifer was the thing standing over me with a mug, steam rising out of it.

She sat on the edge of my bed as the hot water froze my lower lip and made my tongue rough. She molded her lips into a variety of shapes as phrases like "accident" and "Manny laughed" came out. I made out very little, but was having a truly wonderful time. The bottom of the hot water got very sweet and thick, and I savored it as Jen pulled the blanket to my neck. "Second chance," and "You too?" competed with the tick of the wall clock for my attention. Finally, she thanked me for being so understanding, and stood to leave. I dropped my head into the softness of the pillow as she turned the corner and walked toward the door. The lights went out and I closed my eyes. I don't know what it was that led me to open them again, but when I did, I stared in amazement at her silhouette as it undressed itself and laid its naked warmth beside me under the covers.

Chapter thirty-one

I awoke the next day with a chill. The clock read 10:09. Glancing to my right, I realized that I was not alone. Neither was I covered. Sleeping by my side, wrapped in my blanket snug and warm as a burrito, was Jennifer. Apparent checkmate, and here I thought the game had ended two years before. She was lying on her back, motionless, a shard of sunlight piercing the vertical blinds and lighting her hair. Her face in repose was breathtaking, and I stayed perfectly still so as not to awaken her. Only her stomach moved, rising and falling with each breath. Someone had once told me that the truest measure of a man's life was the taste of his first morning breath, and that everything after that was a rationalization. That morning, the air had the taste of a campsite beside a glacial lake.

She stirred a bit and the covers dropped enough to expose one olive-skinned shoulder. I remembered Sensei Zachary's demonstration of clarity and distraction the night before, and smiled at my sleeping Jennifer. They don't come any more clear than her. But if she's so clear, why do I pity as much as admire her? Maybe it's because clarity, to her, is a necessity. Jen was eight years old the morning she awoke to discover she had a three-year-old sister by way of adoption. But her parents had had a bad marriage from the start, and nothing was about to save it. They divorced just six months later and her mother went back to work full time, leaving Jen alone to raise a veritable stranger. She was preparing dinners by the time she was nine—they ate cereal and sandwiches mostly, because she wasn't allowed to use the oven. She checked Gail's homework, picked out her clothes. She had told me about this the night we met, and I had told her how many beatings I took as a kid trying to stay in between Leo and my father. As our friends drank and danced in a reggae bar, Jen and I sat on the patio and talked about raising siblings. I don't think people like us ever know exactly where we fit. We just try to find someone who can understand. Maybe that's why she had come back to me.

Seeing bare shoulder, I couldn't resist. As gently as I could, I lifted up the blanket and peeked underneath. If there's a more godly vision than a beautiful woman in the nude, I've yet to see it. No painting can depict her; no poetry can evoke her.

"Everything still where you remember it?" a voice whispered, and I was embarrassed, but not in a bad way.

I kissed her and we made soft, patient love. In time, hunger set in, so we showered, made pancakes and ate them in bed.

"Your friend Josie is such a nice man," she said, catching a drip of syrup off her bottom lip with her tongue. "He's very fond of you, you know."

"How do you know that?"

"We talked while we drove home last night. That's going to be a great letter of recommendation."

"Aw, Jen, I don't care about the letter. He's my friend." I thought of all the time Josie and I had spent together over the past few years. "Maybe my best friend."

"I know. I'm just saying it's nice."

"You know, he used to clerk for the Supreme Court. He's one of the top constitutional scholars in the world."

"I'm going to get more juice," she said, swinging her legs off the side of the bed. "Want some?"

"No, thanks. Some people say he's already been short-listed for a federal judgeship."

I watched her walk into my kitchen and open the refrigerator. She looked adorable wearing one of my *gi* jackets, my brown belt tied around it to keep it closed. As I watched her fill her glass, I couldn't believe she was back.

"So why's he a teacher?" she called as she put the juice back into the refrigerator.

"I'm sorry—what?"

"Well," she exhaled, sipping juice as she climbed back into bed, "couldn't someone like that earn ten times as much at a law firm or something?"

"We talked about that once. He said it was too stressful and mostly about client cocktail parties and billing, not the things he really cared about."

"So why not be a senator, a judge?"

"Hey, Jen, how come you and Jeff aren't together anymore?"

She stopped drinking. For a moment, she said nothing, just looked into me with those plush, dark eyes. "We talked about this last night," she finally said. "Do we really need to go over it again?"

"Truth be told, Jen, I don't remember that much about last night. I remember you whomping me in the face with a hundred-pound sack of sand and dragging me back here, but beyond that..."

"We should bake a cake," she exclaimed.

"Huh?"

"To celebrate our getting back together. What do you say? Have you got flour?"

"Jen, I don't know how to bake. What about..."

"I do." She popped up out of bed and skipped to the kitchen.

"You didn't answer my question," I called after her as she rummaged through my pantry.

"Baby," she said, "I never really got over you. I never stopped thinking of you."

"So it was more about missing me than anything about Jeff?" Now that I'd managed to say his name, it felt good to repeat it. It reminded me that it was no longer a shadow over me.

"I can't say it was so simple—you do have flour!—Jeff was wonderful, but he just had no direction in life. I don't know, you can't turn feelings into words like turning flour into a cake. It's like trying to explain why you loved a book or a movie. It either makes you cry or it doesn't, and trying to explain the reasons isn't always possible."

I swallowed hard because she'd in fact put her finger precisely on what the problem had been with Jeff. He had no direction. As I've said, one thing Jen was blessed with was clarity—she knew what she wanted her life to look like and who she wanted to be. Problem was, if that was my only trump card over Jeff it put me on shaky ground. I was on the verge of a law degree, sure, but law school hadn't exactly ignited my passions. I didn't read any law outside of my class requirements, no magazines or newspapers. Didn't bring the subject up over meals. Being a D.A. still sounded interesting, but mostly, I was excited that law school was just a couple of months from conclusion.

"All you're missing is icing, butter, eggs and vanilla," she smiled, emerging from the kitchen carrying a bag of flour. "And this flour got wet at some point so it's now officially cement." Her smile faded. "Baby, what's the matter?"

"Nothing."

"You sure?"

"Uh huh."

She put the flour down on the countertop and sat beside me on the bed, her knees folded beneath her. She cupped my face in her hands. "I don't deserve your trust yet, I know that," she said, "but I'm going to earn it back, you'll see. The last time I made it through a day without thinking of you was the day before we met. When was the last time you didn't think of me?"

"Same day," I smiled. I took her hands off my face and held them by our laps.

"Well, there's the reason I came back, and there's the reason you let me. Can't we figure out the rest later, after we finish the cake?"

I kissed her and untied the brown belt that had been holding the *gi* jacket closed. We made love again. But along with being clear, Jen is nothing if not focused, and so my next stop was at the store for cake ingredients.

She mixed while I sat on the countertop, trying to dip a finger into the batter to taste it, then opening the icing and letting her have some off my finger. I remembered a bottle of rum I had and pulled it out of the cabinet while she wasn't looking. I didn't take the cap off, but she didn't know that. I waited until she had turned her back to get the vanilla, then inverted the bottle over the bowl. I held it there so she could turn around and catch me.

"J.J., no," she shouted, then realized that I had fooled her. "Okay, that's all for you." She took me by the hand and started to pull me out of the kitchen, but didn't notice a wet spot on the floor. She slipped and fell, and I fell too, reaching back to try to grab the counter, getting only the bowl of batter instead. She screamed when it toppled over onto us, then scooped up a handful of it and pushed it into my face. I did the same to her, touching off a full-scale food fight that left chocolate icing on her eyebrows and a broken egg atop my head. We eventually collapsed in each other's arms, but just as we settled down, she broke out again in peals of laughter.

"What now?" I sighed.

"I'm...I'm...," she stammered, tears streaming down her face.

"You're what?"

"Look at me!" she yelled. "I'm a battered woman!"

Chapter thirty-two

Terry Steele set a platter of crudités on the coffee table in front of me and Jen, while Josie poured the wine. In the background, the Red Sox were five runs behind the Yankees in the eighth inning, but aside from Josie's father, Ben Sr., no one cared. Josie held a glass of wine aloft.

"To graduation," he said, and everyone reached their glass toward the others as we toasted the end of law school.

"Thanks again for including me," Jen said as we drank. "It was very nice of you."

"Well," Terry rested a hand on my shoulder as she passed behind me, "J.J.'s very special to us. Wouldn't be much of a celebration without you." She leaned over my shoulder and turned to me. "And the Prince of Darkness tells me you're all set to graduate top five in your class."

I covered her hand with my own but said nothing. It was still hard for me to believe that graduation was just a couple of weeks away.

"Number two," Josie said from his seat on a couch against the opposite wall.

Jen's eyes widened. "You're second in your class?"

"Hard to believe, I know."

"Wait a minute," she said, "I don't get something. If you're second, shouldn't you have been *Law Review?*"

"My first-year grades were lower."

"I didn't know that," Terry said. "They couldn't have been that much lower if you're second now."

My eyes met Josie's across the room. "One bad grade cost me."

Terry groaned, "Don't tell me—Vermilyea. *Chulo*, he does this all the time. Somebody's got to—"

"It wasn't Vermilyea," I said. "He actually gave me my highest grade."

"Then who?"

There was a silent moment, then Josie chuckled awkwardly: "Believe me, you're lucky. *Law Review* was the biggest waste of time I ever—"

I compressed my lips to stifle a smile, while all eyes turned toward him. Even his father turned away from the baseball game.

"*Chulo*," Terry said. "How could you?"

"I had no choice," Josie appealed to the ring of disapproving stares. "You should've seen his exam. I've read more coherent desert island rescue notes."

"You said not to be tied down by the rules of law," I pointed at him.

"I said not to use them as a ceiling." He turned to Terry. "I meant, use them as a floor and expand from there. I never told him to advocate the violent overthrow of the Supreme Court."

"That would be cool," Ben said.

"Oh no," Terry said. "Not the *freedom of spirit* speech. Well, J.J., now you know he loves you. He's been drilling that into me for years."

"It's important," Josie said. "Jennifer, back me up."

"I know it is," Terry said as Jen smiled and shrugged, "but time and place, *Chulo*, time and place. You don't plant that in a student's head the night before a final exam."

Josie was silent for a moment, looking from me to Terry, to Jen, to his father. But when he noticed his son awaiting an answer, he shook his head. "No," he said. "I won't undercut this with Ben here. Always is the time, everywhere is the place. This isn't some naive idealism; it's a legitimate truth. It might have cost J.J. an exam, but it'll make him happier for the rest of his life. It's a mindset, a, a...." He struggled for words.

"I think he's gonna sing," Ben, Jr. put in through a mouthful of potato chips.

But Josie didn't hear him. "An uncontained spirit can accomplish anything," he said. "But we all get so shackled by trivialities—grades, rent, personal trainers, heated leather seats."

"Grades matter, *Chulo*. Rent matters."

"They can heat the seats now?" Ben Sr. asked.

"Yes, of course rent matters," Josie answered. "But how much rent, and at what cost? You know how many times I've heard our friends talk about how miserable they are, and rationalize it all because they say they need to take care of their families."

"But that's true of a lot of people," Jen put in. "Sometimes you have to sacrifice for the sake of necessities."

"But, Jennifer," Josie leaned forward, "what's really necessary? Rent, yes, but what about double the rent for the sake of higher ceilings? How much more work, how unpleasant the work, and for how high a ceiling?"

Jen wasn't intimidated. "But you're the one who's trivializing. People don't double their rent for higher ceilings, they double it for better schools, opportunity for their children."

"Okay," Josie smiled, and I could see the glimmer of his classroom eyes. "That's a wonderful, valid point. But let's take a look at that too. Essentially, you're saying the more you have, the better it is for your children. And who wouldn't sacrifice, put in endless work weeks at a tedious job, for the sake of their children? And let's even set aside the issue of whether these things are more valuable to a child than a parent's happiness, because that's too easy. Ben," he turned to his son, "where do normal people live?"

"Normal?" I interjected.

"Bear with me," Josie held up his hand. "Ben, where do normal people live?"

"In homes," Ben answered.

"Describe the homes."

He looked at his mother, who encouraged him with a smile. "Um, with bedrooms, and a living room with paintings and stuff, a kitchen, an elevator," he glanced around the room at the rest of us, suddenly self-conscious, and shrugged, slumping back into the sofa. "Whatever. I don't care."

"Like our home?" Josie asked.

"Yeah, whatever."

"There's my point, Jennifer. Children define 'normal' as whatever it was they grew up with. The more they see growing up, the more they need to recreate in their adult lives. The more they need to recreate, the harder they have to work, and more important," he emphasized with a raised forefinger, "the more narrow their range of choices."

"Wealth creates choice, it doesn't take it away," Jen said, glancing sideways at me.

Josie's eyes instinctively followed Jen's gaze, then returned to her. "It might look that way, but would you agree that someone looking to be wealthy has fewer professional choices?" he asked. "After all, even the best high school teacher can't recreate wealth like the average bond trader. So if my premise is sound—that children need to recreate the standard of living with which they grew up—they have fewer choices of careers that give them that chance."

"Sure," Jen allowed. "That makes sense."

"And they have fewer geographical choices too, because rural areas tend to lack executive jobs."

"Not always."

"No, not always—there are exceptions. I'm just speaking of tendencies. And they tend, I'd also assert, to have fewer intellectual choices—because time for epic novels and art galleries tends to disappear under the onslaught of an eighty-hour work week. So does meditative thought, giving them fewer spiritual choices." He thought for a moment, his eyes averted and unfocused, then turned back to

Jen. "And as sad as it is to acknowledge, one could even argue that they have fewer romantic choices, if you believe that the right spouse is an advantage in the corporate world. And so along they go, their need for comfort making the choices for them. Comfort," he shrugged. "Heated leather seats. High ceilings and treadmills. Comfort—the one thing that has no meaning outside the concept of accommodation, yet it grows from lap dog to bulldog to bulldozer." He aimed an index finger at the group. "And eventually, flattens everything in its path.

"The more you show them," he continued, looking at his son, "the faster you set their treadmill. The faster you set their treadmill, the faster they have to run. J.J., I am sorry about that grade, I truly am. I've felt badly about it ever since I did it, but I want you to know that I didn't make the decision lightly." The room was silent. "I care about you," he said. "I don't want to see you turn into that."

"You can set a treadmill too slow too, you know," Josie's father called over his shoulder, his eyes still on the game.

"How's that, Pop?"

Ben Sr. swiveled the recliner in which he was seated, turning his back on the game. He looked nothing like Josie. Ben was rugged and windburned. Josie bore more resemblance to his mother, they told me. Bore some resemblance to my mother too, come to think of it.

"I said you can set a treadmill too slow for your kids too," he repeated. "Do you have any idea what it was like running my little farm, living my quiet life, then being handed a son with an I.Q. of 185? You know how many nights I lay awake, wondering how in the hell I was going to make the world challenging enough for you? Especially after your mom died?"

"I had no idea, Pop," Josie said. "I didn't mean to imply—"

"Why do you think I got you into law?"

Josie smiled indulgently. "You got me into law?"

On the outskirts of the conversation, I was quietly surprised. I'd always assumed that my mentor had been born with a burning desire to be an attorney. I stayed still, hoping no one would cut the conversation short before I could hear the rest of the story.

"Yes I did. I saw how much you love to argue," he said. "Did it better than anyone I ever knew. Law seemed a natural."

"I don't love to argue."

"Hell you don't. You're ruining this poor young fellow's graduation party doing it."

Josie looked to the rest of us. "We weren't arguing, were we?"

"No," Terry said. "Pop, we're just talking. Josie gets emotional, but trust me, he doesn't love to argue."

"Oh, okay," Ben rolled his eyes. He stood and reached into his back pocket, producing his wallet. He rummaged through the worn black leather, coming around the coffee table as he did, and squeezed himself between me and Jennifer. We slid aside quickly when we realized he was going to sit on us if we didn't. "Let me show you all something," he said. Josie and Terry leaned in too, to see what he had. Ben Jr. stayed slouched into the sofa, feigning disinterest. I watched Ben's thick, weathered fingers as they extracted a yellowed newspaper clipping. As he unfolded it, I could see that it was torn along the fold creases. Unfolded, it was about the size of a greeting card. I leaned in to see better, as Ben carefully smoothed it with his hand. Josie let out a groan when he realized what it was, and straightened up, walking to the opposite side of the room. He slumped into the sofa beside his son.

It was a newspaper article entitled, "White House Welcomes Local Star!" and in the photo that accompanied the article was a smiling, teenage Josie Steele shaking hands with Jimmy Carter.

"What is this?" I asked as I read.

"Well, right there, you see—it's kind of torn through his face—that's Josie, and of course this fellow you'll recognize as former President Jimmy Carter. That's Rosalyn over there."

"But why..."

"Because back in high school, my boy here who doesn't like to argue was the star of the debating team. Won the state championship, then the nationals. The whole team got invited to the White House to meet the President, but Josie was the one he picked for greatness."

"Dad..."

"Well, didn't he?"

Josie didn't respond.

"What did the President say to you, Joze?"

"The man lived on four hours of sleep a night; he wasn't coherent."

"What did he say?" Jennifer asked.

"Said it was an honor to meet a future Supreme Court Justice," Ben announced. "Now what do you think of that, Jennifer?"

"I think he was right," she said, looking at Josie.

Josie acknowledged the compliment, but was obviously embarrassed.

"Now let me ask you all—what would you do if you had a son that the President of the United States of America called a future Supreme Court Justice?" No one said a word. "Hometown paper did a whole story on him, so did the TV news. *New York Times, Washington Post*—they all had at least a few sentences about it. What would you do?"

"What did you do?"

"During my senior year of college, he applied to Harvard Law in my name," Josie said. "But it was my decision to—"

"Got you to take the admission test too," his father pointed out.

"Come to think of it, that's true," Josie sat up. "You told me you'd pay for a plane ticket to Spain that summer."

His father waved him off. "Christ, Joze," he laughed, "I didn't have the money for any damn plane ticket. I had to hock my watch just to scrape up enough for you to take the test."

"So that's how you wound up at Harvard?" I asked.

"Not exactly," he answered.

"No, he'd never make anything that easy on me," Ben continued. "He told me he didn't want to go. Got into Harvard with a scholarship—anyone in our town would've given a limb to have an opportunity like that—and he said he didn't want to go."

"I said I wasn't *ready* to go," Josie corrected him.

"Yeah," Ben snorted, "wasn't ready. You believe that?"

"So what did you do?"

"I'll tell you what he did—he took off for Spain. I still don't know where he got the money from, but he got it. I guess when you got a head full of brains and a heart full of fear, you can do anything."

Josie began to stand. "I beg your pardon."

"Hey, hey," Terry stepped in, "let's not fight. Pop, it turned out pretty good—that's where we met, after all."

Ben aimed a thumb at Terry. "The two of them, both running scared."

"What were you running from?" I asked Terry.

"My family, I guess. I don't talk about it, J.J."

"It's no way to live," Ben said, "running away."

But the smile Josie and Terry now shared suggested otherwise. It was the same mutual delight I'd seen between them the day I met Terry in the Chinese restaurant.

"Those were good years," Terry said, her eyes fixed on Josie. "God, it was romantic. We lived everywhere. What was the street in Madrid, *Chulo,* the one near the university?"

He thought for a moment, squinting up at the ceiling. "*Princesa,*" he said.

"I studied there for a while; Josie was a tour guide in the *Prado.* Then we went to Barcelona."

"*Paseo de Gracia,*" Josie noted.

"Remember the sycamores?"

"And old man Ampuero?"

"He was the one who started calling you *Chulo,*" she remembered.

"I've been dying to ask you what that means," Jen said. "*Chulo?*"

"Oh, it's just a joke," Terry answered. "One day, Josie got it into his head that he had to go running with the bulls in Pamplona, and old man Ampuero," she looked at Josie and laughed, "he was probably all of fifty—he had a car and said he'd take us. Now, the thing about running with the bulls is that, the closer you run to them, the braver it means you are. So me and Ampuero, we're sitting outside the barricades waiting, and out of nowhere here comes Josie, in full sprint." She started to laugh harder and he buried his face in his hands. "No one else anywhere near him. No runners, no bulls. He runs right past us, terrified, arms flailing,"—she waved her arms in the air— "doesn't even hear us yelling to him as he goes past. Then

he's gone and it's quiet again." She shrugged. "We look for other runners, maybe a runaway bull. What was he running from? But there's
nothing," she continued. "It was like we were there on the wrong day.
Must've been a full minute before we finally started to see other people
running, two before we saw a bull. *Chulo*, it doesn't really translate.
Some people say it means brave, some say handsome, but it's more.
In Spain, at least back then, it's like," she rubbed her fingers together
in the air, "calling someone *Chulo* is as high a compliment as you can
pay. It's reserved for the most strong, the most brave, the most handsome. Really you didn't hear it applied to anyone but a bullfighter, so
it was old man Ampuero's little joke. It kind of stuck."

I looked at Josie. "Two minutes ahead of the bulls?"

He lifted his reddened face out of his hands. "Have you ever
seen the size of a bull?"

"Oh man, I don't think I ever laughed so hard in my life,"
Terry said.

"How long did you live there?" Jen asked.

"Barcelona?"

"Spain."

"Three, maybe three and a half years," she said.

"Why'd you come back?"

"Well, we got married and we were ready to come home, I
guess. Josie went to law school then—"

"You're welcome," his father said.

"My dad had already made the arrangements," Josie explained.
"Enrollment, housing—"

"How'd you know they were coming back that year?"

"He made the arrangements every year," Josie said. "They still
tell stories about him in the admissions office."

"And where'd you go after law school?"

"D.C.," Terry said. "Josie clerked for a justice, but then I got
pregnant with Ben."

"All my talk about high ceilings and treadmills," Josie said, "and
I flinched when the moment of truth arrived."

"You didn't flinch," Terry countered, and I could tell by the
way she said it that they'd had this conversation before.

"I took a job with a firm."

"Rent matters," she said. "It's not like you stayed there."

He nodded wearily and turned to me. "I came to B.U. after I left the firm."

"Everyone at school wonders why you didn't teach at Harvard," I said.

"B.U. promised me more flexibility. Said I could specialize in more than one subject, bring more realism into class. Of course, whenever I try to do any of that, they complain."

"Can I ask you something, Terry?" Jennifer asked tentatively. The Steeles looked at her. "Have you been back to Texas since then?"

"No."

An awkward silence followed. I saw a thought occur to Jen and she began to speak, but Terry was a step ahead of her.

"I'd better go check on dinner," she said, and went into the kitchen.

Jen leaned back into the couch. "Smart, Jen," she muttered.

"Don't worry about it," Josie said. "It's not something we talk about. No great secrets, no dramatic revelations. Just a family that doesn't get along."

Two hours later, after dinner, I realized that I hadn't seen Josie in a while. I'd thought he'd been in the kitchen helping Terry clean up, but when I looked for him in there he wasn't around. His dad was flirting with Jen in the living room and Terry was busy with Ben Jr., so I went looking for Josie. I found him in his office, at his desk, with the lights out except for a 40-watt desk lamp. He was holding a glass filled with clear liquid, and staring at nothing.

"There you are," I said. He raised the glass toward his face and looked into it. The desk lamp was a supernova by comparison to him. "You okay?" I asked. His head nodded so slightly it could hardly be considered an affirmation.

"I need some time alone, okay?" he said without looking at me, his voice small and distant.

I watched him as he stared, the light reflecting amber off the glass. "No, I don't think so," I said.

I entered the room and sat down opposite him, the desk between us. Several minutes passed in silence. He closed his eyes, leaned back in his chair. Still, I said nothing, willing to wait however long it took for him to return. I know that abyss, and I know that having someone there can keep you from drifting farther in.

"How long you going to wait?" he asked atonally.

"How long you going to make me wait?"

A punctuated, sardonic laugh came out of him. He took a drink from the glass.

"That stuff's not going to help," I say.

"It's worth a try."

"It's not worth a damn. Come on, Josie, what's going on? You sick? Terry, Ben?"

"No, we're fine."

"You angry at Terry for telling that story?"

He smiled distantly. "I love that story."

"Then what?"

"My father," he admitted, looking at me.

"Your father? What did he do? He's proud of you."

His eyes wandered again, and his head was leaned so far back into his chair it seemed glued to it. "He didn't do anything on purpose," he said. "But that story he told—and here I thought it had been my idea to become a lawyer. You know how deflating it is to wake up one day and realize that you let someone else chart the course of your life?"

I didn't know what to say. I felt young. He'd been such a good friend to me, I knew I owed him better. But I didn't have it to give. I chewed my lip, then ventured: "Maybe it doesn't matter how you got here as long as you're happy."

"I suppose that would make it better, yes."

We sat in silence as I tried to get my mind around that.

"Josie," I said, beginning to stand, "I'm going to get Terry. I think she—"

"No!"

I fell backward a step in surprise, nearly tripping over the chair behind me. "What?!"

"No," he repeated, calmer but still urgently "Please, J.J. Please."

I settled back into the chair. "Are you and Terry having problems?"

He dismissed the notion with a sad chuckle, almost more of an exhale. "God, no. If there's anything right with my life, it's her and Ben. It's just—your life brings you to a crossroads and you take a direction. Years pass, and if you found your way it doesn't matter why you chose the road you did. But if you went the wrong way and got lost, and you're so damn far from where the road forked that you can't even find your way back anymore…especially when it was all someone else's idea…" His voice cracked. He squeezed the bridge of his nose between his thumb and forefinger.

"But you *can* find your way back," I said. "Who says you can't?"

"It's not that easy," he muttered into his fist, then looked at me. "How does a famous lawyer take a job in a museum? How does he tell his wife? No," he shook his head, "sometimes, you have to accept who you are, even if you don't especially like who you are."

"I don't believe that."

His eyes were half closed when he looked at me. "You will," he said. "Or, at least, you may, if you don't take control of your own life."

"What's that supposed to mean?"

"I don't know what motivates you, J.J.," he said wearily, "but I know it isn't a love of law. I've often wondered why you did what you did first year, when you challenged me in class."

"I did it because you were being a jackass."

He shook his head. "I don't think so," he said. "I was being a jackass, true, but that doesn't change the fact that you were reckless with your future. I could've thrown you out of my class if I wanted to." I started to defend myself but he held up his hand. "I'm not saying I considered it. That's not my point."

"Then what the hell is your point?"

He thought for a moment. "I knew," he began. "When Jimmy Carter first uttered those careless words and my father decided to turn them into his life's work, and the town and papers ran with it and I couldn't go get a simple haircut without everyone pointing and talking about the future Supreme Court Justice—I knew I was being dragged in a direction I didn't want to go. I ran all the way to Spain to get away, and though I didn't know at the time that's why I was doing it, my instincts were dead on."

"What's this got to do with me?"

"I can't stop wondering about that day in class," he said, "whether that was your Spain."

"You think I was trying to get thrown out of school?" I asked. He didn't answer. "Well, you're wrong," I spat. "Just because you didn't have the guts to find your own way in the world doesn't mean I don't. I want to be a D.A. And you're wrong about something else too, by the way—your life isn't so bad. You hate your job—welcome to the world—most people do. For crying out loud, man, when I came in here I thought you were dying. And here it's all about money?! And after that speech you gave Jen?"

"That's not what I'm saying."

"You have any idea how lucky you are, how lucky Ben is? Hell, when I was a kid, me and Leo used to pee out the window into the alley if our father was home, just so we wouldn't run into him on our way to the bathroom, 'cause most nights that was enough for a beating. Ben's loved, you're loved."

"And you think that makes it easier?" Tears filmed Josie's eyes. "Don't you get it? That makes it worse." He stood and crossed to the opposite side of the room, and leaned against the window. He drew the drapes back a few inches and looked down to the street. "It's not just about my job. It's about who I am and the life I'm living. I can see myself in a different life, J.J., being a different man in it—a better man—I can really see it. But I'm trapped in my love for my family. If I didn't love them so much, I'd start over, who cares? I'd move into some slum in the Combat Zone and do whatever I damn well pleased." He pushed his hair behind his ears. "But if I loved them as much as I should," he said more softly, "as much as they deserve to be loved, I'd go back into private practice. I'd bring home enough money so that it was no longer such a suffocating issue in our lives—at least the sale of my soul would be complete. But I sit here meekly in the middle, teaching something I don't believe in, a Pied Piper leading the rest of you into the sea because it's convenient for me." He looked back at me. "I'm a coward and the clock is ticking until the day Ben realizes that."

I had no idea how to respond. I was frustrated with Josie—buckled by the very life I was aspiring to, a life that still seemed awfully good to me. And I was surely disappointed in myself, because I sensed there had to be more to it than the pampered problems I could see at the moment. The combination made me angry, at both of us. I stood and looked down at him, trapped in a four-star prison without bars, doors, walls or guards, and it made me angrier still. "You don't want Ben to think of you as a coward," I said evenly, "then stop being a coward." Then I punctuated it with the one word I wish I hadn't said. "*Chulo*."

Chapter thirty-three

Y ou just ran a red light," Jen noted calmly as Ed tried to drive and find his bag at the same time. "Why don't you show us when we get to the bus station?"

"Got it." Ed pulled a wristwatch from his bag and handed it to Jennifer. "It's just a prototype, but that's it—the Tropical Storm Watch. What do y'all think?"

From the back seat of Ed's car I took a quick glance at the watch, but I was more interested in the email I was reading. Leo had sent it this morning, but it was long and I hadn't had time to read it at school, so I'd printed it out and brought it with me. We were on our way to drop Jen off at the bus station for an interview she had in New York later that day. Then Ed and I were going to a park in Cambridge where the law school was having a picnic for the graduating class. Exams had ended the week before. Some people still had a paper or two to hand in, but that was about it.

"It's actually nice," Jen was saying as I turned my attention back to the email. "It's slimmer than I thought it would be."

"That was the challenge," Ed said.

"This thing really forecasts the weather?"

"Well, this one's pretty bare bones. The real one will do more. But yeah, press that button right there. No, wait, it's this one."

"And there goes another red light."

"No, this one."

"It says, 'May 7.'"

"Oh, that's the date function. Try that one."

"Mostly sunny, seventy degrees. Wow."

"Cool, right? Show J.J."

Jen handed the watch over the seat to me and I took a closer look at it.

"But I still don't understand," she said. "You're a lawyer, Ed. Why are you messing with this stuff?"

"What should I do, send out a hundred resumes like your boyfriend back there, just to get ninety-nine rejections and a job I don't want?"

"He's just going to do it for a few years, then he'll have all sorts of options."

"It's nice." I leaned forward to return the watch. "I like it a lot more than that military thing."

"The Mister Potato Missile Head? That would work, I'm telling you. Think about it—you're some foreign country and you see that sumbitch coming at you. You're not going to shoot it down."

"Tell Jen about the other one, the perfume."

"Cologne," Ed corrected me. "See," he addressed Jen, "I read this article that said scientists can now extract behavior-specific pheromones. So I'm thinking, we make a cologne for men that arouses women's, you know, desires."

"You're joking, right?"

"I call it the Afro-disiac." He noticed Jen staring dumbfounded at him. "It's for an urban market," he explained.

Jen swiveled in her seat. "He's kidding, right?"

"I'm telling you, J.J., give up this stupid job search and come with me. Train's leaving the station."

"With you?" Jen arched her eyebrows. "You're lucky I let him go to lunch with you."

"Hey, a McDonald's," I called out. "Ed, pull over."

"We got time?"

"Sure," I said. "Jen, is it okay with you?"

"Remind me again what this is?" she frowned.

"I got a rejection letter yesterday from a firm in Manhattan."

"Who?"

"Let's see." I put Leo's note aside and leafed through my note-book for the envelope. "Smith, Ratchet, Hargrove, Frump and Frump."

"Two Frumps?"

"Apparently."

"You'd think one would be enough."

"You'd think."

"And that's your hundredth rejection?"

I nodded.

"J.J., do you really have to do this?"

"I promised myself, Jen."

Ed pulled the car to the curb and I waited for Jen. "I think it's a bad idea," she finally said, "but I guess if they've already rejected you." She held out her right hand. "Let me see what you wrote."

I handed her the letter.

> J.J. SPENCER
> 141 Kelton Street Apt. 5
> Boston, MA 02143
>
> Leonard A. Frump, Esq.
> Smith, Ratchet, Hargrove, Frump and Frump
> 19 Wall Street, Suite 1500
> New York, N.Y. 10002
>
> Dear Mr. Frump:
>
> It is my privilege to inform you that, with your rejection letter to me dated May 2, your firm gains the distinction of being the ONE HUNDREDTH law firm to reject me.

As a result, you will please find enclosed one (1) TEN DOLLAR ($10.00) book of MCDONALD'S GIFT CERTIFICATES, redeemable at your local McDonald's franchise. Now, make me proud. Don't let me hear about you buying BIG MACS for the partners and nothing for the associates; get FRENCH FRIES or something else you can all share. Also, please note that, pursuant to Pelman v. McDonald's, 237 F. Supp. 2d 512, you won't be able to sue McDonald's if the food makes you fat. Spilling the coffee on your crotch is still your best bet.

Bon Appetite!
J.J. SPENCER

She handed back the letter. "This is our future you're playing with, you know."

"*Our* future?"

She tilted her head and smiled. "No?"

"Wow, well, I always wanted it to be romantic and surprising when it happened—and I never figured on Ed being here, but..."

"No, it's okay," she put her hand to my lips. "Don't say anything. That's what I want too. Sometimes I guess I just need to be reassured."

I was surprised by her diffidence; she didn't show it often. Ed stayed in the car as Jen and I went into the McDonald's.

"I really don't like this," she repeated inside as we waited on line.

"Hey, let me ask you something. What would you think of me taking Ed up on his offer?"

"Please tell me you're joking," she said.

"Why? He's a smart guy." She pressed her lips together and brushed her hair off her face with two fingers. "What?" I laughed.

"It's not funny!" Her eyes teared up and her gaze hardened, and

I realized she was serious. "Honestly, sometimes you terrify me. You can be so self-destructive."

"How is that self-destructive?"

"It's all self-destructive. This stupid letter. Josie Steele. I'm depending on you. Do you get that? I love you and I want to build a life with you—and I understand that you're different, but—" she caught herself and slowed her momentum. "Couldn't you try to tone it down just a little, for me? What are you going to do when you have a boss you don't like, send him gift certificates? Sometimes you have to compromise a little in the real world."

"Josie Steele? What about him?"

"You haven't spoken to him once since last week, and I know things are awkward right now, but do you have any idea how valuable he could be to your career? Contacts like that don't grow on trees, you know."

"I tried to call him," I said. "You know that."

"Once."

"Okay, once, but I did try."

"With that much at stake, couldn't you make a second call?"

Maybe she was right. Maybe I took it too personally when he didn't return my call, or maybe in the back of my mind I'd been expecting it. I'd never had a friendship that didn't eventually succumb to logistics, disappointment or inertia. I never really thought of them as permanent. I always want them to last, but friendships drift like continents—invisible to the eye and impossible to stop anyway.

"Maybe you could talk to him at karate tonight."

"He hasn't been there all week."

"Really?" she asked, and I could see that her focus had shifted. She was—for the moment at least—concerned primarily about Josie, and less preoccupied by the implications of his silence for my career. This was when I liked her best, in the context of her friendships, where she was always so caring. I much preferred it to her self-appointed role as my career counselor. "That's not like him."

I nodded, then took her hand. "Come on," I said. "We don't have to do this."

But she held her ground. "No, now I feel like I'm taking the fun out of your life. I don't want to change who you are; I just want you to temper it a little."

"It was just a joke. It's not that important."

"Tell you what," she smiled. "We'll make a deal. Send the letter, but promise never to go off making Afro-disiacs with Ed."

"What's your problem with Ed?"

"I know he's your friend and all, but you have to admit—he's a bit of an idiot."

I stepped back from her. "Jen," I said, "remember how surprised you were when you found out I'm graduating second in my class?" She nodded. "Well, you might want to sit down—Ed's first." A Big Mac could've fit into her gaping mouth and still left room for fries. "He's a genius, Jen."

"Idiot savant is as far as I'll go."

Chapter thirty-four

After dropping off Jen at the bus station, Ed and I continued to the picnic, where I found a spot under a tree and unfolded Leo's email.

> Hi J.J.,
>
> I've been studying too much, that's the only explanation I can offer for why I did it. Last night in Woodruff Library, I was suddenly overtaken by an irresistible urge to climb up on a bookshelf and dribble droplets of orange juice down onto Carolyn Dubasch. I tried to resist, but the compulsion was stronger than I. (So's Carolyn, but I'm faster.) Before I knew it, I was scaling the shelf, my cheeks bloated round with orange juice. Carolyn escaped dry, however, when I somehow managed to get myself lodged between the bookshelf and ceiling. The Druid Hills fire department came pretty quick, but I had to stay up a while longer, so Clarence could come see. Apparently, Clarence's wife left him last

month, and the guys thought this might cheer him up. He lives kind of far away.

Now, don't freak out, but the reason I've been studying so much is because I switched majors again, and it leaves me pretty far behind. I can tell you're angry, but what else could I do? What's the choice when you have no idea what to do with your life? Sure, you say law school, but lawyers sip their beer and that's just wrong. I don't know…what's law school like? Is it terrible?

What's the matter with me, J.J.? I'm 21 years old. Why can't I choose a career? I started college as a Philosophy major, but gave that up when I realized that I'd developed a permanent headache and ended three straight classroom debates with physical threats. So I switched to Psych. After all, the red paper wasps were no match for my Hannibal Lecteresque marathon mindfuck, when I sat beside them for hours describing the meaninglessness of their insentient lives. (Good technique, bad aim—my roommate swore he'd kill us both if I didn't get rid of the pond margin.) Anyway, like so many of my choices, Psych turned out to be a mistake too and so what if mom does have the hots for me. Onto English Lit, where I read eight classics and didn't understand a word of any of them. Never could figure out why it's such a terrible thing to split an infinitive, and ending sentences with prepositions, I don't even want to talk about.

So now I'm a Biology major. Here's how that happened. The science library smells awful, and since the Centers for Disease Control is just down the road, I stopped by to see if that might be the cause of my rhinitis—hay fever to laymen like you. Vijay and Micah took a liking to me and took me out for Zimas as they exposed me to the world of carpet beetles, silverfish, mold, bacteria and yeast. They explained how fungi are everywhere, and because they lack chlorophyll, they're dependent on external food sources. They gobbled down their Portobello mushrooms as I sat nauseated but transfixed, listening to them tell me how multicellular fungi—mold to morons like you—grow as a mat of intertwined microscopic filaments called hyphae. It's really amazing, J.J. Unbeknownst to most people—especially tinea cruris like you—there's an entire parallel world living right under our noses. It's like Chinatown. I'm not saying it's a career, but maybe it'll keep me off bookshelves.

Anyway, I'm looking forward to seeing you at your graduation. You must be excited to be almost finished. Have you gotten job leads yet? Stick with it, a guy here told me that his brother, who also went to B.U. Law, sent out over 500 resumes before he got a job. But the point is he got one, and today he's one of the most highly respected toll booth collectors in the state, whaddaya think of that?

Love,

Leo

I folded the note, put it into my back pocket and propped myself up on an elbow. I should call him. Beneath the casual tone, I knew he was struggling. I regretted having lost my patience with him the last time he switched majors. It's hard to find your way in life, and it's not even as simple as the crossroad Josie had described. It's more complicated than that, because life isn't a crossroad; it's a river with infinite tributaries and no destination. Josie is lost too, but he's so far downstream that swimming back to choose another tributary seems impossible to him.

I stared out at my classmates, feeling vaguely sad. Maybe it was an accumulation of things. Leo's email, what I'd said to Josie, all the resumes. I felt sad for Jen too. I didn't mean to scare her. But why all the worry? I'm not self-destructive. I started with nothing and was about to graduate law school. I just picked up my box of graduation garb yesterday. And even if it means I'll have to sit draped fabulous in a red satin gown with a purple cowl around my neck and tam and tassel on my head like some sort of flamboyantly gay monk, I'd achieved what I set out to do. In a few months, if I passed the bar exam, I'd be a real lawyer. Didn't that count for something? Jen says that if she doesn't cheer, it's only because she still sees so much more to come for me, and that she wants to help me fulfill my potential. But looking ahead is a cliché—something they tell you when you get fired. Everyone deserves the occasional round of applause.

Around the open park, my classmates looked relaxed. Relaxed with each other, relaxed with school. Some wore shorts, with sunglasses dangling from Croakie cords around their necks. It was so different than the day we'd first met, on the courtyard outside the law school. People knew each other now, had gone through so much together. We'd banded together in study groups and toiled until all hours of the night. We'd debated each other in classes, competed for the attentions of the opposite sex, shared in a drink or a movie. We were no longer strangers with just one thing in common. We weren't all necessarily friends either, but in a way, our collective relationship had more endurance than individual friendships. We had a common academic history and professional future, even as we headed off on a more divergent set of career paths than most of us had even known existed when we began law school.

Bernie Nockowitz was in charge of the barbecue, and was handing out grilled hot dogs to people waiting with buns held open. Bernie had landed a job with a big Boston firm. Past him, Irwin Smuck and a guy I knew only by face were disgracing the sport of football, throwing wobbly passes to each other and dropping most of them. Irwin would be returning to Florida to work with the local chapter of the A.C.L.U.

Ed came toward me with a beer in each hand. He was wearing his Tropical Storm Watch.

"Come on, J.J., have a beer," he said.

"No thanks," I deferred. "I'm going to karate tonight."

"Hell-bent on that black belt, huh?"

"I guess. I'm also kind of hoping Josie'll be there."

"You two still haven't spoken?"

I shook my head.

"It's been a week."

"I don't know what to say to him."

He sat down next to me and drew a breath. "Can I ask you something?"

"Sure."

"It's okay if you don't want me to."

"No, it's fine—ask."

"Well," he pulled up his knees and stared out at the lawn, "I've been informed that there's a two-beer limit here today. Since you're not drinking, can I have your two?"

I laughed and stood up. "I know that was hard for you to say," I extended my hand to him and pulled him to his feet.

Aaron Bocian approached us, characteristically frantic.

"Aaron, you're late," I said. "You're going to lose points for that."

"I can only stay for a half hour," he sputtered. "I've got a ton of work to do."

"Aw, Bocian," Ed sighed, "come on, make a lay-up. Ain't you ever going to change?"

"Easy for you to say," Aaron countered. "You don't have to worry; you're going to be rich."

"I'm going to be rich *because* I don't worry."

A touch-football game was starting across the way, so we dragged Aaron along and made him join in despite his uncertainty over the stability of his epiphysis. I barely noticed the day pass, or the crowd thin out, but before I knew it the air had cooled and it was just me and Ed left. We found a bench and sat down. I checked my cell phone.

"She call?" Ed asked.

"No. Maybe she's still in the interview."

At the other end of the park, a woman was playing with a dog. I squinted to try to see her better. Ed crossed his legs and leaned back.

"Things are moving pretty fast for you two," he said. "Were you serious before, almost proposing?"

"I'm not sure. Probably not, but we're not that far away."

"Moving pretty fast," he repeated.

"I guess once we got back together, that was all we needed."

"Sixty-two degrees in New York," he mused, pushing buttons on his watch. Then he looked at me. "And her timing doesn't bother you at all?"

"Her timing? No, why?"

"Nothing." The woman at the other end of the park threw a tennis ball and the dog took off after it. "It just seems kind of coincidental, is all," he added. "Showing up just as you're finally ready to get your degree."

"Ed, I know you and Jen don't exactly see eye to eye, but trust me, she's not as calculating as you think. She missed me."

"If you say so."

Something about the woman seemed familiar.

"Who is that? I know her."

Ed stood and watched them, hands on his hips. "She's a yellow lab for sure, but I ain't seen her around school."

"Not the dog, you redneck, the girl."

We walked toward them. The girl was kneeling down in front of the dog, trying to pry the tennis ball out of its mouth. "Give it, Linky," I heard her demanding, "give it." I knew immediately by the voice who it was, even before she pulled her face back from the dog.

"Amy!" I shouted, and broke into a jog.

She looked up at the sound of her name, her blue eyes catching the sun. When she saw me, she shrieked and sprang to her feet, diving at me when I got close and nearly knocking me over. I wrapped my arms around her waist and her feet lifted off the ground when I spun with her in a circle. "Hiya, dad," I heard coming from somewhere near my jugular. We hugged for a long while, tightly, like you do when it's pure. It felt so good to see her. It had been too long.

When we finally pulled apart, she said, "I missed you, dad!" then noticed Ed and leapt at him. "Ed, my buddy!"

"Hello, Miss Amy," he said, and they hugged too.

"God, it's been so long. How are you guys?" she asked as Linky pushed her nose into Amy's hand, jealous of her attention. Amy distractedly petted her face as we talked.

"We're good," I said. "Graduating next week."

"Oh my God, has it been three years already?" She stood back and took the measure of us, smiling with pride. "Seems like just yesterday you were sneaking into my bed."

Ed's mouth dropped. "How's that?" he asked.

Amy glanced at him, then back to me. "You kept our secret?" she smiled. "Aw, how chivalrous. Hey, so what are you guys doing in Cambridge?"

"The law school just had a picnic," I gestured vaguely with my thumb over my shoulder. "What about you?"

"I live here."

"Where, that one?" I asked, pointing to a high-rise overlooking the park.

Her eyes followed the direction of my index finger, then looked back at me like I was crazy. "Yeah, sure," she chuckled. "Those are all million dollar condos. No, I live in that little one next to it."

"It looks nice too."

"It's okay. Sometimes when it snows a lot, then melts off their eaves and onto our building and in through our ceilings, they let us keep the puddles."

I smiled at her joke, then tried to ask about Doctor Howard. "How's…" the name kind of caught in my throat.

"Howard?" she prompted, then smiled and shook her head.

"Over?"

"Over," she exhaled. "Too possessive. He thought jealousy was a sign of love; I think it's a sign of insecurity."

"I'm sorry."

"How about you? Jen?"

"We're together," I said. I ignored the sadness in her frozen smile. If there was a part of me still in her, it wasn't my place to expose it. "We're going to move back to New York after graduation."

"You going to live together?"

"No, we'll get separate places. We're not ready for that yet."

"Do you know where you'll be working?"

"Not Frump and Frump," Ed noted.

Amy smiled expectantly. "Who's that?" she asked, and Ed told her about the McDonald's gift certificates.

"I can explain," I started to say, but it wasn't necessary; it would have been like explaining the merits of meat to Linky. Amy understood my passive-aggressive needs.

"You just need to alienate these people, don't you?" she said.

"Working overtime this year," Ed put in.

"What do you mean?"

"Yeah," I said, "what do you mean?"

"I mean Steele."

"Oh, come on, they're completely different situations."

"What?" Amy asked. "Tell me." Linky hopped up on Amy with her front paws, trying to get the tennis ball. Amy took just enough notice to throw the ball across the park, sending Linky off in pursuit.

"He's talking about Josie Steele, a professor."

"I remember him," she nodded. "You two were kind of friends." Her smile dropped incrementally into a frown. "What happened?"

"We sort of had a falling out," I said, and explained as best I could.

"Oh, dad," she shook her head slowly, and there was such disappointment in her eyes. "You've got to make that right."

"That's what Jen says. She says contacts like that don't grow on trees."

"Contacts? When did people become contacts to you? I meant that it sounds like a friend was in pain and all you thought of was yourself."

"Ame, you don't understand. This guy's one of the luckiest people I've ever known. He's brilliant, successful, got a great marriage. He's not crazy about teaching law. Big deal—I'd kill for his problems." She looked straight at me. "What?"

"That's just what Lauren used to say about you when you broke your leg."

"Lauren? What did she say?"

"That you were a smart, successful guy on his way to becoming a lawyer, and all you ever did was complain."

"That's different, I was hurt."

"All pain is real, J.J."

"But I was hurt."

"So is he. You know, when I was little, I had a friend, Clara, who was in a wheelchair," she said, "and sometimes I used to be jealous of her. Now who would've sympathized with me for that? But I swear to you, it hurt."

"You were jealous of someone in a wheelchair?"

"I know it sounds dumb, but everywhere we went, she brought out the best in people. People gave up their seats, held doors for her, smiled at her. A mom could be in the middle of beating her kid, but as soon as she saw Clara," a small smile creased her eyes, "it was like magic. The anger would disappear, and suddenly she's looking at her own kid like it's the first time. And I used to think, I want to be able to do that. Go around restoring people's values just by being there."

She didn't know that was exactly the effect she had on me. I looked at Ed and he nodded. Linky brought the ball back and dropped it at Amy's feet. I knelt to pick it up. Linky waited, her mouth an open smile. I bounced it once, then threw it across the park.

Chapter thirty-five

Graduation weekend swamped the city like a hurricane. With some sixty colleges and universities, Boston's got a higher concentration of students than any other metropolitan area in the country. There wasn't a hotel room or restaurant reservation to be had. Fenway Park was sold out for the Red Sox game. There was a two-hour wait to get into the aquarium and forty-five minutes at Paul Revere's house. You couldn't even hail a cab on Newberry Street.

My mother and Leo arrived Saturday on an afternoon flight. Getting off the plane, my mom was more buoyant than I'd ever seen her, and it felt good to be the cause of it. We spent the day strolling downtown with thousands of other graduates and their parents, then, after dinner, I dropped them off at their hotel. On Sunday morning, we met at the Case Athletic Center on Babcock Street for graduation. I could barely keep my eyes open during the speeches: first the governor, then a professor. Finally, the Dean read off the names. I scanned the audience, spotted Leo waving and returned his wave. He sat between my mother and Jennifer, in the middle of a row about halfway back.

When the Dean called my name I stood, thinking that

September would never again mark the beginning of my year, and never again would I work sixteen-hour days for free. When exactly I would start getting paid, or by whom, was still unsettled. I might've been able to get a job already had I interviewed with some of the law firms that had visited campus, but I just didn't want to work for any of them. Still, that was a problem for another day. For now, all I had to do was grab the diploma like a red baton and keep moving.

A polite round of applause crackled in the room as I made my way to meet the Dean at center stage. I paused and looked out at the audience as I shook his hand and accepted my tube, waiting for the school photographer to snap the picture he'd later sell me for $17.50. In their seats, my mother and Jennifer clapped and Leo let loose with a high-pitched whoop. I raised a victory fist as he pumped his arms in the air and tried unsuccessfully to drag my mother and Jen out of their seats.

After graduation, as people milled about on Babcock Street, Josie came over and introduced himself to my family. They talked for a few minutes, then he pulled me aside and handed me a small, gift-wrapped box. I turned it over in my hand.

"So you're not still angry with me?"

He looked genuinely surprised. "Angry? Oh, that? J.J., give me some credit. I like that I can count on your honesty."

"But you didn't return my call."

"It's been a busy time. Come on, open your gift."

"You didn't have to do this," I said as I unwrapped it.

"It's no big deal, just something to help you study for the bar exam."

"Have you noticed how no one gives amphetamines anymore?" I opened the box and removed a small reading light, designed to clip onto the edge of a book. "I love it," I said. "Thank you."

"You're going to let me hear from you once you move back to New York, right?"

"Definitely, Josie. You and Terry, you're family to me. And, listen, I'm sorry if I stepped over the line, I really am."

"You didn't." He tapped the reading light. "Study like you've never studied in your life," he said. "This test is a bear."

"Okay," I smiled. "Can I be tied down by the rules of law?"

He pointed his index finger at me. "For those two days only."

"It's a deal."

"And anything I can do to help with the job search—a letter, a phone call—just let me know. Or if you want to work with me…"

"I'm going to miss you too," I said. We hugged and wished each other well. "Wait a minute," I realized, "work with you? What do you mean, work with you?"

He tried for a moment to play it off casually, but then sighed. "Okay—I wasn't going to tell you this today…it's not really the time for it—but as it turns out, today is my last day at B.U. too. What you said to me, it was just what I needed."

"Needed for what?"

"The best way to keep my son from discovering that his father's a coward is to stop being a coward. I'm out, J.J.," he said, "I'm leaving B.U."

"What are you talking about?"

"I'm through teaching," he shrugged. "Through."

Romantic, disturbing visions of Josie, Terry and Ben in a cold water flat in the Combat Zone filled my head. "What are you going to do? A gallery?"

"I'm going back to my old firm." He held a steady gaze on me.

"You can't be serious. Private practice? I thought you hated it, that it was all client cocktail parties."

"J.J., our lunch reservation's in ten minutes."

"I'll be right there, Mom."

"I've given it a lot of thought," Josie said. "I need to commit to something. End this gutless life in the middle. It doesn't really matter which way I go as long as it's a bolder path. It's going to feel good to be able to spoil my family. I'll just avoid the cocktail parties."

Determined not to make the same mistake I'd made before, I embraced him. "I'm happy for you, Josie. If it's what you want, I'm happy for you."

I took a few steps to rejoin my family as Josie greeted two alumni who had approached with wide smiles.

"Josie," I called to him. "That monk."

"What monk?

"The one who left the monastery when he smelled the soup."

"Yes?"

"Forget it," I reconsidered.

"What about him?"

"It's nothing," I waved. "We can talk about it later."

"Okay," he said, and turned back to the alumni.

Chapter thirty-six

J ust two months after graduation, I was studying harder than I ever had in law school. The bar exam was just eleven days away, and I sat at a desk in a small, austerely furnished studio apartment that I'd rented for the summer on the Lower East Side of Manhattan. It came with an unfinished wood desk, a closet, and a couch that pulled out into a bed. The floor was uncovered, the air conditioner unreliable, and the neighbors unemployed. All in all, just what I needed. I wanted to be insulated from any distractions, including friends, family and Jennifer. Jen had landed a job in the public relations department of one of the financial giants on Wall Street and gotten her own place on the Upper East Side. We decided that I'd move to the neighborhood after the bar, and once I got a job, but that we'd continue to live apart for a while.

The bar is a twelve-hour exam given every year at the Javits Center over the course of two grueling days. After graduation, I'd taken two weeks off to relax, then started studying. Of the forty-two days since then, I'd studied on forty-one. Fear was my fuel. There was no area of law that was outside the scope of the bar, so I had to study everything: corporate law, contracts, criminal, matrimonial, torts, real property, constitutional, commercial paper—everything. Practicing attorneys often make a living specializing in any one of these areas, yet I was expected to know them all by the end of July. Eight hundred years of jurisprudence. That's why lawyers often say they knew more law the day of the exam than at any other time for the rest of their careers.

And passing was no foregone conclusion. I'd assumed that, having managed to get through three years of law school, I could certainly pass one more test. Then they opened the review course I'd signed up for by telling us that, of the nearly ten thousand law school graduates who took the New York exam last year, one-third had flunked.

The weeks dragged on and the summer heat intensified along with the pressure of the onrushing test. Every day I would wake up at seven and study until five, with breaks only for meals. At five, I'd catch a subway to Centre Street for the review course I was taking, five nights a week for four hours a night—then six hours on Saturdays and Sundays.

I hated going to sleep. Sleep meant the end of the day, and the end of the day meant that the next thing to happen would be the sun rising on a whole new day of studying. Seventeen days before the exam, the review course ended, leaving nothing to break the monotony of each day in that bleak, sweltering apartment. And no longer would studying end at ten. This was the home stretch; this was for all the marbles. My family and Jen had stopped calling, at my request. I'd asked them to wait for me to call, so that I could do so only when I felt that I needed a break.

Had I not seen a newspaper on my way to breakfast that morning, I don't think I would've even known it was Saturday. A magnificent summer Saturday. New York City was virtually empty, due to the weekly exodus to the Fire Island and Hamptons beaches. Jen had bought a half-share in a Westhampton house and was there now. As I walked back to my apartment eating my bagel, I stopped at a light. A cyclist pulled up alongside and balanced himself on one leg as he removed his helmet. He shook his head side-to-side, his long hair slapping against his forehead and spraying my bagel with sweat. He apologized with a series of "dudes," and "totallys" and I gave him the bagel.

That had been my socializing for the day. Now it was just me and the books again. I'd read the same sentence six times. For all I knew, it could've been that one about *stare decisis*. Policy of principle, principle of policy. Principle of principal. This was no longer school, after all; it was the real world.

I studied all day. The sun had set hours ago and I still had a lot more work to do before bed. I stared down at my notebook, the heat from the desk lamp scorching my brain. Through blood-shot eyes, I glanced up at the clock over my bed. 1:47 A.M. In the silence, I monitored my breathing, could hear the fatigue. I took a sip of tepid coffee and scratched at the stubble on my face. Shaving was a luxury, meant only for human beings. In my mind, I was in a foxhole. A foxhole in the Alamo. A foxhole in the Alamo inside the Warsaw Ghetto. A foxhole in the Alamo inside the Warsaw Ghetto, peering out anxiously for bloodthirsty Mexicans and Alpine-yodeling Nazis. A foxhole in the Alamo inside the Warsaw Ghetto, peering out anxiously for bloodthirsty Mexicans and Alpine-yodeling Nazis, and surrounded by little green aliens in…

Stop it, I scolded myself. *No little green aliens tonight. Come on, you don't have to retain it for long. On July 31, you can dump ninety percent of it.*

My bed beckoned from across the room. *J.J., come give me a hug.* I tried to ignore it. The subject at hand was criminal law and my notes claimed: *there is a strong presumption of sanity in New York.* I thought of the cyclist as I heard a group of people belting out the theme song from *Gilligan's Island* outside my window.

Which parts of New York? I asked the book.

Come closer, it said, *and I'll tell you.*

This is another trick, I said, *like the bankruptcy thing yesterday.*

That was true, said the book. *In New York, there's a filing fee to declare bankruptcy. If you can't come up with the dough, you can't go bankrupt. Come*, it whispered, *let me teach you more.*

I leaned into the book but saw nothing, heard nothing. The two top pages suddenly leapt up and pulled my head into the white, soft paper. As everything turned black, a telephone rang in the distance. I stood to answer it but no longer recognized my surroundings. I was no longer in my apartment; I was in some kind of workplace. It was abuzz with activity.

At the end of a long hallway was an open office door. The ringing was coming from down there, so, hesitantly, I went to investigate. I entered the office. Smoke filled the air. Behind the olid haze, an obese, unkempt man in a filthy T-shirt was chewing on a cigar. I stepped farther into the room, then spun back to look behind me—the door and hallway were gone. In their place was an enormous, overstocked warehouse. I turned back to the man when I heard him talk into a speaker phone.

"Spencer brain hippocampus," he said in a flat, rote tone. "Serving your long-term memory needs for twenty-five years."

"Yeah, hi," said the nasal voice over the speaker phone, "this is Sheila in prefrontal cortex. Listen, you guys got any extra room up there? We're loaded down here in Short Term and just got a whole new shipment of facts to store."

"Extra room?" he laughed bitterly, leading to a series of hacking, life-threatening coughs. He spit into a wastepaper basket and took the cigar from his mouth. "You crazy? We got all we can handle."

"Aw, come on. It's just for a week or so."

"What can I tell you, we're full. Why don't you try Fond Memories on five? I ain't seen nobody go up there for a while."

"Can't," the voice said, "I got strict orders. Everything's gotta be stored in one of the two primary banks, regardless of space availability."

"That's ridiculous."

"Tell me about it, but you know this place."

"Christ—I'll straighten this out; get me Logic on the phone."

"What am I, new? Don't you think I tried that? Those offices are closed."

"Then get me Reason."

"On a weekend?"

"Well for crying out loud, who's running things down there?"

"Anxiety," said the voice, "and he's drunk."

"Can't you have Humor talk to him?"

"On vacation till July 31," Sheila answered. "Come on, Lou, can't you make a little room?"

"Make room?"

"Yeah, you know, get rid of the words to *Walk the Dinosaur* or something. Or toss some of those stupid lines from old movies he's always quoting."

"He'd kill me."

"His friends would love you."

"Look, I just store the stuff; I don't make decisions. You'll just have to find room for it down there."

"Fine, have it your way. But if we overload and I lose the wallet again, you're going down with me."

I was awakened again by another phone ringing, but when I opened my eyes this time, I was back in my room. Dazed and confused, I picked up the phone. It continued to ring, and I realized that the sound was coming from my alarm clock. I'd spent the entire night asleep on my desk. My back ached, my neck was stiff, and it was sunrise. Ten days to go.

Chapter thirty-seven

I didn't take any time off after the bar exam, the results of which wouldn't be available for months. I was out of money and, however uninspired I was by the prospect of forty years of law, I needed a job. I made one final adjustment to the knot of a subdued burgundy tie around my neck and stepped back from the bathroom mirror. *I'm not sure who you are or how you got into my mirror,* I thought, as I lifted my chin a bit and moved it side to side, *but you sure look like a lawyer.* The navy blue suit was brand new, and so freshly pressed you couldn't even tell it had cost less than two hundred and fifty dollars. I ran a forefinger over the pants crease. You could slice cheese on it.

I went into the hall and picked up my empty leather briefcase, embossed with the gold letters, "J.J.S.," a graduation gift from Leo and my mother. The forecast was for rain, so I got an umbrella from the closet. It was time to go, but I couldn't resist one last look in the mirror. It felt like Halloween. Ultimately, it made no sense to wear a suit to a full day of job interviews. Considering the task at hand, bare feet and overalls rolled to mid-calf would've been more practical. A slop bucket would've made a nice replacement for the briefcase, maybe a muck shovel instead of the umbrella. But I'd done my research and knew that none of the firms I was visiting encouraged farming implements.

My first interview would be with a general practice firm on Madison Avenue. After that, I'd get my long-awaited shot at the Manhattan D.A.'s office. I would've rather started with the D.A.'s office first thing in the morning while I was fresh, but the scheduling wasn't up to me. As I opened the door and stepped outside the building, I was immediately hit by a blast of hot air, as if I'd just walked behind a bus. The entire city was suffocating in a thick summer heatwave, the sun beating off the glassphalt sidewalks. If it felt like this at only ten in the morning, the rest of the day was sure to be brutal. I removed my jacket and laid it over my forearm. It wouldn't help my cause to stumble into interviews in the midst of a stroke, so I decided to take a taxi and consider it an investment in my future. I stood just off the curb at 3rd Street, my right hand raised. Across the way sat a white, stretch limousine with smoked windows and license plates reading, BUYDRUG. I really had to get a job so I could move out of here. A taxi pulled over perilously close to my foot and I got in. It was a decision unworthy of a lifelong New Yorker—I should've noticed that his windows were open and sent him away. Open windows meant no air conditioning.

We careened from lane to lane, eventually taking 23rd Street west to Madison Avenue, then proceeding north. He told me about his homeland, and how much he missed his family. I leaned over to read his name so I could respond, but couldn't tell which was the first name and which was the last. I didn't want to offend him by addressing him incorrectly, so instead of trying to figure out whether the circle with the diagonal line through it was a vowel, I changed the subject by asking if he had air conditioning. He told me to get my foot off the seat.

"You gonna scuff the upholstery," he complained.

I looked down at the upholstery and wiped my hand over what little I could see between the silver electric tape. At Madison and 51st, he pulled over and I paid the fare. He upbraided me for my bad manners in handing him a twenty and I tried to explain that it hadn't been premeditated, but he wasn't interested.

Alone in the elevator on my way to the twenty-seventh floor, I took advantage of the privacy by smiling as hard and wide as I could, to relax my lips. I hate talking to people with tension in my lips; it makes me self-conscious. On twenty-seven, the doors opened and I quickly folded away the smile and strode purposefully toward the receptionist's desk. On the wall behind her, twelve-inch gold letters proclaimed: FIELDING & CATES.

The receptionist looked up at me and smiled. "May I help you?"

"Good morning," I said. "I have an appointment with Mr. Cates. I'm J.J. Spencer."

"And your name?" she asked as she pressed the intercom.

"J.J. Spencer," I repeated, looking around, trying to envision this for the rest of my life. The waiting room was decorated in conservative cream tones, with framed lithographs on the walls.

"Mr. Cates," I heard her say into the intercom, "there's a Jimmy Spencer here for you."

I didn't bother correcting her; Mr. Cates would know who she meant. He'd personally scheduled my interview just two days before, and had at the time commented on the uniqueness of my name. The fact that he'd mentioned it meant that the first part of my strategy had worked. I'd used J.J. on my resume instead of my formal name, hoping it would stand out.

"Please have a seat," the receptionist looked up at me and smiled. "Mr. Cates will be with you soon."

I sat in a chair instead of on the sofa. Sofas make me slouch. On the coffee table in front of me was a selection of reading material. The *New York Times*, the *New York Law Journal*, *Fortune Magazine*, and a few others. I picked up the *Law Journal* and pretended to read, thinking instead about the upcoming interview. I'd memorized answers for stock questions like, why did you choose to go into law, and what kind of law do you want to practice. But it unsettled me to know just how insincere my prepared responses were. Maybe it would feel different when I got to the D.A.'s office in a few hours. There, the questions would be about why I wanted to fight crime, and I could tell them about Dairian Davis. Plus, Fielding & Cates was looking for a civil litigator. Conflict drains me, and a litigator's life is one continuous series of arguments taking different forms. Letters threatening to sue, phone call one-upsmanship, overheated conference rooms, tattling on each other at judge's benches. At least for D.A.s, the conflict has a noble goal. But for now, I was here, I was broke, and I needed a job.

Fifteen minutes passed before the receptionist finally said, "Mr. Spencer, if you'll follow me, Mr. Cates will see you now."

She led me down a long hallway lined with case books and other legal research material. We passed a man in a charcoal suit who looked at me briefly, but checked his watch and continued on his way. When we came to a closed oak door, she knocked and said, "Mr. Cates, your ten-thirty is here."

"Send it in," a voice answered.

I took a quick breath, then walked into the room with just the right amount of smile on my face.

"Good morning, Mr. Cates," I held out my hand to him.

"Good morning," he answered, looking down at some papers and just barely acknowledging my outstretched hand with his own. With his other hand, he gestured to the green leather chair in front of his desk. "Have a seat," he said, and I lowered myself into it. He picked up my resume off a stack on his desk. "Let me just refresh my memory," he said. "Seen a lot of these over the past few weeks." I folded my hands over my lap and waited. "J.J. Spencer," he said, hanging on the final letter of my last name, seeming to enjoy making the sound. "Peculiar name."

"It stands for Jerome Jonathan," I said, "but I've always gone by J.J."

"So, Jerome," he sat back in his chair and laid his intertwined fingers on his belly, "why law?"

"My father is an attorney," I said, "and ever since childhood I've wanted to follow in his footsteps." ["Excepting perhaps the explosive temper and cirrhotic liver," I thought.]

A fraternal smile curved his lips. "And having now been through school, do you know what field of law you want to practice?"

I glanced over at my slop bucket in the corner by the front door. The muck shovel stood at attention by its side. Holding my hand down by my left thigh, I snapped my fingers sharply. Shovel and bucket fell briskly into place. I removed my shoes and socks, rolled up my pant legs and readied myself. I cleared my throat. "Yes, sir," I said, "I want to be a litigator."

"Good," he said, drawing a red check on my resume. "Why is that?"

"I enjoy the challenge of constructing a case and presenting it in a compelling way," I said as I stood and opened the window to let my soul run for cover. Then I took the shovel and drove it into a fresh, steaming pile of manure. "And the precision of language that's an attorney's stock in trade has always attracted me. I've spent more Saturday afternoons than I can remember with just a cup of coffee and a dictionary, studying why certain words evoke an emotional response while others don't, the use of rhyme and meter, logical pro-gression, advocacy skills." Mr. Cates turned his head as I dumped the first shovel full on his desk blotter.

"Yes," he ate it up, "I've studied language myself. But I'm sure you realize that being a litigator—as lucrative as it is—is not an easy field. Probably the single most difficult area of concentration," he said, clipping off the last six words as sharply as a Monty Python skit.

"I welcome the challenge, sir," I said. *I've had pasta eight nights in a row, sir,* I thought.

"Think you're up to it?"

"Yes, sir," I said. *I spent Sunday morning trolling the grocery store with a pin and sucking out the innards of eggs, sir,* I thought.

"Just so you know, Fielding & Cates requires no fewer than twenty-two hundred billable hours a year, and you may find yourself billing as many as twenty-five. That means there are going to be some very late nights and very long weekends. Are you married?"

I shook my head.

"Girlfriend?"

I nodded.

"You might want to consider letting her go."

"I'll have the papers drafted this afternoon, sir."

"But tell me, Jerome, why would anybody want to work this hard?"

Because raw eggs taste like mucous, sir, I thought. "It would be easy," I called over my shoulder as I turned back to my pile of manure, "to drift through my working years as a nine-to-five man. I could devote my time to other things, and concentrate on being a well-rounded individual. But the Renaissance is over—I want to be great at what I do, and to be great at something means total devotion." I didn't bother walking back and forth from the manure to the desk anymore; it seemed more efficient to hurl each shovel full across the office. Cates flinched when the first load hit him, but eventually adjusted, sitting stoically as he slowly disappeared beneath it. "Nothing against life, Cates," I continued without turning around, "if that's the way you swing. But I prefer work. Tedious, superficial, lucrative work. If you told me that I'd be out of here by five every night, I'd turn around and walk out that door, so help me." I paused halfway through, straightened up and wiped the sweat from my brow with the back of my hand. I looked at what I could still see of Cates, wondering if he could still hear me. Unable to tell, I continued. "At the risk of sounding materialistic, there are certain luxuries I want to enjoy. And the only way to that is through hard work—dreadful, soul-stealing, borderline criminal work."

After a while, he began to wrap up. "Now then," he said, "have you any questions for me?"

A litany, I thought. *Why's there no umlaut in the word,* umlaut? *What do you think of the name Detective for a boy? Why can't you play defense in golf? Don't you think a cement mixer, from behind, looks like an elephant defecating? Stare decisis—what is that?* I thought. "How early is coffee ready in the mornings?" I asked.

He loved me, I thought, as I left Fielding & Cates and immediately caught a taxi downtown to the D.A.'s office. The D.A. job was still the one I wanted, but it was nice to know that I'd have options. As the cab passed 14th Street, I imagined how great it would be to work downtown, near Jen. We'd made tentative plans for lunch, provided I finished with the D.A. in time to coincide with her lunch break.

At the D.A.'s office, I asked for a recruitment coordinator named Swerza. Unfortunately, Mr. Swerza had a moustache. And in Mr. Swerza's moustache, Mr. Swerza kept a little ball of fuzz. Perhaps it was from his coat. Perhaps it was from his secretary's sweater. Maybe it was a fashion statement, I don't know. For whatever reason he had it, that little ball of fuzz effectively ruined any chance I ever had of becoming a prosecutor.

Throughout the interview, the ball of fuzz would disappear into Swerza's nose every time he inhaled, then reappear in the exact same spot with every exhale. Try as I might, I couldn't concentrate on his questions. All I could think of was how badly I wanted to reach over and pluck that fuzzball out of his moustache. The interview didn't go well, needless to say, and I felt very resentful toward Swerza. He couldn't take the time to comb out his moustache before interviews and my career is affected by it. I was out of there in twenty-nine minutes flat.

"Hi baby, can you get lunch?" I shouted into my cell phone, trying to be heard over the street noise. I held my hand to my opposite ear as a muffler but the air was so hot it made my face sweat. I had my jacket off again, but now that it was past midday, that offered little relief.

"J.J.! How's going, honey?"

"What?"

"I said how's it going?"

"Not so good. How's your day?"

"Unbelievably busy. I'm swamped."

"So no lunch?"

"Sorry, I really can't."

"Are we having dinner tonight?"

"Definitely, I'll come over after work. One second, J.J.—Allison, I'm over here. Do you need me?" I didn't hear anything for a minute. "Sorry, J.J., this place is crazy today. You've got to meet these guys, they're a panic."

"Invite some of them out with us tonight if you want."

"Yes, I told you I have it right here. What, J.J.?"

"I said if you want to—"

"I said it's right here. Baby, I've got to go. I'll see you tonight."

"Okay, I'll—" She was gone. I dialed again.

"Josie Steele's office," a voice said.

"Mr. Steele please."

"I'm sorry, he's behind closed doors."

"Hi Amanda, it's J.J."

"Oh, hi J.J., I didn't recognize your voice. Hold on, I'll interrupt him."

As I waited for Josie to pick up, I used my lower lip to clean the perspiration off my upper lip. I pressed my right palm to my ear as a city bus dragged by, belching a cloud of black fumes at me.

"J.J.?" I heard Josie's voice.

"Hi Josie."

"Good to hear from you. Any news?"

"No," I said. "It didn't go so well with the D.A. How are you doing? How's the new firm?"

"My offer still stands," he answered, ignoring my question. "You can come up here and work for me."

"Thanks, maybe I'll take you up on that one day. How's Terry, Ben?"

"Everyone's wonderful."

"What?" I pressed the phone harder to my ear.

"I said everyone's wonderful. We've gone to contract on a house in Newton. We'd love to have you up for a visit once we close on it."

"I'd love to. How're things at the *dojo*?"

"Who knows—I've been so busy here, I haven't worked out in weeks."

"Yeah, me either, between taking the bar and the job search."

"Forgive me," I heard him say to someone else, "it's my star pupil."

"Are you with someone, Josie?"

"A client," he said.

"Oh, I'm sorry. Amanda didn't tell me."

"She wasn't supposed to. She knows that family takes precedence."

"Thanks. Well, I'll let you get back."

"You sure? Nothing else?"

"No, just calling to say hello."

"You know, I know someone at Greer, Babcock and Drew. It's a very good firm."

"I appreciate it," I said. "I just want to see if I can do this on my own."

"It won't get you the job. It'll just get you in the door. You'll still have done it on your own."

I considered the offer, and realized that I was in no position to refuse. I couldn't bank everything on Fielding & Cates. He sensed it in my silence, and spared me my pride by saying: "I'm calling them today no matter what you say, and I'll speak to you tonight. Don't worry—I'm doing them a bigger favor than I'm doing you."

I thanked him and hung up. His confidence inspired me, and I resolved to have great interviews for the rest of the day. Mid-afternoon, I met with Hersh, Coen, Stine and Wysse, a firm from eastern Long Island that had rented an office in Manhattan for a week to hold interviews. And after a very productive hour, the interviewer ruined everything by asking me a question I couldn't resist.

"I certainly admire your academic record, Mr. Spencer," Mr. Hersh said, "and you seem like a nice young man. But we're look-ing for a long-term relationship, so I guess there's one more thing I need to know that's as important as any of that." He paused and I waited for another question for which I'd prepared—Where do you see yourself in ten years? As ludicrous as this question is, they all ask it in order to cover themselves with their partners in case I leave after a year. But just as I cocked my bat to drive the question out of the park, he threw a curve, leaning forward and asking: "Do you sincerely want to work in East Setauket?"

Why do they do this to me? Cates with his litigation, Swerza with his fuzzball. Where I see myself in ten years, that's what you were supposed to ask. I stared at him for a good long while, trying to form words unthinkable to me. I was raised in New York City, for heaven's sake. I went to law school in Boston. I didn't even know where East Setauket was, except that I had reasonable confidence I'd be able to find it if they spotted me West Setauket. I wouldn't have even taken this interview if everyone hadn't warned me about how hard it was going to be to find a job in this economy.

"I want to work in East Setauket," I began, measuring my words, hoping I wouldn't be tempted to say any more. But then I heard myself adding: "I want to live in East Setauket." Stop it, J.J., stop it. "I want to raise my children in East Setauket." Well, I'm finished here anyway. Might as well turn out the lights. "And I want to die in East Setauket."

As I left that interview, all the strength Josie had given me evaporated, replaced by more resentment. I resented having to soft shoe for everyone I met. I resented the fact that I was being tested again. Ever since grade school I've been getting tested; you'd think by now they'd just take my word for it—I'm okay. I resented having to cut my hair and choose my clothes on their terms. In fact, I resented the whole notion that I had to be like they were, in order to be a good lawyer. And, man, was I ever tired of hearing myself talk. That was it, mostly, I was just exhausted. And so when, in my last interview of the day, a Nepalese attorney with a thick accent, a mind-boggling list of accomplishments and a stunningly appointed office asked me, "How do you re-create yourself?" I blew it.

My problem was that I had spent quite a bit of time researching not only his firm, but him personally. He was known as a profound and free thinker. Law.com had profiled him months earlier. It said he was the son of a Sherpa mahatma. He'd grown up on the southern slope of the Himalayas, studying and training. He still did yoga every morning, and dabbled in astral projection as well. The Dalai Lama was a client.

And so I think it's perfectly understandable that I took the question, "How do you re-create yourself?" to invite some sort of metaphysical, stream of consciousness give-and-take. Oh, one other thing. I had spent the previous weekend in the New York Public Library studying Eastern philosophy.

"It is said," I began, holding out both my hands, palms up as I'd seen in the books, "that Milarepa himself had initially set out on a path of greed and vanity, bringing down the wedding tent of his evil uncle. And not until years later did he sing: O Lama Vajradhara, immutable in essence, you know the happiness and difficulties of this mendicant."

I sat back in my chair and nodded. He squinted at me in silence.

"What?" he finally asked. "Why, why are you saying these things?"

His impatience was unbecoming of a sage, and made me nervous to boot. But I was still upset with myself for having been snide in the East Setauket interview. This was a great man I was speaking to, after all.

"I simply meant to make the point that to re-create oneself is the supreme prerogative of all men, and that as the prismal colors of our chakras shimmer and swirl, so do we—"

"What?" he interrupted, so I tried again.

"I see myself as a computer-generated image of how I'd look if I'd had the chance to grow up."

"No, no," he shouted, slapping his own forehead. "Re-create, do you understand? Re-create, re-create."

Maybe he'd grown tired of the mystical thing and was into genetics now.

"I'd need double-stranded DNA and a Petri dish—"

"Re-create, re-create," he was pacing the office now, waving his arms. "How do you re-create yourself? Tennis, golf…"

I walked home with my shirt untucked, my tie in my pocket and my self-confidence shattered, tapping the sidewalk with the umbrella point as I made my way. The summer sky was still light, but the air had cooled and the rush of traffic subsided. I thought about the *dojo* in Greenwich Village to which Zachary had referred me, but I wasn't in the mood to recreate. The evening air had me pining to be somewhere I could better enjoy it. In a park or next to a brook. Maybe walking with Jennifer along the banks of the Charles. I thought about Boston, and wasn't sure if it was the city itself that I missed, or the simplicity of my days there. Everything was so different now. I wanted to go back, although I clearly remembered yearning to move forward just a few months before. I wondered how Leo was doing. He'd decided to stay in Atlanta this summer to do an internship at the C.D.C. before starting his senior year in September. He said it was his last chance to have some fun before having to get serious. Studying fungus and mold at the C.D.C.—strange kid. I made a mental note to call him.

I passed a playground where young mothers sat by as their children played. Nothing ever makes me feel more lonely than watching children play. I used to stand at the fence of a schoolyard on Harvard Avenue in Boston and watch them. And I realized as I stood now and watched a little girl run down the slide-upon, that I wanted to cry.

When I got home, Jen called to say she had to work late and I reacted badly. We argued, but then apologized, albeit tersely, and made plans for the next night. I sat inertly in front of the television set, too disinterested to bother choosing a channel. The phone rang again and I sat up, relieved that she had called back. I didn't like how we'd left things.

"I'm glad you called," I said when I picked up.

"I'd think so," answered Josie. "You've got an interview at Greer, Babcock day after tomorrow."

"Are you serious? Josie, you're a lifesaver, thank you. I did so badly today."

"You're welcome. They're at 452 Madison Avenue and you're to ask for Ted Dietz. He's the managing partner."

"He's your friend?"

"No, my friend is in Tax. They're staffing up in litigation and real estate, so that's where the openings are."

"Ted Dietz." I wrote the name down, along with the address. "And what did you say the name of the firm was?"

"Greer, Babcock and Drew."

Chapter thirty-eight

Being friends with someone, you can forget who he is to the rest of the world. By the time I sat down to interview with Ted Dietz, Josie's recommendation had completely shifted the burden of proof. Dietz interviewed me with expectation, then at the end of the interview, Josie's friend met me at Dietz's office to take me to lunch. They called the next day to offer me the job. Burden of proof is everything.

During my first several months at Greer I did well, despite finding no intrinsic value in the work itself. Truth is, I despised the work, yet it allowed me to find a rhythm for my life, a rhythm that had been lacking for so long. I was well paid and had moved my mother into a better apartment. Jen and I were doing well and even talking about moving in together. I'd found a *dojo* that had a nine o'clock evening class, allowing me to train regularly. Though my new sensei told me that he needed Zachary's blessing to test me for my black belt—a blessing Zachary had yet to give—there was a tournament coming up in three weeks and I planned to make my case for black belt then. All in all, it wasn't a bad time for me, and I came to accept, struggled to accept, that for some, work isn't life, just the price of admission. Having accepted it, I tried not to think about it.

"There's my dynamic duo," Carter Boston exulted as Ira and I arrived at his office late one spring afternoon. He was in shirtsleeves when we got there, holding a fishing rod and pretending to cast. "Have a seat gentlemen." He put the rod aside and walked around to his desk chair. Ira and I looked at each other, then back to Boston. He held his arms out to the sides and allowed himself to fall backward into his chair, his feet sailing up with the inertia of the fall. "I just heard from Heather Sherwin," he said, referring to the head of our Real Estate Group. He opened the bottom drawer of his desk and reached in. "She says Eiderhorn is ours, and I say that calls for a celebration."

When his left hand reappeared from the desk drawer, there was a bottle of Johnnie Walker Blue in it. One by one, he produced three rock glasses from the same drawer.

"But it's only five o'clock, Mr. Boston," Ira said.

"Lighten up, Finowitz," Boston answered. "You've got to take some time to enjoy life, you know." He poured us each a glass and handed them around. "To Stan Eiderhorn," he said, tapping his glass against each of ours, then tilting his head back and savoring a long, slow drink. Ira shrugged and took a sip. I hesitated.

"Come on, Spencer, drink up."

"It's just that, well, you know," I began to explain.

"What, the karate thing?" he waved his hand dismissively. "Don't worry about it; you'll win. Greer Babcock guys always win. When is it, anyway?"

"Three weeks," I said.

"Then here's to you too—to your winning the Yah-Yah! championship."

I smiled and took just a small sip, surprised that it didn't taste as much like embalming fluid as whiskey usually does.

"You know," Boston said, his voice airy from the scotch, "Eiderhorn actually mentioned you to Heather when he told her we got his account."

"Mentioned what? Me?"

"You believe it?" he nodded. "Heather's got twenty years in real estate, I'm the best litigator in New York, but he said all the firms he met with had people like us. He wanted warriors, and that having a karate expert on his team meant a lot to him. As a matter of fact, you know what," he said, reaching out and taking the crystal glass from my hand, "no more of that for you—you've got a tournament to win. Stan's pretty quirky—if the guy that beats you is a lawyer, he might give him the account."

Not long before Ira and I had started at Greer Babcock, Stan Eiderhorn's company, S.E. Capital, had purchased a $188 million package of defaulted mortgages from Penman Mutual Life. Because the loans were all in default, he was able to buy them at just 59 cents on the dollar. Then he hired six firms to collect on the money. Each firm got about $30 million of notes to work out. Eiderhorn had said it was an audition. Whoever collected the most money for him in the least amount of time, spending the least amount of his money on litigation and other legal fees, would be the winner. That firm would get to do the legal work on all future loan packages he bought. Ira and I had been working on those deals under Boston and Sherwin ever since we got to Greer. We got lucky on a couple, managing to negotiate settlements and avoid trials. That was the key. Getting the account was an enormous win for Greer, worth millions of dollars a year.

"Has he bought anything else yet?" Ira asked.

"Just closed on a $144 million package from Parker National Bank. Unbelievable deal—43 cents on the dollar. I don't know how he does it."

I sat forward in my seat. "Parker National? They don't do commercial properties."

Boston pointed at me. "Damn, I like you." He raised his glass again, speaking to Ira as he gestured toward me. "Kid knows the market. And here I wasn't even planning to interview B.U. grads. Who knew they were putting out lawyers like this right across the river, huh, Finowitz? We thought they were just staffing our mailrooms." He laughed alone at his joke. "Anyway," he finished the glass and poured himself another, "you're exactly right, Spencer, and that's going to make our job tougher." He held the bottle out over

Ira's glass and Ira shrugged, so he topped it off. "The new loan package is twelve hundred loans—very labor intensive. The Penman Life package was bigger, but it had only thirty-four loans in it. Plus, all the new deals are residential, so the courts are going to be a lot less sympathetic to our side. We're going to put in a lot more work, for a lot less money."

"So why are we doing it?" I asked.

"Two reasons," he said. "First, Eiderhorn's getting close to a $355 million package from a life company I can't divulge, all commercial property—get this—only nineteen loans. And second," he paused and smiled, raising his glass again, "we got an equity stake in the Parker National deal."

"So we're getting a fee plus a participation in the proceeds?" Ira asked. Boston smiled and Ira whistled softly.

I sank deeper into my chair. It was hard enough to go into conference rooms and courtrooms and foreclose on someone's office building, but at least in those situations, we were competing with real estate professionals over business assets. But with the new package, we'd be taking people's homes. I did some quick math in my head— $144 million total package size, 1,200 loans. That meant an average deal size of $120,000—not even the homes of wealthy people.

Chapter thirty-nine

That night, Jen and I met for dinner at a Chinese restaurant on the Upper East Side, the first time we'd seen each other in almost a week. Between all her business travel and my fourteen-hour days, it was hard. That was one reason we were talking about moving in together. We figured we'd probably live at my place. After I got the Greer job, I'd rented a one-bedroom on the Upper East Side, just five blocks from her.

"A $144-million client told them that you were the main reason he hired the firm?" she smiled in wide-eyed glee. "Look at that, all those years you were right—karate is practical."

"Not the main reason," I said, "one reason. But that's not my point. These are people's homes, Jen. How can I make a career out of foreclosing on people's homes?"

She rolled her eyes. "God, J.J., sometimes you can be such a narcissist. What do you think, if Greer Babcock doesn't do it, everyone will just get to keep their homes? He'll just get someone else."

"So you think I'm being ridiculous."

"No, not ridiculous. You're sensitive; it's sweet. But you have to think of yourself sometimes too, your future. I don't know anyone who hasn't had to do some distasteful work to advance. A guy I work with sold penny stocks to widows for six months, just to get equity sales experience. He doesn't do it anymore."

"He ripped off widows?"

"That's not the point. He did it for six months because he had to. There's people out there doing a lot worse."

"Who is this guy?"

"It doesn't matter, one of our managing partners. Baby, this is an amazing moment in your career. Your firm got a huge account because of you, and you've been there less than a year. You don't think they notice that upstairs?"

A waiter approached with menus in his hand, gave us each one and walked away. Jen stared down at hers as I pretended to look at mine.

"Can I tell you something, Jen?" She looked up with those beautiful, dark eyes, and waited. It made it harder for me to say what I wanted to. I knew it was going to upset her. "I think I might have made a terrible mistake." Her mouth closed into a frown. She leaned back in her chair and folded her arms across her chest. "All this, it feels wrong."

"You don't like law," she said flatly. "Are we really going to do this again? I don't care what you do as long as you're happy. But just put in a couple of years so you have some choices. Then do whatever you want."

"It's not just that, though. So much feels wrong. I don't know, this ambitious, Upper East Side life. Suits, subways, Johnny Walker Blue…me. I feel like I'm in the wrong skin."

"I thought we agreed on the Upper East Side because it's residential. Hey, it's no picnic for me commuting down to Wall Street from here, you know."

"I know," I bowed my head.

"Maybe I shouldn't move in."

"No," I protested. "When I say everything feels wrong, I don't mean you. I love you. It's everything else."

"I love you too, but for the life of me I can't figure you out. What is it you want, J.J.? Just tell me."

The waiter returned and we ordered. When he left, Jen turned her gaze back toward me, her arms still folded across her chest. She reminded me of my mother the one time I dared to bring home poor grades, during my first year of high school. Encouraged by a friend, I'd been dabbling in rebelliousness. Never made the same mistake again.

I rubbed my hands over my face. "Forget it," I said. "Forget I said anything. It's probably just stress." Her face relaxed a little, and I saw a breath of air inflate her chest then leave again. "I'm going to be joined at the hip to this Eiderhorn guy for the next few years, and they're all expecting a lot of me. Then there's the tournament…it's a lot on my mind."

"I know," she said. "But you'll win; you're ready. And as far as Eiderhorn goes, I've actually read about him. I think you'll like him. He's a really interesting guy. He started as a D.J. at some trendy night-club and made contacts there, and before you knew it, he was doing deals with them. Not a bad mentor to have, you know."

"Oh, that reminds me, I have to call Josie tonight. Are we going to go up there this summer?"

"It's still a ways off. Why don't we wait and see. I still have to get my list of weekends for the Westhampton house."

Chapter forty

Just three weeks later, Stan Eiderhorn had already lost patience with us. We'd given a borrower a month extension to try to refinance before foreclosing, and Eiderhorn was furious. He'd just finished shouting at me, Ira and Carter Boston over a speaker phone, and Ira and I were riding the elevator back to our office, saying unflattering things about clients. This Parker National deal had changed everything, it had cost me my rhythm.

"We help people who don't need help, to beat up the ones who do," I muttered as we got to our office. "Ridiculous."

"Absurd."

"I don't want to be doing this anymore."

"Me either."

"Really? Because there's a career seminar at the Y tonight, you know," I said. "I'm going to meet Jen at my place and go, if you want to join us."

He stared at me. "You quitting?"

"No, just looking into my options."

"Good, because I was just talking about maybe asking for a transfer to a different department, not quitting."

"All the departments are the same, Finny. They're all the same."

He continued to his desk and peeled a yellow Post-it note off his phone receiver. "What's this?"

"I got one too."

"Damn, a lunch invitation from Dietz." He looked up at me. "You?"

I nodded. As managing partner, Dietz made it a point to have lunch with first-year associates every couple of months.

"It says one o'clock. We'd better get up there."

We went immediately back to the elevator, and sat in Mr. Dietz's office as he finished dictating a letter. I snuck a peek at Ira and we winced at the sight of Dietz practically swallowing the microphone, his perpetually moist lower lip pressed to it.

"Okay, all done," he announced. "Ready to go?"

But as we stood to leave, Dietz's secretary came into the office. "Excuse me, there's someone waiting in Reception for Mr. Spencer."

Dietz and Ira looked at me and I shrugged.

"A client?" Dietz asked.

"A Mr. Steele," she answered.

"Josie Steele?" I said. "That's my old law school professor."

"Well, come on, introduce Mr. Finowitz and me," said Dietz.

We took the elevator down to reception, and as soon as I saw Josie standing there, I knew something was wrong. Even dressed in an expensive suit, he didn't look well. He was even thinner than usual, and very pale. "Josie," I said, walking over to him and taking his hand. "What are you doing in New York?"

He shook my hand and patted my left shoulder with his other hand. "I had a deposition downtown this morning, so I thought I'd stop by and take my prize pupil to lunch."

"I wish I knew you were coming. I've already got lunch plans." Peripherally, I noticed Dietz standing stiffly at my shoulder. "I'm sorry, Ted Dietz, this is Josie Steele. Josie, Mr. Dietz, our managing partner."

"Call me Ted," Dietz said as he took Josie's hand.

"Pleasure," Josie said.

"And this is Ira Finowitz," I continued.

"Mr. Steele," Ira said.

"Anyway, like I said," I continued, "we were just on our way out to lunch."

"Why don't you join us?" Dietz offered.

Josie accepted, and over lunch he and Dietz swapped war stories as Ira and I, having nothing to add, sat quietly, deferential still-life smiles on our faces. On the walk back from the restaurant, Josie noticed the brick wall of Central Park.

"Is that Central Park?" he asked, and we said it was. "I've never seen it. Ted, would it be too much of an inconvenience if I borrowed J.J. for a while so he could show me?"

"No problem at all," Dietz said.

"Thank you, sir," I said. "I won't be long."

"Take your time," he said, then added slyly, "bill it to Eiderhorn."

Ira is fortunate to be so tall, because the saliva that sprayed off Dietz's lower lip with his spurt of laughter landed harmlessly on Ira's lapel. I laughed along until they crossed Fifth Avenue away from us.

"You must be getting pretty tired of that," Josie observed as we turned toward the park.

"You have no idea," I rolled my eyes.

"So how is everything? They treating you well?"

"Oh, they're fine. You look tired."

"Long drive down."

"Important deposition?"

"Actually," he smiled, "there was no deposition. I just felt like doing something different today. Didn't tell Terry, didn't even know myself. I got into the car this morning to drive to work, and when I reached the entrance for the Mass Pike east, I turned west."

"You sure you're all right?"

"I'm fine," he insisted. "Didn't you ever just feel like going west?"

I let it drop. Though I knew it was masking something, his good mood was infectious. "Why don't I show you Sheep's Meadow," I said. "It's my favorite part of the park."

"And then the bandshell. So," he said as we entered the park at Fifth Avenue and 61st, "your tournament's tomorrow night, isn't it?"

"I was kind of hoping you'd enter."

"I wish," he scoffed. "I haven't been to the *dojo* in months. I barely have time to see Terry and Ben. We're defending an insurance company against a hundred-million-dollar class action."

"But don't give up karate. You can make a little time. What if you—"

"Don't you think I'd like to?" he cut me off. "There's no time— I've got a family to support."

"Don't give me that. I know your family. And you look thin and tired."

He exhaled. "It's just that things are very busy at work right now. I'm sorry if I seem fractious."

"Aw," I waved my hand, "you don't seem fractious."

"No?"

"Definitely not."

"You have no idea what 'fractious' means, do you?"

"None." We walked a bit farther and something occurred to me. "If you're so busy, how did you find the time to drive to New York?"

"You know," he reflected, "sometimes in the office, I'll find myself staring out the window at the building across the street. I see everyone in their offices, going about their business, and they look just like animals in a zoo. They think they're in their natural habitat, but I've got a better vantage point. I can see that they're in cages. And it amuses me until I realize that when they look back at me, I'm in a cage too. I have my little room and I'm locked up in there until it's time to leave." We walked beneath an overpass and he continued, as the shadow enveloped him. "I'm a monk, and that office is my monastery. I don't know, this morning, the open road, it smelled too good to resist."

"You told me that monk never went back."

We approached a footbridge that crossed over a stream. On the stone wall of the bridge a man was passed out, plastic bags covering his torn shoes, engulfed by the stench of whiskey, urine and despair. Josie and I stopped talking as we passed him.

"I'm going back," Josie said.

Past the footbridge, the path forked. We veered right toward the Wollman ice skating rink.

"Did I mention that I'm going to a career seminar tonight?" I said.

"Really? That's great, J.J.—very smart of you."

With Wollman on our right, Josie pointed up toward a bluff above a rock wall to our left. "What's up there?" he asked.

"Nothing."

"No such thing."

"Well, I don't know. The path doesn't go there."

"The path goes anywhere you want it to. Come on," he said, and started climbing the wall.

"Josie, my suit," I protested, but he ignored me, clawing his way up, his tie tossed over his shoulder. When he reached the top, he stood on the wall with his hands on his hips. "Let's go, old man."

I don't know why I followed him up there, but I did.

"You're going to win that tournament easy," he said when I reached the top, my suit pants dusty. "You're in the best shape I've ever seen you."

"Thanks," I said. "Now can we—"

"Come on." He lifted his hands into sparring position and bounced on the balls of his feet.

"Josie, I'm not sparring in my suit."

"Come on," he repeated, pushing me at the shoulder. "I'll go easy on you."

I tried to ignore his bizarre behavior. There was another path fifty yards away. But as I walked past him, he playfully slapped me on the head. "Come on, Mr. Spencer."

"What are you, insane?" I laughed, unable to resist him. "Okay, this is going to be for that Con Law grade."

We circled and threw a few harmless punches and kicks, as cars slowed on the road above to watch the two men in business suits karate fighting in Central Park. But even at half-speed, I was starting to perspire, and didn't want to go back to the office any more of a mess than I already was. "Enough, enough," I called, covering my head. "I give."

Josie backed up, laughing and breathing heavily. He was in terrible condition. Too thin, too pale, no wind. He bent over and put his hands on his knees, then sank to the ground. He pulled his knees up and rested his forehead on them, his back still rising and falling as he tried to catch his breath. I sat beside him. He stayed quiet too long. Even once his breathing regulated, he left his head on his knees.

"You okay?" I put my hand on his back.

He raised his head and looked at me, all the cheer gone. "Terry's pregnant," he said.

I stared into his weary eyes, trying to read the thoughts behind them. "That's great, isn't it?" I asked tentatively.

"Yes," he said softly, "it's great."

"But it's not."

"No," he said, and looked straight ahead.

"Because it's a deeper pit. The more people you love, the more confined you feel."

"One more set of eyes looking to me for something I can't provide."

"You do provide."

"I thought so," his eyes cornered toward me, "but it turns out, they need more. They need me happy. But I can only be happy or rich—I can't be both."

"For God's sake choose happy."

He shook his head and spoke evenly. "You have no right to say that. You've never looked into the eyes. Starving the eyes for the sake of my own happiness—"

"Makes you unhappy."

He nodded silently.

"You know, Josie, maybe that monk got lucky, to go over the right wall the first time. Maybe you've got to jump more than one wall before you land right."

"Maybe," he said, the trace of a smile tugging at the corners of his mouth.

As small as it was, his smile pleased me. I felt that I'd helped, just a bit. Maybe come just a little closer to being the friend he deserved, and to the man I wanted to be. We sat silently for a while, inhaling the spring air. From that isolated bluff, the city seemed peaceful and life seemed at hand. But within a few hours, I'd begin a downward spiral that wouldn't stop until an unamused New York City cop cuffed my hands behind my back and pushed my bloodied, drug-addled head into the back of his patrol car.

Chapter forty-one

It came like a fist out of a blind alley.

After walking Josie to his car, I went back to the office and finished my day of work. Then I went home to wait for Jen, so we could go to the Y. I waited until after seven, then called her cell phone. There was no answer. The career seminar would be starting at seven-thirty. I tried her office and her apartment phones, and got nothing. When I'd heard about the seminar, I'd been so excited that I'd called her right away to ask if she'd come along. She'd agreed quickly. But it was getting close to eight o'clock and she still wasn't here. I tried the cell phone again and got a recorded message. She'd been getting less and less reliable over the past few weeks, and the truth is, by nine o'clock, I had convinced myself that she was with another man.

Shortly after eleven, I reeled out of my apartment in a rage, ran the five blocks to her place and hammered my fists against the door. When she let me in, however, there was no other man. All she'd been in bed with was a pint of ice cream. But through the surreal fog that had descended upon me, I could no longer make out shapes. For over a year, she'd never forgotten plans. For over a year, we'd spoken on the phone nightly. For over a year, the future had been clear. It was me, and it was her. And whether it was surrounded by Boston, New York, law or looting, it was me and it was her. And now, something was telling me that maybe it wasn't, after all. I was hurt, and I was frightened, and I lashed out.

"What's happened to you?" I demanded. "What's the matter with you?"

"Nothing," she protested. "I just, I'm a little confused right now. It's not you. I love you so much," she insisted. But her tone was strained, like she was trying to convince herself.

"If you're confused, let me help you. That's what we're here for, isn't it?" I didn't realize what a lost battle I was fighting. Her mind was made up. I couldn't help with the problem because I was the problem.

"I do that too easily," she answered. "I want to depend on myself for a while."

I could recount the whole miserable night if I wanted to—I remember every word—but I'd really rather not degrade myself any further. She said a lot of things—indistinct, generic things—few of which I understood. She said it wasn't working right now for either of us, and that we should look forward, not back. That it would be good for us both. She said she really loved her job, felt like she belonged there, and that besides, everything always turns out for the best. The clichés infuriated me and I spat venom at them. She responded with more clichés, and we never really did meet in the middle. But so what—trying to save a relationship with words is like trying to douse a fire with a picture of water.

"You're in love with someone else, aren't you?" I accused, never for a moment imagining that I was right.

She backed up a step, sat at the foot of her bed and looked at me in silence.

"You are?" I sank down on the floor and stared at her. "Who?"

"It doesn't matter. Nothing's happened with him."

"Him? Who? The guy who sold penny stocks to widows?"

"He only did it for six months," she shouted.

"You mean I'm right? That's who you're in love with?"

"Nothing's happened. But yes." She watched me steadily as I

stared at her. "Anyway, it's not about him—we've grown apart, J.J. We have. We want different things now."

"How can we want different things? I don't even know what I want."

"You *do* know what you want. And it's not what I want. Can't you see that?"

I felt queasy. Everything was far away and out of focus. Love isn't supposed to be explainable; it's supposed to be sacred and hazy. You don't decide to love, you surrender to it. It should never be exposed as mutual ambition; it should never be understood. And God damn it, even if you are an investment banker you shouldn't bring your laptop into bed—it's backwards—if anything, you should bring your dreams to work. But if she didn't believe any of this, why didn't I just turn and go?

"So that's it," I stood and puffed out my shattered chest. "We want different things now. All the time, love, trust—everything—trash it all because we want different things now."

"Look, I'm sorry. I'm sorry! I wish I could do this better, but this is the best I know!" She lowered her voice and tried again to console me. She said more than once that no one knows what the future holds, that we might end up together after all, but come on. Love is like anything else that dies. Once it's dead, it's dead.

I woke up the next morning—it might have been a Tuesday—on the hardwood floor of my new *dojo*, kicked at the heavy bag for a while, then called in sick to work. I spent the whole day at the *dojo*, feeling like I'd been disemboweled with a pick-ax. Around midday, I stood to go home, but as afternoon became dusk, I found myself seated in that same far corner, my knees to my chest.

People started to arrive for the evening workout, earlier than I'd expected. Over the next twenty minutes, more people arrived than I'd ever seen for a weeknight class, and they weren't all students. Friends and family members took seats along the side wall. There was even an Asian newspaper reporter, who spoke quietly with a few people while writing into a notepad. As I watched quietly from the corner, two men used white tape to mark off a large square in the center of the floor.

I was in no mood to compete in the tournament. I felt so empty, so drained. But when Sensei Zachary and Manny entered the room, I knew I'd have to fight. They'd come because of me; there was no other explanation for their presence. Zachary hated tournaments. But no one had ever stalled on brown belt as long as I. He had come to see if I was ready to advance, I was sure of it.

So I thought about Jennifer. I thought about her dark eyes staring up at me from the foot of her bed, and her telling me that we want different things, and that what she wanted was a guy who sold penny stocks to widows. The more I thought about her, the more I thought about myself, the angrier I grew. I greeted Zachary and Manny, then went into the locker room and chose a *gi* from the linen closet. When the tournament started, I fought ruthlessly. I destroyed three brown belts, one after another. The last one had to be helped from the floor. I walked over to where Zachary and Manny stood, and waited silently for my invitation to test for black belt.

Zachary looked at me for a moment, then shook his head and walked away. I turned to Manny.

"You flunked, counselor," he said.

"What do you mean, flunked? I killed those guys out there."

"Oh, you won the tournament all right." Tilting his head, he motioned toward the sparring floor, where two black belts were preparing to begin the next division. "But that was also your black belt test."

My arms dropped to my sides. From behind, guttural shouts filled the room as two black belts sparred. I wanted to shout too, or cry, at the pile of failure in my heart, at the helplessness in which I insist on wrapping myself. I live my life at the mercy and whim of everyone who matters to me. Everything I want rests in someone else's hands, and I'm so sick of it. I do my best and get nowhere. And even now, all I can seem to ask is: "Why does he hate me?"

"Shut up, he don't hate you. You think he drives down to New York for everyone?" He checked over his shoulder, then got close to me. "That guy, he's the worst driver I ever rode with. He don't drive, he aims."

"So it's just my karate that stinks. Tell me what I have to do,

Manny. Tell me and I'll do it. I'll come to Boston every damn week-end, I'll—"

"Your karate's fine. Hell, it's better than fine. I'm not even sure I could beat you anymore. Nah, I could."

"Then what?"

He turned me by the shoulders and pointed to one of the brown belts I'd injured. He had an ice pack to his jaw and someone was helping him gather his belongings. "That's what," he said. He reached over to the table full of trophies, grabbed one at random, and handed it to me. "Congratulations, counselor," he said, and walked away.

Chapter forty-two

Decorating his various apartments over the years, Ed had apparently just continued to transfer the furnishings from the first college dorm room he'd ever had. Even now, living in a West Side doorman building, his apartment had a distinct frat house flavor: big plastic backlit beer bottle on the wall, posters of bikini-clad women strewn over red sports cars, and speakers the size of a dog house. It had been weeks since I'd seen Ed, weeks since I'd seen anyone outside of work. I knew it was inevitable, that I'd eventually have to talk about what had happened with Jennifer and at the *dojo*, but I'd tried to avoid it as long as I could.

I sat on a tan vinyl couch that ran the length of the wall, my feet on the coffee table, and drank from a bottle of beer. Ed was sunk deep into a yellow bean bag chair across from me. He'd climbed into it an hour ago—before his first beer—and now, on his eighth, seemed to be stuck. He aimed the stereo remote over his right shoulder, and without looking, backed the CD up a track. He smiled at me and raised the volume.

"I'm begging you, Ed," I shouted over the music, "can we please play something other than *I Fought the Law*?"

"I told you, son, it stays on until you come clean," he answered. "Worked on Noriega, it'll work on you."

"But there's nothing else to say." I sighed and took a swallow of beer. "She just up and left. If I understood it, I swear I'd tell you."

He looked at me, unimpressed. I stood and crossed behind him to turn down the music. He tried to grab my wrist, but was too drunk and awkward to stop me. I'd only had four beers.

"I just wish I'd seen it coming," I said once it was quieter. "Might've been easier." I walked back to the couch, sat down and picked up another potato chip, then put it back in the bowl. They were starting to nauseate me. "If things had been deteriorating for a while, you know? If there'd been a progression. I think that would've at least lessened the shock. But me and Jen had a great relationship until the day it ended."

"No you didn't," he said evenly. "J.J., I swear, I've never met anyone who could build a fantasy world like you. You should have rides there, and get people to walk around in costumes of Jennifers and Amys and lawyers and everything."

"Amys?"

"Maybe a log flume."

"Stop it."

"It's so," he insisted, and I rolled my eyes and picked up the day's newspaper off the coffee table. I thumbed through it until I got to the horoscopes. Mine was the usual stuff about Mercury blocking my sun and ruining my tan. Jen's was now on the twentieth consecutive day of "Free! Free! You must be free! Rid yourself of past commitments! It's not so bad to sell penny stocks to widows!" I closed the paper and looked at Ed.

"What fantasy?"

"Aw, I ain't getting into all that; I ain't your shrink. All's I'm saying is, why don't you stop worrying for once about who you want to be, and just be whoever the hell you are? You know the difference between us?"

"Your parents are first cousins."

"You know the other difference between us?"

"Tell me."

"You always looking to fulfill some grand vision of yourself. I know who the hell I am and I just try to find things that fit."

He had a point. And one thing was for certain, Ed never got bogged down in second guessing. While everyone was telling him during third year of law school that it was wrong for a valedictorian to waste three years of study without even giving law a try, he ignored them. He got a partner for his Tropical Storm Watches, then bought late-night television time to sell them. He said there was nothing he could sell that a beautiful young woman couldn't sell better, so he hired several for the commercial and went right over the top with it, no apologies, no hand-wringing. He called it a nymphomercial, and the watches sold in a heartbeat, so he made ones that measured heartbeat too. They sold just as fast, and some company hired him to write and direct a nymphomercial for them. That one was in progress now, and he had three other companies under contract. Suddenly, he was out of the watch business and into the nymphomercial business, and he had never planned a bit of it. Never wondered whether it would work, never figured out why it couldn't work, never took his eye off the work itself.

"Okay then," I relented, "tell me how you do it."

"Go on."

"No, I'm serious. I think you're right. How do you do it?"

"Do what?"

"Come on, Ed. You know what I mean. You can't start this then not finish it."

Silently, he considered me for a moment. "Alright," he finally said, "but I do not want this thrown back in my face if it sounds stupid."

He struggled until he'd rolled himself out of the bean bag chair, then picked up the newspaper I'd discarded. He sat beside me on the couch and laid the newspaper out on the coffee table as I leaned forward. He turned pages for a while, until he came to the obituaries.

"That's how I do it," he said.

I looked to where he was pointing. An obituary read: "Graeme Delaney, 80, War Hero and Founder of Delaney Industries, dies." After the word "dies," in blue ink, Ed had carroted in the word "anyway."

I looked at him, then to the next obituary. "Ludek Brakhage, 68, Chessmaster, Philanthropist, dies," and again, inserted at the end of the sentence, the word "anyway."

"Your problem," he said, "is that you see your life as profound. The more profound you see your life, the more important each decision becomes. What's going to be the result of this, where is that leading. I know where it's leading. And ain't nothing I'm going to do going to change it. You love karate—I know it, I see you when you talk about it—but you ain't worked out once since you failed your black belt test weeks ago. You hate law, but there you go off to work every dang morning."

"I'd quit but I—"

"I know," he interrupted, "but I. But I don't know what else I'd do. I'd leave New York City but I don't know where I'd go. I'd find a nicer girl to date who didn't have my whole life planned out for me, but I don't know where to find her."

"I miss karate," I said aloud, to myself.

"So get your butt to the gym."

"You don't understand. It was so embarrassing. They said I was all anger, no content." I sighed, linked my fingers behind my head and leaned back.

"Well, they're right. You broke a guy's jaw."

"It was an accident."

"Hell it was."

"I let everyone down," I remembered, thinking of the expressions on Zachary's and Manny's faces.

"You'd like to find another girl too, wouldn't you?"

I said nothing. This was starting to hurt.

"So why don't you?"

"Can't I heal a little first?"

"Yeah," he allowed. "Come on, I don't mean to be hard on you. I'd just like to see you do one thing in your life that's your own choice."

"Jennifer was my choice."

"You were Jennifer's choice."

I wasn't sure if Ed was right, but I wasn't sure he was wrong either. One thing I knew, I was unhappy. I felt alone in a city of millions. I hated the life I'd chosen, everything from the city, to the suits, to the work, to the empty pit it all left in me. I hated it for all it was, and sometimes, even more for what it wasn't. I hated who I was in this life. When I was small, I used to think my arrival was inevitable; now, it seemed farther away than ever. But I didn't see any way out.

New York
Present Day

Chapter forty-three

It's the Friday of Labor Day weekend and I'm so glad this miserable summer is almost over. Though the sun is just beginning to rise directly ahead of me, the eastbound traffic on the Long Island Expressway is already bad. Beside me, the sixteen-ounce cup of coffee I bought before leaving the city is empty. I'm on about two hours sleep today, having spent last night going through the Eagan file at Greer Babcock's offices. I'm so tired my eyes burn. I veer off the highway at Exit 32, just over the Queens/Nassau border. Today's going to be a hot one, but it's also the end of August and in a few weeks the air will cool. It seems like yesterday that I met my future classmates on a courtyard outside B.U. law school, on a morning just like this. It had been a new beginning for all of us, and as I drive, I shake my head at the thought that everything that started that day, might end today. Today would be the final day of testimony before the disciplinary committee, and if we didn't convince them that I was worthy of my license to practice law, they would revoke it.

As I check over my right shoulder and turn left onto Little Neck Parkway, I'm not even sure I still want the license. I've spent the past two days hearing people testify about my supposed passion for law, wondering why the need to lie.

I travel north on Little Neck Parkway, just a few hundred yards, until I reach the entrance to the Eagans' townhome community. It's quiet in the car. I have the radio off because Leo is asleep in the passenger seat. He's flying back up to Boston today for orientation at Harvard Law. Classes begin next week. I'm taking him to the airport, but have to stop at the Eagans' first to pick up their bankruptcy papers. I'd been shocked when Leo told me he'd decided on law school, and doubly so when he told me which school he'd gotten into. I'm a little worried because he doesn't seem to have any more reason for going to law school than I had four years ago, but who am I to argue, he's going to Harvard.

As I pull the car into the Eagans' driveway, the dawn sun, now behind me, reflects off the upstairs windows. Leo awakens when I cut the engine. He looks at me, then out at the Eagans' house.

"Where's all the planes?" he asks groggily.

"Just a quick stop," I explain. "It's too early to drop you off anyway."

Emily answers the door on the first ring. She's still in her bathrobe, holding a mug of black coffee. Behind her, two children sprint haphazardly back and forth. I introduce her to Leo as we step inside. A pillow flies between us.

"Michael," she scolds her son.

"Sorry again that I had to come by so early," I say. "I've still got to drop my brother off at the airport, go home to put my car away, and be at the hearings by ten."

"Please," she answers, "you're doing this for us. I should be the one apologizing." She hands me a sealed manila envelope. "Here are the papers. Can I get you some coffee? Leo, coffee?"

Leo declines. I'm prepared for the offer, and hand her the empty sixteen-ounce cup. "I know it's impolite, but if I could get it to go?"

"Of course."

"Hi Dali," I say as the border collie hops up on me with her two front paws. I lift her paws off my suit, squat down to pet her, and look around. "Where's Jared?"

"Still sleeping," she calls over her shoulder as she goes into the kitchen to fill my coffee. "He had a bad night."

I follow her so that I don't have to raise my voice. "What happened?"

"Asthma attack," she shrugs.

"Your husband has asthma?" Leo asks. Emily nods as she hands me back the cup.

"Did he always?"

"For a couple of years now."

I notice that Leo has a peculiar expression on his face. He's crinkling his nose and looking around the house.

"What?" I ask.

"Oh, the smell," Emily laughs. She puts her hand on my shoulder and speaks to Leo. "You'll get used to it, your brother did."

"It's awful," Leo says, not looking at us.

"Leo," I admonish him. He looks at me and Emily.

"No, that's not what I mean," he answers. "Ms. Eagan, do you mind if I take a look around your home?"

"No, just please don't wake up Jared."

Leo walks the inside perimeter of the house, getting close to walls, looking them up and down. I watch him, wondering what he's doing. In the far corner of the living room, he squats behind an end table and pulls back a corner of carpet. "It's bad," he says to no one in particular, "but not bad enough to explain asthma. Ms. Eagan," he looks up, "do you have a basement?"

Emily nods and leads us to a closed door off the kitchen. As soon as she opens it, the musty smell gets so strong I instinctively revert to mouth breathing. She flicks on a light and the three of us walk down a narrow staircase. Leo pulls some storage boxes from the wall, exposing more of the green-black slime I'd seen upstairs the last time I was here. But here, it's thicker, and there's much more of it. It covers the entire wall behind the boxes, like wet paint.

"Ms. Eagan," Leo says, "I think I know why your husband is sick."

The smell down here is too strong to stay, so we go back upstairs and sit on the sofa.

"What you have growing all over your walls," Leo says, "is a kind of mold called Stachybotrys. Now, nothing's been proven for sure yet, but I know a lot of people who say Stachybotrys is really toxic stuff. I've heard stories of it causing chronic fatigue syndrome, pulmonary hemorrhaging, cancer."

"Asthma?" Emily asks.

"I've heard asthma a lot," Leo nods.

"Wait a second, Leo," I interrupt. I know how fragile the Eagans are and I don't want their hopes raised. "I've read a little about toxic mold and they say the whole uproar is bogus, just some new panic."

"New?" Leo smiles. "Ms. Eagan, do you have a bible?"

"Sure," she says, and goes upstairs. Once she's gone, I check to make sure the kids aren't around.

"Be careful with these people, Leo," I say. "They've been through a lot."

Emily returns with the bible, Jared following behind sleepily. She hands the book to Leo and he thumbs through it.

"Leviticus 14," he says. "Look, J.J.," he hands me the book. "Detailed steps for getting rid of mold."

"In the bible?"

"At the very least, it's an allergen," he says to the Eagans. "Whether it's as dangerous as people say, I don't know, but you've got a ton of it. It could be why you've got asthma."

"So what do we do?" Jared asks as he takes the bible from me and looks for himself. "We had the insurance company out here, what, two years ago, Em? They said they took care of it."

"They cleaned it with bleach," Leo smiles, and Jared nods. "And they painted over it with an anti-microbial paint."

"That's right," Jared says.

Leo shakes his head. "Useless. All the bleach does is kill living spores. The dead ones are just as dangerous. And that paint's a joke too. All it does is cover it. The mold keeps growing underneath until it grows right through. I'm telling you, get rid of this mold and I bet you'll feel a lot better."

"Get rid of it how?"

"Well, first you've got to figure out where the moisture's coming from and fix that. Then, I'm not sure. There are companies that specialize in this stuff. They'll know what to do."

Emily laughs unhappily. "What's the point? They're foreclosing on us anyway. Let them deal with it."

"Let me worry about that," I say. "For now, I think you should listen to Leo. At least find out what it'll cost. You might still be here a while if I can stall them in bankruptcy court."

"The kids," Jared realizes. "Em, we've got to move to a motel, or your sister's."

"Move?"

"At least until we take care of this."

She turns to Leo. "Is that necessary?"

"It's not a bad idea," he answers.

As we drive from the Eagans' home to LaGuardia Airport, I can tell that Leo's mind is racing.

"You've got to help those people, J.J.," he finally says. "They need you."

"I'm trying," I answer as a taxicab cuts me off. I get to my right and exit into the airport.

"What do you think you're going to do?"

"Don't ask me. You're the one going to Harvard; I'm getting disbarred."

"They won't disbar you." He looks out his window. "And they don't teach you how to be a lawyer in law school, everyone knows that." He turns to me. "So I'm asking you—how do you help them?'

"You look for the moving part," I shrug.

"Moving part?"

"It's like sparring," I say as we arrive at the terminal. "When a guy's got both feet planted and his hands up, it's hard to hit him. So you've got to get him moving. If he lifts a leg to kick or block, he's vulnerable. If he punches, that's an opening too. There's always a moving part. Like the bogus fees Eiderhorn's hitting them with— that's a moving part."

"Can you hit him?"

"Not hard." We pull alongside the curb and park. I get out

with him to help him get his bag out of the trunk. "I could use that to reduce their payoff, but it won't save the house."

"How about the mold?"

"How about it?"

"Couldn't you threaten to sue Eiderhorn for it?"

I shake my head. "I could probably sue their insurance company, but their lender? I doubt it. Eiderhorn didn't even make the loan; he just bought it. It's a negligence case, which means you've got to prove a duty to prevent a foreseeable harm. I just don't see it. Plus, you said there's no connection between mold and asthma."

"No *proven* connection," he corrects as I hand him his bag. "There might be one day."

"Well, anyway," I sigh, "safe trip." We hug and I give him a kiss on the temple. "Thanks for coming in."

"Let me know what happens."

He turns and goes into the airport, and I get back into my car. There has to be a moving part, but I still haven't found it.

Chapter forty-four

I'm already seated at our table in the hearing room, my left leg jackhammering from all the coffee, when Ira comes in. "Funny story," he says as he lays his briefcase on the table. The committee isn't here yet, neither are any of my witnesses. Ed said he'd be here even though his testimony is over. My mother too. The only person left to testify is Josie, but still, no one's been able to get in touch with him. "I went to the office this morning to get some work done. Care to tell me why my key card wouldn't work?"

"I had to, Finny," I say. "You know that." I retrieve his card from my pocket and reach up with it.

"Idiot," he mutters as he takes it from me. He sits down beside me and starts to unpack his briefcase. "So what did you find out?"

"It's air-tight," I say. "Title's clean, docs are perfect."

He absorbs the information calmly, as always. "Okay, well, first things first. We'll talk about the Eagans later, after we take care of things here. It's a big day for you."

"I guess."

He continues to empty the briefcase. "You guess?"

"It's been strange, that's all. I sat here Wednesday and yesterday listening to people talk about how much I love law, and I'm realizing that, not only isn't it true—it's never been true."

He turns away from the briefcase, toward me. "Never?" I just shrug. He looks at me for a long moment. "You know," he finally says, "maybe the problem isn't the license but the way we're using it."

"What do you mean?"

"The other night," he leans toward me, "when we were out at the Eagans' house. Weren't you energized? I was energized."

"It felt a lot better than foreclosing on people," I admit.

"Right, so I'm thinking, maybe you and I start our own firm. Take on the clients we want. People who really need us, like the Eagans."

"Our own firm? Finny, we're just a year out of law school—who's going to hire us?"

"The Eagans."

"And you'd give up your cushy, high-paying job for that?"

"It's going to come to a head anyway."

"It is?"

"It's inevitable, J.J. Once the propeller quits, your only choice is to jump or find someone to push you. Someone like a disciplinary committee," he adds.

"Well, it sounds like a nice idea and it probably would've been great, but they're going to disbar me."

"Maybe not."

"But maybe."

He narrows his eyes. "So let me ask you something—you're sleep-deprived; you betrayed your friend; you have no idea what to do for the Eagans; and you think you're about to be disbarred. Why don't you seem upset?"

Despite my best effort, I can't suppress a small smile. "Jen called."

His eyes widen. "When?"

"This morning. I was out taking Leo to the airport, and when I got home there was a message."

"What did she say?"

"That she missed me. That I was right about the other guy."

"Wow—so on again, off again, is on again. You're happy about this, right?"

"I think I'm happy about it."

"God, she's pretty. Have you called her?"

"Not yet—she'd have been gone to work by the time I heard the message anyway."

His cell phone rings. "Maybe that's Steele," he says, and takes the phone to the window for better reception.

After a moment, he holds out his thumb toward me, pointed up. Finally, Josie's on his way. I knew he'd come through. Someone thumps me on the back and I turn to say good morning to Ed. I decide not to tell him about Jennifer's call. My mother comes in and—noticing the committee filing in from the opposite side of the room—breaks into a heel-clopping trot, kisses me quickly and goes with Ed back to the witness bench. As I watch them walk away, I feel vaguely guilty. They're all here fighting for me and I'm losing the will to fight. Ira returns and sits beside me. "Good news," he says.

"That was Josie?"

"No, it was the prosecutor I've been negotiating with on your criminal case. They're going to let you off with community service and a suspended driver's license, as a first-time offender."

"That's great," I say. "Ira, thank you."

"Yeah, but we've still got to convince these guys to let you keep practicing law," he points out. "Damn Josie Steele, if he doesn't show up today, so help me...."

Ira's agitated but I'm not. Maybe it's because the specter of a prison term is gone, and the worst that can happen now is that I can't practice law. I think about my circumstance, and wonder how it all came to this. Somewhere along the way I must have followed the wrong path. Dreams begin with an impulse, some motivating force. And sometimes, the force is not the silver cup itself, but the anticipation of how sweet its nectar will taste.

The entrepreneur who starts his own business—the car dealer or linen-distributor—is he motivated by cars and sheets, or the vision of independence? How many celebrities lay crossways on their beds as children, feet on the wall, dreaming of the perfect note, the perfect characterization, the perfect turn of a phrase? Few, I think. Most of those who did probably aren't even celebrities today. They're unknown artists, living quiet lives, eyes closed and headphones on. Or acting in obscure summer stock productions. Or stuffing short stories away in desk drawers. Because their motivating force *was* the note or phrase. For those who became famous, I suspect, the real dream was the glitter their celebrity would bring. Suddenly the stream forks, and those who forget the initial impulse and instead follow the manifestation, get lost. Dreams are fluid if you remember why you first had them. And fluid dreams aren't impossible, they're inevitable. No bird ever obsessed over a specific worm. When hunger is the motivation, any worm will do.

The door behind me swings open and I turn, expecting to see Josie. Instead, I stare in amazement as Carter Boston enters the room. Just like that, I want to win again. He avoids my eyes, even as I watch his full stride toward the witness bench. My cell phone rings just as the committee is calling the session to order.

"Turn off your cell phone please, Mr. Spencer," Carlysle says.

I hear him but it doesn't register, preoccupied as I am with Boston. He's not here as a witness against me—they don't do that in disciplinary proceedings because they file papers laying out their case—he's just here to watch the kill.

I flip open my cell phone, still staring at Boston, wanting nothing more than to keep my license, if only to crumble it into a ball and push it down his throat.

"Hello?" I ask.

"I asked you to turn off that phone," Carlysle calls.

"J.J.?"

"Terry!" I exult. "It's Terry Steele," I tell Ira, who smiles and pumps his fist. I feel triumphant, and turn to face the committee and Boston as I speak. Carlysle is watching with the laser focus of a child waiting for someone to get the cellophane off a lollipop.

"We've been dying to hear from you. Is Josie on his way?"

"J.J.," she begins again, and I'm struck by the huskiness of her voice. It shakes so badly she can barely speak. I wait, suddenly too frightened to speak. "Could you please come right away? I…" she stammers, "I found Josie," she draws another breath, "locked in the garage this morning...in the Toyota, with the engine...." She breaks. "Oh God, *Chulo*."

"Terry!" I call loudly to get her attention. I don't want to ask the next question. "Is he...?"

I hear someone comforting her on the other end of the line, and from the background sounds I realize she's in a hospital. I call to her again, unsure whether the phone is still next to her ear. "Terry!" All eyes are on me.

"They don't know yet," she finally says. "He's on a respirator."

"He's going to be fine," I say, trying to sound confident. "I'm on my way. Where's Ben?"

"In Boulder with his grandfather. Please come right away, Newton-Wellesley Hospital. I'm so sorry J.J., I don't have anyone else to call, I wanted to call my folks, but I—"

"I'll be right there," I say, and I'm already scrambling to my feet, sending my chair clattering across the floor behind me.

"Oh *Chulo*," I hear her say softly to herself as I hang up, "why didn't you just tell me?"

The first face I see is Ed's. He's already left the witness bench and is on his way toward me.

"She found Josie in the garage with the car engine running," I tell Ira. "I've got to go."

"My car's parked nearby," Ed says as he reaches me. "I'll drive you to Boston."

"No thanks, I'm going to fly, but can you get me to the airport? I'll call Amy and see if she can pick me up at Logan."

"What's going on?" Carlysle is demanding, but I haven't got the time to answer him. Ira will explain. "Mr. Spencer, if you leave now, don't expect..." I hear him say, but Ed and I are out the door before he finishes the sentence.

Chapter forty-five

The clouds have rolled in over the course of the morning and enveloped the entire Northeast. But despite the cloud cover, it's a hot, humid day in Boston. My dress shirt sticks to my back as Amy races along Washington Street. She veers sharply into the hospital's circular driveway and pulls to an abrupt halt at the entrance. I scramble out and she does the same. I start for the front door but she grabs me by the sleeve. When I turn, she hands me my jacket, my necktie balled up but hanging partially out of one of the pockets.

"You going to park and meet me upstairs?" I ask.

"No," she says, handing me her car keys. "I'm going home. Terry's not going to want strangers around. Here's the keys. Just give me a call later whenever you can."

"You sure?"

"Just go," she says. "Give the keys to that guy over there," she points to a man in a yellow windbreaker. "They've got valet parking."

I stop to hug her, and she briefly allows it. But before I'm ready to let her go, I feel her hands on my chest, pushing me off. "Hurry," she says. I hand off the keys to the valet and sprint for the hospital.

Inside, someone points me toward the Emergency Room. I've got my jacket clenched in my fist and can feel a breeze up my untucked shirt tail as I run through the antiseptic halls. By the time I find the E.R. waiting room, I'm winded and coated in a chilly sweat. I push open one of two swinging doors. The air in here is as thick as it is outside, and everybody sits in sweat-soaked shirts, wearing looks ranging from hysteria to resignation to anger. As I run a sticky hand through my hair, I scan the room for Terry. I spot her in the far corner, behind two women trying to comfort an old man. I move past the man, who sits leaning forward with his hands clasped behind his head, repeating no, no, no. Terry sits in a quiet daze, strands of her soft auburn hair dangling over her eyes. I kneel down in front of her, and from here I can see that her eyes are red and swollen. She looks so frightened that seeing her tightens my throat.

"Terry?"

Her eyes raise and focus on me. They fill in an instant and she falls forward, wrapping her arms around my neck. On my knees in front of her, I feel her body shudder. Her hair sticks to my face and I squeeze my arms tight around her. I cup the back of her head in my hand and for a long while, we don't move. I feel her pregnant belly against me, and try to angle myself so as not to press on it.

"Ms. Steele?" a voice above us asks, and we separate from each other to look up. A young, prematurely balding man in powder blue scrubs stands above us. What's left of his hair is stark orange, and his forehead is huge. "Doctor Caruso will be out in a while to talk to you, but he asked me to come and let you know that everything is going well so far. Your husband seems to be responding to the medication— the blood sample we drew showed a good, strong oxygen level—so we've taken him off the respirator. That's very good news."

"Can I see him?"

"He's not conscious yet."

"I don't care," she insists. "I just want to see him. Please, I'm so scared."

"Let her see him," I echo. "Just for a minute?"

"Okay," he nods, "come with me."

We leave the waiting room, bypass the E.R. and head down a

hallway of individual rooms. As we follow the resident through the halls, I'm searching for any reason to be optimistic. "That's a good sign," I say to Terry as we walk, "they've got him out of the E.R." She doesn't seem convinced. When we reach Josie's room, someone intercepts the resident.

"He's right in there," he tells us, pointing to a room before stopping to talk to the doctor who spoke to him. I hold the door for Terry and she begins to enter but stops and stands aside as a nurse exits. The nurse stops me when I try to follow Terry in. "Just the wife," she whispers.

Terry turns back to me, brushes her hair back and reaches up to kiss me on the cheek. "Thank you for being here," she says, then disappears into the room. I lean against the wall, watching a clock above the nurse's station. According to the clock, she's only been gone five minutes—it seems longer. Finally, she emerges from the room, looks at me and sighs heavily. I flex my shoulder blades to push myself off the wall.

"How is he?"

"Sleeping," she says, taking my place on the wall, then adds with a trace of anger, "not a care in the world." She takes a closer look at me and she caresses my arm. "Don't mind me; I'm in a state."

"Did they tell you anything?"

"They say he'll live, but it's too early to know if he did himself any permanent harm, you know, mentally. No, no," she says, brushing my cheek, "don't do that. He'll be fine."

We walk the halls slowly, toward another waiting room. That's where they'll know to find us with any news. Reports filter in throughout the next couple of hours, each one progressively better than the last. We sit beside each other on an orange vinyl couch, the position of which I rearrange to face the window. I recline on the couch and put my feet on the window sill, staring outside as the grey-blue Boston drizzle becomes a steady rain. Still no Doctor Caruso, but the resident—Fox, I think he said—comes in again and says he's continuing to stabilize. "Who?" Terry asks with a faint smile, and we all laugh wearily. All situations find equilibrium, and besides, he's continuing to stabilize. We buy newspapers and pretend to read. To my left, a chunky little girl inverts a pack of M&Ms over her open mouth, trying to pour in the entire contents. It reminds me that I haven't eaten today. When Fox returns, Terry and I are beside a candy machine gathering change for a snack. Smiling, he gives us the news we've been waiting for—Josie has regained consciousness. Exhausted and relieved, we collapse into each other's arms. I even reach over and pull Fox into the scrum.

"I can see him again?" Terry asks, rhetorically now.

"Sure," he answers. "He's still very groggy, but he did ask for you."

"How about me?"

"Soon, I promise."

Terry's gone for longer this time, but looks much better when she returns. "Come on," she says, "coffee's on me. It's going to be a long night."

I pepper her with questions as we take the elevator down to the hospital cafeteria. "What did he say? Was his speech alright?"

"He didn't say much," she answers. "Apologized a lot, then kind of passed out again."

"But he's okay, right?" I persist. She seems encouraged now that she's seen him, and I want some of that for myself. "I mean, it'll take time, but he's going to be fine."

"They said it could be weeks until we know for sure," she answers, watching the numbers over the elevator door light up as we descend, then realizes that I'm waiting for more, and adds, "but they're optimistic."

When the doors open, several people are waiting to get on. They stand aside when they see Terry's distended belly.

"By the way," I motion toward her stomach, "I didn't want to bring it up before, but you look great. Are you feeling well?"

"Carrying through the summer's a drag, but all in all, it's a good pregnancy."

In the cafeteria, we buy blueberry muffins, french fries and an apple that, were we in a grocery store, we'd have scorned. I pour myself a cup of coffee and hold an empty cup toward Terry.

"Decaf?" I ask.

"Not today," she smiles wanly.

We pay, then settle into a small round table in the corner of the cafeteria. I offer her cream and sugar for her coffee but she declines both. Around us, tables are filled with doctors, nurses, candy-stripers. There are also other visitors—you can tell by their expressions how sick their loved one is.

"How are you doing?" she suddenly asks.

"Me? I'm okay. Tired."

"I mean, the hearings and all."

"Oh, that." My face rests in the palm of my right hand. I watch the line at the cash register. "I guess I let things get a little out of control."

"Just a little," she smiles. "But he's proud of you, you know."

I have to laugh.

"It's true," she says. I can't bring myself to look at her. "J.J.," she reaches across the table and shakes my forearm, "get yourself straightened out. Don't wait until you end up in a garage."

"He should've told you he was unhappy."

She releases my arm and leans back. "Maybe this *was* his way of telling me."

"What do you mean?"

"Aw, he knows when I leave the house for work. He could've got into that car hours earlier if it was what he really wanted."

"You're just angry, Terry," I say. "You know he's not like that."

"I'm not saying he thought about it. But if deep down he really wanted to do this…," her voice breaks, betraying her outward calm. She swallows and continues. "I mean, honestly, when's the last time you remember him failing at anything he wanted to do?" She looks directly at me, her eyes moist. She attempts a fatalistic shrug, and smiles a tense, thin line.

"He still should've told you. He owes you that much."

"I knew," she drops her gaze into her coffee. "It's just, I try so hard not to be a Donahue. I grew up in a family where everyone just loved to tell everyone else how to live. And everyone was just so perfect 'til you got to know them and see how miserable they all were. Perfect dads who never made it to a dance recital lecturing other dads about priorities; cheating tennis wives telling daughters to pray before bed." She takes a french fry and turns it over for a moment before putting it back on the tray. "I just swore I would never do that to anyone else, especially not Josie."

"You just did it to me."

"I'm not telling you how to straighten yourself out, just to do it." I say nothing, and she smiles. "Alright, I guess it's the same thing. Maybe I'm a Donahue after all."

I smile too. "And I'm a Spencer. Damn Prince Spencer, never allowed to fail, never allowed to doubt."

"Too many people counting on you to succeed."

"Or fail."

Her brow furrows. "Who's counting on you to fail?"

"Oh, no one really," I say, then admit: "My father."

"I thought you don't speak."

"Doesn't mean I don't hear him."

"Ah, the voices—I get those. They're awful, aren't they? Cause that's when you know they've got you. When they don't even have to be around to make you feel bad."

We nod at each other, then share a laugh. "So what now?" I ask.

"Well, they said they'd give me the names of some therapists; I guess that's a good place to start. Past that," she sighs, "damned if I know."

At the far end of the room, I see Fox standing in the doorway scanning the cafeteria. I stand and catch his attention, in case it's us he's looking for. He nods when he sees me, and walks purposefully in our direction. For an instant, a chill surges through my chest and arms. For reasons I can't explain, I'm sure he's come to tell us that Josie is dead.

"He's up," Fox calls to Terry before he even reaches our table, and I exhale. "He'd like to see you again."

"How about me?" I ask.

"If it were up to me," he shakes his head. "He's just not ready to face anyone yet."

"Why don't you go take a drive, clear your head," Terry says to me as she stands to go. "I'll give you a call later."

"It's okay, I'll wait," I say.

"No, don't," she says. "I'm going to stay with him a while."

She embraces me, then steps back and takes my hand. She begins to speak, but reconsiders. To thank me again for coming, in a way, would be depreciative. Etiquette can cheapen a friendship. She reaches up and touches my face with her hand, nods just a bit, then takes a deep breath and follows Fox out of the cafeteria. I sit back down for a while before leaving. I eat part of a blueberry muffin. I was sure he was dead.

Chapter forty-six

I've been driving through the pouring rain, no destination in mind, for an hour now. The drizzle has become a downpour. My eyes are heavy and I can feel my breathing as I stare straight ahead, focused on nothing. I leave the radio off. It only gets AM anyway. He's been dead and gone many times in my mind today, and I still don't know to what extent he'll recover. Brain cells don't regenerate. It frightens me, and infuriates me. I notice that the windshield wiper is moving more slowly than my heart, so I set it at high speed.

Every random turn I now make turns back on me. I pass a mailbox outside McDonald's and see me and Jen dropping the book of gift certificates into it. A ways down the street, the T stops near Brookline and lets me out to go study Con Law with Josie the night before my first-year exam. The wind is sweeping the rain now, and I slow down to let a jogger pass who has evidently taken the case for good health full circle. Near Kenmore Square, I see myself seated on the curb, my head down, my crutches lying in the middle of Comm Ave. Through the I.H.O.P. window, Jen and I laugh as we choose names for our children. The sun is setting, or is that the rain? Eventually, I find myself at the *dojo*, always the *dojo*. Where Josie and I first became friends. In school, I'd met Josiah Steele, the Advocate's Devil. But in the *dojo* I met Josie. With the car's engine still running, I rifle through my suit jacket and find my keys. The key to the *dojo*, which Zachary gave me the day I left Boston, is still there. I switch off the ignition, look at the key for a moment, turn it over in my palm. I dash through the rain to the front door, go in and take the stairs two at a time. After bowing at the threshold, I find the linen closet and pull out a *gi*.

Stretching feels so good, so calming and dry. It reminds me of the night Josie and I rushed in through the pouring rain. It makes me want to call him and tell him to come down here and meet me. We could spar. He seems closer than he is. Who knows what's left of him now? Maybe bits of him made it over the wall and are now scattered across the dry dust.

I close my eyes and breathe. The musty smell of the old floor is a refreshing change from the swelter of the hospital. Vibrations from my brief jog around the room cause the heavy bag to rock slightly, and the squeak of the chain catches my attention. I walk slowly toward it. A quick counterclockwise spin and I lash a strong back kick into it at head level. I catch the bag on its return and set it still. Beginning to warm up, I throw slow crescent kicks with my right leg. Knee, midsection, head. Knee, midsection, head. Now the left leg. Knee, midsection, head. Knee, midsection, head.

"Passion alone is never a trap," I mutter with disdain. "What do you know?" Knee, midsection, head. Knee, midsection, head. "Who gave you the right to do this?" I sneer as I follow up three right-handed jabs with a left cross and right uppercut. Knee, midsection, head. "How dare you? What if Terry left late today?" Knee, midsection, head, head. "Why can't you just laugh at things every now and then?" Knee, midsection, head, head, head. "Did you even try to compromise some of your damn ideals? Did you ever think of your wife and child, you selfish son-of a-bitch?!" Spinning right back kick explodes into a vicious left elbow and then several more. My voice bounces off the walls. "Did you think about me?!" The heavy bag is harder to see now, like the road through the windshield of Amy's car. "I looked up to you—we all did! Where do we look now? Where do we look now? What do I believe in now?" I slam wild, ragged punches and kicks into the bag. Sweat flies from my hair and sprays the bag. I feel my wrist sprain forward but don't care. "Did you try everything?" I demand. "Every goddamn thing? What's left now, huh? What's left?! What's left?!" I leap with a cleansing, guttural shout and hitch in the air for a roundhouse kick. I land slightly off balance and lurch forward, grabbing the bag for balance. I pull my legs back beneath me and hang on to the bag with my right arm, gasping for air. Two more harmless lefts to the midsection, then silence but for my breath.

I close my eyes and try to steady my head. What if he never recovers? What would become of Terry and Ben? The baby would never know its father. What if she'd been late leaving for work? Who would've told Ben? He wouldn't have reacted at first; some news is too big to hear. But when whoever was delivering the news of his father's death held their adult stare on him, or tried to embrace him or explain the unexplainable, his eyes—his father's eyes—would've filled, his lips would've drooped. He might've screamed but probably not—he has a lot of his father within. He'd have cried, that's for sure. He'd have cried for a long time. He'd have asked questions no one could answer; he'd have blamed himself; he'd have felt guilty, angry, betrayed, alone and scared. Worst of all, he'd have grown up far too soon.

"I just heard," a deep voice says from the front door. "I'm sorry." It's Sensei Zachary. I want to say something but no words come. He walks toward me, gently takes me by the arm. "Let's walk, J.J."

I'm not in the mood for a lecture, but he's always had a hold over me. He releases my arm and starts walking across the floor, knowing I'll follow. Side by side, we walk from one end of the room to the other. I keep my eyes forward. Neither of us says anything at first.

"You're a lot like him, you know," he finally says.

"Thank you."

"A man who should have the world at his feet," he continues without pause, "but for some reason chooses to carry it on his shoulders." I realize that I've taken a compliment where none was intended. "Why do you think he's like that?"

"He had to get over the wall," I say as we reach the far end of the room, turn and head back the other way.

"The wall?"

"A story he told me once," I explain, "about a monk who smelled soup cooking on the other side of the monastery wall and went over to get some."

"It's a good soup," Zachary nods and smiles softly. "Personally, I could do without the gall bladder."

I look up at him as we pass the heavy bags. "You've had it?"

"Yeah," he says, "I've had it." We pass the front door to the *dojo* on our right. I absently reach out and touch the wall that runs perpendicular to it before we turn and head back the other way. "So what's it like in there with Josie gone?"

"Lonely."

"I'll bet," he says. "When are you going over?"

"Never."

"You're going to die in there if you stay."

"At least I'll get to live a while first."

He shakes his head. "You won't have lived at all. If you've smelled the soup, it's already too late to stay."

I stop walking and turn to face him. "So what am I supposed to do, sensei?" I say. It's not a question; it's a challenge. We're near the far wall. Down by the other end, people have started to file into the *dojo* for class, chattering at first, but turning silent when they see us. One begins to approach but sensei raises his hand and the man stops and returns to the group. Some disperse to the locker room to change, others remain, watching us. Still more enter. "Seriously, tell me, what am I supposed to do? Follow Josie? Why, because it worked out so well for him?"

"At least he's out."

"He's half dead!" I shout. "He's not out of anything. There's nothing romantic about it. His wife was almost a widow, his son..." My throat seizes up and I have to stop speaking. I walk away from him and go over to the wall, turn and lean back against it. Zachary comes over and leans on the wall beside me, saying nothing. I close my eyes and lift my face toward the ceiling, trying to catch my breath. "Damn," I exhale. I hear people gathering at the other end of the room, by the heavy bags and front door. I don't want to look down from the ceiling.

"You're missing the point," he finally says. "Climbing walls is dangerous, yes. But he had to use the wall, you don't. You can still use the door—it hasn't shut behind you yet."

"No more metaphors, sensei," I look at him, "please? Just tell me in English—what am I supposed to do now?"

"I can't answer that," he says. "You've got to hear your own, clear voice—that's the only way you're going to figure it out. If Josie could've heard his, he would've lived a different life. Look at me—you have to hear your voice."

"I can hear my voice."

"You haven't heard your voice in years."

"Then whose do I hear?"

"I don't know," he says. He notices the group of students standing on the opposite side of the room. "Let's find out."

He walks to where the others stand. I push off the wall and follow.

"Close your eyes," he tells me when we're near them.

My balance wavers with my eyes closed, but his hand on my triceps steadies me. After a moment, he tells me to open them again, and when I do, I see a man kneeling in front of me, several feet away. He has a round face and straight black hair. He's Asian. It takes me a moment to place him, but then I remember his name as Larry something. He started working out here just a few weeks before I moved away. Kneeling in front of me, he stares straight ahead, not acknowledging me. "This figure prostrated before you," says Zachary, "try to imagine it as the single strongest voice that lives in your head. The one you hear most often, above all the others. Look at it and tell me, what does it say?"

I look at Zachary instead. "You've got to be kidding."

"That's what Josie said when I tried to do this with him last week," he says.

"Do it, J.J.," Manny adds from a few feet away.

I nod, and Zachary says, "Good. Now, look at the figure. Don't see it as a man, try to see it as a voice. Tell me what it says."

At first, there's just silence. My strongest voice is a vacuum. I concentrate harder, trying to hear my innermost driving force. I begin to hear them—there are many, everyone talking at once—but they slowly fade away, leaving just one. Then I hear myself murmur: "What are you waiting for, a round of applause?" My single strongest voice, and it's not even my own. I stand frozen, exposed. I don't want to look at anyone.

"Close your eyes," Zachary says and I do, grateful to be alone. "Concentrate—see that voice. See it in green neon, spelled out in the darkness of your closed eyes. Listen to it closely. Let it echo. *What are you waiting for, a round of applause?*"

I feel my body waver again but keep my feet. I adore my mother; I don't want to blame her for my failings. She meant nothing by it. It's just an expression. It's not her fault I heard more than she said.

"Open your eyes," I hear Zachary say, "and tell me what's the next voice you see."

Beside the Asian man is a teenage girl, her floral skirt splayed about her on the applewood floor. Thunder rumbles outside the window. I feel the perspiration on my brow. My hands lift, against what I don't know. But everyone is awaiting an answer and I can't avoid it.

"What do you see?" Zachary repeats, his voice close by.

The words now ringing in my head sicken me. It shouldn't be. Not after all this time.

"Why was I cursed with this family of losers?" is what I hear myself say.

I want to explain that that's not my mother's voice, that she would never say such a thing, but Zachary is already telling me to close my eyes again. "See it pure," he says, and I do. I see it all. I see my father reeling about the kitchen, bottle in hand, whiskey slopping up the inside as he gestures to the three of us in the doorway between the kitchen and living room. He'd moved out weeks before and why he's back, I can't imagine. I have Leo pinned behind me with one arm, and though my mother stands in front of me, I have my left leg crossed in front of her. Get out, she's shrieking at him. I already called Dairian. Get out. It's a plea and a threat at once, but he doesn't seem to hear. "Why was I cursed with this family of losers?" he's shouting toward the ceiling. "White trash, low rent, go nowhere losers, sucking me down with you. No more, I got better now—a nice family." He turns on her and screams, "Nice family! Not some been nowhere, going nowhere," he fires the bottle at the wall and it shatters, "Brooklyn trash!"

"My boys ain't trash," my mother screams, and the sight of shattering glass sends her flying toward him, tripping momentarily over my leg, but scrambling to her feet and swinging a metal teapot by the handle. She rears it back and smacks him with it full force. "My boys ain't trash! My boys'll do more than you ever did! Get out! Get out!"

"Open your eyes," Zachary says, and I do, but I can barely see anything. I'm still in the night as Zachary repeatedly shouts, "What do you see?"

My father's hand goes to his head when the teapot strikes him, then he wheels and throws a wild roundhouse punch. He hits her, not with his fist but his forearm. I feel Leo start to push past my arm, but I shove him back into the living room and grab a broom that had been leaning in the corner. I hit my father as hard as I can.

"What do you see?"

"Nothing."

"What do you see?!"

"Nothing!"

The impact of the broomstick against my father's two-hundred-pound frame knocks me off balance and suddenly I'm spun around and he's got me pinned to the wall, his forearm under my throat, jammed so hard into me I can barely breathe. His face is close to mine, sweaty and disoriented. His eyes are insane. I can see the saliva between his teeth and smell the whiskey on his breath. There's a commotion behind him but he ignores it as he snarls at me.

"What do you see?!"

I'm breathing too hard to see anything, to hear anything. You can't goddamn see voices anyway. I'm not trash, neither is my brother, neither is my mother. "Nothing!"

"You," my father growls, as he drives his forearm farther into my throat so hard it makes me gag. "I wish you were never born."

"I wish you were never born," I say aloud.

No sooner were the words out of his mouth when two dark hands slammed down onto his shoulders and tore him off me. I sank to the floor, pulled my knees to my chest and watched as Dairian choked the night back to silence, leaving me forever unaware of what would've happened next.

"No, don't close your eyes," Zachary commands. "Don't close your eyes. Look at them, look at them. Here they are. These are your voices. These are what've been running your life. Look at them, kneeling in front of you. Say something to them, J.J."

But I can do nothing of the sort. I can barely even see them, just three stumps somewhere in front of me. I try to take a step backward and stumble, and with uncanny speed Zachary is behind me, holding me up.

"Don't you retreat now. You're already here, you're right here. Don't speak to them if you can't—speak to me. What do you want to say to the voices? How about the young one?" he asks, pointing to the girl. They come into focus, but they're too terrifying to address directly. "Come on, tell me. How about that one?" he points to the Asian man.

I can't speak. I feel a shivering chill and try again to back away, feeling my legs stronger beneath me now. My head is shaking. I try to turn my shoulders and run.

"Speak up for yourself," Zachary insists.

He throws his full weight behind me but I'm getting the better of him. "Someone help me!" he shouts, wrapping his arms around my waist. "I can't hold him! Someone get over here! Talk to them, J.J. Talk to them."

From the side, someone springs forward and now I feel two people restraining me. Another comes and I try to sink to the floor but they won't let me.

"Tell them, man!" I hear someone shout from the side, and some dam breaks in the group. Everyone is suddenly shouting at me, imploring me to say something. I flail and twist, trying to break free, but they've got me so wrapped up I can't get away.

"Stand up for yourself," someone yells.

"Tell them you don't care what they think," exhorts another.

"Tell them it's your life!"

Then I remember. It starts as a whisper, a memory from later that same night. Dairian is seated at the foot of my bed, a bloody washcloth pressed to his head. I'm under my blanket and Leo is on my bed, legs crossed. The hallway light reflects off Dairian's head as he says: "You can spend the rest of your life trying to get even with a memory, or you can just tell him to fuck off."

I'm still trying to change that night, I realize. To win a fight from sixteen years ago. To choke the air out of a man whose heart suffocated in a bottle long ago, and gain the approval of a woman— any woman—as long as I can be absolutely sure that she doesn't have it to give.

I feel my lips start to move, and a sound, imperceptible at first, comes from me. I'm just muttering, but I force my gaze to remain on the three voices, who sit still before me.

"Fuck off," I mumble. I feel the arms still restraining me but they needn't—I no longer want to run.

"Yeah!" someone shouts.

"Yes!" Zachary echoes. "Tell them again!"

"Fuck off," I repeat, stronger this time, as the crowd shouts approval. "Fuck off," I say more loudly, and my right arm breaks away from the hands restraining it. I raise my fist and shake it at the voices. The hysteria overtaking me feels perfect. "Fuck off! Fuck off!" My voice ricochets off the concrete walls, a hysterical piercing scream. The group cheers.

Someone steps in front of me and starts pushing me backward, as I strain to get at the voices. Screaming wildly, I'm senseless and primal. I have no idea of how long I've been screaming, but my throat begins to hurt. I stop screaming and stand wide-eyed, panting. I'm sweating profusely. When my breathing subsides, I feel Zachary's hand on the back of my neck. I grasp it, then let it go.

Chapter forty-seven

I'm seated beside Amy as she drives us to Harvard. Zachary had invited me to stay and work out, but I thanked him and declined. There's something else I need to do. Just a few miles away, Leo is starting law school. How can that be? What is my little brother—with his lighthearted style, irresistible charm and inexplicable fascination with carpet beetles, diatomaceous earth and multicellular fungi (mold, to morons like me)—doing in law school? And how will he try to escape when his time comes?

Too frightened to scale the wall on my own, I'd once tried to manipulate Josie into tossing me over during my first year of law school. When he refused, I sent prank mail to one of the most prestigious law firms in New York. Still, no one stepped forward with a toe-hold. So I grew increasingly desperate—smart-mouthing interviewers, betraying clients, bringing drugs to work. Each step less subtle, until I started attacking the very law I'd sworn just a year before to uphold. But even after brawling in the street and driving drunk, I couldn't get anyone to help me over the wall, because I'd made another mistake—I'd hired myself one hell of a lawyer.

What would have been my next step, had Josie not disrupted

my carefully orchestrated plan with his own? An unattended garage?

And I was lucky. As hard as I'd tried to escape, I always had enough fear of the fall to keep me alive. But Leo knows no fear, never has. What would his escape look like? Ed Coleman's unapologetic exit, or the unattended garage?

How many others of us are out there, quietly toiling, denying the storm ever rising in our chests? Especially the lifelong students among us, who so often choose our careers because the lack of structure in the post-graduate world is too terrifying to face. Maybe that's why there are so many unhappy lawyers. All of us, lost in tributaries and too damn worn out by fourteen-hour days to turn and head back upstream. Are we really the industry of misanthropes we're portrayed to be, or are we just unhappy?

Who else? Who else? Who lives a life he never chose, worships a truth he's never seen, loves a lifestyle more than the person sharing it, dies silently and piecemeal, day by day, week by week, month by month, year by year?

Not my little brother. I won't let it happen. But I knew persuading him could be hard, so I drove to Amy's apartment and asked if she'd come with me, knowing she would. It's always been so painless with Amy. As we drive, I tell her about Josie and about what happened in the *dojo*. I stare out my window at the streetlights. Amy drives slowly now, nothing like the mad rush to the hospital earlier in the day. The streetlights give off an ochre glow, within which I can still see the remains of today's rain. It's just a mist now though, vaporous raindrops barely thicker than a fog.

We park the car and walk to the Harvard law library. Leo didn't answer his cellphone, so I figure that's a good place to find him. It's an enormous building, and we go from floor to floor, searching. Finally, we spot him. He's seated at an eighteen-foot-long table beneath a crystal chandelier, his back to us and his head cast down at a 45-degree angle, staring at a thick book that I'm sure is lousy with Latin phrases. Two other students sit opposite him, staring at computer screens. Leo's plugged in too. We never had anything like this at B.U.

"Time to go," I say to him, standing at his right shoulder as Amy stands at his left.

"J.J.!" he looks up and smiles. His eyes shift to Amy, then back to me. His smile fades. I hate when I do that to him. "What are you doing here? How did it go today? They didn't—"

"Come on," I repeat, "time to go."

"Shh," someone says.

"Is it Mom? Is she okay?"

"She's fine, it's nothing like that. Come on."

"Okay, let's get a cup of coffee," he says.

"No cups of coffee. We're getting you out of here for good."

He looks back to Amy, who offers only a shrug and a smile.

"What are you talking about? Did they disbar you?"

"Shh!"

"Josie tried to kill himself," I hear myself say, and while there's a logical nexus there for me, I realize it can't make much sense to him.

"What?" he asks as he pushes back his chair and stands up. He reaches out for me and before I know why, I've got him in a bear hug and I'm dragging him toward the front door of the reading room.

"My stuff," he exclaims.

"You don't need it."

"Hey, what are you—" the woman across the table begins to say.

"He quits," I call to her.

I manage to wrestle him out of the reading room and into an empty lounge area. In front of a window overlooking an athletic field, he stomps on my foot. "Get off me," he shouts, pulling free as I recoil from the pain in my foot. "What's the matter with you? What's the matter with him?" he asks Amy.

"Dad, just talk to him," Amy says to me, putting herself between us. "Just talk."

I'm not exactly sure what to say. I turn my back to them and limp toward the other side of the room, then back. Amy hasn't moved. In her eyes, I find the words I need.

"Leo," I say past her, "please don't make the mistake I did. I went to law school for all the wrong reasons and I think you might be doing the same thing." He doesn't say anything, just looks from me to Amy and back again. "It's okay," I persist. "I understand. We had a rotten childhood, but we've got to let that go, both of us. It doesn't matter what anyone else wants, we've got to live our own lives."

"Um, Amy," he begins, "it's Amy, right?" She nods. "Could you possibly score me some of whatever you've got him on?"

"Josie tried to kill himself," I repeat, as though this has some secondary meaning to him too.

"I'm so sorry, J.J.," he says, and Amy stands aside as he embraces me. "I know how close you were."

"You have no idea how close I was," I say. I put my hands on his biceps and hold him at arms length. "So you understand why I'm here?"

"I really don't," he confesses.

"Why are you in law school, Leo?" Amy interjects. "I think that's what J.J.'s worried about."

"Why I'm in law school?"

I cross my arms over my chest and wait for his admission of guilt.

"Well," he shrugs, speaking more to her than to me, "in college I got into microbiology. You know, bioeffluents, mycotoxins." She nods. "I first thought about getting a PhD but I didn't really want to research or teach. So I decided to get my law degree so that I could represent people who've gotten sick because of indoor molds and other environmental factors. I met with a lawyer in Atlanta who specializes in it and he said the field was just beginning to evolve, and that lawyers like me that already have a background in science will be in huge demand."

Amy turns to me while Leo is still talking. She crosses her arms over her chest and waits, then draws a deep breath for dramatic effect. On her face is the hint of a smirk. I'd feel like an utter fool if I weren't so relieved. I'm proud of Leo for the thoughtful way he's gone about this.

"By the way," he continues, "you were right—you can't sue the lender. They can foreclose on the Eagans if they want."

I step forward and hug him, then throw him over my shoulder and carry him back to his books. I set him down and smooth out his shirt.

"Wrong guy," I whisper to the woman across the table.

Chapter forty-eight

I t's gotten pretty late, and though I might be able to catch a flight back to New York, I'm in no rush. I still have a lot to do up here. I spoke with Terry a little while ago and she said Josie was doing well, sleeping a lot. I told her I'd come by the hospital tomorrow. Amy and I go back to her apartment.

"When's the last time you ate?" she asks as we come through the door. Linky, her yellow lab, greets us with a tennis ball in her mouth and tail wagging. Amy pets her head but doesn't engage her past that.

"I had a muffin at the hospital," I say.

"Have a seat, I'll get us something."

I sit on the sofa while she goes into the kitchen. It's been the most draining day of my life but I'm still too wound up to sleep. It's hard to believe today's the same day I started at the Eagans' house with Leo. I feel like a week has passed. Amy brings some pear juice, hummus and bread, and sits beside me.

"Where are you?" she asks, noticing my faraway stare.

"Oh, sorry," I say. "I was just thinking of something Zachary said tonight. Just before he went to teach the class and I came to

347

meet you, I asked him what made him think my voice would be any smarter than the others I'd been listening to."

"Uh huh." She pours us each a glass of juice.

"He said you don't follow your voice because it's right; you follow it because it's yours. That it won't necessarily lead to the things you want today, but in time it'll—how did he put it?—it'll create an expression of yourself that's your best self, the highest potential self you can be. And that changes everything: the work you do, how you live, who you love. And the things my lower expression wants today will be of no use to my higher expression. What do you think of that?"

She chews on a piece of bread and thinks for a moment, then swallows and says: "Not to be cute, but I think his point is that it doesn't matter what I think."

"Okay," I smile. "I'm just saying, it makes me wonder about cause and effect."

"Cause and effect?"

"Jennifer called this morning."

Her chewing slows, but other than that, she doesn't react. "How is she?" she asks casually.

"I didn't speak to her. She left a message. She wants to get back together."

"And you're wondering whether she's the cause of your lower expression, or just one of the effects of living in it." I nod. "What do you think?" she asks.

"Maybe a little of both. I can't blame it all on her; hell, I was no better off when we met. But maybe someone else would've dragged me higher by now."

I look at her and her blue eyes are staring at me from above the glass of juice she holds to her lips. I wait, and she lowers the glass.

"Does it matter?" she asks.

"What do you mean?"

"I mean, you seem to be thinking more clearly now than you have in all the years I've known you. So when you listen to this new voice in your head, does it still want Jen?"

"Good question," I chuckle. "I'm not sure. I've wanted her for so long it's kind of hard to hit the brakes."

We talk a while longer, then fall asleep in each other's arms, fully clothed on the sofa. It's the deepest sleep of my life, and I don't wake until near noon. On Saturday we visit the hospital and bring Terry clean clothing. Josie sleeps the entire time we're there. Terry says his condition has stabilized, but that they're facing a long rehabilitation, both physically and emotionally. Ben is coming home today from Colorado, so Amy and I pick him up from the airport and stay with him until Terry gets home. She hasn't decided yet what she's going to tell him. On Sunday afternoon, Amy drives me to the airport.

"Thanks for everything, Ame," I say as we stand beside her car, the engine running.

She reaches up and wraps her arms around my neck. "Let me know how everything turns out," she says as we hug. "I love you."

"I love you too," I say.

We've said that to each other a hundred times, but for some reason, this time it strikes us as funny. We pull our heads back, consider each other's startled expressions, and laugh. Her hands rest on my waist.

"I…" is the most eloquent thing I can come up with, my face blushing.

"Yeah," she agrees, straightening her arms. "It's been an emotional couple of days. Go, you big dummy. Catch your plane."

I kiss her goodbye, then pause, then kiss her goodbye again, and it's less funny now.

As I'm sitting and waiting to board my flight back to New York, my thoughts of Amy are interrupted by something Leo had said: They can foreclose on the Eagans *if they want*. I mull that over, and it sparks a series of legal chain reactions.

If they want, I repeat to myself, and smile.

I've just found the moving part.

Chapter forty-nine

Carter Boston's secretary leads the Eagans and me through the hallways of Greer, Babcock and Drew toward Conference Room IV. It hasn't been that long since I called this place home, but it feels like another life. Attorneys, paralegals and receptionists regard me with either disinterest or pity as we pass, and objectively, I suppose they're right. But I know something they don't—the strategy I've devised to save the Eagans' home is going to work. And so as I make my way past former colleagues, I feel like the high school gymnasium whipping boy made good, striding into the reunion party.

This morning, following my instructions, the Eagans called Carter Boston and said they were ready to settle their foreclosure suit. Because he faces the prospect of getting held up for a long time in bankruptcy court, Boston agreed to meet. He doesn't know that I'm coming.

The door to the conference room is closed when we arrive. Boston's secretary opens it and holds it for us as we enter. Boston is leaning over the shoulder of Heather Sherwin, looking down and pointing at something in her ledger. Two first-year associates sit silently on the opposite side of the rectangular table. They're the show of force but they look like mannequins to me. The one on the left could even be wearing one of my old suits, except it's not a real suit, just a one-piece replica velcroed around his neck. Seamlessly replaceable, just like me. Ira sits next to them, and meets my eye as I enter. We spoke last night and he knows exactly what I have planned—even helped to fine-tune my pitch—but doesn't want to give anything away. For now, it's best if he pretends to remain loyal to Greer Babcock.

"What's this?" Boston scoffs when he sees me. "Aren't you suspended?"

"Not as far as I know," I say. There's been no final decision yet from the Disciplinary Committee. "Besides, I'm just here in an unofficial capacity."

"He's our family advisor," Jared adds.

"Well, he's not welcome in this meeting," Boston says. He pulls out a chair and sits down. "So if you want to settle this, I suggest you tell him to wait outside."

"There you are," comes a voice from the open conference room door. It's Stan Eiderhorn.

"Stan, what are you doing here?" Heather asks. I'm as surprised as anyone that he's here, but his presence doesn't change my strategy. It might even help.

She and Boston rise to greet him, and the associates do the same. Ira begrudgingly joins them. Eiderhorn is in his late forties, but looks a lot younger. He's fairly short and of diminutive physique, and looks lost in a poorly tailored, designer navy blue suit. He has bright blue eyes and a salesman's smile. He runs marathons and is sure that he could sell us our own thumbs if he were of a mind to.

"Weren't we going to go over progress today?" he asks Heather.

"Oh, my goodness, it completely slipped my mind," she says. She notices his displeased expression. "An unexpected meeting came up on one of your loans."

"One of mine?" he smiles. "You don't mind if I sit in, do you?"

"Of course not," she says. "Emily and Jared Eagan, this is Mr. Eiderhorn." He smiles and shakes Jared's hand, then Emily's. He covers her right hand with his left as he does. She tries to return the smile but doesn't quite succeed.

Then he notices me. He recognizes me, but I can see that his instinct has already told him that something is wrong. For one, I'm standing with the Eagans. He shakes my hand while looking back toward Sherwin and Boston.

"That's Mr. Spencer," Boston says. "He used to work here."

"Used to?"

"He's moved on."

"Then why's he here?"

"He was just leaving," Boston says.

"Mr. Eiderhorn," I say, "I'm advising the Eagans in the foreclosure. We can settle all this today, but only if I stay."

"Then you stay," he says.

I show no satisfaction when Boston nods me in. I don't want this to degenerate into a grudge match. Besides, staying is a small victory. I'm after bigger wins today.

As everyone takes seats, I open my briefcase and remove a series of photographs. I lay them down on the table in front of Eiderhorn, Sherwin and Boston. The first-year's and Ira crane their necks to see.

"These are pictures of the walls in the Eagans' home, the one you're trying to foreclose on." I notice Eiderhorn's brow furrow. Sherwin leans forward and maintains a poker face while she looks from one photograph to the next. Boston barely considers them worthy of his attention, but I notice the pen between his fingers oscillating at hummingbird speed.

"What am I looking at?" Eiderhorn asks.

"It's is a kind of mold called Stachybotrys," I say. "It's also called toxic mold, because it causes chronic fatigue syndrome, pulmonary hemorrhaging, cancer. Actually it causes a lot of things, including asthma, from which Mr. Eagan here suffers." I give this a moment to sink in, then place several more photographs down on the table. "This one is a picture of the upstairs hallway, with the carpeting pulled back. Here's the living room; this one's the master bedroom; and over here's the basement."

Eiderhorn looks to Sherwin and Boston. He's not wise, but he's clever. "What do you say, team?" he asks lightly. "Does this have anything to do with us?"

Boston still hasn't deemed the photos worth more than a cursory glance.

"Not a thing," he says. "First of all, Stan, there's no proven connection between indoor mold and any of the sicknesses Mr. Spencer just listed. Second, if they wanted to sue us for negligence, they'd have to prove that we knew or should've known both about the existence of the mold in the Eagans' home, and that it's toxic. Since they obviously can't do that, they'd have to sue in strict liability, which doesn't stand a chance."

He stares directly into my eyes, and I stare back into his as I address Eiderhorn. "No proven connection," I repeat, nodding. I open a manila folder and toss a stack of stapled paper on the table. "Here's a $32 million verdict from Texas that says different, Mr. Eiderhorn. I'd say Mr. Boston is playing pretty high-stakes poker with your money. Second, as far as foreseeability…" I reach into my briefcase and produce a bible, with a yellow Post-it note marking a page. I slide it across the table to Eiderhorn. "Leviticus 14—take a look. Detailed steps for getting rid of mold." I shrug. "I think a jury could find foreseeability."

Eiderhorn hasn't gone from D.J. to multimillionaire for nothing. He leans back in his chair and smiles at me. "Room full of lawyers, I knew someone was going to get sued sooner or later. How about I sue you for breaching attorney-client confidentiality?"

"They're already taking my license away and I've got no money," I answer immediately. "But I understand Greer Babcock has a big malpractice insurance policy. That's a nice deep pocket. If I were you…"

Eiderhorn laughs and pats my leg. "I like this guy," he says to Boston and Sherwin. "A real warrior. So tell me, counselors, how strong is his case?"

"He's got no case," Boston repeats, and I know that he's right. But I also know that doesn't matter—that's not my end game. "Could he sue? Sure, anyone can sue anyone in America. Could he even get an idiot jury like the Ballard case in Texas? I suppose it's possible. But legally speaking, he's nowhere. And by the way, the Ballard verdict was knocked down to $4 million on appeal."

"Okay, so let's say I don't sue, just for the sake of argument," I begin. I lean forward, my elbows and forearms both flat on the table. My sternum rests on my hands, to keep them from shaking. This was one of Ira's suggestions last night, something he picked up over the course of the last year that he said had worked for him. Everything rides on how well I sell the next few minutes. Maybe years down the line I'll be able to do this kind of thing and stay calm. But the truth is, right now I'm terrified.

"Let's say your foreclosure sails through without a hitch. What then?" I speak directly to Eiderhorn. "Mr. Eiderhorn, the last thing in the world you want is to own this house. Because once you own it, what are you going to do with it? You can't sell it; it's a swamp. Anyone you sell it to could turn around and sue you for latent defects, or a lot more if they get sick. The statute of limitations for children doesn't even begin to run until they turn eighteen, so if the family you sell to has kids, you could be looking at liability twenty years from now. Right now, I agree with Mr. Boston—I don't have a great case. That doesn't mean I wouldn't try it, but I don't know if I'll win. After all, you're just the lender. But once you own it and sell it, then you've got real liability."

· "I'll remediate it," he says.

"If it can even be remediated," I counter. "Look at these pictures," I say, pushing the batch in front of him. "It's a swamp. People all over the country are knocking down homes infested with toxic mold, because the cost of remediation is more than the home is worth."

"So I'll just bleach and paint."

"And that would work until I knock on the door of the new owners and tell them that I'm going to make them rich." Just the slightest bit of air escapes him, but I know this is a turning point. All negotiations reach this point, but it can be hard to recognize. "Look, Mr. Eiderhorn, the Eagans are already in bankruptcy. I can drag out this foreclosure for a couple of years—that takes away from your IRR.

Then take away the cost of remediating the mold and doing it right, and the fact that the house isn't worth more than a hundred grand to begin with. Add all that together and you've got a loan here that's a hell of a lot more trouble than it's worth."

I glance across the table at Ira. He's leaning forward, his elbows and forearms flat on the table, his sternum resting on his hands.

"Let us pay off the loan at the price you paid for it," I make my final pitch, "and we'll go away."

He doesn't even blink as he stares at me, his blue eyes searching for weakness. I return his stare and don't dare move. I don't smile; I don't shift in my seat.

"What are the numbers, Heather?" he asks, still looking at me, and I know I've just won. I don't let the Eagans know this because the only thing that can mess things up now is if egos get involved. I need to let Eiderhorn save face, to appear to be backing voluntarily into a corner.

"Principal balance is $92,000, plus thirty-three in interest and fees. You're in for $53,750."

"I'll settle it at par," he says to me. "Ninety-two thousand."

"Fifty-three, seven-fifty."

"Forget it, I'll take my chances," he says, and stands to leave. "Heather, Carter, one day you'll have to tell me how you managed to lose this guy."

He turns and opens the conference room door, then strides down the hall as though he hasn't a care in the world. For the first time, I see the Eagans' confidence in me waver.

"I might be able to come up with a little more," Jared whispers in my ear.

I don't acknowledge him. I look at Boston across from me. We both know that Eiderhorn will accept my offer, but didn't want to do it in person.

"Maybe someone should go after him," one of the first-year's suggests.

Sherwin winces slightly and Boston and I actually share the slightest hint of a smile. We know the associate is right, but I can't go because it would undercut my position. Boston refuses to go because it's me. Ira breaks the stalemate.

"I'll see if I can talk to him," he says, not waiting for permission, and with three lanky steps is out the door. In the wake of his departure, we sit in total silence.

Emily stands and walks around Jared's chair toward me. She bends down and puts her hand on my left shoulder while she whispers in my ear. "Could it really cost more to fix the house than it's worth?"

With my right hand, I cover hers, then signal her to hold the thought. I'll tell her later that I've already spoken with their insurance company. I think they're going to honor the policy, but if they don't, assuming I get to keep my license, I'll force them to. Ira and I have already talked a little more about going out on our own if I keep my license, opening a firm dedicated to fighting these kinds of claims. I've even fantasized about Leo joining us once he graduates. But all that's a long way off. A lot of unanswered questions still remain.

"Can the Eagans come up with the fifty-three, seven-fifty quickly?" Ira asks me when he returns.

"Absolutely," I answer. "Do we have a deal?"

"Only if they'll sign a release," he says sternly, "waiving all rights against Mr. Eiderhorn. That means everything—they can't sue him for anything to do with the house or Jared's or the children's health, forever."

Only the Eagans think this is a compromise. The rest of us know that signing a release is part of every settlement. It's entirely for show, to let Eiderhorn save face.

"What do you say?" I ask them.

"What do you think?" Jared responds.

"I think you should take it." They nod at each other and then eagerly at me. "Looks like we have a deal, Mr. Finowitz," I say.

Chapter fifty

I return to my apartment after the meeting, having nowhere else to go. I'll have to keep track of the Eagans—make sure they get their mortgage satisfaction documents from Eiderhorn, follow through with their insurance company. Still, that's no full-time job. I turn the key in the lock and open my front door. The light on my answering machine is flashing. Maybe it's Terry, or Ira with news from the disciplinary committee.

No job, no Jen, no voices ringing in my head. I should really spend some time in Boston now, help Terry. Zachary offered me a job in the *dojo*, and a chance to take the black belt test again. Maybe I'll take the job. Maybe I'll stay with Amy for a while. Maybe I'll just crawl into bed and come up with a better plan tomorrow, and maybe I won't.

It's been a long time since I had no plan. It feels comforting to plan, as though it endows the future with order. Talented young people course like water through the academic pipeline, clinging futilely to graduate school when we realize we're soon to be spit out the other end into chaos. Graduate school offers the promise of order, even if for just a while longer.

But it's an illusion. It's all an illusion. The world is chaotic by nature, and if you can't find a corner of happiness within the chaos, you might as well stop trying. I press the button on my answering machine and listen as I walk into the kitchen and pour a glass of water. It's not a new message after all, just the one from Jen from a few days ago. A smile comes to my lips as I hear her melodic voice. But as I walk back toward the telephone, glass of water in hand, it rings. I wait three rings before picking up.

"You were great," Ira says. "You'll be a worthy partner for me one day."

"Thanks, Finny," I smile. "I guess we'll have to wait and see if we have that choice."

"We do," he says. "That's why I'm calling. I just heard from Carlysle. They're suspending your license for six months."

"I'm not disbarred?"

"Nope. So I'm thinking, maybe you take some time to clear your head, then get to work finding us some cheap office space. There's a Chinese restaurant in my neighborhood that only uses half its kitchen."

"I don't know," I sigh. "Finny, I was so scared today. I'm not sure I'm cut out for this stuff."

"You're surely cut out for this stuff, J.J. You just outfoxed the best in the game. And there's a lot more Eagans out there who need people like us in their corner."

"That's true," I say. "Might be fun."

"Might be."

"Okay, how about this? You stay at Greer and save your money—if you partner with me, you're going to need it—and we'll see where we are in six months."

"What are you going to do?"

"Well," I say, looking around my apartment, "first of all, I guess I'll have to move out of this swank place. They only use half the kitchen, you say?"

"Seriously, what are you going to do?"

"I think I'll spend some time in Boston," I say as I reach down and erase Jen's message. "I'd like to be there for Josie."

"Sounds like a good idea. Look, don't feel obligated to me. You do whatever you want. Just think about it."

"I will. And thanks, Finny, for everything."

"You'll be getting my bill."

It's early evening by the time I arrive at Amy's front door. I haven't called in advance because I wasn't sure I'd wind up here. I put my bag down beside me and knock. From inside, I hear talking. She answers the door, telephone by her ear. Her eyes widen and a smile lights her face. "I've got to go," she says into the phone. "I'll call you back." She tosses the phone onto her sofa and aims her blue eyes at me. "What are you doing here?"

"They let me keep my license," I say, "but suspended me for six months."

"I'm sorry."

"I'm not. I took a job up here in the *dojo*, but the pay's not much. Do you think it would be okay if I stayed with you for a while, just until I scrape up enough for a place of my own?"

She steps through the doorway and links her arm in mine. "You know something, dad?" she smiles as she leads me inside. "You're not very perceptive. I like that in a guy."

Acknowledgments

I would like to express my profound gratitude to the many people who helped breathe life into this book during the twenty years it was in the making:

First, to my mother and father, the two people who nurtured in me whatever it is that allows books to emerge, and who threw a book party to celebrate the completion of *A Monk Jumped Over a Wall*...in 1988. Might've jumped the gun a bit there. For your love, encouragement, and sometimes inexplicable optimism, thank you.

To everyone at Toby Press for your hard work and dedication: Deborah Meghnagi, Isha Smole-Esses, Roger Mehl and Tani Bayer. And a special thanks to Matthew Miller for your integrity, sincerity and keen eye for talent.

To my agent, Luke Janklow, for your unshakeable faith in the manuscript, tireless work on its behalf, and magnificent editorial eye. But more than that, for your utter disdain for the corporatization of publishing—the sworn enemy of authors and readers everywhere. On the other hand, tuck your shirt in, kid.

And to the others at Janklow & Nesbit who contributed their

own unique and substantial talents: Morton Janklow, Claire Dippel, Michael Steger, and Bennett Ashley, thank you all so very much.

To my early readers, possibly in order, but after twenty years and innumerable drafts, it's hard to remember: Wendy Klein, Carolyn Nichols, Dr. Timothy Radomisli and Milda DeVoe, thank you.

And to all of the others who have donated advice, encouragement, feedback, or the experiences that fed the narrative: David Nussbaum, Richard Nussbaum, John Aherne, Sara Kriegel, Dr. Fred Levy, John Paine, Tim Farrell, Yvonne Chan, Anthony Fine, Steven Samuel, David Finkelstein, Evelyn Letfuss, Bruce Tulgan, George Mattson, Eric Verch, Leslie Payne and Felix Martinez.

Finally, and most importantly, thank you to those who take the time to read what I write. I hope there is something for you in here.

About the Author

Jay Nussbaum

Jay Nussbaum is a writer, lawyer and teacher. *A Monk Jumped Over a Wall* is his second novel, his first being *Blue Road to Atlantis* (Warner Books, 2002). From 1997 to 2000, he taught Eastern philosophy and martial arts at Cornell University. He lives in New York with his wife and these two—whom he suspects were sent to live with him by the Folgers people.

The fonts used in this book are from the Garamond family